HAPPY STATE

By Samantha Fitzgibbons

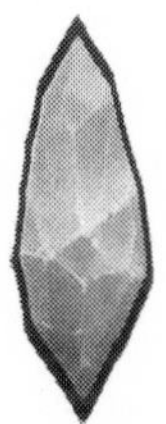

Crystal Peake Publisher
www.crystalpeake.co.uk

First edition published in July 2022 by Crystal Peake Publisher

Print I S B N 978-1-912948-45-1
eBook I S B N 978-1-912948-46-8

A catalogue copy of this book is available from the British Library.

Typeset by Crystal Peake Publisher
Cover designed by Richard Heathcote

Visit www.crystalpeake.co.uk for any further information.

HAPPY STATE

By Samantha Fitzgibbons

'There is nothing either good or bad but thinking makes it so.'

-William Shakespeare

Reviews are the most powerful tools for a publisher and an author. They help to gain attention for the books you enjoy reading. Honest reviews of our books helps to bring them to the attention of other readers.

If you have enjoyed this book, or any of our other books, we would be very grateful if you could spend just five minutes leaving a review. These reviews can be as short or as long as you like.

To Nikki,
For your unwavering faith and support.

Prologue

'*Happiness; the state of being happy,*' that's what the dictionary tells us.

We all seek happiness in some way or another; an eternal quest to grasp hold of a fluid and unseeable phenomenon that continually slips through our fingers. But really, it's only ever slices of happiness that we experience. Just as we have moments of sadness, distress, grief, and mourning. Happiness is a retrospective emotion and often, when we feel it, we don't even know it's present. Sometimes, we're disappointed when we find it, selfishly yearning for more.

We all have our own ideas of happiness; our own perceptions of what happiness looks like. Feels like.

Soon, you will understand how very different these perceptions can be.

I thought I knew what happiness might look like.

I didn't have the first clue.

The year is 2029. The United Kingdom has revolutionised.

If you don't know what I'm referring to, then you haven't been affected yet.

You will be.

My name is Rafella Crowe, and this is my story.

Chapter 1

The bustling city street lay in eerie silence. Usually a hub of activity, it surrendered to a harrowing stillness. Evenly situated street lights projected a glimmer of ominous light, serving to magnify the feeling of impending danger that loomed in the air.

The old, disused subway tunnel was situated halfway down the long road. No longer used by commuters, it existed as a meeting point for the underhanded practices of juvenile misfits, or at least that was the reputation it carried.

In the near distance, the laboured grinding of wheels rumbled along the pavement like the faint echo of thunder. Moments later, a young man on a skateboard appeared at the opening of the tunnel. He was dressed all in black, his hood pulled up; a dark, menacing face covering revealed only his eyes.

He came to an eventual standstill as he approached the top of the street; a well-practiced and effortless stamp of his foot as he caught the board in his right hand. As he took a step closer to the brick wall, he glanced at the graffiti that adorned it; bright neon colours cried tears of injustice.

Within a matter of seconds, a large, rolled up poster was removed from his backpack; a quick smear of adhesive before he attached it to the wall.

'Freedom is coming!'

Finally, he sprayed his unique tag across the bottom of the

poster; the essential finishing touch.

His work was done.

Within seconds, he had disappeared like a ghost into the ether.

Chapter 2

'Pops!' I shouted from the bottom of the staircase.

He didn't respond. The man was senile, not deaf. I could hear a rustling sound. I bounded up the stairs and into Dad's room. An inflated hot water bottle on the floor sent me flying towards Dad's bed.

'For God's sake, Pop…'

I stopped in my tracks. Dad was leaning against the wall, staring at a photo of Mum. An open crisp packet lay in his lap and there were broken crisps all over the floor. He rocked gently with silent tears streaming down his porcelain cheeks.

I clenched my jaw. Please don't let it be happening yet.

'Hey, Pops,' I whispered.

I slowly crawled towards him, my left knee throbbing from its impact with the bedside cabinet. I sat beside him and took his free hand. He looked at me with immeasurable sadness in his eyes. I leaned into him and touched the photo. Mum's blue eyes were staring directly into the camera. For a second, I felt like she was looking at me; like her soul was present in the room. Dad squeezed my hand, then gently touched the bracelet that remained firmly attached to my wrist. Mum's bracelet, the one she passed on to me during her illness. I hadn't taken it off since the day she'd left this world.

Silently and thoughtfully, we shared the moment.

*

I was always a daddy's girl. Maybe it was because I'd been a tomboy, though I suspect he'd have embraced a "girl's girl" equally. Either way, Dad had always been my best friend. My soulmate. My fun loving and mischievous partner in crime.

When we lost Mum to cancer, Dad had to step in and take on the role of both parents. He nailed it. It was a happy and fulfilling childhood.

Dad had been an established and well-known artist for thirty years. Many of my happiest childhood memories involved proudly perching next to him on a highchair with my own tiny easel, plastic apron and a pink paintbrush. One of my paintings still unashamedly adorned the walls of our home; a girl with an oversized head, a shock of yellow hair that sprouted like clock springs, and a red smile that overlapped her face and merged into the background.

'Her first piece of art,' Dad had proudly declared to anyone that entered our home.

I knew from an early age that the artistic gene had bypassed me.

His success hadn't come easily. He'd faced rejection after rejection; he was told that his paintings were average, unimaginative, and bland. It hadn't phased him; he'd continued to feed his passion until a small gallery owner had asked him if he could commission some of his paintings. The rest was history.

He found no joy in making money. His real love came from teaching at a local university. Guiding and nurturing the yet to be recognised talent of hungry, passionate art students; nothing gave Dad more joy than paving a creative path for enthusiastic proteges. Mum had been one of his students and had frequently told me the story of how she had signed up to evening art classes, and essentially maintained her attendance because of Phillip, the "*charismatic art teacher*". Dad joked he had subtly encouraged her not to give up her day job, yet blushed every time he was in close proximity to her. Before long, they were dating. She said he was captivating; he said she was useless at art but gloriously enchanting. Within a year, they were married. Mum gave up the art classes and became a yoga teacher.

Losing Mum had been a hard passing, but Dad's courage had been colossal. He comforted me when I yearned for her; encouraged me to laugh at memories of her bohemian eccentricity and cried with me as we shared memories of happier times. He watched me grow with pride, shed tears of joy when I passed my exams, lectured me about my first boyfriend and taught me the morals and values that have made me who I am today.

On a bad day, I try to remember to like myself because that pays testament to all the work that Mum and Dad did.

Life continued for us, as it does, but the absence of Mum was ever present. I'd still pick up my phone to call her when I needed guidance or had news to share. Those habits were hard to break. But Dad encouraged me to continue talking to her, despite feeling a little stupid at times.

'Don't ask me, ask your mum,' he'd say.

'Dad, don't be silly!'

'Ask her,' he'd urge.

'Okay! Mum…' I'd said awkwardly on one particular

occasion. 'Which subject should I choose? Art or history?'

Dad looked at me truculently. 'What did she say?'

'She said history. *Definitely* history.'

'There you go,' he cooed. 'She never lets you down.'

During Mum's last weeks, she'd talked about how she wanted for nothing with Dad. She could count on one hand how many times she'd argued with him; never having to ask twice, nag or clean up after him.

When he started having a few silly accidents, it was even more apparent that something wasn't right. Leaving the gas on, the car engine running, leaving his bedroom curtains drawn for three days in a row which, surprisingly, was the one that triggered alarm bells. Dad was regimental at the best of times, but Mum's "clean house, clean mind" mantra had ensured that we left things as we found them. In our home, unopened curtains meant a great deal more than just unopened curtains.

It didn't take long for the doctors to diagnose vascular dementia. That was the day my world should have fallen apart. It should have been the worst day of my life.

It didn't even come close.

*

I finally managed to get Dad downstairs and into his favourite chair. He took my hand and mouthed the words '*you're magic*' to me. He'd said it to me since I was a toddler, but on this day, it left me heavy-hearted. I needed to be grateful that I had my dad in body, mind, and soul. One day, these moments would be few and far between. Another day, they'd cease to exist.

I selected a piece of classical music from our high-tech music station and turned the television off. Some days, he watched the meditation channels for hours in the hope of clearing his mind, easing the anxiety that he stored inside. For me, they did anything but; the endless stream of soporific music made me both irritable and lethargic, not to mention vaguely murderous.

But that might not resonate with you.

Not yet.

I sat back down and touched Dad's hand. He looked at me and smiled.

Sometimes, I wondered if Dad's illness had eased his experience of the immense changes that we had all endured. Sometimes I questioned if there really was a God and wondered if Dad had been saved.

I left Dad in a calmer emotional state as I drew the curtains in the living room. It was four minutes to ten. Four minutes before curfew.

The sweepers would arrive any minute.

*

We'd learnt to find inventive ways of drowning out the wailing of the siren that marked the beginning of curfew. Often, the television or music at a high volume would be a sufficient distraction, but on other occasions, Dad and I would decimate verses of our favourite songs at full pelt. Fortunately, we didn't have neighbours in close proximity, as we'd have no doubt received an ASBO of sorts.

That night, we didn't feel much like singing. Dad had taken

himself to bed to read his magazine, so I'd opted for the sofa with a soothing hot chocolate.

I mindlessly flicked through the multiple channels that made up Happy State TV, the toxin that it was. A gritty drama would have suited my mood perfectly, but we were no longer privy to such luxuries. Instead, a plethora of uplifting films and documentaries now monopolised the laborious television package that had been forced upon us. Boring wasn't the word.

I grabbed one of Dad's books from the side table and half-heartedly skimmed the pages. However hard I tried; European sculpture would never be my thing.

It was the distinctive tone of our leader, Edwin Oakes, that made me glance up at the TV. It was another unrelenting documentary about our transition to The Happy State. I should have turned over straight away, but the coverage of the United Kingdom crashing to its feet, the rapid uprising of the new, fastidious government and the plans for The Happy State sparked my attention.

As I mused at the transparency of the overconfident Oakes, I considered the extreme changes that both myself and the inhabitants of the United Kingdom had endured over the last two years. Sometimes, when I thought back to the trauma that it had induced, it played out like an action film in my mind. I wondered who the leading character might be.

Myself and around seven million others had watched in horror as the government was overthrown. Civil war, they'd called it. I'd found it hard to believe that a war of any kind could occur in the twenty-first century. They talked about it, threatened it even, but I never expected to witness anything of the sort during my lifetime.

The documentary played out the pre-transition chaos that had brought our country to a standstill. I balked at images of rioting and looting in the large cities, marvelled at the barbaric actions of some of its occupants, and empathised with those that merely craved peace. Living in the small village of Thendra had served us well, as we'd remained relatively unaffected. For that alone, I was blessed.

Nathaniel Frost appeared; his military regalia impeccably tailored, as always. There was no doubt that he looked the part as he spoke of his role in leading the military. '*It's all for the greater good,*' he reiterated at least five times.

He grinned smugly as he looked at the camera and explained the regenerative and nurturing benefits of martial law. I laughed to myself; the contradiction wasn't lost on me, despite my vast disinterest in politics.

I thought back to Dad's expression when they'd announced The Happy State at a national press conference just a year prior. He'd reluctantly watched, uttering phrases like "cobblers" and "nut jobs" under his breath. He'd made his views on it all abundantly clear from the outset.

Frustrated at the stream of rubbish being spouted by our newfound leaders, I glanced around the room at the artwork that Dad had created. I rarely spent time simply appreciating his talent. I think it saddened me if the truth be known. What once took him days to create had turned into months, such a tragic tale of decline that I'd yet to come to grips with. Sometimes it was easier to forget about his wonderful creativity and impossibly clever brain.

I felt irritable. It was moments like these that I missed my mobile phone. I missed the opportunity to waste time as I ingested mind-numbing information from the worldwide web. They'd taken those from us straight away; a 'deeply damaging phenomenon,' they'd called them, or some such phrase. We'd evolved to be antisocial, and we needed to relearn the basic ability to converse, apparently. I could see their point, but I sometimes missed the escapism.

Begrudgingly, I hit the power button on the remote control to save myself the arduous task of finding a suitable program to watch.

Sometimes, boredom was all there was.

Chapter 3

It was a beautiful spring morning as I prepared Dad's breakfast. My enforced early night had enabled me a satisfactory sleep which had left me feeling unusually cheerful.

I laid his plate of runny scrambled egg on the table while he sipped his tea. The egg looked uninviting, far too liquidised for my liking. The two slices of brown toast were cut into triangles; there was a thin layer of butter and the egg was placed in the centre. As fussy as he was about such things, I was starting to realise that I lived for these moments. One day I'd miss these fastidious habits.

'Min here yet?' he asked as he sliced into his toast.

'Not yet, Pop. She doesn't start until nine. She needs a lie in if she's got you to deal with all day.'

He winked at me.

My eyes welled up, and I turned to face the window. That was my dad. The cheeky crooked grin, the twinkle in his eye. I missed him, and he hadn't gone anywhere yet. Anticipation can be a cruel thing.

'Don't be daft. That one's got more energy than a six-year-old,' he muttered.

Min. Dad's carer. The salvation that we'd unknowingly craved, who pulled Dad and I from the depths of despair just ten months prior. A larger-than-life character that shared an endearing love/hate relationship with Dad.

Dad groaned at her a lot, frequently pulling faces or making hand gestures behind her back, but he wouldn't be without her, and neither would I.

With just a couple of days spent at the local surgery, Min spent the rest of her time at my dad's beck and call. In truth, we didn't need her full time, as Dad was perfectly capable. At least for now. He had the funds to pay her handsomely, and he secretly loved her companionship. Their relationship was nothing if not comical, and I'd spent many hours laughing at the discourse that took place between them. Dad, with his abject stubbornness and Min, with her no-nonsense attitude; they were comparable to a comedy duo.

Sometimes I envied her time spent with Dad. Other times, I appreciated the respite.

That day, like every other morning, I did the handover with Min before leaving for the café. The walk was a saviour in the warmer months, less so in the cold of winter. I loved days like these, when the sun bounced off my face and gave me cause to smile. Often, I'd leave half an hour early just to enjoy the tranquillity of nature that existed in our quiet village. Other days, when I was feeling energetic, I'd opt for a gentle run. I was eternally grateful to my parents for choosing such a beautiful, picturesque village to live in. With one small church, an array of independent shops, and a large, well-kept park, we were truly blessed in our surroundings.

I arrived at work to a vision that never ceased to delight. Dahlia had ingratiated herself at a customer's table, where she offered a free tarot reading in-between orders. Jo, on the other hand, was pulling not-so-subtle faces at a troublesome child.

I smiled to myself. My work was my sanctuary; the time spent around the girls and the customers gave me light relief from the underlying sadness within my personal life.

Three days off with Dad had given me numerous moments of delight, but I wasn't disappointed to be around people again, back to the sound of clinking coffee cups and idle chatter.

Jo, dressed in her customary skinny jeans and grungy t-shirt, opened the doors at nine sharp and the usual flow of late starters rolled in for their morning caffeine shot. "Whingey" Winnie was the first in; within ten minutes of ordering, she'd be offering tips to improve the taste of the tea. I waved at her as she entered and took a seat. Her routine was like clockwork, so no verbal exchange was necessary.

Graham followed. I glanced at Jo as we anticipated the inevitable.

'Morning ladies! Don't worry, I'll settle my bill today,' he whispered with a cheeky wink to boot. He never did, God Bless him. He'd had a rigorous battle with cancer and I didn't have the heart to bother him with a few pence.

Dahlia floated towards me like an ethereal being in her long, loose skirt. 'That really was the best reading I've ever done!' I nodded in encouragement. She said that after every reading. 'Morning, Anne,' she beamed as she offered a welcoming smile to another regular. She leaned in towards me and spoke through gritted teeth. 'If she dares to say the milk's off…'

I laughed. 'Miracles can happen, you know?'

I wandered around the tables and collected a few empty cups as the girls started on the coffee. 'You okay, Lennie?' I asked as I picked up his barely consumed coffee cup.

'Not bad,' he grimaced. 'But I'd much rather be sat over there.' He pointed to the table in the centre of the café.

'I'm sure you would,' I laughed. 'But we know precisely what'll happen. More coffee?'

He shrugged his shoulders, nodded his head reluctantly.

'I see you've shoved Lennie to the back today,' I grinned as I loaded the cups into the dishwasher.

Jo widened her eyes. 'I had to! He'd been here for less than five minutes and he started talking to that woman over there.' She nodded her head towards an elderly, well-to-do woman, tucked away with her head in a magazine. 'It's every day, Raff! He's relentless.'

'Give him a break,' I said as I glanced over at him. 'He's lonely, that's all.'

Jo rolled her eyes at me. 'Tell that to the customers.'

When the next customer entered, she disappeared in a flash. I watched her playfully twiddle with her cute top-knots as she leant over the counter, giggling with the local police.

'The milk's definitely off. Can I have a fresh cup?' I looked up to see Anne stood before me. Miracles weren't happening, clearly.

They say that familiarity breeds contempt, but to me, it was the devil I knew. When it's the only certainty you have in life, it's quite the comfort.

*

I was one of the lucky few that retained my job with the transition. As we became an independent state, many local businesses had been forced into closure with the vast changes that our country had undergone.

I owned a small coffee shop in the village and, despite what was occurring in the world, people still drank coffee. Mum had always wanted a coffee shop of her own and Dad had uncompromisingly bought her a perfectly petite building in the centre of the village, presenting it to her just weeks before her diagnosis.

She never got to experience the joy of making plans and sampling a multitude of different flavoured coffees. She asked that I take over and make it my own, which, at first, I'd been reticent about. Owning a business was no mean feat, and I wasn't a natural entrepreneur. I'd had plans to go to university and study a subject that I'd never quite decided upon, a notion that Dad still encouraged me to follow. He insisted that he'd sell the building with minimal issue but I wanted to create a legacy for Mum. In time, I surprised myself with my passion to create and manage.

The building consisted of a downstairs coffee shop and an upstairs apartment that had been unused for several years. Initially, it was intended that I would move in and make it my own. I'd make the dreaded transition into adulthood. My walk to work a mere trundle down the stairs. But Dad's diagnosis dictated that I stay close to him. I wanted to stay close to him, and I valued separating my work and home life.

We needlessly spent time decorating and furnishing the apartment, mainly because Dad had insisted on it. He'd enjoyed taking charge of something, probably because he felt like he had no control over anything else in his life.

It wasn't my place to deny him of his dignity.

We'd spent weeks testing the colours of paint, comparing carpets and organising electricians and plumbers who would later fit a sink, a shower and a toilet. It was all fruitless, but it made Dad happy to be useful; to be doing something for his daughter.

He wanted to feel needed.

'What are you going to call it then?' he'd finally asked.

'Call what?'

'The café. It needs a name!'

I'd pondered for a minute, then smiled broadly.

'The Café,' I said. 'I'm going to call it The Café.'

Chapter 4

I caught Dahlia glaring at me. No doubt, she'd seen me frantically chewing on my lower lip, a growing habit that had become quite involuntary.

The café was full to brimming.

'Can you just hurry the back table up?' I whispered. 'They've been here for over an hour without ordering.'

'They're regulars. I can't kick them out!' she protested.

I made a huffing sound, and Dahlia started to laugh.

'You're in the wrong job,' she laughed as she wiped the units with her plant based disinfectant. Her arms made a rattling sound each time she moved with the number of bracelets she wore. 'You don't even like people, especially when there's a lot of them in one place.'

'I'm fine,' I mumbled.

She stopped what she was doing. 'You're a hippy at heart, I'm telling you.'

I rolled my eyes.

'Just look at your bracelet,' she winked as she headed over to the back table.

Dahlia was determined to recruit me into her vegan and meditative lifestyle. When she'd heard about Mum being a yoga teacher, she'd almost fainted with excitement. Ever since, she'd not so subtly worked her magic on me, but was yet to succeed.

It didn't stop her tenacity.

I glanced down at the bracelet around my wrist. I'd been told that in times of stress, I subconsciously stroked or toyed with it.

Mum had visited India in her late twenties and freely offered her services to a local school. Before her departure, an elderly lady had handed her a blessing bracelet and told her to wear it at all times. She was so moved by the gesture that it had remained fixed to her wrist ever since. She had given it to me before she died. I only had to look at it to remember her.

*

I arrived home at around two o'clock, having popped in to check on Dad. Min had a last-minute meeting at the surgery and I wanted to ensure that he was coping. She often tried to assure me that I worried too much, but a simple error in judgement could be fatal and I wasn't prepared to chance it. Predictably, Dad was absolutely fine and caught up in yet another painstaking program about The Happy State.

'Why do you watch this rubbish, Pop?' I asked as I unloaded the few bits of shopping that I'd collected on the way home. 'It only winds you up.'

His eyes were fixated on the screen. 'It makes me feel better to know that there are less fortunate souls in the world than me.'

'Who are you on about?'

'These prats! Oakes and Frost. They actually believe their own diatribe! I'd rather have dementia than be responsible for the mess they've created.'

I stopped in my tracks. 'Dad, that's an awful thing to say. Nobody wants dementia.'

He shrugged. He was in one of his stubborn moods. I'd come to learn that watching anything political only served to aggravate him.

'You're mad enough without it,' I joked, as I attempted to lighten the mood.

'Well, just listen to them. They reckon this Happy State rubbish is going to turn us all into smiling idiots. I know, let's send in the military and give them a curfew. That'll do the trick!'

I snatched the remote control and turned the TV off; I wasn't enabling his mood any further. It was sometimes hard to snap him out of it and could take him several days to simmer.

'Oi! I was watching that!' he groaned.

'No, you weren't. You were shouting at it!'

He rose from his chair and marched out of the room. 'I'm off to blinking bed to read my book then.'

I sensed I was playing parent for the next few days.

'Oh, and Min's just arrived,' he roared from halfway up the stairs. 'Tell her I'm busy and not accepting visitors.'

As I made my way to the front door, I laughed at loud at his petulance. He was such an infant at times. Should we dare to ignore him, we'd no doubt be accused of neglect.

It came as quite a shock when the front door burst open to reveal Min, armed with a large vacuum cleaner.

'Min, what on earth are you doing?'

She barged past me. 'I just can't use your useless excuse for a vacuum anymore. It drops more bits than it collects. That thing will be the death of me.'

'Here, let me help,' I insisted.

'It's fine. I've got it.' She was as stubborn as a mule.

I'm not entirely sure what happened next. Somehow, Min lost her grip, and as the vacuum headed for the floor, we both reached out to save it from imminent death. Somewhere along the way, Min leant forward and our heads collided, which, in turn, sent us both tumbling to the ground.

The debacle was entirely farcical.

The room lay in silence for a few moments. I lay perfectly still, mentally assessing all potential injuries. Someone started to laugh; a third person that most definitely wasn't Dad. It was male, that much was apparent. It was impossible to gain any insight into the mystery man because of my awkward positioning, so I wriggled my body out from under Min.

'Min, you okay?' I wheezed.

'I've got you. You're alright,' said the mystery voice.

As she moved, the weight against my back lessened and I was able to roll over. I felt a stinging sensation on the side of my face, but all of my limbs seemed to be intact. I was bewildered as a tall, slim, dark-haired man settled Min into a chair. Curiously, I propped myself onto my elbows as he turned to look at me.

The face belonged to someone that I hadn't seen for a very long time. A face that I hadn't wanted to see in a long time.

It was Jed.

'Oh! It's you.'

'Nice to see you too!' he grinned.

Jed was Min's obnoxiously arrogant son that I'd had the pleasure of going to school with and hadn't seen for several years. He'd worked a summer or two in the United States after finishing college, something about teaching underprivileged kids. I almost choked when I heard that one. I'd either misheard or there was a definitive underlying motive for his move. Either way, I hadn't missed him.

'Nice cut, Fella,' he said as he eyed my face.

Fella. I hated him calling me that. I hated it as much as he knew I hated it. I chose to overlook his comment.

'Long time no see,' I mused as I gently touched my cheek to assess the damage.

As I moved my hand from my face, fresh blood smudged my finger like red paint. I winced.

Min gasped. 'Oh love, I'm so sorry!'

Naturally, she insisted on recruiting the first aid kit and delegated Jed to the position. Within seconds, Jed was attending to my grazed cheek with an antibacterial lotion of sorts. I felt uncomfortable being so close to him.

'This really isn't necessary,' I muttered as I ducked out of his way. 'It's a scratch. I'm sure I'll survive.'

'Flesh wound actually.'

I rolled my eyes. 'Same thing.'

'Just following orders.'

I conceded solely to satisfy Min.

With his face just inches away from mine, I fixedly stared at the wall to the side of him to avoid any awkwardness. His facial features were apparent in my peripheral vision, and I couldn't deny that he was handsome. Dark hair, tanned skin with the whitest teeth I'd ever seen; he looked like an all-American football star. His stay in America looked good on him, and I had no doubt that he'd have had his fair share of admirers. Despite my incessant dislike of him, I couldn't help but feel somewhat drab in comparison.

I was certain that he was deliberately taking his time to annoy me. 'Okay, enough!' I demanded, as I forcefully pushed his hand away.

I snatched the cloth from him and glanced in the mirror. At the top of my right cheek was a tiny and indiscernible scratch. It certainly didn't require the help of a nurse.

Min, on the other hand, found the whole incident quite hilarious. Even Jed had acquired a fit of the giggles. They say that laughter is contagious and in time, I found myself laughing with them.

I still hated him

With my limbs intact, I went upstairs to say goodbye to Dad before I headed back to work. He was glued to an art magazine that he'd subscribed to for as long as I could remember. Min and I often joked that he spent more time criticising art than relishing it.

'A ten-year-old could paint this crap!' he muttered as I leant in to kiss him goodbye.

'I don't know why you bother reading it, Pop.'

'What's that on your cheek?' he asked as he lowered his glasses and stared at my face.

'Cut myself shaving,' I winked. 'Nothing for you to worry about.'

He looked at me with adoring eyes. Eyes that openly reflected the eternal love he had for me. 'You look more like your mum every day.'

Sometimes, his love for me was an overbearing burden. Though I would never be without it, being loved wasn't without its issues. We could read each other's facial expressions; we could feel one another's pain. A love so raw was as painful as it was pleasant, as melancholy as it was happy. Perhaps I should have revelled in Dad's proclamation, but my stomach turned each time he said it to me. Looking like Mum was a daily reminder of the life he once had, the wife and soul mate he had lost to a cruel and painful disease.

I hoped I didn't cause him pain.

Heavy-hearted, I left for work; a small butterfly stitch on my cheek courtesy of Nurse Jed. As I stepped outdoors, the bright spring sun shone down onto my face. I closed my eyes for a moment and allowed the warmth to soak into my skin.

Jed's familiar tone destroyed the moment. I turned to see his annoyingly smug grin.

'Not going to say goodbye then?'

'Can't say I'd planned on it.'

'See you soon!' he called as I turned my back on him and took giant strides to put as much distance in between us as possible.

All those years later, and he still had the ability to make my cheeks flush with irritation.

I detested that guy.

Chapter 5

Oakes sat nervously in the back of the off-road vehicle as the driver frenziedly sped across the dirt track. Despite his seatbelt, he felt safer clinging to the door handle for extra protection. He loosened his tie with his free hand; the warm weather made him feel hot and irritable, especially in a three-piece suit. After a two-hour drive from the City, they arrived in a small village called Thendra, the site of their largest and most resplendent Zone.

He leant forward and tapped Frost on the shoulder. 'How far?'

Frost glanced at the in-built navigation system. 'ETA sixteen seventeen.'

Oakes looked at his watch. They had nine minutes to go, and he desperately wanted a cigarette. He leant back into his seat; he was in no rush to see what lay ahead of him.

The vehicle slowed as it neared two enormous metal gates that resembled something from an old horror film. He wound down his window to allow some fresh air to enter as Frost spoke into the intercom. The gates opened, and they continued down a long and winding path until a large Victorian building came into view.

The building was affluent and inviting, but locals were all too aware of its history. Once a well-established psychiatric hospital, a large media campaign in the late nineties had unveiled stories of the cruel and barbaric treatment of its patients. The news had caused uproar, and the hospital had been forced to close down. Oakes felt uncomfortable merely thinking about it.

As the vehicle came to a standstill, he hastily jumped out and lit a cigarette. He allowed the pleasurable sensation of calm to wash over him as the nicotine worked its magic. Instantly relaxed, he watched as Frost strode into the building with the efficacy of a president. His ego angered him, so he inhaled more deeply.

He and Frost had been in talks about the Zones for nearly three years, but since they'd been implemented, he felt nothing short of dread. At the time, the premise of a Zoning system had seemed practical. Efficient, if not extreme. But Frost had sold the idea to him like a supercharged salesman and he'd concurred.

There was no turning back.

He'd taken a mere four drags when Frost returned and urged him to cut it short. Highly dissatisfied, he tossed it to the ground and stubbed it out with his shoe. It wasn't a good start. He reached into his pocket for his breath freshener as they approached the doorway; no one cared for the smell of smoker's breath. He pumped it into his mouth four times, placed it back into his pocket, and straightened his tie. Appearances were everything.

He was just glad that they couldn't read his mind.

As he stepped inside the lavish foyer, he was immediately taken aback at the alignment of staff that eagerly awaited his arrival. Like a member of royalty, he worked his way along the line, drowning in overly sycophantic dialogue as he shook hands with each member of staff. When he finally reached the end, he was greeted by an annoyingly overenthusiastic lady who was keen to introduce herself.

'Mr Oakes, I'm so delighted to meet you finally,' she balked as she cupped his hand in her own. 'I'm Jude, general manager of Zone Seven. We are honoured to have you here.'

'The pleasure is all mine, I assure you,' he beamed. Lying had become second nature to him.

'Might I interest you in a guided tour?'

Oakes turned cold. The last thing he wanted was a guided tour. That wasn't the deal. Get in, meet a few of the staff and get out, that's what Frost had assured him. The vague knowledge that he possessed of the Zones was sufficient to keep him awake at night. He didn't want to add any visuals to the experience.

'Oh, that won't be necessary,' he laughed. 'I'm sure you have it all under control. And of course, we're running a very tight ship. We just don't have the time, I'm afraid.'

Jude looked crestfallen.

'Of course you do!' interjected Frost. 'It would be a travesty for the leader of The Happy State to come all this way and not ingratiate himself with the Zone, would it not?' He added extra emphasis to the word "ingratiate." He was toying with him.

Oakes clenched his jaw. Frost got off on being an annoying creep.

'Wonderful!' exclaimed Jude like an excitable teenager. 'In that case, I'll be sure to have tea and cake waiting for us afterwards.'

Oakes produced his best smile. 'Oh, how very kind,' he lied.

Jude ushered him to the wide marble steps that belonged in a historical drama. The building was large and opulent, but eerily silent. He scrunched his nose as he took in the stench of illness that loomed in the air, the white clinical walls and the lack of furniture. Jude talked the entire time, but he paid little attention besides the occasional acknowledgment.

They stopped at the top of the stairs; he was slightly breathless from the climb but did his utmost to disguise the fact. Jude guided him through the corridor as she explained the history of the building and the service that they were providing the patients. She thanked him numerous times for trusting her with such a prestigious role; a role that he knew nothing about. He desperately wished that he could mute her.

'And now, let me introduce you to one of the patients. She's been so excited to meet Edwin Oakes!'

He glanced at his watch, prepared to concoct another excuse when the door swung open. He stood still, bewildered as to his next move.

'Please, come,' she urged as she steered him towards the door.

He stared directly into a bedroom; a loose term to describe the plain white walls, the plastic chair in the corner, and the single bed. The barred windows offered an extra touch. It was less than inviting, barely even comparable to the rest of the building. A woman, possibly in her mid-thirties, sat on the edge of her bed. Her hair was greasy and her face was heavily lined. She was painfully thin, if not malnourished.

Jude slowed her words as if she was speaking to a ten-year-old. 'Hello Tegan, there's a very important guest here to see you.'

Oakes watched with concern as Tegan struggled to even raise her head.

'Are you going to introduce yourself?' asked Jude as she

hauled Tegan to her feet and roughly kicked a pair of shoes out of her way. 'Say hello to Mr Oakes. He's a very important man, Tegan.' She spoke with syrup-laden kindness that oozed insincerity.

He moved forward, desperate to alleviate some of Tegan's discomfort.

'Hello, Tegan, I'm Edwin. It's nice to meet you.'

Her inability to focus made it glaringly apparent that she was heavily drugged on medication.

Jude tugged at her hand to move her closer to Oakes. She wobbled as she fought to ground herself.

'Hello, Mr... Oakes,' she slurred.

'That's a good girl,' said Jude in a perfectly condescending tone. 'Tegan has been here for three weeks. She suffers from paranoid schizophrenia and has a very hard time managing it, don't you, Tegan?'

Tegan clung tightly to Jude's arm; it was clear that her balance was entirely dependent upon support.

'She has sensibly decided that she'd like to stop being a burden to everyone around her. Your poor family have had a terrible time with your moods, haven't they?'

Tegan nodded. Or, at least, tried to.

Oakes winced at Jude's brazen attitude. Tegan had no concept of reality. In those few moments, it had all become alarmingly real to him. He didn't want to know the fine details, and this was a sublimely fine detail.

Jude raised a large smile. 'It's time for you to have a rest, isn't it, Tegan?'

Relieved, Oakes made a gesture to shake her hand, but given

the speed at which she moved, he withdrew it in a bid to protect her from further depravity.

'It was nice to meet you,' he muttered as he made his way to the door.

Jude followed and pulled the door behind her. 'I'm so glad you got to see her. She's been keen to meet you.'

He was quite certain that Tegan could not express any such sentiment in her current state.

Jude lowered her voice and ushered him away from the door. He was aghast at her futile gesture; Tegan could barely focus, much less eavesdrop.

'Tegan is a very poorly lady. We took her in after her family failed to cope with her. They bought her an apartment to give them some space. Her poor mother was a wreck, apparently. She had several breakdowns herself as a result.'

Oakes blinked his eyes as he attempted to keep up with Jude's incessant gabbling.

'She's had several sessions with the councillor and has given her full consent. It's wonderful when they make it so easy. Some patients make it very difficult for us. Some of them…'

Having largely tuned out of the conversation, he stopped her mid flow. 'Sorry, consent?'

'Yes, Mr Oakes. It makes things so much easier when they don't put up a fight. She signed her name without hesitation, which means that in just a few days…'

'Yes. Absolutely!' he interrupted. 'It's been a long day.'

He was fully aware of what would be happening in a few days. He didn't require a picture.

Frost was adamant that their consent deemed it humane.

Evolution, he called it. Natural selection. Weaning out the weak to enable a greater race. The "mopers" as he'd so eloquently named them, the instigators of problems, the chronic complainers. Those that drained the health service of an immeasurable number of resources for problems they claimed were to do with their minds.

A purist race. Didn't Hitler have similar visions?

A cold shiver swept over him as he considered the things that he had agreed to; how he had been blindsided into endorsing such barbarism.

'I can show you some of the patient records if you'd like? I'm sure you're keen to see our progress?'

'No, I really must dash,' he said as he took giant strides towards the staircase.

'Of course, you're a busy man. Silly me,' she giggled.

He turned his back on her and headed down the stairs.

The stark reality of the Zones would now fester in his mind permanently. He despised Frost for subjecting him to this visit.

Chapter 6

'He's asked me on a date,' beamed Jo. 'Can you believe it? He asked me on a date.'

I rolled my eyes as I cleaned the table in front of me. One of our morning customers had brought three small children in with them and they'd managed to massacre two tables and four chairs with orange squash and chocolate mousse.

'Er… hello? Earth to…'

'Yes, I heard you,' I snapped. 'Those grubby… look!' I said, waving my filthy dish cloth in the air.

I was quite used to problematic children and usually wouldn't fuss about such things. I was still irked by Jed and his surprise visit; the mere knowledge that he was in the area was sufficient to make my blood boil.

'Who is it then?' I asked, certain that this was the desired response.

'You're serious, aren't you?'

I stared at her blankly.

'Honestly, do you not pay attention to anything that happens in here? He's been coming in for a couple of weeks. His name is Aron, and he's incredibly good looking. Oh, and he's a policeman!'

Before I could respond, Jo had skipped over to Dahlia, who had just walked in. It was lovely to see someone appreciate the small things in life.

The rest of my day went with little interest, but I couldn't help but notice that "Anne of the stale milk" had failed to show. In truth, I did more than notice. I actively looked out for her. When you had a regular chronic complainer, you tended to adapt to their visiting habits. You became accustomed to the same faces, sitting in the same seats, ordering the same drinks and quibbling about the same old things. There was something comforting in routine and expectations, and when someone failed to appear, it made us question their whereabouts. Well, made me question their whereabouts.

'You realise she doesn't have to come in every day, don't you?' Jo had said.

'Well, yeah. But she does come in every day,' I replied.

'Maybe she's ill? People do get ill, you know.'

'She's never ill!'

'Everyone gets ill!'

She was right. I needed to give it a rest.

The main action of the day decided to wait until I got home that evening. I entered a warm and comforting house; the smell of home cooking oozed into the atmosphere. Min didn't need to cook for us, but it was an absolute blessing that she did. After a day of waiting on people, the thought of preparing food was often a bridge too far.

Min was spreadeagled on the sofa, her reading glasses perched on her head and an open paperback strewn across her stomach. I giggled at Dad as he dozed in his armchair, his head continually drooping then jerking back up again.

'Hey, Pop,' I whispered.

His eyes widened, his arms flailed as he frantically searched for the magazine that had fallen from his grip and onto the carpet.

'Just resting my eyes. I was wide awake.'

'You're allowed to fall asleep, Pop,' I laughed as I handed him his magazine. 'Good to see you keeping busy.'

He rubbed his red-rimmed eyes. 'Where is she?'

I eyed Min as she snored contentedly. Her mouth was wide open with a fine trail of dribble on her chin.

A large grin swept across Dad's face. 'Help! Help me!' he shouted at the top of his voice.

I was unable to suppress a smile as Min jumped out of her skin. Her eyes darted left and right as she attempted to identify the imminent threat.

'You bleeder,' she chided. 'You'll give me a heart attack one of these days.'

They were like a couple of overgrown kids.

'Dinner's prepped. It just needs reheating, love,' she said as she forced her swollen feet into her shoes. 'I'll be getting myself home now that I've been rudely awakened.'

She couldn't help but draw the curtains on her way out, a customary pre-curfew habit of hers. After refusing a lift home, insistent on stretching her legs "to get the blood flowing," Dad and I wasted no time in tucking into an outrageously large portion of her homemade risotto.

With our stomachs suitably bloated, we collapsed into our usual seats in front of the TV. Half-heartedly, we watched an old British film about a bunch of armed robbers who ended up double crossing each other. I didn't have a clue about what happened. Dad provided a full running commentary while I strained to hear the dialogue.

Moments like those I cherished.

The pre-curfew news followed and neither of us had any inclination to move from our seats to hunt for the ever-disappearing remote control. We were forced to watch as the broadcast depicted serenity and calm across the nation. The City streets looked peaceful, or at least that's what they wanted us to see. They applauded martial law; the riots had diminished, and the country was now in harmony. This would only improve, they said. We will continue to go from strength to strength, they promised.

'What do you make of that then, Pop?' I asked whilst simultaneously yawning. I knew precisely what he'd make of it.

I glanced over. He was fast asleep; a delicate whistling sound emanated from his pouted lips.

With nothing but drivel to watch, I too must have dozed, and I woke a while later feeling disorientated. Dad was no longer in his chair and the TV played an arduous gardening program that seemed to loop every couple of weeks. Looking at my watch, I realised it was seven minutes to eleven. Dad had obviously taken himself to bed and left me to sleep on the sofa. Disgruntled that I probably wouldn't sleep well that night, I turned the TV off and headed for bed. It was only when I reached the hallway that a cool draught caught the back of my neck.

The front door was wide open.

My resting heart rate increased tenfold. A parent with dementia meant that you couldn't take your eye off the ball for even a second. Without considering the ramifications of my actions, I stepped out onto the driveway; my head spun one way, then the other in rapid succession. He could be anywhere. He could have been run over, taken to hospital. I had no idea where to begin.

It was then that I spotted him, crouched by the shrubbery in next door's garden. I placed the door on the latch to ensure that I didn't lock myself out, and with bare feet, I tiptoed over to him.

'Dad, what are you doing? You shouldn't be out here,' I whispered, conscious of the fact that we were violating curfew and that the neighbour might be suitably unimpressed.

He frantically rooted through the shrubbery like a dog searching for a bone.

'I think I dropped them here, but I can't find them.' His tone was urgent and breathy, his hands and face were black with dirt.

It was the moment that I'd dreaded for so long.

Dad had lost his mind.

As the panic crept over me, I heard Min's voice in my mind. 'When in doubt, switch off the emotion until you've dealt with the practical.'

Deal with the practical. I needed to get him indoors before a sweeper went by. There was plenty of time to fall apart later.

Fervently, I looked up and down the street in both directions. The road lay in still silence, apart from the sound of Dad's manic rummaging. With no knowledge of the frequency of the sweepers, my mission required immediate action. The ramifications of being caught outside were too great to consider.

'Dad, you need to get up. We can look together in the morning.'

'They're here somewhere, I'm certain of it.'

'Dad, the sweepers will be here any minute. Can you please

just come inside?'

'Just give me a sec,' he muttered as his hands wildly scrambled through the dirt.

I placed my hands underneath his armpits in a feeble attempt to haul him to his feet. The combination of our comparable sizes and his abject stubbornness rendered it a futile exercise.

'Dad! We have to get inside,' I gasped.

Numerous images played out in my mind's eye, and none of the outcomes provided me with comfort. In desperation, I dropped to my knees; cupped his head in my hands and forced him to look into my eyes.

'We have to go inside, Dad. Whatever you've lost, we can find it tomorrow, I promise.'

'Any second, love…'

'Dad!' I begged, agitated at his reticence. 'There's nothing there, my darling. Please, we really have to go.'

I blamed myself. I'd been working too much and had taken my finger off the pulse.

And then I heard the sound that I feared the most.

The thunderous roar of its engine, the rumble of its oversized tyres on concrete. Hesitantly, I rose to my feet. Approximately one hundred feet from where I stood, a sweeper turned the corner and headed towards me. For a moment, I was frozen to the spot, like someone had hit the pause button on reality. I glared ahead of me, transfixed by the dazzling white headlights; two large menacing eyes contemplating their next move. It crawled towards me in a slow and predatory manner, as if stalking its prey.

'Dad!' I shouted as I burst into action. 'It's coming. We have to go right now!'

He ignored me and continued to forage through the greenery. I made further attempts to rouse him, but his focus alone was rigid and uncompromising. As the sweeper drew closer, I knew I had to take action. If I was unable to get him indoors, I had to hide him.

Without forethought, I threw my entire body weight over him and awkwardly rolled us both into the shrubbery. He winced as his body hit the ground. I don't know where the strength came from, maybe it was adrenalin fuelled desperation, but I was somehow able to pin him to the spot.

I saw the headlights first. The surrounding foliage lit up like a garden feature as they swept over us, except it was me that felt like the feature. Never had I felt so exposed. My cold body was rigid in its deathly stillness. I was fearful to breathe aloud.

As the lights passed over us, a tiny, bright red light sped past my eyeline and gave me cause to blink. I wondered if I'd imagined it, if it was my mind playing tricks. When the light reappeared, it confirmed my fears.

On this occasion, it lingered, and like the beam of a sniper, it slowly and meticulously wavered in front of us. I held my breath and forcibly squeezed down on Dad's mouth; my eyes firmly focused on the red dot. If it was a motion sensor, it was only a matter of time before we were caught. If it was a sniper, then I'd surely transcended reality and landed in a movie.

It shifted to the side of me, just inches away from my face. I pushed harder on Dad's mouth, urging him to remain silent. I was barely breathing, and despite being of no religious affiliation, I said a silent prayer.

In an instant, it had disappeared, but I remained committed to the cause. I'd seen too many films to know that capture always came when the prey became complacent. A few moments later, the headlights faded and, once again, we lay in the dark of night.

I listened intently for the diminishing roar as the sweeper faded into the distance and even then; I persisted. There was no point in time that I was certain that we were safe, rather a time that I needed to trust in something far greater than us. Aware that we couldn't remain in place all night, I removed my hand from Dad's mouth and dropped my head onto his chest. I allowed myself to breathe freely as the sensation in my limbs returned.

'Found them!' whispered Dad, as he waved a pair of glasses in his extended right hand. 'We went for a walk earlier and I dropped them. Forgot to go back for them. Good specs these.'

I think I stopped breathing for a second or two.

Sometimes, there just weren't any words.

*

I could tell from the expression on Min's face that she wasn't sure whether to laugh or cry. Whilst it was undoubtedly concerning that Dad had showed sheer rebellion during curfew, there was no denying the fact that he had a lucid recollection of losing his glasses.

Min had a twisted sense of humour at the best of times, a trait that had warmed us to her from the outset. During our first meeting, she had marched through the house and demanded to see Dad. I was taken aback at her boldness, but my requirement for help had outweighed any emotion I might afford. Once she'd located him, she'd brazenly approached him and told him that she couldn't have him 'trying to cook his dinner in the washing machine,' and that she was here to take over such duties.

Over time, I'd come to realise that it was this very frankness that had saved us.

'She thought I'd finally lost it, Min,' he laughed. 'The look on her face was priceless!'

I remained expressionless.

'She had her hand over my mouth like a gag! What did she think I was going to do?'

Min burst into raucous laughter; a laugh that belonged to an oversized comedienne.

And just like that, the severity of the situation diluted fifty-fold.

'You're a walking liability, Raff,' said Min as she wiped tears of laughter from the corners of her eyes. 'You've spent more time on your face than you have on your feet this week!'

'I'm going to work,' I interrupted. 'Don't lose your glasses or I'm disowning you.'

I left the two of them laughing about the absurdity of it all while I took a step closer to my inevitable nervous breakdown.

Chapter 7

The members of the cabinet were seated around a long breakfast table as they studied a selection of photographs. An array of brightly coloured fruit garnished the table top along with a limitless supply of expensive coffee. Amongst them were images captured from the riots, many of which were undeniably vivid. One in particular showed a soldier with his hands around a man's throat. The individual held his arms above his head in an undisputable act of surrender. Another portrayed a backdrop of chaos; a soldier smiling gleefully with his foot perched on an injured woman's stomach. Others showed soldiers lashing out at civilians as they lay on the ground, their arms serving as their only available shield.

Frost looked smug as he picked up a photograph and carelessly tossed it across the table.

'Selective editing can make anything appear one-sided.'

Chief of Staff Albin Larson shifted in his seat. 'It doesn't look good for us. What protection do we have over these images?'

'The same protection that you always have,' replied Frost in his usual self-confident tone. 'None! There is no assurance that these won't be leaked to the public.'

'The public aren't aware of the riots and it's going to stay that way,' said Oakes agreeably. 'An image is an image. It doesn't mean it played out that way.'

'Did it?' asked Larson.

Oakes rolled his eyes. 'Irrelevant!'

Albin looked directly at Oakes, 'You realise that we'd be heavily compromised should these be released?'

Frost stared at him directly. 'If you do your job correctly, that won't be an issue. What are they going to do without the media? Photocopy them, and stick them to the wall?'

'Well, hardly. But there's always a way.'

The demise of the mainstream media had made whistleblowing an arduous task. Frost was resolute that no resistance group would embark on a national campaign to leak photographs that could easily have been doctored. It would be both time-consuming and pointless.

Frost produced another set of photographs. Zone Seven, their grandest creation, was clearly depicted in each shot. 'If you want something to worry about, these might be more suitable.'

Albin's jaw dropped. 'These are legitimate images of you standing outside Zone Seven. The date and time are clearly printed on each one. Someone clearly has access; they could circulate them with ease.'

Frost sighed. 'And what is it you think that these amateur terrorists plan to do with them? We're more powerful than them.'

Albin took a beat before he answered. 'The media could turn on a sixpence. We've always known that. They'd take the hit to get a story like this on the news.'

'We own them, Albin. The only news that goes out is the news that we advocate.'

Oakes let out a hearty laugh, and everyone turned to face him. 'Or fabricate.'

Frost couldn't resist a smile. 'Well, quite!'

Albin's clenched jaw and flushed cheeks showed his grievance at the exchange.

'We also have footage from the city,' he retaliated. 'How long before this gets out then?'

He pressed play on the video recorder and stood beside the unfolding footage in an act of defiance. His jaw was jutted forward, his arms were tightly folded.

Oakes wasn't blind to the tension between Frost and Albin. Over the last few months, every meeting had turned into a battle of the wits; an array of caustic comments, perpetually hurled back and forth. It wasn't maintainable. At some point, he'd have to choose between a loyal colleague and a man that could make him powerful.

He dreaded the day. His newfound desire for power made it a simple decision.

As Albin glared at him, he winced at the scenes of chaos and anarchy. An array of colour decorated the screen as multicoloured flags and banners blew in the wind above the heads of city protesters. Thousands of anti-government activists chanted of dictatorship, loss of civil rights and a corrupt government. Protest signs displayed messages of hatred and resentment; 'Welcome to the Unhappy State!' and 'It's all lies!'

Of much greater concern was the obvious presence of Freedom. A rapidly evolving resistance group. In recent months, anti-political, urban graffiti depicting political dissatisfaction with the state of the country had appeared more regularly; the group's signature logo was always evident. Oakes strained his eyes to seek evidence of their involvement within the footage and when he failed to, he relaxed a little. That was until Albin pressed pause on the video.

'Here, you can see Freedom's logo,' he stated as he pointed at a large flag that depicted the infamous "F". He hit play again and Oakes leant back in his seat. One mere flag bearer could be rendered a fan, so to speak.

Albin had a faint smirk on his face, a rarity to say the least. As he hovered over the television, he pushed his finger on the pause button with unnecessary drama. Oakes was uncertain as to where Albin was leading with his cocksure attitude.

'Look again.' He pointed at five separate individuals that wore white face coverings, often associated with the notorious resistance group. They carried banners and posters, all depicting the same logo.

Oakes felt his stomach turn as he looked at Frost for assurance. His blank expression gave nothing away.

'So, it's Freedom,' shrugged Frost. 'We're fully aware of their following. You bring us nothing new, Albin. Just because they spout nonsense doesn't mean that the public will believe them!'

Albin shuffled from one foot to the other. 'Their following is huge. We have a problem here. We've just brought the country back from a breakdown, but we're still only teetering on the edge. If they continue to rise, it could break us again.'

Oakes chewed at a loose fingernail. He hadn't been overly concerned about Freedom at first, but then he'd begun to receive threatening letters. They generally condemned Frost's extreme right wing opinions, more recently advocating for his instant dismissal. They were well-scripted, far too elaborate to be amateurs. Each letter had been surreptitiously hand delivered to his office, so much so that apprehension was impossible. They left no trace; they knew what they were doing. Freedom knew precisely of their plans for The Happy State and it concerned him. The Zones were a top government secret, yet, somehow, they were privy to information.

Frost blamed him for the poor security; shocked to the core that a resistance member could gain access to a government building.

'You're too soft with your employees,' Frost had argued. 'Without fear, people become slack and make mistakes. You treat them like they're friends. It won't serve you well.'

The current incident with the photographs had merely strengthened Frost's argument. The stakes had risen, and he needed impeccable protection. He would be forced to concede and utilise Frost's security detail.

He hated it when he was proven wrong.

Frost had stipulated that he dispose of the hate mail. He said that it served no purpose; that it would be cathartic to destroy it.

Oakes had shredded each of the letters. He hadn't felt better for it.

Having tuned out of the conversation between Frost and Albin, he turned his attention back to the screen; to brutal images of the military as they knocked protesters to the ground. Seemingly innocent onlookers were punched, kicked, and restrained by soldiers. All of them were inadvertently embroiled in a war that they weren't fighting.

He chose to believe that Frost's men felt justified in their actions, or he'd send himself mad thinking about it.

When the film had ended, Oakes abruptly dismissed

everyone from his office. With his nerves on edge, he pulled open the secret drawer underneath his desk and removed a small bottle of whiskey. He relaxed into his chair as he devoured the contents of two glasses.

He had a speech later that afternoon, but there was no harm in Dutch courage. Besides, no one would have to know.

Frost had a way of getting under his skin.

*

After publicly garbling a response to a number of concerns regarding martial law, the cabinet descended upon a small, private bar that they frequented. It was an informal debrief, though barely eligible to qualify as business due to the amount of whiskey consumed.

The secret underground bar was a favourite of politicians and journalists; a bustling, champagne drinkers' haven where "off the record" took on a whole new meaning. While the larger media houses were void since the governmental changes, they still liked to know what was going on. They were eternally hungry for a story and would stop at nothing to encounter a mere inkling of information. Frost disliked it immensely. He didn't like alcohol, and he certainly didn't like being within earshot of non-allies.

He watched as attractive women flirtatiously greeted notable public figures. They'd do anything to get their vulgar little world back up and running, anything to get a story that would make them untouchable once again. He'd fight it to the death. The media only served to destroy good intentions.

Seated in a small booth at the back of the bar, the mood

turned serious as Albin begun to criticise Oakes for his candid public speech.

'Of great concern is the valour in which fine details were articulated,' he complained. 'Do we deem it necessary to impart such finite details of our proposition? The resistance didn't require a mention.'

'I assume that's meant for me,' snorted Oakes as he studied the menu.

Frost couldn't resist a chuckle at Albin's expense. It was him that had devised the speech and Albin knew it; the comment was indirectly aimed at him. Not that he cared much, but most of the staff hadn't taken too well to his influence, and it was painfully obvious. He was used to being disliked. There were no friends in politics.

'The people are scared. Speculation of a threat from a resistance movement will serve no benefit,' Albin urged.

Oakes shot forward in his seat. 'Are you serious? The public aren't stupid, Albin. They've seen the posters and the graffiti; those that live in the cities have even seen the protests. Although we choose to keep that information away from the smaller towns, they all need to know that Freedom is threatening their dreams of a Happy State. We need to get the public on our side early on, or we're screwed.'

Albin attempted to speak, but Oakes raised his voice.

'The public are innately suspicious regarding politicians. Who can blame them? They've been governed by trash up to this point. We'll continue to feed them manipulated news updates, but, once in a while, a little bit of unsettle is necessary. That's how you gain trust.'

Frost leant back in his seat as he smugly observed the body language of the group. Oakes secretary, Anneka, looked uncomfortable. She always did; she was far too nice to have a role of such prestige. A woman of her ilk would be better suited to teaching a bunch of preschool kids. He made a mental note to add her to his exit list and recruit someone worthwhile.

He turned his attention to Albin, who relentlessly whittled on about his concerns. He was already on the list. Right at the top.

'But asking the public to report the resistance is going to trigger a war,' continued Albin. 'We'll have cell groups and lone actors doing our work for us. That very thing happened with Islamic fundamentalists. In spreading the hate, the government ended up with a heap of right-wing defence organisations that caused equally as many problems.'

Oakes snorted in disapproval.

Frost culled his urge to intervene and educate Larson on real world politics. The sole reason for social unrest was substandard governing. It was never people. The right amount of control could govern any group or individual.

'There's no harm in involving the public,' slurred Oakes as the whiskey began to take effect. 'It makes our job a little easier, and I believe it's the approach that's necessary for this transition. The public are on a need-to-know basis.'

Frost smiled to himself as Anneka and Albin recoiled at Oakes' brash tone. It was always going to cause a stir when a placid politician reassessed his outlook and took the hard line. Frost had no doubt that they blamed him personally for the extreme change in Oakes' character. But you couldn't afford to be naïve in politics. There was always an element of secrecy and corruption.

'But suggesting extreme measures for the resistance?' asked Larson. 'Thank God you didn't spell it out! It hardly makes for a Happy State. What even are these measures?'

Frost leant forward and placed his elbows on the table. The conversation had become heated, and he couldn't risk being overheard.

'We have yet to decide on the nature of these precise measures. It is something that is under consideration. As we keep telling the public, Albin, it's going to get tough before it gets easier. You don't create a Happy State by just winging it. You have to set a few rules and make a few harsh decisions. Reducing crime is an integral first step.'

Oakes reached into his jacket and pulled out his cigarettes. 'To offer an ounce of power is to disarm. Consider this a decoy from the real truth.' He stood and made his way towards the door.

'Don't worry, Albin,' whispered Frost as he rose from his seat. 'There, there. You'll be alright.'

He didn't stick around to see his reaction.

Hot on Oakes trail to the outdoor smoking area, he steered him into a quiet corner, away from prying eyes and ears. He noticed that three well-known reporters had chosen the same moment to opt for a cigarette break; it was painfully tactless. He didn't trust public conversations, especially with all the hacks mulling about.

He kept his voice low as he spoke. 'We had sightings of several known resistance members in the city today. Don't worry, we had eyes on them at all times.'

Oakes was visibly shocked by this admission. 'How the hell did that happen?' he fumed. 'I could have been…'

'We had it under control,' reassured Frost. 'But the time has come to employ more regimental detail.'

'Where are you holding them?'

'We aren't.'

'Why on earth not?'

'They're small fry. We need them to lead us to the big boys.'

Oakes wiped a visible bead of sweat from his brow. 'Maybe we'd have got something out of them,' he contested. 'Did that cross your mind at any point?'

Frost had encountered resistance groups aplenty in the line of duty and they seldom to never offered information of their comrades, regardless of the level of scrutiny. He could have spun rhetoric on the subject, offered specific examples, educated him on the criminal mind, but he didn't have the patience.

'We wouldn't have. Trust me.'

Oakes leaned in closer. 'It's your responsibility to see them coming. It's your responsibility to stop them from coming anywhere near me. And if they do, it's your responsibility to do whatever is necessary to ensure it's the last time they ever do!'

Frost opened his mouth to speak but stopped himself. It was a deliberate move. He was becoming too adept at subtle manipulation.

'So, can I assume that we at least have locations of the individuals in question?'

Frost remained silent. Another deliberate move.

He threw his cigarette to the ground. 'Well then, if I care to remain safe, I suppose I need to look at alternative arrangements.'

'Perhaps we could implement new security?'

He couldn't get rid of Oakes' half-soaked security team quick enough; they'd get more use out of a flock of sheep.

Oakes paused.

Frost waited.

He'd become quite accustomed to Oakes frivolous and childish ways. He'd make him sweat for a moment or two while he enjoyed the power trip. Next, he'd either light another cigarette or use that ridiculous breath freshener to elongate the silence.

Oakes removed his breath freshener and sprayed it into his mouth four times. He turned his back on Frost and opened the door to the restaurant.

'Deal with it,' he snapped as he disappeared through the doorway.

'Like clockwork,' Frost muttered under his breath.

Frost was elated. There hadn't been a single member of Freedom present at Oakes speech, but he didn't need to know that. It had proven to be the perfect opportunity to recruit his own men. He knew Oakes would be grinning his imbecilic head off as he entered the restaurant. A few glasses of whiskey and he thought he was impenetrable.

The irony was extraordinary.

He too was smiling.

Chapter 8

As I walked to work in the morning sunshine, I thought about Anne's four-day absence from the café. Despite my attempts to realign my thoughts with my own concerns rather than those of a woman that I knew very little about, my mind seemed to be stubbornly fixated on her.

I slowed down as I reached The Comms Wall. It had become quite the habit to interrupt my journey with a voyeuristic insight into other people's lives. I wasn't the only one. In the early days of the transition, there had often been a gathering of people, keen to pass on a message or simply pry. It had been quite the novelty.

Communication had become testing to say the least, so people had taken to leaving each other notes or pictures on the wall. When things had been at their worst, you would often witness an entire conversation between two parties, though more recently they'd taken to leaving a series of marks that were indistinguishable to anyone outside their circle. On this particular day, there were numerous dots, lines and slashes that might as well have been a foreign language for all they represented. Feeling somewhat despondent at the lack of creativity, I continued towards the village, which was much busier than usual. I noticed a large group of people walking towards the local park and, inquisitively, followed a family as they approached the large arch that marked its entrance. There were military stationed either side, questioning and inspecting people before they entered. Mindlessly, I found myself next in line as the family passed through.

A poker-faced soldier searched the contents of my bag before giving me the once over with his eyes and nodding his approval. I assumed that was English for "you're not a threat."

The park was bustling with people, so I instinctively followed the direction of the slow-moving crowd. Kids ambled behind their parents while couples casually meandered, hand in hand. When I reached the halfway point, I started to regret my decision. The crowd seemed to be increasing in size and there was an oppressive mugginess in the air, which made me feel irritable. As an avid hater of busy areas, I decided that it might be a good time to abandon my plight and head back in the direction that I came. If it was anything notable, I'd no doubt hear about it from each and every one of my customers. Numerous times. For at least a week.

My mission wasn't quite as smooth as my intention. As I attempted to weave through the evergrowing crowd, people forcefully moved towards me, impatient at my desire to move around them. Others stood rigidly in place, determined not to lose their place. The more that I moved, the more my legs weakened; a thin veil of sweat had manifested across my brow and upper lip and my head was spinning.

I recognised the symptoms. I was going to have a panic attack.

The pre-panic anticipation merely served to worsen my mental state. I was glued to the spot as a plethora of blurry faces busied around me. I felt sick.

In spite of the dark veil that rapidly enveloped me, I heard someone call my name. I looked up to see a figure standing before me, my impaired vision denying me any lucidity.

'Rafella, are you okay?'

I don't remember what happened next. I know my legs buckled, and the world started to spin as I remained hopelessly fixed to the spot. I might have even lost consciousness for a few seconds. The next thing I recall was awkwardly hanging over someone's shoulder as they manoeuvred me through the crowd.

When we stopped, the person, presumably male due to their excessive strength, sat me down on a hard surface. I stayed perfectly still for a minute or two with my head leant forward. The voices around me seemed loud and animated. I could smell the aroma of a smoky barbecue.

It was inevitable; I cupped my hand to my mouth as the acid rose from my stomach and, eyeing an empty area of grass, I lurched forward and vomited.

After emptying the contents of my stomach, a hand reached out and kindly offered me a tissue. I didn't dare look up and examine the level of embarrassment that I would be privy to. Instead, I remained crouched on the floor where I was passed a further three tissues. It was only then that I glanced upward to identify the person who had rescued me from my own stupidity.

He was tall and stocky; his eyes were gentle. He looked to be in his mid-fifties and was handsome in a rugged way.

He unscrewed the lid on a water bottle and handed it to me. 'You looked in a bad way back there. Are you alright?'

I nodded. I definitely wasn't alright, but I was vastly improved from the preceding ten minutes.

'Crowds,' I croaked as I took a sip of lukewarm water. 'I think I'm allergic to them.'

He smiled. 'People are overrated. Do you feel better?'

'I think so.'

I glanced at my surroundings. Stationed to my left was a small, custom-built stage that was manned by angry-faced security guards. Their robust chests stuck out as they attempted to project an air of authority. Three army trucks were parked nearby and an abundance of military were scattered in various positions, their oversized rifles ready for action, visible to everyone and sundry. There were people everywhere, all hungry for an occasion that I knew nothing about.

'How do I not have a clue what's going on?' I asked.

He laughed. 'You have a life, perhaps?'

'You clearly don't know me,' I snorted.

'Except I do,' he replied. He stared at me. 'You don't remember me, do you?'

My mind was ninety percent off kilter already. It was unlikely that I'd have recognised my own reflection.

'The café,' I said with a confident smile. That was how I knew the majority of people that I failed to recognise, my fail-safe response.

He shook his head.

Damn!

'I used to be good friends with Phil, your dad. It was some years back, mind,' he confirmed. 'I haven't seen you since you were a kid.'

I was ashamed. Not only had he rescued me, but he knew me from old.

'Christmas of 2012,' he recalled. 'The dinner burnt. Pretty sure we ate ravioli?'

'Ravioli shapes, in fact! With stuffing and sprouts. How could I forget that?'

'I think we were too drunk to care,' he laughed. 'The adults, that is. You were only...'

'Five, six maybe.'

A significant period of my childhood, submerged in the depths of my memory. It made me wonder what else was down there.

He smiled warmly as he offered me his hand. 'Do you think you could stand?'

I took his hand and slowly rose to my feet. Apart from the brutal headache, I felt a lot less sickly.

'I think you'll live to see another day,' he said as he cautiously let go of my hand. He glanced around as if to survey his surroundings. 'You should get yourself out of here,' he urged. 'It's going to get even busier.'

I noticed that he continuously turned his head like an on duty policeman. Each time someone passed by, his eyes darted in their direction.

'Are you with someone?' I asked, suddenly aware that I might have held him up. 'I'm so sorry for taking up your time.'

'Not at all. Just thinking of you.'

'Sorry,' I repeated.

'Don't apologise.' His head spun as a woman passed by with her dog. She recoiled slightly, as though she felt threatened.

I hurled my bag over my shoulder with the effort of an invalid. It felt like someone had loaded it with bricks. 'I only came to see what was going on. What is going on?'

'Edwin Oakes is addressing the people. Everyone's favourite person.'

I rolled my eyes. I was too familiar with Oakes' endless rambles and had no desire to be a part of it.

Stan laughed. I sensed he shared my opinion.

'Well, I think you're okay now,' he reassured. 'Please give my best to Phil.'

I felt my eyes well up at the mention of Dad's name. It was so comforting to see someone that shared a history with Dad and I. Despite the drastic nature of our encounter, it had offered me a strange sense of comfort.

'Are you alright?' he asked.

I nodded over enthusiastically, a bid to stifle the tears.

It didn't work; I sobbed like an injured toddler. A surge of tears streamed from my eyes and showed no signs of relenting. Stan urged me to sit as he squatted down in front of me. Certain that I was embarrassing myself, I hid my face in my hands to retain some semblance of dignity while Stan simply waited for the moment to pass.

'I am so embarrassed,' I sniffed, roughly wiping my eyes.

'Don't be,' he soothed. He glanced at a soldier who was standing nearby. 'Seeing that doesn't help, we're living in tough times.'

I followed his eyeline. 'Oh, I'm used to that. Quite the norm now,' I laughed. 'What's a park without an armed soldier?'

He nodded. His eyes were kind.

'Dad has dementia,' I blurted. I took a deep breath and made a strange snorting sound. The act made me laugh out loud, and the laughter morphed into sobs.

'I am so sorry,' I said, rubbing my hands over my face. 'I can't believe I'm doing this to you. You must think I'm crazy.'

'I'm upset to hear about your dad.'

I looked at my feet and shuffled them back and forth. 'Yeah. Diagnosed two years ago.'

'Sorry.'

I waved my arm nonchalantly as I attempted to refrain from crying. 'It is what it is. He's so well loved. And spoilt rotten!' I laughed.

A wave of applause from the crowd dissected the awkwardness. I was thankful; I'd never been happier to see Edwin Oakes.

'I have to go, Raff. You and your dad are forever in my thoughts. Be sure to look after yourself.'

I smiled.

'...and I'd stay away from crowded places.'

'Thank you!' I called after him.

I watched him duck and dive between a few people in a stealth-like fashion. There was something about him, something edgy perhaps. I couldn't put my finger on it, but I picked up a distinctly strange vibe.

I rolled my eyes at my own idiocy and wondered when I'd stopped acknowledging the good in people. Only I could have come to such a conclusion. He'd shown nothing but kindness and I'd chosen to over-analyse. I dismissed the thought instantly. I had the gall to think his behaviour strange when I'd fainted, vomited and sobbed in a twenty-minute window.

The crowd made their way towards the stage and I lingered

in a barren patch of grass to regain my strength. Oakes' speech was in full swing, and his audience was transfixed as he spewed the same old rhetoric. I had no intention of staying.

As I neared the café, I found myself laughing at my ineptitude. Mum could never understand how a pacifist like herself had given birth to such a worrywart. She often reminded me that my eccentricity was nothing short of endearing. We both knew that it was Dad's gene pool that was responsible. Until Dad had begun earning a salary, he'd worried desperately about the future; how he'd support his family if he didn't get a break, what he'd do for work if he couldn't earn a living from his art. But each time, Mum had placated him, consistently telling him to have faith, to prepare himself for his big break. Mum was a believer. She had a cast iron faith that his tenacity and talent would prevail.

She was right.

I hadn't inherited that gene either.

*

I fell back onto my comfortable mattress and glanced out of the window. The night was darker than usual. The sky looked black and angry, as though a storm was imminent. The sweepers were out and their headlights were casting ominous shadows on my window. I hated this time of night, when the fear of the unknown encircled me like a vulture. I closed my eyes, but the alternating light and shade teased my eyelids. Panic was draining beyond the moment itself.

Despite my attempts to clear my mind, the events of the

day played over and over. There was something about Stan's demeanour that had unsettled me. His altruism was to be admired, and I remained thankful of his presence, yet he had obviously been distracted.

Then again, I hadn't proven to be the most enticing of company.

My tears. My deluge of heartfelt tears that had come from a deeply embedded place. My emotions were like a caged tiger of late; ready to pounce at the first opportunity.

I thought back to a book that I'd read as a young child. The story was about a boy that couldn't cry, no matter how hard he tried. All the things that made him sad built inside him until one day, he cried at something trivial and couldn't stop. As the story progressed, he cried more often, each time a little less, and eventually, having imparted all of his burdens, he stopped. I always thought it was a silly book, yet all those years later, I found myself in a similar predicament.

Aware that I was allowing myself to wallow in self-pity, I redirected my thoughts to Oakes' speech. He had captivated the attention of the masses with his half-baked, phoney speech. I failed to see beyond his arrogant and smarmy exterior. He'd waved as the crowd had cheered, attempted coyness at the applause. I could see that he was soaking it up, allowing his ego to breed.

In the brief time that I was present, he talked about the positive changes that had already materialised due to martial law. He stated statistics that correlated a happier state with lower crime rates. The incessant cheers had significantly lessened as he talked about the resistance.

'The new enemy is the resistance. Although more prominent in cities, they're slowly moving out to smaller areas and we, the people, must remain vigilant and report any suspicious behaviour. The resistance will be treated with extreme measures.'

I'd left at that point. Extreme measures and a Happy State in the same sentence; it didn't make sense to me. A leader that expected his public to do the work for him seemed nothing short of absurd; the concept of a rebellion habituating in a sleepy village like Thendra, even more so. It was futile scaremongering that would merely aggravate the peace.

I wanted to switch my brain off. I needed to switch my brain off.

I looked across at Grey Bear, who was proudly seated in the wicker chair. His big brown eyes openly peered at me. I walked over and scooped him up, firmly embedding him in my arms.

Grey Bear was a comfort blanket. He always reminded me of Mum.

*

I'd been given Grey Bear when I was around five years old. I'd fallen in love with him at first sight and set about my childhood endeavours with him firmly attached to my side at all times. Bath time had been a battle of the wits to prize him away from me; my only compromise was that he perched on the side of the bathtub. I loved him with every inch of my heart, the only way that I knew how to love.

A month or so after having him, Mum had asked me what I was going to call my nameless accomplice. I'd giggled.

'What's so funny?' Mum had asked.

'That's the silliest question ever,' I'd replied, apparently rolling my eyes.

Mum had been taken aback at my response. 'Oh! Well, I'm so sorry. Does he have a name?'

'Grey Bear,' I replied, immediately and incontestably. As deadpan as a satirical comedian.

Mum and Dad had been endeared by my no nonsense take on life at such a young age.

Grey Bear went on to spend over one thousand nights cuddled up to me at night. He'd been on numerous family holidays, had his fur "blow dried" as Mum called it, lost an eye, and had the eye replaced with a slightly smaller version of the previous eye.

I can vividly remember the day that Mum had approached me in the garden while I was watering the plants with my mini watering can. In her arms sat Grey Bear.

'Darling, why have I just found Grey Bear in the dustbin?'

'I'm too old for him now, Mummy,' I'd replied, eyes firmly focused on the task before me. 'And besides, he got too needy for me.'

Mum later revealed that she'd had to suppress a giggle. Instead, she tried to convince me to keep him, though to maybe consider a more "casual" coupling.

'No thanks!' I'd replied, 'He takes up all of my time, and I have things to do.'

With that, Mum took Grey Bear and placed him in her wardrobe for safe keeping. She reintroduced him to me when I was sixteen, along with the tale of our break-up, and I've kept him in my room ever since.

We had a much more relaxed relationship after that, but the odd cuddle here and there still magically transported me to happier times.

*

The next day at work, I sought nothing more than normality. I considered routine and familiarity to be as valuable as gold when I felt off-kilter.

The unnaturally warm weather had given me a fitful sleep the previous night, and I craved a busy shift to tire me naturally. The steady flux of customers failed to provide, and my mood soured as the day progressed. On another day, a slow to moderate pace might satisfy me, but a mere five customers prior to lunch only made me irritable.

Sometime during the afternoon, I started flagging and found myself slouching a lot. I was in a strange mood, out of sorts almost. I half-expected Dahlia to attribute it to a full moon.

'You're in one of your weird ones, aren't you?' she said.

I shrugged. 'I'm not sure what I am, to be honest.'

'Life as we know it has changed. You're allowed to feel that way.'

I raised my eyebrows. 'It isn't a full moon?'

She offered a sarcastic smile. 'It's waxing gibbous, but nice try. It might be that you're not eating enough.'

'Waxing who?'

'Forget it,' she laughed. 'Did you eat breakfast?'

I thought for a couple of seconds. 'You know, I honestly can't remember.'

The next thing I knew, she'd thrust a piece of cake and a cup of tea in front of me.

'I'm not hungry,' I whined. 'And even if I was, I'm too tired to eat.'

'Eat!' she demanded as she pulled out a chair and sat me in it.

My eyes became heavy as I pushed the cake around the plate.

'I'm watching you,' Dahlia called from the counter. 'You're not moving until that plate is empty.'

Disapprovingly, I scrunched my nose up at her.

My feet throbbed from the work shoes that I'd recently purchased, so I slipped them off and stretched my tired and aching feet. I slowly worked my way through the gargantuan slice of cake and attempted to enjoy a few moments of relaxation. It dawned on me that my clothes had begun to feel looser. Somewhere between looking after Dad and my daily shift at the café, I'd forgotten to look after myself.

I could hear Mum in my mind, 'You'll be no use to your son or daughter if you can't look after yourself.' I shook my head at the sound of her voice. It didn't matter how many times I told her I wasn't the parenting type; she'd always thrown me that knowing look.

Every day, I hoped that I lived up to her expectations.

I glanced around the café. Two friends caught up over coffee and cake, and a mother stole some reading time as her newborn rested contentedly in its pram. The ambient music in the background masked the clinking of cutlery; the low hanging lights projected a warm, dim light that complimented the atmosphere. I was proud of what we'd created, a tiny slice of escapism from the darkness that surrounded us. My only sadness was that Mum never got to experience it herself.

I blinked the tears from my eyes and turned to look out of the window. As my gaze wandered, a newly hung poster on the wall caught my attention. It didn't require close inspection to spot the imposing government warning.

H.S. GOVERNMENT WARNING.

It is a crime of the state to be a member, affiliate, or enabler of a resistance group. The punishment is severe for both terrorist-related activity and for harbouring a known member.

If you have any information that would be useful to us, contact us immediately.

Your help will be rewarded.

I tore the poster from the wall.

While I actively encouraged the support of local businesses, I refused to be an advocate for an individual's ruination. Ironically, The Happy State laws seemed to grow more rigid by the day; Oakes hadn't paused for breath before implementing his latest strategy.

In no way did I endorse a resistance group of any kind, but it was not in my nature to promote turmoil in my personal space. The café was a place to relax; a governmental call to action contradicted the spirit of all that it stood for. During moments of anger or frustration at the actions of others, Mum had always lectured me on the profoundness of life and taught me never to judge even the worst of actions. Remaining true to her free-spirited views, she philosophised that everyone had a story, and there was usually a rationality to individual behaviour.

I rolled the poster into a ball and hurled it into the waste basket.

And then I cut myself another piece of cake.

Chapter 9

It took me nine minutes to nip to the newsagent two doors away and exchange a few bank notes for loose change. On my return, I hadn't expected to see Jo recoiling as a forceful male customer pinned her to the counter. An array of scattered leaflets decorated the wooden floor.

Aghast, I dropped the bags of change and headed in their direction. 'What's going on?'

To my surprise, the man relented at once.

'What on earth do you think you're doing?' I demanded. His clothes looked worn and grubby; his hair was overgrown and unkempt. It crossed my mind that he might be homeless, a sad consequence of post-war unemployment.

Concerned, I looked at Jo. 'Are you alright?'

She nodded. Apart from a slightly twisted t-shirt, she seemed to have survived the ordeal.

A shuffling sound distracted us. We turned to see the man scrambling on the floor as he fervently gathered the fallen leaflets. The café fell into silence; I had no idea what I was dealing with. We watched in disbelief as he scurried and gathered his belongings with the desperation of a scavenger.

When he started to cry, it was like nothing I had ever encountered. It was neither sob nor squall, but more animalistic in nature. He rocked back and forth, consumed with gut-wrenching pain. I beckoned to Jo to switch the door sign to closed and crouched down next to him. Jo cast me a look of disapproval, but I felt no sense of fear or threat.

'I'm sorry,' he whispered.

I lifted a fallen leaflet and studied its contents. A dark-skinned, wild-haired girl beamed back at me; she was undeniably beautiful and charismatic. In bold lettering, the word "Missing" lay above the image.

'My daughter, isn't she beautiful?'

'Yes, she is,' I smiled. 'I'm really sorry.'

He gently took the leaflet from my hands and stroked his finger over her face as tears fell from his haunted eyes. 'That's Layla, my baby girl. It's been five weeks.'

With no inclination as to what I could say, I chose to remain silent. There were only so many times a person could hear a bunch of euphemisms. I knew that from experience.

'We've asked her friends, but no one's heard anything. I'm not holding out for good news.'

'Hey, you mustn't think like that,' I said. 'You don't know anything yet.'

He squeezed his eyes shut, held the photograph to his chest. 'I love her so much. She's my world. I don't know how I'll live without her.'

Jo stepped forward and kneeled in front of him. 'You've contacted the police?'

He nodded. 'Numerous times. As soon as I told them she had a condition, they lost interest. Didn't even put a missing person's report in.'

I wouldn't have enquired further, but Jo had more front than me.

'A condition?'

'Manic depression. It's a tough ride. She can be up one day and down the next. Police probably think she's topped herself.'

'Is that possible?'

I felt my neck stiffen at Jo's brashness.

'Definitely not. I've told them as much, but they aren't interested.'

'My boyfriend is a policeman,' Jo lamented. 'I can ask him for you?'

He smiled. 'Thanks, but you won't get a different response. They won't even let me put posters up anywhere, something about scaremongering. She's my daughter, for God's sake.'

At last, it all started to make sense. 'That's why you were here…'

'Yes. I'm sorry. I'm just asking a few local businesses… seeing if they'd mind putting something up. It all helps. When she… your colleague, said no, I just…'

Jo smiled. 'It's okay, honestly. I understand.'

'I'm truly sorry for scaring you. I shouldn't have reacted that way. I've had a few refusals today and, I suppose, you got the wrath. People aren't like they used to be. They're just too scared of the ramifications of taking a few leaflets. This world that we live in…'

'You're telling me,' I muttered. 'Look, I'm more than happy to take some and pass a few around.'

He placed his hand on my forearm, a gentle clutch. 'Thank you. You have no idea what that would mean to me.'

He thanked us at least a further nine times before he left, and, to our great fortune, he'd already departed when a mildly inebriated Lennie rose from his seat and made his way to the front door.

'Been livening up your coffee again, Lennie?' I frowned.

He was already on a second warning for the sneaky hip flask he occasionally smuggled in with him. Once more, and I'd be forced to ban him from future visits, which was the last thing I wanted to do.

'Don't know what you mean,' he slurred.

'Last warning, Lennie. I'll have to ban you if you do it again.'

He attempted to salute me, but his hand fell short of his head. Jo rushed to the door to hold it open for him as he took a large stride backwards.

No more drama. Please!

'That man… his girl's gone, you know. They have her. They'll have us all soon.'

Jo steered him to the door and forced him outside. 'Okay, Lennie. Thank you. Take care and see you soon.'

With Lennie safely removed, I pinned a poster on the board and placed another at the back of the café. I knew I could talk to a few of the neighbouring shops and convince them to do the same.

I mused at the reticence of the police. I was sure that they still had a duty to serve and protect, regardless of the influx of military. A missing person would fall under police jurisdiction, so their apparent negligence mithered me.

If we were incapable of helping our fellow citizens, what hope was there for any of us?

*

I raced down the stairs with my jacket hanging over my shoulder.

'Min, why didn't you wake me?' I blurted.

'Well, given that you're not six years old, I didn't realise it was my job!' she mused. 'And I thought you looked like you could do with the extra sleep. You got in late?'

'Yeah. Dahlia worked over and helped me with the accounts,' I offered, grateful that Dahlia had made a tedious job slightly less so.

'You missed dinner, I expect?'

'No, actually. We got crepes from over the road and washed them down with a beer.' We'd eaten a healthy salad with sparkling water, but sometimes I couldn't resist.

She shook her head. 'Honestly, Raff!'

I darted around the kitchen as I gathered my belongings. Having woken with yesterday's clothes on and having no time to shower, I felt suitably groggy.

'Your Dad told me about that poor gent that came in,' she said. 'I'll pop some posters up in the surgery if you like?'

I frantically scanned the room for my car keys, so I didn't fully acknowledge what Min had said. In such circumstances, I'd learnt it best to agree. 'Er... yeah. Thanks, Min.'

She dangled a keyring in front of her face. 'Is this what you're after?'

'Ah! Yes!'

She pulled her hand away as I reached out. 'You're not looking too well.'

'Oh, not you too!' I groaned.

'Well, I won't lie. You look...'

'Thin!' I snapped. 'Yes, so I've been told. Thank you for your concern.' I held my hand out, and she dropped the keys into my palm. 'And late. Really late!'

I noticed that she'd made a couple of slices of toast for herself, so I defiantly stole one from her plate and shoved it into my mouth to placate her. 'Happy now?'

'I give up!'

I spotted Dad in the lounge as I gathered my belongings. He precariously waved a screwdriver in his hand as he muttered an array of choice words under his breath.

'What's he fixing?' I whispered.

'Don't ask,' Min urged. 'I've told him it's DIY for a reason. Don't involve yourself! It always ends badly when he starts meddling.'

She was right. Dad wasn't a particularly patient individual, despite his numerous attempts to toy with things of a domestic nature. It usually ended in a power cut.

'I'll sneak out,' I said. 'Just tell him I said bye.'

I snatched Min's second piece of toast as I walked past her.

'Thanks for the breakfast!' I called as I made my way to the front door.

Chapter 10

I sat in the passenger seat of Jed's car while his fingers irritatingly drummed on the steering wheel to the beat of the noxious music that was playing. He was the last person I wanted to share a lift with, but when he conveniently passed as I made my way home in monsoon-like weather, my jacket held awkwardly above my head, the decision to avoid drowning had seemed logical.

He had opted for the long way home, so the journey was jerky, to say the least. As he weaved in and out of the small side roads, his sudden, erratic movements forced me back and forth in my seat. He'd muttered something about 'avoiding the military,' and I hadn't questioned him further. I sort of got it. There was nothing like seeing a bunch of armed soldiers to dispel a decent mood.

As we meandered through one particular avenue, the surroundings seemed overly familiar. I didn't know the area, but I felt like I did at the same time. Any semblance of automatic recognition was crippled by Jed's insufferable music that would likely damage my eardrums for life. I tried to think, to piece it together, but I just couldn't pinpoint it.

No longer able to cope with the tedious, high-pitched screech that incessantly spewed out of the speakers, I leaned forward and changed the channel. He glared at me, unsatisfied with the relaxing music that monopolised every other radio station. I too found it mind-numbing, but it was better than the alternative.

A pretty, pale blue house sparked my attention and added to the teetering memory. It differed from its neighbouring homes with its peculiarly ornate structure.

It was something to do with Anne. I was almost certain of it.

And then it came to me.

Several months back, I'd driven Anne home after she'd developed a severe migraine at the cafe. It had seemed inappropriate to allow her to walk under the circumstances. At the time, I'd commented on the quaintness of the pretty blue house that we'd passed.

I grabbed hold of Jed's wrist and demanded that he stop the car. He applied the brake with such force that I jerked forward, despite my seat belt.

'Jesus! A bit of notice would have been nice!'

I climbed out of the car and ambled down the road, scrutinising each and every house. Jed followed behind like a lost child, puzzled as to my plight.

'What are we doing?'

I stopped in my tracks and turned back to look at him. 'We are doing nothing,' I bluntly retorted. 'But I'm checking up on a friend. You can go if you want.'

I continued ahead while he muttered something under his breath. Derogatory, no doubt.

A man on the other side of the road made no attempt to conceal his scepticism as he cleaned his car. His edginess came as little surprise. Conjecture had become commonplace in Thendra; new faces were often regarded as a threat to the safety of the inhabitants, especially since the transition. It had never made much sense to me.

A few steps further and Anne's house seemed to glare at me from the end of the grove. It was tucked away behind a large oak tree and a plethora of greenery. I recalled commenting on the satisfying seclusion of her home. Her hanging baskets were immaculate. The grass, though slightly overgrown, was clearly well maintained.

I marched down her driveway like a woman on a mission and tapped at her front door. When I failed to elicit a response, I tried again until I was certain that she wasn't home. Jed lingered at the end of her driveway and abruptly tilted his head in a gesture that beckoned me to leave. I wasn't ready to concede.

The front room curtains were closed, which made it impossible to catch a glimpse inside. Instinctively, I headed for the gate and followed a narrow entry; another gate opened up to her back garden.

Jed caught up with me. 'Seriously, what are we doing?'

This "we" business irked me. There was no "we" now, or at any point in the foreseeable future.

I considered his words. What was I doing here? It wasn't like I knew Anne particularly well. I wasn't a relative or close friend, even. But for some reason, unbeknownst to me, I'd become increasingly consumed by her evasiveness. A customer who made it to your front door during gale force winds and heavy snowfall was surely justification for concern.

When there was no response at the back door, I lowered the handle and the door opened with ease. I surprised myself with my boldness.

'Really?' quipped Jed.

'Will you be quiet?' I snapped. 'You're putting me on edge.'

'I'm putting you on edge?'

'Shut it, Jed!' I snapped as I furtively placed my foot inside Anne's kitchen. I called out her name before heading further into her home.

'I hate to break it to you, but breaking and entering is a criminal offense.'

'Thanks for reminding me,' I snorted.

His mouth burst into a huge, smug grin. 'I guess this makes you a criminal then.'

'Then I guess it makes you one too!'

With Jed on my heel, I tiptoed towards the lounge area. The closed curtains projected a dreary darkness throughout the room. I fought my urge to open them up and allow the natural light to enter her home.

'What are we looking for exactly?' he asked as he lifted an ornament from a cabinet and inspected it. I snatched it out of his hand. 'Has it dawned on you that she might not like your coffee anymore? There's a really nice coffee place…'

'Grow up, Jed!'

With trepidation, I continued through the house. I was taken aback at the tidiness and the orderly fashion in which her numerous ornaments and keepsakes were positioned. It looked more like a show home than a residential property. The cushions on her sofa were neatly stacked; the sofa looked in pristine condition. Her ornaments, of which there were several, were immaculately polished and placed with careful thought. A collection of assorted animals sat on one shelf and a group of finely crafted women were elegantly poised on another. There was a certain obsessiveness amongst the neatly displayed trinkets and spotless furniture which urged me to consider her character.

Her fascination with stale milk started to make more sense.

I spotted three pairs of shoes that were regimentally lined up against the wall. Slippers, long grey boots and a pair of slip-on plimsolls. Hanging overhead was a thin grey jacket and a purple winter coat, both of which I recognised from her numerous visits.

'She's clearly not here,' said Jed as he perched himself on the arm of the sofa. 'We should go.'

An adjoining door led to a dining area where a large table took up the majority of the room. Draped in a stunning antique tablecloth, table mats, cutlery and napkins were positioned at every seat, as though a dinner party might be imminent.

The end chair lay on the floor as if it had tipped over backwards. Nearby, an empty plate and its contents were scattered across the carpet.

Jed crouched on the ground and looked under the table. 'She didn't like her pasta much.'

'I very much doubt she's under there,' I quipped.

'You never know.'

I was perturbed by a woman's need to vacate her home so suddenly, particularly one as freakishly spotless as Anne. I hadn't even considered the prospect of finding her...

'Maybe she was rushed into hospital,' I suggested.

Jed rose to his feet. In a flash, his joviality had dissipated. 'We need to get out of here.'

'What's the problem?'

'Besides breaking into someone's home?'

Touché.

I followed his lead as he hastily exited through the house like a doomed burglar. A medication bottle caught my eye; perched on the kitchen unit in prime view, presumably so that she wouldn't forget to take whatever contents it contained. I double backed and read the label; the brand name was immediately recognisable as commonplace antidepressants, prescribed to an Annabelle K. Sinclair.

Mum had been given a course of the same medication after her diagnosis, but they'd done little more than neglect her of all human emotions. It transpired that she'd only taken them to prevent her from being upset around Dad and I; her last undertaking as selfless as the rest. The tablets needed to be taken on a daily basis to avoid a number of disturbing side effects. Wherever Anne had gone, she'd struggle without them.

More alarm bells.

Back at the car, Jed hit the accelerator before I even closed the door.

'What's up?' I asked as I pulled the door and hastily fastened my seatbelt.

He didn't respond, and remained aloof for the duration of the journey home. Granted, I'd taken a dubious risk, but Jed was anything but a scaredy cat. Fear of reprisal was far more likely to have an adverse effect on me than him.

The rain had started to fall heavily by the time he reached my house. I wasted no time in thanking him for the lift and opened the door to make a run for it. I wanted to beat the rain as much as I wanted to escape Jed's company.

I was halfway out of the car when he decided to speak. 'How well do you know this… Anne?'

I clambered back inside and closed the door to prevent the rain from entering.

'Wow! Timing!'

'Sorry.'

'Not very well. Why?'

'No reason,' he muttered.

There clearly was a reason. Just like there was a reason for his solemn expression. I placed my hand on the door handle, ready to abscond.

'So, why are you so worried about her then?' he continued. 'If you don't know her, I mean.'

'If you have something to say, will you just say it?'

'Just curious, that's all.'

'She's a diehard regular. I haven't seen her for five days. That's why. Okay?'

He shifted in his seat, then turned to face me. He opened his mouth to speak, then bit down on his lip. I waited.

Finally, he spoke. 'Can I trust you, Raff?'

I fell silent. I really didn't know how to answer the question. Just because I didn't like him didn't necessarily mean that he couldn't confide in me.

'It's not a trick question. You either can or you can't. It's that simple.'

'It depends,' I surmised.

'On what?'

'On what you're confiding.'

He stared at me intensely, as if desperately trying to mind read.

'Mum told me about the man in your café. The one looking for his daughter.'

I hesitated. 'What's that got to do with anything?'

'Well, there's Anne, and this man's daughter. Coincidence, don't you think?'

I hadn't given it a second thought. As far as I was concerned, the two were isolated incidents. I looked on with incredulity, hopeful that another pearl of wisdom might offer me some insight into the offbeat conversation that we were having. It never came.

'Well, thanks for the talk. It was weird.'

'Yeah.' He glanced at my hand, poised on the handle. 'Tell Mum to meet me in the car.'

Before he was able to lure me into any more cryptic conversation, I opened the door and sprinted to the front door. The sleet-like rain felt like small rocks as it bounced off my skull, and within seconds, my clothes were soaked through. I stepped inside the warm house and shook myself like a wet dog.

A hostile stare from Min made me feel like a naughty teenager. 'All over the clean carpet. Lovely!' she alluded.

I glared at her through my rain sodden hair. 'Your chariot awaits.'

She gave me a wide berth as she passed me by. 'He's away with the fairies,' she whispered, pointing to the living room. 'I've put some dinner aside for you.'

'Thanks, Min.'

Quite alien to the concept of relaxation, I decided to use the time that Dad was asleep to unwind and have a little me time. I poured myself a bath and added an overly generous amount of honey-scented bath wash that was probably long out of date. As large, translucent bubbles formed on the water's surface, I lit a sweet-smelling candle that had simply gathered dust while lying dormant. When the tub was full to the brim, I climbed in and invited the warm, soapy water to caress my damp and aching body.

For a minute or two, I revelled in comfort and allowed myself to drift away to a thought-free paradise. It didn't take long for my mind to wander back to Jed's words; 'a coincidence…'

Two missing persons in a short space of time was coincidental. Two missing persons that were linked to the café was even more so. If he was trying to tell me that something was amiss at the café, he was delusional. I chided myself for wasting too much mental energy on the topic and made a mental note to avoid further contact with him. I still couldn't understand why he was so keen to ingratiate himself in my company of late, and it unsettled me. Back in the school days, I wasn't deemed worthy of a public greeting. What had changed?

As far back as I could remember, he had always been surrounded by a harem of fawning girls. The sort that pouted like fish and uploaded every inconsequential pose to social media. Life was different back then, of course, but I'd never had much interest in superficial attention seekers.

Living in such close proximity, we'd occasionally bumped into each other on the journey home; he'd either be on his skateboard or carrying it under his arm. It had surprised me how different he was with me, a stark contrast to his public persona.

He hadn't been glued to a mobile phone like most, instead he'd actually conversed with me. He was sweet and funny and he'd walk me to my door even though it meant going out of his way. I'd warmed to his gentler side and, in time, we started to meet at the gates to share our journey home. He tried to teach me to skate, but I hadn't taken to it remarkably well. The visible scar on my right forearm was living proof. He even started talking to me at school, occasionally sitting by me at lunchtime. Eventually, when the mask fell, I realised that I was simply the stooge of one of his jokes.

I tried to dispel the memories, but they seemed intent on pushing through. It's not even like anything terrible had happened, but it was obviously sufficient to have affected me on some level. His reappearance seemed to have reignited all that was quashed.

I relaxed further into the tub and tried to think of pleasant things. Anything but Jed.

I failed.

It was a hot, balmy day in our final year of school and I was sitting in the school field as I chatted with a couple of friends. Jed had walked past with his entourage. My friends had rolled their eyes and made suitably inappropriate comments about the girls hanging off his sleeve. I'd subtly glanced over; it was too tempting not too. I noticed Jed looking over in our direction and was sure that he was laughing.

My friends joked we weren't cool enough; that he was merely fulfilling his duty to shame those that fell short of his level of perfection. We had laughed together, bonded by kindred spirits; jointly rejected by the popularity so desired by a million adolescents.

I had no issue with Jed's necessity to maintain a certain amount of credibility amongst his peers. It was what it was. I didn't seek assurance like he did.

He headed in our direction as his "girlfriends" giggled in the background like vacuous airheads. I fully anticipated that he'd strut towards us with his ego-filled aura, sprinkle some of his righteousness and reroute as he drew near. It caught us off guard when he stopped next to us.

He stood there for a few seconds as he waited for a reaction. A few wide-eyed stares shifted back and forth between me and my friends.

'Can I speak to you, Fella?' he asked. He knew how much I hated that nickname. He never called me that when it was just the two of us.

My friends tried to suppress a smile but failed. They too, knew how much I hated the nickname.

'Sorry, Raff! Can I have a word?'

I continued to ignore him. I could play that game too.

'Raff?'

'What?' I snapped.

I looked up at him as he hovered over me. I may have been mistaken, but I was sure that he blushed.

'Er… can I speak to you?' he mumbled.

He eyed a quiet area to the left of us, away from other students. He clearly didn't want to be seen with uncool sorts like us.

'Speak to me here,' I said bluntly.

Out of the corner of my eye, I spotted his tightly huddled

entourage as they incessantly giggled and made unsubtle physical references towards us. Jed looked awkward.

After a lengthy and uncomfortable silence, I turned back to my friends, who were intently focused on their school books. I wasn't going to be the beneficiary of one of his public acts of humiliation.

And then he said it. 'Will you go out with me?'

Jaws dropped.

Jed's cheeks flushed a deep shade of red.

I hadn't seen that coming.

While I couldn't deny a certain pleasure in seeing him squirm, I had to keep on my toes. My retorts needed to be sufficient in order to retain the upper hand.

'Go where?' I asked innocently.

'Anywhere. Just... I don't know,' he stammered.

I delayed my response as I rapidly tried to anticipate the punchline of the joke. With no notion of how to react, I laughed out loud. Whether it was a defence mechanism; a fake laugh that served to mask a deep-rooted degradation, or a genuine "laugh-out-loud laugh" at his stupidity. I couldn't be sure.

One thing was certain. He wasn't going to humiliate me in front of his minions. I wasn't going to fawn all over him and cling to his ankles while I begged for his love and adoration. He'd picked the wrong stooge.

'Get lost, Jed,' I replied.

It was the best I could muster under the circumstances. I had no doubt that I'd spend the remainder of the day ruminating more effective retorts.

Jed returned to his selfie-loving harem without so much as a backward glance. No doubt they'd all have a good laugh about it.

If I'd have reacted as anticipated, I imagine the response would have cut me like a knife. They'd have laughed in unison like the caricatures that they were and taken snapshots of the moment. Leaving me, the innocent victim, publicly humiliated and hurt.

Except it hadn't gone to plan and for that, I was grateful.

Despite my brash exterior, I was deeply disappointed and upset. I'd started to enjoy Jed's company during our alone time and developed quite a fondness for him. Not that I'd have admitted it in a million years. The moment he publicly humiliated me was the moment that I'd internally planted my hatred for him.

I'd ignored him after that.

Just like Grey Bear, Jed, metaphorically speaking, had gone straight into the dustbin.

So why couldn't I stop thinking about it?

*

After an irritable and fitful night's sleep, I woke thinking of Anne and my impromptu visit to her home. In retrospect, I was astounded at my brazenness.

Frustrated at the obscurity of it all, I stopped at the police station on my way to work and reported her disappearance. They reluctantly took a few details, but due to my relationship with Ann, or lack of, I was informed that the issue didn't warrant concern, let alone manpower.

I left feeling deflated and saddened by the absence of concern for an individual with no known relations or peers. Instead, her existence constituted the manager of a local coffee shop reporting her disappearance to a station full of unconcerned police.

This was her legacy.

Chapter 11

Oakes had delivered a public speech in the city on "moving forward to a happier state". He knew it sounded trite, but thought the people would go for it. They did; many congratulated him on his "wonderful service" afterwards.

He seldom had an autonomy of the speeches he delivered. More often than not, he was handed the topics by a public speaking expert and expected to merely deliver the content. Regardless of his preconceptions, he had come to realise that working with advisors at this level was a winning formula. They were trained to know what would resonate, whether he agreed with it or not. It was all just "fluff", they'd told him.

After a productive morning, he'd been urgently summoned to the meeting room. Anything urgent in nature panicked him and he'd fought the urge to crack the whiskey open.

When he arrived, Frost, Albin, and three other high-ranking team members were present. An additional two men were sat scribbling notes, but he failed to recognise them. It didn't bode well for Albin.

He spotted his ever-faithful secretary, Anneka, sat alone at the end of the table. Her head was bowed, and she wrung her hands so rigorously that one might assume she faced certain death. She looked deceivingly small in the high-backed executive chair, so much so that he felt inclined to protect her from an unknown fate. He took a seat beside her and noticed her visibly jump when the heavy oak door slammed shut.

'Seems we're all present,' said Frost, as he took a seat and glanced around the table. 'Let's begin. This morning, we received another threat. It was addressed to Edwin.'

Oakes felt his heart skip a beat. He leaned forward in his seat and clasped his shaking hands together.

'A few personal details were included, such as Edwin's home address…'

'I'm in the room. Feel free to direct this towards me,' Oakes blurted, perturbed by Frost's third-person address. 'This letter…' he continued. 'Do I get to see it?'

Frost eyed him. 'We'll get to that. First, the security team need to ask a few questions.'

One of the two men looked up at him. His stocky, muscular arms looked as though they were about to explode through his t-shirt. His crooked nose suggested it had been broken numerous times.

'Just a few questions. Have you noticed anything unusual or concerning in your personal residence of late? Anything that you couldn't put your finger on, but struck you as strange?'

Oakes couldn't think. His brain matter had turned to jelly. He wracked his brain but could see little besides a white void. 'No, not that I can think of. Should I have?'

'Not at all. Just covering all angles,' said the security man. 'Strange phone calls?'

'None.'

'Any close relatives?'

Oakes' legs started to fidget underneath the table. 'None to speak of.'

'Any at all, Sir?'

'A brother overseas and a sister in the city. We're not close.'

'I'll need their details at a later stage.'

Oakes nodded. He hadn't spoken to them in years and wasn't sure he even knew where they lived.

'Girlfriend? Significant other?'

He sighed. 'Is this really necessary?'

'Absolutely, Sir.'

'No.'

'No companion?'

He wriggled in his seat. He could almost feel the stares as they burnt into his flesh. 'No! No companion.'

'Okay. We'll need to place you in secure residence for the time being. We can't take any chances.'

Oakes slid his chair back and rose to his feet. 'Can someone please tell me what the hell is going on here? I refuse to answer another damn question until I know what this is about.'

Frost glared at him. 'The letter is with forensics as we speak. We're holding out for CCTV footage and a forensic match for fingerprints. The perpetrator dropped the note in Anneka's tray this morning. It's the usual drivel.'

'What drivel?' he urged. 'This is my life we're talking about.'

'They want rid of me. It's an empty threat. Nothing to worry about.'

'If it's nothing to worry about, then why am I moving to a secure house?'

The security man cut in. 'It's a precaution, Sir. Nothing more.'

'Do you think it's Freedom?'

The security man glanced at Frost, then back to Oakes. 'You

don't need to concern yourself with that at this stage.'

'I do, actually. Don't keep me in the dark.'

The security man was hesitant with his response. It was obvious that he sought Frost's approval in confiding information.

'Anyone?'

Frost nodded, and the man continued. 'It's likely. They're highly professional. I'd hypothesise that they have ex-military or intelligence in their group based on the sophistication of their work. This incident has demonstrated the same level of sophistication.'

Frost interrupted. 'Moving on. Take a look at these.' He slid a photograph across the table and Oakes leant in to study it. 'As you can see, image one depicts a truck, or a "sweeper" as the civvies call them, parked outside a civilian property.'

He circulated the next photo. 'Image two shows a soldier walking towards the house.'

He produced another three photographs and passed them around. His tone was undeniably nonchalant. 'Three, a soldier carries a woman from her house. Four, the woman attempts to escape and, five, the soldier has her by the arm.'

The members remained silent as they leafed through the photographs. The close-up images depicted a slightly more rigorous depiction than Frost's version. Strained faces and clenched fists were apparent from both the military and the middle-aged woman. In one shot, she had been physically lifted off the ground in what could only be described as an abduction.

Oakes felt a lump of acid rise into his mouth. 'Jesus!'

Albin fell back against his chair in a look of defeat. 'You've been followed; you've been photographed, and now you're being blackmailed.'

Oakes reached for the jug of water and poured himself a long glass. He knocked it back in one go, then poured another. In that very instant, he yearned for his old life. The life before he became leader of The Happy State, before it was even a notion. It was so much simpler back then.

'And here is a copy of the pièce de résistance,' said Frost as he presented the death threat. A sheet of paper lay in a clear plastic bag, with a sticker that read "Evidence – F5".

Edwin,

You claim to seek a Happy State for the British people, yet your secretive actions are to the contrary. Your arrogance in assuming that your actions go unnoticed is illiterate at best. Do you honestly believe that no one is aware of your agenda? The people seem to like you. At one moment in time, you showed humanity and offered hope for our country. Nathaniel Frost was your downfall, and we endeavour to act accordingly in order to have him removed from office. There are still ways of reaching people, so do not underestimate our ability.

There is hope for you, should you reconsider your actions. We know about the Zones and Frost's big plans. There is time to make changes.

Release the innocent people that deserve a future. Destroy the Zones, dismiss Frost.

We are not amateurs. Our plans can be expedited at any given moment and the outcome would be devastating for you. We will not cease until we see that justice has prevailed.

We look forward to your next speech. As always, we'll be close.

P.S Have we got the right address overleaf? We'd love to send you a Christmas card.

Oakes glanced up. 'Was it the correct address?'

Frost nodded.

Oakes lit a cigarette. It never made him popular for doing so indoors, but there had to be some perks to being a leader. He needed some sort of stimulant if he was going to avoid keeling over and having a stroke. Frost showed his distaste at once. He turned to face Anneka as he slid his chair back a few inches.

'Anneka. Let's go over it again,' he urged. 'Whenever you're ready.'

Anneka nodded. 'I arrived at around… two minutes to seven in the morning. There were a couple of letters in the tray, nothing that needed urgent attention. I left them there with the intention of organising them later and went to make myself coffee. I came back and delivered the post to Albin at twenty past eight.'

'So, the letter definitely wasn't there when you first looked?' asked Frost.

'Definitely not. I scanned the post, as I do every morning, to see if anything needed my urgent attention. It wasn't there at that point.'

'You're confident that it appeared sometime between seven o'clock and twenty past eight?'

'Yes… well, I suppose so. I'd hardly say confident. I just know it definitely wasn't there first thing.'

Frost glared at her. 'That's a yes, then?'

She nodded as she further retreated into her coiled position. Oakes cringed at the unnecessary interrogation technique that she was being subjected to.

'You don't remember seeing anyone that you might not have

seen before? A cleaner, a plumber, a visitor, anyone?'

'No. I saw Albin and a few other members of staff. Apart from that, I didn't see anyone.'

'Are you absolutely sure?'

'Absolutely sure.'

She turned to face Oakes. He wanted to support her, but he hadn't been in the office that morning. He offered her a reassuring smile.

'I'm so sorry, Mr Oakes,' she pleaded. 'I wish I could be more helpful.'

'You're not to blame, Anneka. You were just doing your job.' He glanced at Frost. 'Is this necessary?'

'Absolutely! It plays out one of two ways. She knows more than she's letting on, or she's slack at her job.'

Oakes rolled his eyes. He was incensed at his arrogance with Anneka seated in such close proximity. 'She made herself a cup of coffee. That's hardly slacking.'

'The fact that someone entered the office and planted something with tremendous ease highlights a problem. Next time, it might be a bomb.'

'Kick a man when he's down, why don't you?'

'I understand that you're nervous. That's why we need to make a few changes.'

Oakes clenched his fists in a bid to stop his hands from shaking. It was all about implementing his security team. He should have seen that coming.

'Of course, if you're concerned, and would rather reschedule your visits…' he continued.

'Definitely not!' He knew that Frost was testing him. 'The

thought never even crossed my mind.'

The thought had crossed his mind on numerous occasions.

Frost lay his hands on the table as he addressed the security team. 'So, are we in agreement that this looks to be the work of Freedom?'

They nodded in unison.

'Okay then. Meeting complete. We'll reconvene later today.'

When everyone had left the room, Oakes waited for Anneka while she fumbled with her belongings. He wanted a quiet moment with just the two of them present.

'Are you alright?'

She nodded.

'You didn't deserve that. I'll speak to him and ensure that he never does that again.'

'That won't be necessary,' she whispered.

'It's perfectly necessary! It's his fault that the security failed, though he'd have me believe that it's my...'

'That isn't what I mean,' she interrupted.

He closed the door to allow them some privacy. 'What is it? Is there anything I can do?'

She paused for a moment, then glanced up at him. It was the first time he'd seen her eyes all morning. 'Yes, there is actually.'

'Anything. Just say the word.'

'I'd like you to accept my resignation, as of this moment.'

He was taken aback at her admission. 'Anneka, don't be absurd. You're not going anywhere. Look, ignore Frost and his scare tactics. I'll speak to him and...'

'You don't understand what I'm saying, Edwin. I'm leaving. I have to leave. I can't be around that monster of a man for another minute.'

She spoke with conviction; it had been a while since he'd seen evidence of the tenacious and fiery secretary that he once knew.

'I'll sign as many non-disclosures as you want, but I'm out of here. It's up to you whether you'll support me or not.'

'Of course, anything that you want. I'm so sorry that it has come to this.'

She offered a half-smile and opened the door. As she made her way out, she turned back to look at him. 'If I were you, I'd do the same. This is going to get ugly and I genuinely fear for you. Get out of here, Edwin. Go back to being the good guy.'

With that, she turned and walked away. Oakes was left dumbfounded.

Anneka had been with him from the very beginning of his political career. Her gut instincts had driven him forward on many occasions. He feared a world without her loyal guidance.

Deeply saddened, he returned to his private office, and overwhelmed with tiredness, slumped against the door. An array of former Prime Ministers and leaders glared at him from overhead; their faces aligned throughout the vast room. They'd all made their mark in some small way, but none of them had been extraordinary. None of them had surpassed public expectation.

Change required sacrifice, and it would be tough before it was easy.

This was only the beginning.

*

Chapter 12

Dad had been in great spirits for a few days, which had prompted me to reminisce about days gone by. It seemed so recent that we had been a complete family. Time had flown by at an alarming rate.

In light of my reflection, I spontaneously decided to take a few days away from work. Jo and Dahlia had made it effortless to do so, graciously accepting the offer of extra shifts. I hadn't taken time off in a while. Granted, I'd taken the odd day here and there, but I hadn't given myself a sufficient holiday. Instead, I'd worked myself into the ground and allowed my health to suffer.

The temperature had increased sufficiently, which allowed us days outdoors. I felt it time to spend some quality time with the person who meant the most to me.

We spent our days enjoying lazy mornings, long walks, picnics in the sunshine, and rest when desired. Dad painted enthusiastically, and I sat alongside him as I used to. I reread a few of my favourite novels and lost myself in a world of love and innocence.

We dug the bikes out of the shed, dusted them off and cycled to the park for old times' sake as we shared fond memories of my childhood. Dad looked happy, and I felt happy. Had it not been for the presence of the military and the absence of Mum, each day would have perfectly emulated a snapshot from one of our old photo albums.

Mum had always highlighted the need to set aside quality family time, though I hadn't appreciated it as a young child. If only I could go back and savour every moment. I wasn't going to make that mistake with Dad.

The amount I loved him hurt my soul.

On my final day off, I mentally committed to a thorough spring clean. With the day as glorious as the previous, I opened the doors and windows to clear out the cobwebs and allow the warmth of the sun to enter. For the first time in weeks, I felt energised; the combination of fresh air, rest, sunshine and good food had brought me back to life. Mum always told me that I was like a baby bear; only good for hibernation in the colder months, but springing to life in the summer.

Some things never changed.

By late morning, the rooms were aired and vacuumed and fresh bed sheets were applied. Lavender essence had been sprayed into the atmosphere, which offered a homely and calming ambience.

After tidying Dad's room, I lay myself down on his bedroom floor for a brief interlude. I was pleasantly tired from my painstaking efforts, and as the sun cascaded through the open window, I allowed myself to embrace the moment. I closed my eyes and spread my arms on either side of me; the soft fabric of the carpet creeped between my fingers. I stretched my limbs as I inhaled the gentle aroma that circulated around me.

I stretched my arms further to release the tension in my neck and shoulders. My right arm reached underneath Dad's bed. When my hand met resistance from a sturdy and immovable object, I glanced to my right and spotted a wooden box. Curiously, I rolled onto my stomach and manipulated the box from its position. I gently ran my finger over its beautiful carvings. It looked as though it was handmade.

Inside were hundreds of old family photographs. There were pictures of Mum, of Dad, of Mum and Dad, of me. Even Grey Bear made an appearance in a few. Randomly clutching a wad of photos, I positioned myself on the bed and began to sift through.

A life of memories confined to tiny pieces of paper.

Memories were in our minds, of course, but it frightened me how things were so easily forgotten. Sometimes only to be sparked by a chance conversation with loved ones or a complete stranger. Photographs can be such a beautiful thing, but there's no denying the invincible power that they possess; the incessant distress and heartache they can generate. A picture of Mum just days before she died; the smile on her face told no story of her battle. Despite her frail and ailing body, she looked radiant and rich in abundance. I was only thankful that life was normal in her final weeks. There were no wars, curfews or military presence; those things would have simply destroyed her pure soul.

She was always at her happiest when she was with Dad and I. The authenticity of her love escaped from the still image and forced me to smile at her cast iron bravery. Dad looked tired, but well; his arms were firmly wrapped around us. His girls, as he called us.

It was the images of myself that shocked me most. Despite the inner battle I was facing at the time, I looked healthy and happy. My skin was lightly tanned, and my face looked fuller. I had colour in my cheeks. When did I stop glowing? At what point had my complexion become so grey?

I looked up and caught my reflection in the dressing table mirror. My complexion, though improved in recent days, still lacked a spark. Despite my attempts to eat healthily and stay fit, a few bad blows in life, combined with the upheaval of our country, had taken its toll.

I kept hold of one of the photographs before replacing the box under Dad's bed. It was a lovely shot of the three of us on a beach when I was no more than three or four. I could still remember screaming with excitement as the cold sea splashed around my ankles.

Memories. Sometimes it's all we have.

*

The next day, I called Jo at the café and told her I'd be in sometime late morning. The weather was warm, so I opted for a gentle, leisurely run. Thendra was such a pretty village that running was a joy in the summer months. The buildings were pretty and bijou, and the gardens blossomed with brightly coloured flowers. With the military positioned at the end of the high street and scattered in a few of the smaller roads, I selected a route that bypassed them.

As I ran down the main street towards the centre of the village. I imagined how the larger cities would look at this moment in time. There would be military at the end of every street, no doubt. I thought back to my innocent childhood and felt sadness for the young children that would come to know no different. This would be their version of normality. The people that resided there would be unable to escape a life that had been forced upon them. At least I had country walks and greenery in abundance, which aided me with a certain amount of escapism.

It was all for the greater good, apparently. Accelerating us to a happier state, apparently. During these dark times, it would be very easy to slip into a dark place and allow our inner world to cave in.

I ran a little faster as I fought to strengthen both my physical and mental health.

*

As I served a customer their third latte, I noticed another resistance poster on the notice board. I politely excused myself and subtly tore it from its position. Jo appeared next to me with an empty coffee cup in each hand.

I slammed the poster on the counter with more force than intended. 'Who put this up?'

She didn't respond.

'Jo?'

'Okay! Some guy came in and asked me to put it on the board.'

'I told you I don't want them in here!' I snapped.

'I didn't read it,' she replied nonchalantly 'I don't even know what it says.'

My cheeks flushed with irritation. 'Please don't put anymore up.'

She made a lot of cluttering sounds as she loaded several cups into the dishwasher, then stopped abruptly and glared at me.

'You said that before, and then you put that man's poster up the other day. I can't keep up, Raff!'

I rolled my eyes. 'That was completely different! A missing poster, yes! Resistance posters, no!'

She vigorously closed the dishwasher door before she hit the start button. 'Nice to see you're in a good mood today!'

I wasn't, but I had no idea why. I'd been fine up until the moment I'd spotted the resistance poster. Why it irked me on such a great level, I had no idea. Maybe there was more of Mum in my genes than I realised.

'The guy looked official. Like, government or something. He wouldn't leave until I put it up. What could I do?'

I sighed. 'Okay, I get it. Just... no more, okay?'

'Sorry,' she murmured. 'I didn't realise you were so anti-establishment.'

I glanced around the café to ensure that no one could hear our conversation as I took a step closer to her. It was difficult to trust anyone in such uncertain times. I leant across the counter and lowered my voice.

'I'm not, but I don't want to take sides in any of this. A missing person is a missing person, and I'll do anything I can to help find them. You saw the state of that man the other day. To encourage people to report someone, that's wrong. Not our business!'

She frowned. 'But... the resistance is precisely who's causing the trouble. Surely you want to put a stop to that.'

I placed my finger on my lips to quieten her. 'I just don't want to get involved. That's all,' I said in a low tone.

My extreme reactions confused me as much as they baffled Jo.

Having overheard our conversation, Dahlia appeared. She was never one to miss a political debate.

'It's disgusting! The government expects us to do their dirty work for them? That's exactly how you start a war.'

I was wary of Dahlia when she had a bee in her bonnet. She wasn't hopeful about The Happy State and didn't need any encouragement to trigger one of her infamous rants.

'…and everyone has a story, you know? A rebellion isn't for me, personally, but there's a reason that people sign up to these things. Broken homes, dysfunctional lives, homelessness, loads of reasons. We have no right to judge anyone's choice in life…'

Jo's eyes widened. 'You two are something else. We're talking about a poster?'

'We're so not!' protested Dahlia. She picked up the poster and waved it at Jo. 'This poster represents choice and hope, maybe desperation for some. And that's if you even believe any of it.'

'Okay, you two…' I interjected.

I lowered my voice to a whisper in the hope that it would encourage Dahlia to do the same.

'Open your mind, Jo! You're too stuck in here,' she said as she pointed at her head. 'Stop believing everything so easily. You really need me to do a cleansing on you!'

I smirked. It was impossible not to admire Dahlia's staunch faith in healing the soul through the art of therapy.

Jo rolled her eyes at her. 'You almost sound like you're part of the rebellion. Maybe I should stick a poster up with you on it!'

Dahlia and I surrendered to laughter at Jo's expense.

'You're such an idiot!' laughed Dahlia as she disappeared into the café.

I agreed with Dahlia's sentiment wholeheartedly. The act of asking people to prey on others was devious, and should be practiced by those invested in protecting the country. Perhaps, at some point, I'd have good reason to display the posters, but until that point, I didn't care to align myself with pro-government or anti-rebellion individuals.

My life didn't need any further complications.

*

'We've had some great news!' whispered Min as she watered the plants in the back garden.

Dad was out of earshot as he got to grips with a few stubborn weeds.

I gave her a quizzical look.

'The doctor's this morning? You've been so busy, love. I'm not surprised you forgot.'

I looked at the sky and sighed. 'His appointment. Of course. I completely forgot about it!'

Min chuckled to herself. 'There's an irony in there somewhere.'

I looked up at Dad. He was positioned on his knees as he yanked a stubborn weed from the earth. I was sure I heard him swear.

'What did they say?' I asked eagerly.

Min lay the watering can down and glanced up the garden.

Dad didn't appreciate it when Min and I discussed his personal matters, though we did so on a three-hourly basis.

'It seems they're very happy with your dad's progress. She's satisfied that he's doing well and has no intention of increasing his medication at this stage.'

My eyes brimmed with tears. Min smiled and touched my arm.

I perched myself on the wall and took a couple of deep breaths. Despite my non-affiliation with religion, I mouthed the words 'thank you' towards the Heavens.

'So… I told her it's all the healthy food we're making him eat,' Min laughed. 'All that stinky green stuff is keeping him in good form.'

I smiled at her.

'Thank you, Min.'

Maybe it was the food. Maybe it wasn't.

But I was taking it.

*

I'd been in a jovial mood since hearing about Dad's health. Good news was few and far between in the times we lived in. The next morning, I opted for another run, much to Min's dissatisfaction.

'You need to put weight on, not lose it,' she chided.

'It relaxes me,' I urged. 'You should try it.'

She almost choked on her tea. 'Christ, I'd cause an earthquake! I can't even run for a bus.'

Dad couldn't resist an opportunity to wind her up. 'Don't

encourage her,' he said in a loud whisper. 'No one needs to see that while they're eating breakfast.'

When a damp tea towel hurtled through the air in Dad's direction, I snuck out and left them to it.

I took my usual military free route and revelled in the birdsong that greeted me. Dad's health and the warm weather had given me hope. A female neighbour mowed her lawn and offered me a large smile. I waved at her, hopeful that our world was changing for the better. After a long, cold winter, the warmer months could re-energise and nurture even the emptiest of souls; an inkling of reassurance that change was on its way.

I turned right along the road that ran parallel to the café; whilst not the prettiest of routes, it was a military-free zone. Behind the lengthy row of shops and apartments, I weaved in and out of large industrial skips and overloaded bins, exhilarated by the need to dodge in and out, back and forth.

In spite of the narrow turns, I increased my speed as the adrenaline rushed through my body. It was only as I approached the alley that led to the shop that I slowed my pace. I took a few deep breaths and reduced to a walking pace. I was forced to come to an abrupt halt when I spotted Jo and her boyfriend, Aron, in the alleyway. Instinctively, I stepped back, concerned that I might interrupt a romantic interlude. I backed up and positioned myself behind the wall, hopeful that the encounter would be short-lived.

My heart beat rapidly, a sure sign that I'd pushed my body beyond its comfort zone. As I leaned against the wall, I felt a thin veil of perspiration trickle down my forehead. I exhaled, encouraging my heartbeat to return to a normal pace.

I was taken aback at the sound of raised voices that emanated from the direction of Jo and Aron.

'It isn't as simple as that, Aron!' said Jo in a low, but clearly angered tone. 'It isn't my decision to make. I don't know how many times we can have this conversation.'

I heard a deep sigh that I could only assume came from Aron.

'You really need to let this go,' she continued. 'Raff won't allow it. End of story.'

My ears pricked up at the mention of my name. I had somehow, inadvertently, become embroiled in a lover's tiff. I edged a little closer to the alley, carefully ensuring that I remained hidden.

Aron spoke. 'It's making things really difficult for me at work. The police have a duty to circulate these posters, and when my own girlfriend refuses to go along with it, it puts me in a really awkward position. The lads are taking the mickey!'

'How do they even know?' she asked. 'I doubt they care about a coffee shop!'

'You'd be surprised,' argued Aron. 'The government is all over this, and anyone that doesn't comply is going to be held accountable.'

'This is nuts!' protested Jo. 'We're talking about putting a poster on the wall. It isn't our job to find your resistance lot, you do realise that?'

'You're my girlfriend! You at least need to be on the same page as me,' he snapped.

The voices lowered, then muted for a couple of moments; a passer-by in front of the shop, perhaps. When they resumed, they spoke more quietly, so I moved a little closer.

'Try seeing it from my point of view,' pleaded Jo. 'Raff doesn't want the posters up. I tried to put another one up even after she'd told me not to, and she wasn't best pleased. Do you want me to lose my job?'

'Of course I don't,' said Aron. 'But I have a job too! I'm trying to get a promotion, and it doesn't look good if my girlfriend's boss refuses to support the peace,' He paused. 'Maybe she's got something to hide.'

It took every inch of my being to remain in place. I'd been denied the opportunity to defend myself, and it infuriated me. I was sympathetic to Jo's plea as she attempted to gratify both her employer and boyfriend, but I wasn't going to be bullied into doing something that I didn't believe in, especially in my own shop.

I remained painfully still throughout the lengthy silence that followed. For a moment, I feared that they'd become aware of my presence and, any second, would appear in front of me. I wracked my brain for a compelling excuse that would validate my furtive looming.

'I have to get to work,' said Jo, her tone short and abrupt. 'Speak whenever.'

The footsteps on the gravel gradually quietened until there was silence. It took me a few moments to build the courage to peep around the corner; fearful that one of them might still be looming. Satisfied that it was clear, I made my way towards the coffee shop. I was grateful for the reprieve.

As violated as I felt by Aron's words, I wasn't going to be bullied into doing anything that I didn't agree with. And given the way, my luck tended to fall; I'd probably have something new to worry about tomorrow.

I entered the café discreetly via the back door, headed straight upstairs and showered myself in the apartment. Afterwards, I took a few moments to sit back and recalibrate; gather my breath after an active morning. The apartment had a magical way of putting me at ease. Though small in size, it was rich with memories of Dad and I from the lengthy renovation project. With calming pastel colours throughout, and large windows that allowed natural light to fill the rooms, it felt like a second home to me.

Sometimes, it was a welcome respite from demanding customers and the pain that befell me at home.

I closed up and made my way down to begin my shift; Dahlia intercepted me halfway down the stairs.

'We heard water running, so we assumed you were up here,' she said. 'Good run?'

I nodded.

She peeped behind her the way that people do when they're about to confide something secretive, then dramatically pointed down the stairs whilst she shook her head in displeasure.

I raised my arms questioningly, oblivious to her signals. 'I literally have no idea what you're trying to tell me.'

'Jo is in the worst mood ever!' she over-dramatically stage whispered. She did a double take over her shoulder.

I wasn't surprised after the awkward conversation I'd been privy to.

'Nothing a few miserable customers can't correct,' I joked. I made my way past her and continued down the stairs.

She placed her hand on my arm and stopped me in my tracks. 'I mean, like, terrible. She virtually chucked a woman's chamomile at her. I think her and lover boy might be, you know… finito… game over.'

Her attention fell to her hand, which remained rested on my arm.

'You're so skinny. You need to get a few carbs down your neck,' she appealed as she screwed her nose up.

I pushed her hand away. 'I'm fine.'

'You don't look well, Raff. Even Winnie has commented on how thin you look.'

A complaint from Winnie was hardly groundbreaking.

The morning's pleasure bomb had well and truly exploded. First, accused of being part of the resistance, then being told I looked unwell. I chose to ignore it and walked past her.

'You've got a blockage somewhere,' she continued as she overtook me on the stairs. 'If you'd just let me realign your basal chakra for you…'

'Honestly, I'm fine,' I protested.

We were mercifully interrupted by Jo, who looked every bit as miserable as Dahlia had described.

'Morning, Jo!' I beamed in an over exuberant manner. I refused to succumb to further torment.

'You may not have noticed, but I don't have twelve arms, so some help would be really nice about now!' she moaned as she turned her back on us and walked away.

'Told you,' whispered Dahlia. 'She's turned into a dragon overnight!'

I smiled to myself as Dahlia followed her into the café.

Despite Jo's mood, she was adept at graciously projecting her warmth amongst the customers that demanded her attention. The smile on her face told nothing of her inner angst.

The art of deception; they'd got it down to a fine art like I had.

*

Chapter 13

'You need to do something, Raff,' insisted Min. 'How about dinner?'

It was the eve of my birthday, and Min was being as tenacious as usual. She was insistent on throwing me some sort of celebration. It didn't matter how many times I opposed the offers and invites; people just didn't seem to get it. Min especially.

'She's right, sweetheart,' replied Dad, as his fingers worked away at a pencil drawing.

'I don't want to do anything,' I insisted.

Since losing Mum, my birthday was a non-event as far as I was concerned. She'd always gone overboard with celebrations, so to overlook it was a lot less painful than trying to match her achievements and acknowledge the loss. It simply drew attention to the fact that she'd gone. I didn't need any more reminders.

After disappearing to my bedroom, I lay back on my bed and gazed at the photograph that I'd taken from Dad's collection. I felt melancholy about my birthday and equally angry at myself for succumbing to my wallowing mood.

A light spring shower had interrupted the sunshine that we'd gratefully embraced for the last week. I watched as the rain fell against my partially open window; a cool draft replenished the air and lessened the muggy atmosphere.

At around ten thirty, I closed my window and drew the

curtains. The sound of the sweepers was too evident; the oversized tyres sloshing through the rain. Whilst I welcomed the distraction, I didn't want to be reminded of military and curfews or of vehicles that crept around our streets like predators while the rest of us were confined to our homes. Whatever purpose they served, I hated it.

I closed my window in spite of the mugginess and allowed the music to distract me.

I was determined to write the next day off.

*

The cake was bright and beautiful, and two real sunflowers poked out of the top. Dad clutched hold of it tightly while Min stood nearby to ensure that it remained in one piece. A dubious rendition of "Happy Birthday" was frighteningly annihilated by the loud, shrill voices of Min and Dad, but the gesture was undeniably perfect. When the serenade ended, Dad carefully placed the cake on the table and he and Min each removed a sunflower.

'Happy Birthday, darling girl,' said Dad as he handed me a flower.

Embarrassed, I pulled him into a tight hug. 'Thanks, Pop,' I smiled.

Min waved the flower in my face before she enveloped me in a bear hug. 'Happy Birthday, Raff!' she gushed.

I smiled. A longstanding tradition in our home involved the handing of flowers to the birthday recipient. Mum had always chosen lilies. Dad opted for yellow roses, not due to any affiliation but largely because they were hard to buy and he liked to give us the challenge. For me, it was always sunflowers. They were the happiest of flowers and brought light and life to their surroundings. Later, Min had been introduced to the game, and she liked to surprise us by changing her mind each year.

'Thanks, guys,' I said demurely. 'The cake is amazing.'

Min handed me a freshly brewed cup of coffee and proceeded to slice the cake. Another family tradition; cake for breakfast was essential on birthday day. Left alone at the table, I sunk my teeth into a delicious slice of lemon and banana cake topped with buttercream icing.

They were well trained in abstaining from relentless fuss and bluster.

'Oh, you get your present later,' whispered Dad as he popped his head round the door.

Not trained well enough.

*

Human emotions are the strangest of phenomenon. Despite my blatant dislike of birthday celebrations, I was slightly taken aback when, by late afternoon that day, no one had so much as wished me a happy birthday. Jo had been particularly edgy and, whether or not I was justified in my resolve, had made every effort to avoid me. I wondered if I'd offended her with my authoritative request regarding the posters. Perhaps she blamed me for her altercation with Aron. Either way, there was a certain remoteness to her demeanour.

Dahlia had been her usual happy self, but had simply

neglected to acknowledge the day. I was certain I was being stupid. I couldn't have my cake and eat it, so to speak. I'd firmly laid the foundations with the sentiment I attached to birthdays, so I had no right to complain. Not really.

One of my regular casual workers was also on shift. Rex was a strikingly handsome, twenty-year-old budding film maker. I was sure he'd wish me a happy birthday. He had a wonderfully contagious sense of humour and a heart of gold. Rex didn't forget anything.

He forgot.

By the end of my shift, I felt overlooked and depleted and couldn't wait to get home. At least Dad and Min had made the effort.

As I locked up the shop with the numerous keys required, the staff lingered outside behind me. Rex often encouraged us to hit one of the local pubs after his shift, so I imagined they were all going somewhere. Clearly, I wasn't invited.

Just as I removed the key from the lock, Rex announced that he'd left his wallet upstairs in the apartment. As was often the way with staff, he'd taken his lunch break up there and must have dropped it. With heavy legs and a damaged ego, retrieving it was the last thing I wanted to do.

I dangled the keys in front of him. 'Do you want to go and get it?'

'I'll just wait here,' he smiled. 'Thanks, sweetie!'

Begrudgingly, I unlocked the door that I'd just locked, went back inside, and turned off the alarm. Rex followed me inside, and Dahlia and Jo accompanied him. They collapsed on the sofas while I made my way upstairs.

'Don't mind me,' I muttered to myself as I sluggishly made my way up the stairs.

When I opened the door to the apartment, I was greeted by a mass of balloons that read "Happy Birthday" and a selection of neatly wrapped gifts. Seconds later, Jo appeared at the door with a candlelit cake, Dahlia tightly gripped a fancy-looking bottle, and Rex adorned a red bow tie as he clinked four champagne flutes. I was serenaded with a chorus of 'Happy Birthday' for the second time that day.

'It has been like… really hard today, Raff!' said Dahlia playfully. 'You looked so annoyed.'

Jo planted a kiss on my cheek as she vigilantly clutched the cake. 'Sorry, Raff. It was awful having to ignore you.'

She placed the cake in front of me and urged me to blow out the candles and make a wish. I wished for Dad. I always wished for Dad.

Rex tuned into an illegal radio station that played upbeat music and we drank champagne from sugar rimmed glasses. We talked, and we laughed as we soaked up the atmosphere. After a few glasses of champagne, I felt pleasantly lightheaded and relaxed. I fell back onto the sofa and reflected on the day. Dahlia spotted me and threw herself down next to me.

'You do know that you need to start talking about stuff,' she said as she stroked my hair. 'You can always talk to me, you know.'

I nodded.

'Emotions manifest, Raff. Suppress as much as you want, but they'll come back to haunt you.'

'Yeah, I know,' I lied.

'Enough of the deep and meaningful,' insisted Jo as she topped up our glasses. 'I propose a toast!'

She held her glass above her head. 'To our favourite manager, friend and…'

Rex raised his glass. 'Emotional wreck?'

His comic timing and painful accuracy couldn't be denied.

'Cheers, Rex!' I snorted.

'From your valued staff members who love you dearly. Here's to a wonderful birthday. Happy Birthday, Raff!'

Despite my disdain for celebrations, I was suitably placated. They'd surpassed themselves.

Jo drained the last few drops of champagne. 'Right, we're off to Liaison.'

It came as little surprise that they were carrying on into the evening. Perhaps I'd be doing the same thing if…

I stopped the thought right there.

I reached out to embrace Jo. 'I have no doubt that this was your brainchild. Thank you.'

She stepped back. 'You're coming with us.'

The sentiment was kind, but Jo knew it wasn't an option. I had to get back to Dad. I wondered if I'd want to go to Liaison, even if I could. Probably not. Possibly. I honestly didn't know; the concept was too implausible.

'You know I can't,' I said. I heard the sadness in my own voice.

Jo marched over to her bag as Rex straightened his bow tie in front of the mirror. I glanced at Dahlia. She would understand.

'You know I can't. Dad's doing something for my birthday, so I…'

'...and this is precisely what he's doing,' blurted Jo as she thrust a card in my hand.

Quizzically, I pulled the card from the envelope. The message on the front read '*To my Best Friend.*' I opened it up:

To my daughter, my best friend, my soul mate,
Go and enjoy yourself with your friends. You deserve it.
See you before curfew!
Be safe, sweetheart. Love you always.
Dad xx

I clutched the card to my chest as my eyes brimmed with tears.

Jo interlinked her arm in mine. 'Let's go before she starts again!' She nuzzled her face into my cheek. 'You deserve this.'

The tears fell silently as we left the café and walked to Liaison. The others knew of my difficult situation but said nothing. It was better that way.

Liaison was one of the busiest pubs in the village prior to martial law. It had always attracted the younger generation with its modern music and late license. I hadn't visited it, or any other venue, in over a year. As I walked inside, I felt like an imposter, certain that people were watching me.

Jo squeezed my hand. 'Relax! You look like you've seen a ghost.'

Everything looked different. The fast music had been replaced with chilled, urban vibes; the dance floor area was filled with luxurious sofas and quirky chairs, and the teenage crowd had morphed into twenty-somethings like me. Five years ago, it would have been frightfully loud, full of drunken adolescents that sought to free themselves of their inhibitions. Now it was calm and inviting. I felt my anxiety diffuse as I adapted to my surroundings.

'Bit different, eh?' said Jo.

I nodded. 'Very!'

'Did you honestly think we'd drag you to a messy sweat-fest full of kids?'

I smiled. 'It crossed my mind.'

'Happy State regulations,' she said in an affected, posh voice. 'Everything has to be calmer, apparently. Better for the soul. Or something.'

I nodded my approval. 'Finally, a sentiment that I agree with.'

We were led to an outdoor seated area where a reserved sign lay upon the centre of the table. Two silver buckets of champagne were placed each side. We sipped our drinks as we were greeted by village acquaintances. Each one handed me a celebratory drink that differed from the former.

By around seven o'clock, the alcohol had taken effect, and the conversation had become suitably animated. Familiar faces came and went as they offered their best wishes and caught up after lengthy absences. Idle chatter often reverted to The Happy State, and each person had their own theory as to its intention for the nation. I found myself nodding a lot, determined to remain neutral in all things political.

When I received a tap on my shoulder, I turned to greet another well-wisher. My heart dropped when I saw Jed.

'Happy Birthday, Raff!' he beamed as he thrust a bottle of beer towards me.

'Jed! What a surprise!'

He raised a cynical eyebrow. 'My presence brings you such joy, I see.'

'Always!'

We made small talk for a minute or two until I spotted Jo wander past. I excused myself and made a beeline for her as she attempted to dodge me.

'Really?' I quipped as I eyeballed Jed.

She bit down on her lip. 'Yeah. That. He came in to the café first thing this morning to wish you a Happy Birthday. It just sort of… well, slipped out.'

'I'm sure.'

'Oh, he's alright. Very cute!'

'Feel free!' I offered.

'Oh, come on! He was in at half-nine hoping to see you,' she teased. 'You've got an admirer there.'

'Don't even go there,' I muttered.

She lifted a bottle of champagne from the bucket and topped up my glass. 'This might help,' she grinned. 'You won't hate him as much when you're drunk.'

I was already well on the way.

'How are you affording this?' I asked. 'I don't pay you enough to justify all of this champagne.'

She pointed to an on-trend, angular faced man that was engaged in conversation with Aron. 'Aron knows the new owner. Perks of having a popular boyfriend.'

'Oh, you two are still getting on, then?' It came out before I'd had a chance to vet it. I blamed the champagne.

She tilted her head and furrowed her brow. 'Of course! Why wouldn't we be?'

I beamed an awkward smile and opted for a change of conversation. 'You really pulled out all the stops. Thanks. I really needed this.'

'It's my pleasure,' she beamed. 'You deserve it.'

As I threw my arms around her, my eyes filled with tears. The alcohol had gone to town on my emotions.

'Don't you start crying,' she insisted.

She knew me too well.

*

By nine o'clock, the alcohol had taken full effect. There had been bear hugs, exaggerated laughter, declarations of love, and promises of future meet ups that would never escalate. On the way back from the bathroom, I spotted Lennie, our local and loyal café customer. I might have drunk my bodyweight in champagne, but there was no mistaking his inebriated stagger. He seemed to bounce off the walls as he made his way towards the staircase. I felt a bit unsteady on my feet so opted to steer clear. I ventured back outside and immediately ran into Jo.

'Hey! We need to head off soon, it's nearly curfew.' She scrunched up her nose in disappointment. 'I could stay here all night.'

Curfew. For a short time, I'd forgotten the restrictions that we lived under.

I stumbled over a step as I followed her. 'Did I say thank you?' I slurred as the cool spring air hit me like a sharp gust of wind.

'Only about a thousand times. Oh, someone wants to speak

to you.'

My reaction was slow as I tried to follow her gaze. The only person that I could see was Jed.

'Ha! No thanks,' I mumbled as I turned to walk away.

She took me by the shoulders and manoeuvred me towards him. My feet had a mind of their own as they struggled to hold my bodyweight. As soon as her work was done, she disappeared again.

'Hey, birthday girl!'

'You wanted to see me?'

'Well, er… yeah, of course! That's why I'm here.'

'You don't… have to speak to me,' I blabbed. 'I'd hate to… force you or anything.' I wasn't articulating as well as I'd have hoped. I'd gone from pleasantly tipsy to a drunken mess within the shortest amount of time.

'Looks like you're having a good time.' I could see two of him.

'Oh yay! He does want to speak to me. Hurrah! Aren't I the lucky one?'

He put his drink on a nearby table and guided me to a seat. 'I think you need to sit down, birthday girl.'

I dramatically struggled out of his grip. 'No! You… I… don't need to do anything and I don't need… me… you to tell me anything that I should or shouldn't do because… well… you think you know everything, don't… I… you?'

I felt myself wobble. He held onto my shoulders and lowered me onto a seat. I jolted as my backside hit the chair harder than expected.

'Leave… will… you leave me alone!' I snapped as I flailed my arms around. 'Where's Jo?'

'You'll be alright,' he said. 'You've just had a few too many.' Could he have been any more patronising?

'Where is Jo?' I shouted like a petulant child.

I wanted him to leave. I wanted him to know how horrible I thought he was. I wanted him to know that I remembered the cruel joke he played on me in front of my friends. With no prior warning, I started to cry.

Damn my emotions!

In a moment of sheer panic and hopelessness, Jed summoned Jo to assist.

'Thank you for saving me!' I sobbed as I squeezed Jo's hand tightly.

'It's okay. I'm here,' she soothed.

I clutched onto her as though my life depended on it. I cried until I burnt out, until my sobbing reduced to a mere sniffle.

'Before you apologise, let me stop you,' she said. She moved a chunk of hair that had stuck to my teary face. 'If anyone's sorry, it's me. Maybe this was all too much.'

I shook my head incessantly.

'We need to get you home,' she whispered. 'It's nearly curfew.'

As I stood, I wavered. Someone supported me and helped me walk through the pub car park and onto a side street. I thought I saw a policeman watching me, but I wasn't sure.

I remember lying in the back seat of a moving car. The vibration from the bumpy road reverberated on my head and the faint sound of gentle music played.

Then it all went dark.

*

It was pitch black and deathly silent. I couldn't make out where I was. I tried to feel my way around, but there was nothing, just an empty space. My breathing was heavy and my hands shook. I was scared. I blinked a few times, but still, there was nothing. I was enveloped by a suffocating darkness.

Had I gone blind? Panic, sheer panic. I moved around more quickly. I needed to feel something, anything. I raised my arms on either side of me, but only darkness brushed my fingertips. The only sound was of my own breath.

Suddenly, I was in a corridor. A white-walled and white-floored corridor. My breathing was heavy, and the blinding brightness of the overhead light forced me to cover my eyes. I started to run down the corridor. Did I know where I was headed? Maybe I did, for my body moved with purpose. I ran for what seemed like minutes until I reached a small room.

I stopped outside. I could hear people laughing. Loud, exaggerated laughter. It seemed unnatural and forced. A woman walked towards me; she pushed a trolley that held a container of water. She was dressed all in white and her hair was neatly scraped off her face. As she drew closer, she looked up at me and smiled.

It was Mum.

Except it wasn't Mum. She didn't look like Mum, but she emanated her spirit. She looked old and frail, her hair was grey and coarse, and she was tall in stature. Her face looked worn and withered.

Yes, it was Mum. I could feel that it was Mum. I wanted to

hug her but I couldn't, so I didn't even try to. I just knew that I wouldn't be able to.

I followed her with my eyes as she wheeled the trolley into the room. A man sat on the end of the bed with his back to me. Mum walked over to him and touched his face. She looked happy to be with him. She started to talk but there was no sound, just a mouth that moved as it enunciated. She reacted to his words. She laughed. I was frustrated. Why couldn't I hear them?

Mum looked over at me while she spoke, then pointed towards me. She gently adjusted his position so that he too, could look at me. As he turned, his features became familiar. I could see his face.

Dad.

He raised a large smile when he saw me. It was a tired smile, one that required effort. As he gazed at me, his face began to change. A dark, ominous feeling overwhelmed me. Something wasn't right. In front of my eyes, his face grew thin and withered and his skin turned a shade of grey. He tried to raise his hand and his fingers were long and bony. His movements were slow and fatigued.

He was dying.

I was submerged into a sadness like none I'd ever experienced.

My Dad. My world.

At that moment, I learned that losing Dad was my greatest fear. I tried to scream, but I was mute. I wanted to cry, but there were no tears.

Someone started laughing. I don't know who it was, but it became louder and louder…

*

I woke with a start, saturated in sweat. Instinctively, I kicked at the quilt with my feet to allow my body to cool. I opened my eyes with trepidation, uncertain as my reality. There was a sound of laughter in the distance. I blinked my eyes a few times and looked at my surroundings. It all looked familiar. It took a few moments for me to establish that I was home and safe.

As I sat up in bed, I groaned at the dull ache in my neck and the sharp stabbing pain in my head. I could still hear laughter; it sounded like Min and Dad. Was I dreaming?

I sat on the edge of my bed for a minute. I felt sick. Really sick. As I cricked my neck into place, I spotted my shoes strewn across the floor. I was still wearing my clothes from the previous day. Why was I still dressed?

A slideshow of mental images interrupted my contemplation. I'd drunk champagne at Liaison. Too much champagne. I'd been with Jo and Dahlia. I'd seen Lennie from the café. Did I speak to him? Jed! He'd wished me a Happy Birthday, but I couldn't remember anything else.

I cried. Oh God! I remembered crying. Worse still, Jed had seen me cry.

How did I get home? I checked my wrist to ensure that Mum's bracelet was still intact. It was.

Parched with thirst, I reached for the tall glass of water on my dressing table and knocked it back in one go. My chest and stomach made a gurgling sound as the water travelled through my system. As it reached my lower stomach, I felt a disconcerting, churning sensation. My mouth filled with saliva and a sudden warmth washed over me. Hand over mouth, I raced to the bathroom and emptied the contents of my stomach down the toilet. The relentless retching merely magnified the piercing pain in my head, as though a drill was being driven through my temples.

When I was certain that my body had suitably expelled the poison from my system, I flushed the toilet and pulled myself to stand with the aid of everything within grasp. I looked at my grey face in the mirror. The remnants of the previous night greeted me; there was more mascara on my cheeks than my eyes and my hair was plastered to my head with perspiration.

Not my finest hour.

I sat next to the toilet for a while, confident that under the circumstances, I was in the most suitable environment. When I was sure that I could move without unwanted activity, I took a refreshing shower and changed into some loose, comfortable clothes.

I mentally prepared myself for the onslaught from Min and Dad as I stealthily crept down the stairs.

Min didn't take a breath. 'It rises!'

'Dear God!' exclaimed Dad as he lowered his glasses and intensely examined me from head to toe. 'All in one piece then?'

I bypassed them and went straight into the kitchen. Scavenger like, I examined the richly stocked cupboards for something that would satisfy my desire for stodge.

'Is there anything unhealthy in this damn house?' I moaned as I delved into the fridge. The vast array of green leaves and vegetables merely magnified my frustration.

Min barged past me in her usual efficacious manner, which irritated me further. Aggrieved at my inability to satisfy my stomach, I poured myself some fresh coffee, grabbed an oatmeal biscuit, and hurled myself down on the sofa.

'Decent lie in?' asked Dad as he eyed the clock. It was gone one o'clock in the afternoon. I hadn't slept that late since I was a teenager.

'No way! Why didn't anyone wake me?'

'You needed the rest, sweetheart,' said Dad. He repositioned his glasses and returned to his drawing, satisfied that he'd teased me sufficiently.

It came as a relief that I'd booked the day off. Dahlia had harangued me about taking some time off and I'd reluctantly agreed to it. Only in that moment did it cross my mind that she'd subtly urged me to take the day after my birthday. All part of the major plan. Their forethought made me want to hug them.

An oversized plate of toast and scrambled egg, and a fresh mug of coffee, was placed down in front of me. I devoured the feast in its entirety in a matter of moments.

'Someone's hungry,' Min chided. She removed my plate and forcefully ushered Dad into his studio to do some painting.

Satisfied from my feed and feeling mildly improved, I lay back on the sofa and closed my eyes. A dark shadow overhead gave me cause to open them almost immediately. Min hovered over me with her hands on her hips.

'I have a bone to pick with you!' I knew Min well enough to recognise her angry stance. It was definitely her angry stance. 'Do you realise what a mess you were last night? Do you know how dangerous it could have been, drinking and making a scene in public?'

I lay still as I allowed my brain to engage. I was still on catch-up.

'Are you going to say anything?'

'You haven't asked me a question!'

Min sat down on the arm of the sofa. Her generous backside forced me to recoil slightly.

'Don't get all uppity on me, girl! Do you know how pro-active they are with drunks at the moment? The police hang around those places. Things aren't like they used to be. This isn't five years ago when you could roll in drunk at four in the morning. Think about how your dad would react if anything happened to you.'

I pushed myself to a seated position as she relentlessly moaned at me. I'd anticipated a little sarcasm, but certainly not a rap on the knuckles. I didn't have the brain capacity to listen to a lecture.

I waited for a pause in her rant, a breath even. 'It was you and Dad that encouraged me to go out!' I protested.

She nodded. 'Yes, but I didn't expect you to go all gung-ho!'

'That's unfair!' I spat, 'I didn't even want to go out. I'm not going to be held responsible for other people getting me drunk!'

She groaned as she conceded to my win on a technicality. I noticed that she changed the subject. 'And you should be so grateful to Jed for looking out for you. If it weren't for him…'

With that, she had my full attention. In what lifetime should I ever be grateful to Jed?

'What has Jed got to do with it?' I glowered. 'Jed does

nothing that warrants gratitude, and certainly not from me!'

Min fell silent. I was grateful for the breather.

I slumped back against a cushion and folded my arms like a rebuked teenager. 'It's always about Jed!' I spat.

'Have you quite finished?'

'No, actually I haven't. I don't like him. There, I've said it.'

She sighed.

'Oh, come on! You're honestly shocked to hear that precious Jed is not so perfect?' I intentionally over-emphasised Jed's name each time I said it.

She stared at me without blinking. I stared back. I could play that game too. 'Well, go on then. What should I be so grateful for?'

'Well, if you don't know, then it's not worth me telling you.' She turned her head away from me.

I stared at the wall directly ahead of me. I could see Min's chest heaving with silent rage. I felt guilty.

'Sorry. I didn't mean to shout.'

She remained silent. A guilt trip, for sure.

'Do you remember anything? Do you remember seeing any police? Do you remember Jed and Jo frantically trying to get you into Jed's car when you could barely stand? Do you have any recollection of him bringing you home? To safety?'

As things went, I had forgotten, but her admission prompted me into some semblance of recall. I think I saw a policeman but wouldn't have bet my life on it, and I vaguely remembered being in the back of a car. I'd neither known nor cared where I was. My incapacitated state was so great. So, it was Jed that had driven me home. Things were starting to make sense.

'I wasn't that bad,' I protested. 'And yes, it was... I suppose... decent of him to bring me home.' It hurt me to say the words.

Min raised a single eyebrow; an expression that she'd mastered. It dared me to keep arguing and assured me that I'd be the runner up in our verbal battle.

I shrugged my shoulders. 'What do you want?'

'An apology would be a good start.'

'He isn't here,' I said.

She rolled her eyes, but her tone softened. That was something. 'Unlike you, my son is aware of the dangers of being drunk in public. These are different times, Raff. People have been strung up for less.'

'I got drunk. I didn't kill anyone.' I paused. 'Did I?'

'The government is all over this at the moment. Happy State, remember? There's zero tolerance for people that break the peace. Apparently, people were looking at you. The barman even told Jed to get you out of there. Luckily, he was a decent sort. Someone else might have had you locked up.'

I yawned. 'I think you're really over egging this, Min.'

I was fully aware of the implications, largely because Jo talked about Aron and his job ninety percent of the time. Only recently, she'd informed me of the harsh treatment of drunks under the new government. Seemingly, pub owners were urged to report insupportable behaviour to avoid losing their license. It acted as an incentive for them to remain in operation. The sentiment was plausible, but habits were hard to break.

Min shrugged her shoulders. 'Well, I think you owe him an apology.'

The prospect of apologising to Jed made me feel nauseous.

'Fine! I'll say sorry,' I snapped.

She got up and walked into the kitchen. 'Thank you!'

I let out an exaggerated sigh. It was all I could do to inform her that her verdict didn't sit well with me. I stood and made my way to the door. Sleep couldn't come quick enough.

'Oh! One more thing,' she added.

I clenched my jaw as I turned to face her. 'Yes?'

'You took a swing at him when he tried to help you out of the car!'

I smiled; I couldn't help myself. Despite my cloudy recollection, I felt a sense of pride. I was sure that Min smiled too.

I opened my bedroom door and spotted two small but perfectly wrapped gifts on my bed. Dad had bought me a beautiful silver ring that I'd pointed out in town a few weeks prior. I slid it on my finger. It fit perfectly. Min had given me a matching bracelet with my name inscribed on the inside.

She knew how to make me feel guilty.

I raised a smile as I imagined myself taking a swipe at Jed. It was wholly satisfying; my only regret was being too inebriated to appreciate it. It was sorely out of character for me to demonstrate physical violence. I could only assume that Jed had somehow provoked me. He was good at that. Or perhaps it was another of his fabrications. That was more like it.

I'd speak to him alright. But it wouldn't be the apology that Min hoped for.

Chapter 14

Frost knocked on Oakes' hotel room door. He waited for approximately five seconds and knocked again. Oakes appeared with a lit cigarette in one hand and a half-filled glass of whiskey in the other. It was two o'clock in the afternoon.

The doors to the balcony were wide open. The view of the city was astounding; the bright afternoon sun cascaded over the buildings and projected the illusion of twinkling diamonds.

'Quite spectacular,' said Oakes as he took a seat outside. 'It never ceases to amaze me how peaceful it is up here.'

Frost lingered at the patio door. 'Indeed.' He didn't do small talk, and he certainly didn't want to discuss the scenery.

He handed a thin folder to Oakes. 'Figures from last night's arrests. We reached an all-time high.'

As he opened it up and scanned the documentation, Frost noticed how tired he looked. He'd probably been drinking until the early hours.

'Mainly drinking related incidents, but there were also minor attacks on three cabinet members. Nothing serious. Taunting mainly, with a few punches thrown.' Frost continued.

'Anything from Freedom?'

'Nothing specific. Protests are still taking place in a number of areas but Freedom are never present.'

Oakes let out a sigh. 'Why can't they just protest like every other rebel? It'd make our lives a lot easier.'

'For that very reason. They're smarter than that. They set up a protest, incite hatred and remain anonymous. The protesters themselves don't even know who Freedom is.'

'Then we need greater incentives to report members of the resistance.' His voice sounded weak and tired.

'Indeed. We also need to start prosecuting those affiliated with Freedom. Protests should be banned full stop. In the meantime, it's essential that we urge the public to assist.'

It was a tricky topic. Frost would arrest and punish every last protester if he had his way. Oakes was less willing. He always spouted some rubbish about human rights.

Oakes lit another cigarette as soon as he'd extinguished the previous. 'Another sweep with resistance posters?'

On the last run, they'd targeted over ninety thousand businesses and residential properties with resistance posters, but many had shunned involvement. A surprising amount of people wanted to remain non-affiliated to either side after the riots. They'd seen the damage that came with loyalty and realised it was safer to remain neutral. Take a side and you'd be burned, one way or another.

Frost knew he had to play the game. Allow Oakes to think that it was he who called the shots. Tread carefully. 'If you'd adhere to it, it would be my suggestion that we apply more pressure this time round. Make it less… negotiable?' He paused. 'Of course, it's your call.'

Oakes leant back in his seat and gazed at the city.

'Quite the view,' said Frost nonchalantly.

'Yes, you're right. More pressure.'

And that's how you got results!

'If this doesn't make a difference, then we'll have to consider further options,' said Oakes. 'There's no way a group of hippies are running things.'

'Absolutely!' agreed Frost. It was going better than he'd anticipated. 'In other news, approximately seven hundred people were arrested for drinking related issues last night. It's a significant decrease from last month but still too high. Many of them were in smaller areas, which is of concern. It seems that rebellions are moving out to smaller areas.'

He produced another document and glanced at the figures.

'We had twelve drink related arrests near Zone Seven in the village of Thendra. Its population is just nineteen hundred. We also had a tip off about the area from a local police officer.'

'About what?'

'He seemed to think that there might be an influx of resistance there. He was overly eager to impress, so I think he might be looking for a promotion. I question his motive.'

'Can we get him in? Might be worth a conversation.'

'I'll set it up. And as for the drunks, any suggestions?' He'd gladly send them to a Zone and eliminate them. There was no place for them in The Happy State. There was also no way Oakes was ready for such a drastic measure.

'These damn drunks, they're time and effort. We need to be harsher on all crime. This drinking-related crap is time wasting.'

Frost considered the irony of a hardened drinker requesting harsher punishments for drunks.

'Send them to the appropriate Zones. It's time to put a stop to this circus.'

Suitably taken aback at Oakes' instruction, Frost smiled.

'Yes, absolutely. Consider it done.'

He was shocked to the core at Oakes admission, but elated at his progress in remodelling his lenient strategies.

His subtle conditioning was beginning to work.

*

Later that evening, Oakes and Frost sat in a high-profile restaurant as they gorged on a ridiculously expensive dinner. The next day marked the beginning of a monumental national campaign and they'd determined that they could justify a bit of luxury due to the gruelling schedule ahead of them.

Their undertaking wasn't an easy one. It was their quest to assure the public that they were doing everything for them; that their sole purpose was to keep the people happy while leading them towards a Happy State with as few issues as possible. He'd advise them that the challenging pre-state transition would be "ultimately justifiable" as they led them into what would be a "marvellous boost for the former UK." They would announce an amnesty for informers of the resistance and in time, they might even consider a monetary award for those that adhered.

In truth, the prospect of visiting over one hundred towns and cities to deliver the same heartless speech was abysmal. It wasn't easy to convey joy all the time, so he was thankful for the endless supply of whiskey that was joining him on tour.

He drained his glass of red wine and immediately demanded another from the waiter. There were no pleasantries, but he didn't feel guilty. He always gave this particular waiter a generous tip for seating them in a quiet area and ensuring that the other hotel guests didn't bother them. The perks of being high profile.

'We had another one,' whispered Frost as he slid a brown envelope across the table.

Oakes glared at him. He surveyed the room and pushed it away from him.

'Not in here.'

He rose from his seat and headed out to the delegated smoking area. As he lit a cigarette, he took a moment to prepare himself for what he was about to learn.

Frost produced two photographs. The first showed Oakes standing outside a Zone in discussion with Albin. The second was a close up of Oakes. This time, he was laughing with a cigarette in his hand. Oakes handed the photographs back and deeply inhaled on his cigarette.

'It doesn't prove anything,' he muttered. 'There's nothing concerning about them.'

Frost nodded in agreement. 'It does show that someone knows what's going on. That's the real concern.'

'Another hand delivery?'

Frost nodded. 'Same as last time.'

'Tell me that someone saw something,' he pleaded.

'We have nothing.'

'When was it delivered?'

'This morning. The temporary secretary discovered it at around midday. They're brave, I'll give them that.'

He took a final drag of his cigarette and threw it to the floor.

'Find them. And stop them!' he demanded.

He wasn't sure how much more of it he could take.

Chapter 15

I endured the sarcasm and the playful insults from my work colleagues for the duration of the morning. Rex had made an appearance, despite not being scheduled to work. He'd positioned himself by the counter and divulged details of my drunkenness to anyone that would listen. Eventually, I asked him to leave. I had to start showing some semblance of authority.

'Did you hear about Lennie?' offered Jo as she passed me by.

I glanced up at her. 'No, what happened?'

She moved in closer. 'He was arrested outside Liaison just after you left. It was awful. He was so drunk.'

'Poor Lennie!' I muttered.

'He hasn't been in since, either. I'm not sure what's happened to him. Aron doesn't know either.'

'That's strange,' I said. 'Surely he'd know, being a policeman?'

She shrugged her shoulders. 'He doesn't even know where he is. Not at Thendra station, apparently.'

Min was right. That could quite easily have been me.

After lunch, Jed made an appearance. I had no desire to converse with him, so spent the most part of an hour successfully dodging him. We inevitably came face to face.

'How are you feeling?' he asked as I scooped up his empty coffee mug.

'Fine, thanks.'

'Raff, we need to talk.'

'You don't want another drink, do you?' The question was rhetorical.

He shook his head. 'It's important.'

'Look, I shouldn't have let myself get so drunk. And I'm sorry for trying to hit you.' I'd said it. I was still breathing.

I spotted Jo in my eyeline; she threw me an overly dramatic wink.

'It's nothing to do with the other night,' Jed replied. 'Really, Raff. I'm not joking. We need to talk.'

Jo started to blow silent kisses in my direction. I stifled the urge to giggle at her childishness.

'Raff?'

'Sorry,' I muttered, distracted by my immature colleague. I'd deal with her later.

'So, tonight?'

All things considered; a lift home would be an improvement on walking home after a long, laborious day, even if it did mean a quick detour. But the thought didn't thrill me. 'Will you take no for an answer?'

'Nope.'

Too tired to argue, I nodded. 'Yeah okay, whatever.'

'Can I pick you up after work?'

'Meet me here at six.'

He smiled. 'Thanks. I appreciate it. Things have got… weird.'

As he turned to leave, he looked back at me.

'Oh, and you're forgiven for trying to punch me. You might want to work on your aim though.'

With that, he was gone.

If this was another attempt at annoying me, he'd receive my

wrath once and for all.

*

As predicted, Jed arrived at the café ten minutes early, ever the conscientious type. It had been a quiet afternoon, so a lot of the cleaning had been done during work time. I was anxious at the prospect of having to spend time with him, so it didn't stop me from dragging things out a little. Eventually, with nothing left to clean, I reluctantly gathered my belongings and locked up.

As I followed Jed to his car, a feeling of self-consciousness crept over me. Alone in his presence, I'd inadvertently regressed back to my school days and felt like a doe eyed devotee. Distressed that an onlooker might think I was anything of the sort, I overtook him and boldly marched to the car. I was keen to depict an illusion of confidence and independence.

A bright purple skateboard was wedged across the seat and prevented me from sitting down.

'Chuck it in the back,' he called from the other side of the car.

'I didn't know you still skated,' I remarked. I thought back to the shabby-looking board that had followed him everywhere for several years. At least he'd upgraded.

I forced the large, cumbersome board over the seat and let it drop into the back footwell. As I climbed into the passenger seat, I noticed Jed staring at me.

'What?'

'When I said toss it, I didn't literally mean toss it. That's precious cargo back there.'

I shrugged my shoulders as he started the engine. Like I cared what he meant. I wanted to get this over with as quickly as humanly possible.

'Mum was asking questions about our meeting. She seemed happy about it.'

I rolled my eyes. 'I bet.'

'I told her you felt really bad about the other night and wanted to buy me a drink,' he grinned.

My head spun in his direction. 'Are you serious?'

'I had to say something, didn't I?'

I felt sick at the prospect. Min would no doubt be shopping for a wedding hat and sharing the news with everyone that she came into contact with.

He drove to a small pub that was situated slightly further out of the village. With the sun shining, we opted for the outdoor area. Leaving me to find a seat, Jed went to the bar and bought a couple of soft drinks before he sat down opposite me. There was a long, uncomfortable silence before anyone spoke.

'Good day at work?' he asked.

'Yeah, great.'

'That's good.'

'Yep.'

Pause.

'Many customers?'

'What do you want to talk about, Jed?' The small talk was excruciating.

'Yeah, that,' he murmured. 'It's er... it's not your everyday conversation.'

I'd wracked my brain all afternoon trying to decipher what he could possibly need to talk to me about. With no common interests, the thought struck me that it could only really concern Dad or Min.

'Min, she's sick, isn't she?' I blurted.

His eyes flickered with worry. 'No! Well, I hope not. Why do you say that?'

'Isn't that what you're going to tell me?'

'No, God no!' he spouted as the colour returned to his cheeks. 'Don't do that to me!'

'Well, what else would you want to talk to me about?'

He tapped his fingers on the table. There was another lengthy and painful pause.

'Can you just get to the point?' I urged. 'I'm tired and really want to get home.'

I looked at him as he stared down at his drink. Despite his good looks, I felt no attraction to him whatsoever. Perhaps, if our paths had crossed under different circumstances, my knees might have weakened at his big puppy dog eyes. As things would have it, I felt nothing but disdain for him.

'Are you trying to apologise?' I'd figured it out. Boom! 'Listen, Jed, I have so many things to think about right now, that sitting in a pub garden waiting for you to speak is, quite frankly, destroying my soul. I can see that you probably feel guilty for being an idiot all those years ago, so yeah, I forgive you. Job done, discussion over. Can we go now?'

'Apologise? Apologise for what?'

'Yeah, right. Are you serious?' I choked.

'Hang on, if you're on about the other night then you should be apologising to me!'

'Oh, please…' I interrupted.

'It was you that tried to knock me out, not the other way around. And I made sure I got you home without being arrested. So, what exactly should I be apologising for?'

'I'm only sorry that my aim wasn't better,' I retorted.

'Unreal,' he muttered under his breath.

I shifted in my seat as I felt a raging anger rise from the pit of my stomach. I was conscious that people were sitting nearby, so I spoke through gritted teeth.

'I already apologised for that, but no, that's not what I'm referring to. I'm talking about the times when you were a vile pig and humiliated me in front of my friends. And the time that you asked me out, just to make me look stupid. Or maybe the other times when you publicly laughed at me. Take your pick, plenty to choose from.'

He stared at me; his face was aghast. 'Oh my God, Raff. You're talking about school?'

'Yes, I'm talking about school. You were a pig! Not just to me, but to loads of people. That stuff gives people lifelong complexes, you know.'

'You have got it all so wrong,' he appealed. 'I am truly shocked.'

I pulled my jacket from the back of the chair. 'Whatever! I think we're done here.'

'This was crazy of me,' he spat. 'To think that I really believed that I could have a normal conversation with you.'

'Oh, is that why you wanted me to come? To have a normal conversation? Save that for your girlfriends.'

'Girlfriends? You're off your head, you know. Yeah, I might have been a bit cocky when I was younger, so what? I have never gone out of my way to upset you or anyone else. Quite the opposite, in fact!'

'Yeah, course!' I glowered as I jumped to my feet.

His face was blank of expression. 'Thanks, Raff. You have no idea about the world you're living in, and I wanted to help you. I shouldn't have bothered.'

He rose to his feet and stomped to the car without looking back.

I was deeply embarrassed at my admission. Why had I raised an issue from all those years ago? Why had I told him that I'd carried a grudge for all this time? I'd made myself look like a bitter admirer who'd suffered at the hands of an unrequited love. Good work, Raff! I willed the ground to swallow me whole.

I could feel the penetrating stares from a nearby couple. Despite their attempts at subtlety, they were clearly gossiping about the girl that was just ditched by her boyfriend. I gave an awkward smile and rolled my eyes as if to say, 'oh, we're fine!' The girl offered a half smile and clearly felt sorry for me.

Excellent!

I pottered around in my bag to kill a bit of time before I mustered the courage to head to the car. If there even was a car.

The engine was running when I reached him. Mid-stomp, I'd decided to apologise and clear the air. That would be grown up and civilised. Instead, I hurled myself into the passenger seat like a truculent teenager, slammed the door behind me and turned my entire body towards the window. We spent the journey in silence, and when we pulled up outside my house, I opened the door before the car had fully stopped. I realised that I was being ridiculously childish, but having committed to the cause, I felt unable to retreat.

Without so much as a glance behind me, I confidently strutted towards the front door and slammed it behind me. I took a moment to scold myself for acting like such a pathetic idiot.

I heard muted voices, a faint snuffling sound. I wandered into the lounge and spotted Dad and Min on the sofa. Dad consoled her as she cried into a handkerchief.

'Is everything alright?'

Min's face was red and puffy from crying. Her large brown eyes were filled with tears that threatened to escape. I crouched down next to her.

'What is it?' I asked.

Her voice was low and croaky, a far cry from her usual bubbly tone.

'It's Abigail's daughter, Lina. She's gone missing.'

Abigail and Min had met at nursing school and remained friends ever since. Their children, Lina and Jed, were born within just days of each other. Min had looked upon Lina as she would her own daughter. I'd only met her a couple of times, but she was a nice girl. Always keen to put others before herself.

'What do you mean, missing?' I asked. I was all too aware that this was becoming a little too common.

'Abi hasn't seen her in eleven days.'

'I'm certain she'll show up,' I assured her, if only to lessen some of the heaviness that sat on Min's heart.

'Abi let herself into her flat and all of her things were still there. It's like she just vanished.'

A persistent tapping sound caught our attention. Jed was peering through the patio door. I slid the glass door open and let him in.

'You locked me out. I was waiting for Mum.'

Min rushed over as soon as she caught sight of him. 'Lina's gone missing, son.'

There was no mistaking the emotion that washed over him; his complexion seemed to fade to grey in that instant.

'When?'

'A few days ago. I'm so sorry, son. I know how much she means to you.' She caught him in a tight embrace; his arms remain glued to his side.

I placed my hand on Dad's and he squeezed it tightly.

'I don't know what to do,' said Min. 'I feel so helpless.' She glanced at Jed; his body was rigidly fixed in position. 'Are you okay, son?'

'Have you tried her friends? Boyfriend?'

Min nodded. 'They're all as worried as we are.'

His eyes darted from left to right as his brain went into overdrive. 'Right. Let's go,' he demanded as he pulled at Min's arm.

Of all the reactions, I hadn't seen that coming. 'Hang on, give her a minute,' I urged.

He glared at me with vacant eyes; his pupils looked dark. Black, almost.

'This is bull!' he spat. 'How many more people need to go missing before we address the elephant in the room?'

Min's hand reached out, but he rebuked her.

'Come on, son, let's get off home. I need to get the dinner on,' she gabbled as she attempted to alleviate the awkward atmosphere.

Jed stopped her in her tracks and placed his hands on her shoulders. 'Mum, stop it. This isn't a coincidence.'

'I don't want to hear any of your conspiracy theories, son,' she said calmly. 'Not right now, love.'

'But people don't just go missing, Mum. And certainly not this amount!'

I was horrified at his timing. The boy was truly incapable of selflessness.

Min hurriedly gathered her belongings and dashed out to the car. Instinctively, Dad followed her. I urged Jed to hold back, to give them a moment.

'Why on earth did you have to say that?' I snapped. 'You could see that she was upset.'

'Because it isn't a coincidence, and Mum knows it as well as I do.'

'Oh, come on, Jed. There's a time and place for all this.'

'Some people just can't handle the truth,' he sneered.

'Some people just don't buy into idiotic conspiracy theories,' I retorted.

'Not everything in life is a conspiracy, you know.'

Irate at his relentless ramblings, I let out an exasperated sigh. 'So, what then, do you think that people are being abducted by aliens? Because I really can't see where you're going with this.'

He turned his back on me. 'It's not a joke.'

'Oh, come on, your friend has gone missing. It's terrible, but it happens. Chances are…'

'That's where you're wrong,' he interrupted. 'It doesn't just happen.'

'It sounds to me like you're looking for something to argue about,' I snapped. 'Give it up, Jed!'

'Maybe it does, but I'm the only one that can see what's really happening. Don't you think it's a coincidence that your friend from the cafe has just vanished into thin air? And that other girl you mentioned, and now Lina?' He approached me and stared into my eyes. 'Think about it, Raff. We have restrictions. We live under martial law. We can't travel far. We're pretty isolated here. How come no one can find any of these people? You have to agree that it's a bit strange.'

I shrugged. 'I don't know. Yes, it's strange, I grant you that. But it is what it is, people go missing. We can't change any of it.'

'Well, you didn't seem to think that when you went rooting through Anne's house, did you?'

Damn him!

I frantically chewed at my lower lip. 'Look, I just think that kicking your mum while she's down is way out of line.'

I noticed his toe tapping on the ground. Up and down, up and down in quick succession. It was extremely annoying.

'I need to go,' he said as he stormed out of the room. Just short of the front door, he stopped and turned to face me. 'I know things. Things that I actually need to share with you. I tried to tell you earlier, but the conversation didn't go quite as planned. If you want to know, I'm here. I won't push you anymore, Raff. You know where I am.'

I remained silent as he walked to the car. It seemed that each time I parted ways with him, I was tied in knots by his endless psychobabble.

Dad approached me and draped his arm around my shoulder.

'Is she alright?' I asked.

'Not really. Poor thing.'

We stayed out front as we waited for them to leave. I watched as Jed leaned in towards Min and securely fastened her seatbelt. I observed him as he tenderly kissed her on the cheek before he started the engine.

That boy was such an enigma.

Chapter 16

It was too easy.

There were military stationed across the entire city, but it hadn't scuppered their plans. It hadn't even compromised them. They'd created false passes and successfully entered the governmental headquarters.

For the first visit, they'd sent in one of the younger girls in the guise of a nervous interviewee. The receptionist hadn't asked any questions and willingly guided her to the fourth floor. The girl had graciously thanked her and made her way upstairs. She'd literally passed Oakes' secretary in the corridor before she'd casually dropped the envelope into her tray. It was embarrassingly easy.

After she'd made the delivery, she'd swiftly made her exit, removed her wig and within just twenty minutes was on her way home.

The second time was equally as painless.

They'd opted for a classic stereotype; the man who'd come to fix the water machine. They sent in one of the more elderly members, though his age was of no consequence to his ability. As an ex-soldier turned martial arts instructor, he was fitter than most half his age. They'd suggested a limp and an unenthusiastic demeanour to add a touch of authenticity.

He fabricated a name to sign in with; Arnie Swinson. It sounded legitimate. Like his predecessor, he was led directly to the lift with no questions asked. A friendly worker had even taken pity and offered to help him with his large tool bag. He declined and inwardly chuckled to himself.

With tremendous ease, he meandered into Oakes' office as he whistled a playful tune, and slid the envelope into the tray before exiting via a private door at the back of the building.

If Oakes and Frost wanted a fight, they at least needed to challenge them.

Chapter 17

The café had been quiet for a couple of weeks. I liked quiet. I'd come to like boring, even. Quiet and boring meant that things were ticking along without interruption. Quiet and boring felt safe. Jed had kept his distance, which pleased me greatly. The lack of contact had allowed any anxiety to remain at bay.

It had just gone ten in the morning, and I was in the apartment attempting to get to grips with an evergrowing pile of administrative duties. I was easily distracted at the best of times, but on this day, Jed's words were intent on circulating my brain until I addressed them.

'It isn't a coincidence that people are going missing.'

They sounded far-fetched and implausible; a perfect blurb for a thriller novel, perhaps. Lost in thought, I stared blankly at the wall ahead of me, drastically jumping as the temporary waitress appeared at the door.

'God, sorry!' she laughed. 'I didn't mean to startle you.'

I clumsily gathered the papers that had fallen from my grasp. 'No, absolutely fine,' I garbled. 'All okay?'

'There's a man here to see you,' she said as she peered around the door. She stepped a little closer and lowered her voice to a whisper. 'He looks important.'

'Could you deal with him?' I asked, hopefully.

'Afraid not. He said it needs to be the owner.'

I sighed. 'Right, okay. I'll follow you down.'

Jed's conspiracy theories had monopolised my thoughts to the point that I could barely think straight.

I couldn't help myself. I had to ask. Even though the answer could potentially launch me a step closer towards Jed's camp.

I glanced up at the waitress. 'Has Lennie been in today?'

It was as though she lingered on purpose to add intrigue. She didn't, of course. My stomach tossed as I awaited her answer, like the torturous moment that precedes an exam result.

'Lennie hasn't been in for days. It's like he's disappeared off the face of the earth.'

I nodded. 'Thanks, I'll see you down there.'

I felt physically sick as I abandoned my work and ran down the stairs.

*

A stern faced, smartly dressed man with a briefcase in his hand stood at the front counter. He offered no pleasantries as he flashed an identification badge in front of me.

'Ethan Moya, investigator with HSG; The Happy State Government. Can we go somewhere to talk?'

To say I panicked would have been the understatement of the year.

He glanced at the other two members of staff that eyed him curiously. 'Privately?'

I led him to a table at the back of the café and sat opposite to put some distance between us. His surly expression gave me the distinct impression that I was about to be reprimanded. I wracked my brain for any potential misdeeds that I may have committed. Had I forgotten something? Overlooked a bill?

'You're aware of Edwin Oakes and his campaign, I assume?' he asked.

There was a palpable tension in the air, and the saliva in my mouth had all but dried up.

I nodded.

'And you're aware of the transition that we are undergoing in order to implement The Happy State?'

'Yes... yes, of course,' I stammered. I was unsure how anyone could be unaware of it.

'Then you're probably also aware that the reduction of crime is an integral aspect of the transition.' He spared no emotion as he spoke. His tone was sharp and unfriendly,

I nodded. Eagerly.

He removed a sheet of paper from his briefcase and laid it on the table. I adjusted the angle of my head in an attempt to read the upside down writing. He leant back in his seat and regarded me with a look of superiority. It was apparent that he didn't consider me his intellectual equal. Slowly and torturously, he turned the paper around; his gaze remained fixed on mine all the while.

I waited, fearful to glance at what fate had in store for me.

'You might want to read it,' he taunted.

My hands trembled as I slid it a little closer. It wasn't difficult to discern that it was a resistance poster, similar to those that I'd recently refuted.

'I see that you aren't displaying any.'

He was well aware of this fact prior to his visit, of that I had no doubt. I felt it unnecessary to offer my opinion toward the sentiment of the posters, and what I'd done with the last two.

'We'd be disappointed to penalise any individual or business that refused to support our cause. I'm sure you can understand that.'

I nodded. His objective had become clear.

The waitress appeared with two cups of coffee. I took a huge sip before the saucer reached the table. The drink was so hot that I scolded my mouth and winced.

'I think we understand each other, Miss Crown,' he offered. The corners of his mouth were slightly upturned.

I overlooked his error for fear of reprisal. 'Yes, absolutely.'

'Excellent! It's so much better when things are simple.'

He handed me an envelope containing an array of leaflets and posters. 'I'm sure you'll find plenty of room for these in such a spacious unit.'

I nodded. It seemed that I was incapable of articulation.

He took a small sip of coffee, then placed his hands on the table. 'My work here is done. Nice to meet you, Miss Crown.'

'Crowe,' I mumbled. 'It's Crowe.' I held my breath, shocked at my own brevity.

He offered a half smile as he lifted his briefcase and strode to the door.

'Nice coffee, by the way,' he called out as the door slammed behind him.

I breathed a sigh of relief as Dahlia approached me. She didn't take a beat.

'What was that about? He looked vicious. Are we in trouble? They aren't closing us, are they?'

Despite my distaste at the concept of decorating the café with wanted posters, I had no wish to promote unease. With the stricter laws and regulations firmly in place, I couldn't risk repercussions. I'd worked too hard to build the café and its clientele, I certainly wasn't about to self-sabotage.

It didn't mean I had to like it.

*

The next morning, I woke feeling lethargic and faint. When I struggled to summon the energy to get out of bed, Min booked me an appointment at the surgery. Begrudgingly, I agreed.

I arrived at the surgery to bedlam. Workmen paced in and out of the doors as they transported oversized boxes into a parked van. There were two other patients in the waiting room, which was fortuitous, as the remainder of the seating area was covered in boxes. The main desk was barely visible; a tiny gap in the glass panel offered minimal access to the receptionist. Somewhat harassed, and quite understandably so, she took my details and apologised for the state of the surgery. They were having a major clear out, apparently, though she knew little more. 'It was a living nightmare,' she discreetly added.

Crammed into a mere third of the reception area along with the other patients, I was relieved when the doctor appeared and called my name. Her vaguely dishevelled appearance gave me the impression that she was feeling the strain of the commotion.

'Rafella, please come in,' she urged, as she quickly ushered me into her room. 'Is it okay if I lock the door? There are so many people wandering about that I'm concerned someone will just walk right on in.'

I nodded my approval.

'Right, what can I do to help?' she asked. The unrelenting bangs and clutters made it difficult to think clearly.

I explained how I'd been feeling; the weight loss, tiredness, irritability, emotional outbursts, and overall malaise. She focused on my moods and asked numerous questions about my personal situation. As a colleague of Min's, she was already aware of Dad's illness. She sympathised with my plight and suggested a few basic tests to eliminate physical illness.

'How's your dad doing?' she asked as she removed the blood pressure cuff from my arm.

On cue, my eyes welled up, but I managed to contain my tears. Noticing my vulnerability, the doctor handed me a tissue.

'Well, I think we've found the answer,' she reassured as she took my hand in her own. 'Your blood pressure is fine. You're carrying a lot of stress since your father's diagnosis. It's no surprise that you're feeling so low.'

'It just keeps happening,' I said as I wiped a single tear from my cheek. 'One second I'm fine, the next…'

'Yes, grief has a way of doing that. It hits you like a ton of bricks,' she offered. 'Negative emotions create stress which, in turn, leads to weight loss. Weight loss causes tiredness and anxiety and, before you know it, you've got yourself a vicious cycle.'

I nodded vigorously.

'I think you're experiencing mild trauma. I'm aware that you lost your mum a few years ago too, that can't have been easy. Do you experience flashbacks, vivid dreams?'

'Vivid dreams, yes. All the time,' I concurred, delighted that someone understood.

'All very normal,' she soothed. 'And you're still continuing to manage that wonderful coffee shop. Quite incredible.'

I smiled. 'So, I'm not ill?'

'Physically, no. You're fine. You just need to give yourself a bit of self-love,' she appealed. 'You've been through a lot of trauma for someone of your age. I'd rather not prescribe anything just yet. Let's see if we can control it first. Exercise, eat regularly and some free advice? Try not to think too much. It doesn't tend to serve us human folk well.'

A loud bang at the door startled us. The doctor's face turned blood red as she rose from her seat. She unlocked the door and pulled it open. A man in a smart black suit stood on the other side with a chair in his hand.

'I don't know who you people are, but will you please have some respect! We are seeing patients behind these doors!'

She slammed the door and returned to her seat. I sensed it wasn't the first time she'd had to reprimand them.

'I apologise profusely, Rafella. I appreciate that these people have been sent over to do a job, but they have no respect for any of the staff or patients. I can barely hear myself think!'

'What's going on?' I asked. 'It's chaotic out there.'

She sighed. 'Rearranging our systems, seemingly. It's not like we get a say or anything, we're only the doctors!'

I had the distinct feeling that she'd be cracking open a bottle of wine as soon as she arrived home.

I left the surgery and passed two newly parked black vans at the entrance. The entire enterprise looked chaotic as the workforce diligently checked the boxes and shouted their orders at the removal team. It made no sense to be undertaking such an arduous task during operational hours. I wondered why they couldn't grant a little consideration for the staff and patients.

I heard the doctor's voice in my head, 'Don't think too much.' Two minutes out of the surgery and I was straight back to auto pilot.

When I arrived home, Min was alarmingly nonplussed about my appointment. After twenty unconcerned minutes, I felt compelled to share my news voluntarily.

'I'm fine, by the way,' I coaxed.

She sliced a knife through the cheese and onion sandwich that she'd prepared for Dad. He was at work in the studio.

'I know, love.'

'How do you know?' I asked.

She lifted the plate and turned to face me. 'I just needed you to hear it from the doctor. You don't listen to me and your dad.'

'Oh!'

'There's some salad left over in the bowl. Make yourself a nice sandwich,' she said as she headed for the study.

The prospect of salad wasn't particularly enticing, but I thought it sensible to eat something. Doctor's orders. Half-heartedly, I chucked a few things together and by the time I'd sat down at the table, Min had reappeared.

'I don't know how you're working in a mess like that,' I said. 'It's absolute bedlam at the surgery.'

'It's a living hell, love,' she sighed as she began to clear the kitchen. 'Patient care has gone well and truly out of the window. One benefit to it all,' she added. 'They've shortened everyone's shifts so I can spend more time here. More rest for you, love.'

Time off work and she was selfless enough to think about me and Dad.

'Any idea what they're actually doing?' I enquired.

'Ever the inquisitive, just like my son,' she laughed.

Being compared to Jed prompted an overproduction of saliva in my mouth.

'I shouldn't be telling you this. We've been sworn to secrecy,' she whispered, as though someone might hear her. 'We've signed disclosure forms.'

My curiosity increased tenfold.

She took a seat at the table next to me. 'Something to do with the government. They want access to medical records, or something. You know me, love. Even when I'm listening, I'm only half listening.'

'Why does the government want access to our medical records?'

'Who knows?' she shrugged. 'But what the government wants, the government gets. Even if it does cause chaos!'

'Strange,' I mused as I took a bite of my sandwich. It tasted bland and boring.

'You can imagine Jed's views on it,' she laughed. 'He knew about it before I did.'

I raised an eyebrow questioningly.

She waved her arms in the air. 'Who knows? My son seems to have access to information that the rest of us aren't privy to. He's always a step ahead.'

'Isn't he just…?' I sniped.

'And those computer systems,' she added. 'They're updating

them, and that's not without problems. None of us can get our heads around it all, to be honest. The old system was hard enough, but we got used to it. Then they go and blinking change them again. Sandwich short of a picnic, that lot.'

'Maybe they're making them more efficient?'

'Oh, hardly. Some nonsense about seeing a patient's entire medical history at a glance. A waste of money, if you ask me. Click here and click there. You know me and technology…'

'…definitely don't mix,' I interrupted as I thought back to the days when mobile phones were permitted.

It could take Min up to two days to respond to a text and she'd frequently hit 'send' mid-sentence.

She laughed to herself as she started on the dishes. I poked my sandwich around my plate before I decided that I wasn't going to eat it.

Things had become a bit too strange for me of late and I had an overwhelming urge to speak to Jed. Lennie's evasiveness had been the real catalyst, but my trip to the surgery was the final nail in the coffin, so to speak. It was time to hear what he had to say. Only then could I consider whether or not his information was valid and worthwhile.

I had nothing to lose. I didn't like him, anyway.

'Min, would you ask Jed to pop by the café one day?' I casually asked. 'I need to have a word with him.'

A huge smile spread across her face.

'Work stuff!' I lied. 'I need a man's help.'

'Of course,' she beamed.

I tipped my half-nibbled sandwich into the bin. 'Don't even go there.'

'He'll be over the moon, love.'

'Just some help, Min. That's all.'

One day she'd realise that I wasn't going to marry her son.

*

The next morning, I placed a staff advertisement on the door of the café. I'd buried my head in the sand for long enough and the endless shifts were clearly having an ill effect on my health.

It was such a warm day that Jo and I had decided to eat lunch at Liaison. She suggested a glass of wine but I declined; bad memories and worse hangovers. Instead, I tucked into a spicy salad while Jo waxed lyrical about Aron. He'd moaned at her for something or other, and she wasn't speaking to him. I zoned out after the first five minutes; I didn't have the brain capacity to consider lovers' quarrels.

When we returned, Dahlia handed me a handwritten note that had been personally delivered to the cafe.

'Skater boy was sorry he missed you,' she teased as she nudged me with her elbow.

'Don't you start,' I remarked.

Jo leaned in over my shoulder as I opened it out. 'Is it a love letter?'

I glared at her, and she took the hint.

The messily scrawled note informed me he'd be at my house just after nine that night. As if anticipating my reaction and a barrage of questions, it further stated that I needed to trust him and he'd explain everything.

I was ready to listen.

I hated cryptic.

Chapter 18

I felt edgy for the remainder of the day as I anticipated Jed's imminent visit. Given that his arrival was a mere hour before curfew offered a minute sense of ease. His stay would be minimal. He'd be out in half an hour and I'd be in bed by ten thirty. Perfect.

When I saw Min in the early evening, I kept Jed's visit on the down low. She'd have inevitably bombarded me with questions that I didn't know the answers to; lecture me on the dangers of pre-curfew dalliances.

Dad went to bed at eight, which was standard for him these days. Over the last year, he'd come to rely on daily naps, early nights and a solid nine hours of sleep a night. Maybe it was his illness, perhaps it was the medication. It could even be his age. It made me nervous, regardless. As soon as he passed out, a hurricane couldn't wake him.

With Dad in bed, I clock watched as I waited. Incapable of settling, I found myself peeping through the blind every few minutes.

At ten minutes to nine, I saw him walk up the driveway towards the house. Having not given it a second thought until the moment presented itself, I praised him for having the presence of mind to park his car elsewhere.

I opened the door quickly and ushered him into the lounge. While it was highly unlikely that Dad would wake, I didn't want to chance it. If Dad were to see Jed at such a late hour, he'd either assume that we were romantically linked or suspect foul play. Both outcomes were equally undesirable.

A swarm of fluttering butterflies had taken shelter in my stomach, so I sat down to alleviate the discomfort. Jed allowed his backpack to slide from his shoulders before perching on the sofa.

I glanced at his oversized bag. 'Going somewhere?'

'Force of habit. I always carry it.'

There was an awkward silence, much like a first date. I cringed at the prospect.

'So then, what do you want to talk about?' I asked.

'You don't mess about, do you?'

'We don't have much time,' I stressed as I looked at the clock. 'It's almost curfew.'

Jed pursed his lips together. 'I need to know that you're okay with me telling you this. It's pretty heavy stuff.'

My eyes widened in surprise. 'You're offering me a choice now? Will you make your mind up, Jed? You either tell me or you don't, but this is your last chance.'

I allowed him a moment to gather his courage, or do whatever it was he had to do. He didn't speak.

'I haven't got time for this,' I spat. 'This was a bad idea. Maybe it's better if you just go.'

'No, I don't want to go.'

'Jed, you're killing me!'

'I need you to do me a favour.'

I scowled. 'You're kidding, right?'

He shook his head. 'I need you to come somewhere with

me.'

'When?'

'Now.'

I paused for a moment.

Four minutes to nine.

Curfew at ten.

Dad, asleep in bed.

'Are you actually delusional?' I blurted.

'Far from it.'

'Go where?'

'I just need you to trust me.'

'Are you having a laugh?' I snapped. 'Trust has to be earned. Why would I trust you? And more importantly, where, on God's green earth, would you need me to accompany you at nine o'clock at night?'

I did trust him for what it was worth. He respected his mum enough to look out for me. I just thought he was an idiot.

He took a breath. 'The things we've talked about, the disappearances. You'll get a clear picture if you come with me. I swear on my mum's life that you can trust me. I would never put you in danger. It's much better than trying to explain and, in truth, I don't think you'd believe me, anyway. Come with me tonight and you'll see the truth.'

He stopped to take a breath.

'What about curfew? We can't go out after ten.'

He raised an eyebrow. 'Technically, no. It's just about being careful and having your wits about you. Which I do.'

'You've done this before, haven't you?' I already knew the answer.

He nodded.

It came as no surprise. Others had done the same. You didn't get to work in a busy café and not hear a few scandalous stories of curfew rebels. And the one thing that I did know about Jed was that he had his wits about him.

'What about Dad?' I asked as I furiously picked at my thumbnail.

'Sleeps like a log.'

I narrowed my eyes. He was right, of course. Over time, Min would have undoubtedly relayed snippets of information about Dad's habits.

'You literally have no excuse,' he said with a half-smile on his face.

I was consumed by an inner battle of morals. On the one hand, Jed's suggestion was redundant and unworthy of discussion. It was reckless at best. On the other, it might curb my curiosity, not to mention the fact that it was abound with opportunity; a chance to be spontaneous and live on the edge for once. Having lived a regimented life for so many years, excitement had become a non-event. The prospect of an adventure accelerated the already present butterflies in my stomach and gave me a tingling sensation in my skin; all indications of an authentic feeling of exhilaration that had been suppressed for so long.

Mum would tell me to seize the moment.

Dad would tell me I was being foolish and irresponsible.

'Why can't you just tell me?' I begged.

'Because it's far easier to show you.'

He shuffled forward in his seat; his eyes were directly focused on mine.

'Take a risk, Raff. I won't let anything happen to you.'

'Even if I was to agree to go anywhere at this time of night, what makes you think I'd go with you?'

'Because you want to know what's going on,' he replied. 'That's the only reason. I'm under no illusion that you want to go anywhere with me.'

I was considering it. I couldn't believe it, but I was. 'If this is some sort of conspiracy…'

I could see from his expression that he was satisfied at being a mere stone's throw from turning me. 'It is not a conspiracy. Come with me and you'll see for yourself.'

I chewed my gum as my thoughts raced in one direction and then the other. Should I? Shouldn't I? It was quite compelling, even if it was illegal.

'You might even enjoy yourself,' he added with a touch of sarcasm.

Why did I have such an urge to step outside my comfort zone? Why was I so tempted to go with him? The sweepers would be out, and there were numerous implications. What about Dad? What if he woke, and I wasn't there? What if he had a turn and lost his memory? What if he wandered into the street again?

'Your Dad will be fine. Asleep, in fact,' he reasoned, as if he'd read my mind. 'Aren't you slightly tempted to be daring for once?'

Yes! I really was.

'If I were to get into trouble…'

'I've done this a hundred times. You're safe.'

'I can't believe I'm considering this,' I stated. There was an unmistakable taste of blood in my mouth where I'd frantically chewed at my inner cheek.

He rose to his feet and lifted his backpack 'Put some comfortable shoes on. And a hat. Black, preferably. We've got a long walk.'

Before I allowed myself time to reconsider, I jumped into action. I checked that the back door and all of the windows were locked. I examined the cooker and ensured that the knobs were all set to zero. When I'd completed my safety checks, I quietly snuck upstairs, put my trainers on and pulled a beanie hat onto my head. Halfway down the stairs, I turned back. A quick check on Dad assured me that he was out for the count.

'Let's do this before I change my mind,' I said as I picked up my house keys and opened the front door.

*

As soon as we hit the pavement, I struggled to keep up with Jed's pace. With legs that were several inches longer than mine, he effortlessly breezed ahead. I asked him to slow down, but he insisted that we moved quickly for the first part of the journey. Within a matter of minutes, my shins began to ache.

We walked through the village and passed a few people on the way; some had left pubs and restaurants, while others carried shopping bags from the local supermarket. I couldn't recall the last time I'd ventured out at such a late hour. I felt like a criminal.

We reached the end of the road that led to the village and turned down a discreet path that guided us through to a back road. Towards the end of the road, we took a shortcut via a narrow alley that lay adjacent to a row of houses.

The alley had been referred to as "lovers' alley" when we were kids. We'd often spotted teenage couples that were hidden away from the world, captivated by loves sweet dream. It looked quite different all these years later. Overhanging trees crowded the walkway and brushed against my face as I passed through.

As we followed the bumpy, uneven pavement, we reached a vast grassy area. I looked ahead at the open field and felt saddened at its deterioration. Once well groomed and cared for, it had since been neglected with its overgrown grass and run-down appearance.

I moved quicker as Jed traipsed ahead. He increased at such a pace that I was forced to stop.

'Just give me a second,' I gasped.

'I thought you were super fit?' he mocked.

'Not at speed walking, clearly!'

He looked at his watch. 'We need to keep going.'

A narrow alley took us closer to a main road. As we reached the end, the bright street lights illuminated the road ahead of us.

I came to a drastic halt as he thrust his arm across the exit and forced me to take a step backwards.

'Wait!' he demanded as he stared at his watch.

The ominous and unmistakable sound of the curfew siren was deafening; its shrill tone was all-encompassing as it relentlessly sounded, over and over. I placed my hands over my ears and pressed down hard. I felt suffocated by its thunderous volume.

After two minutes, the sound stopped, though the faint remnants of its tedious pitch remained present in my eardrums for longer. For a moment, there was nothing. Just the two of as we waited in silence. Without a word, Jed raised his hand, urging me to remain in place. In the near distance, the loud engines of the military trucks roared as they prepared to make their first rounds.

A cold shiver travelled through my body as I realised that my pursuit had become alarmingly real. Curfew had begun. The sweepers were out.

We waited in silence for what seemed like several minutes. As the roar of the engine drew nearer, I protectively pulled my hat further over my head and wrapped my arms around my body.

The truck moved at a slow pace; its bright white headlights beamed a giant spotlight that accentuated all that lay in its path. I instinctively took a few steps backwards and huddled closer to the wall.

As it passed, I turned my head in the opposite direction, as if it might further conceal me. If I couldn't see them, maybe they couldn't see me. When the sound eventually faded, Jed beckoned me to follow as he stepped out of the alley.

His precision was impeccable.

We ventured down the road that lay ahead. A menacing silence replaced the usual sounds of people and traffic. It felt like the early hours of the morning; the time when the world slept, yet I was very much awake, and the hour was suitably premature to justify such a void. As we walked, the lack of noise merely emphasised the sound of our footsteps. I felt exposed, as though a greater force might be watching our every move.

I continued to lag a few feet behind until we reached another open field; "the wreck" as it had once been known. It had been a popular place to play during our formative years. I was always convinced that the large trees must house over a hundred tennis balls and shuttlecocks.

My feet squelched through the wet grass as we crossed the field. I attempted to awkwardly manoeuvre my footsteps to avoid sinking into a soggy puddle until it became clear that the entire field was rain soaked. I resigned myself to the fact that my feet and ankles were cold, wet and mud-splattered and there was little that I could do about it.

We walked across the open field for a few kilometres. It seemed to grow darker by the minute, and our line of vision had begun to diminish. Jed stopped and pulled a torch from his backpack. We continued in silence until we reached a large wire fence that exhibited an oversized "Do not trespass" sign. Directly underneath, another sign read "trespassers will be prosecuted."

I stopped. Jed must have heard me grumble as he turned to look at me.

'Don't tell me we're going in there?'

I was all too aware that I was breaking the law and didn't want to add trespassing to the list.

'Come on,' he stressed as he skirted the length of the fence

I stayed in place, unsure if I'd reached the limit in my participation of illegal acts.

'Jed!'

His head spun to face me.

'Be quiet!' he demanded in a loud whisper.

He turned his body and shone the bright light directly in my face. I recoiled and covered my eyes with my hands.

'What's up?' he asked.

'Apart from breaking the law? I don't feel comfortable with this at all.'

'Bit late for that! Come on, we're nearly there.'

I reluctantly dragged behind until we reached a small break in the wire. It was of sufficient size to allow a small animal to squeeze through.

'Go through,' he ordered as he placed his hand on the small of my back and gently shunted me forward.

Stubbornly, I dug my cold feet further into the ground.

'Are you kidding me?'

'We're nearly there, I promise,' he implored.

I let out an irritated sigh and carefully manoeuvred my way through the metal wire. I moaned as several spikes poked into various parts of my body. As Jed followed, he projected the torch ahead of us. There was a vast open space that consisted of piles and piles of rubble. They were clearly the remnants of a demolished building.

He stood aside me as he highlighted the area.

'It used to be an electrical plant.'

'Looks more like a war zone!'

I carefully followed his path as he led me around and through the remains; his route was concise and patently stored to memory. As we reached a large chunk of rubble, he took my hand and helped me climb up and over. Such an intimate gesture would usually have instigated a negative reaction, but my temporary state of bewilderment had monopolised my mental intake capacity. I'd let it slip.

For a few minutes, we continued to climb over metal, wood, and concrete. As my frustration grew, I once again prepared myself to question his objective, until he stopped in his tracks. He handed me the torch as he shrugged his backpack from his shoulders and dropped it on the ground.

'Hold it here,' he said as he pointed to an area a couple of feet ahead of us.

I shone the torch as requested. The ground was flat, but we were still firmly positioned on waste land. A number of large boards were stacked on top of each other, and Jed proceeded to remove them, one by one. His strained facial expression suggested that the boards were heavy, but I denied him any assistance as I waved the torch at him. As he removed the last board, a large metal hatch in the earth became visible.

'Really?' I asked. There was a definitive element of sarcasm in my tone.

He looked up at me. 'Are you ready?'

I stared at him quizzically.

He dropped to his knees and awkwardly lifted one half of the hatch. I stepped back and repositioned myself behind him; there was an eagerness to catch a glimpse of what lay beneath me, combined with a foreboding fear.

As the hatch opened, a dim light from below became visible.

He took the torch from my hand and placed it in his backpack as we crouched side by side on the ground. A long concrete staircase lay beneath us.

For the first time that night, he smiled at me.

'Welcome to the biggest secret you'll ever need to keep.'

*

Jed was first down the wide staircase. When he was a few steps ahead, he reached back and took my hand. It was almost fairytale-like, as the prince escorts his elegant beau down the golden staircase to proudly present her to the masses. Except we were heading down a concrete staircase into the depths of the earth and he was anything but a Prince. In spite of the opposing reality, I clung to his hand as I familiarised myself with my surroundings.

As I stepped into the unknown, I could see old brick walls and a network of intertwined metal pipes positioned at various points and angles. An old basement, perhaps. The air was damp and musty, yet a faint, sweet aroma lingered in the air. A plethora of eye-catching murals decorated the walls in bright, bold colours; the graffiti artwork looked as professional as I'd ever seen.

A group of individuals were randomly scattered throughout the sparse area below. Divided into separate small groups, they socialised and chatted amongst themselves as the faint sound of music trickled out of a speaker. The scene could have been extracted from a busy city bar on a Saturday evening several years ago.

A man with a mass of blonde dreadlocks appeared out of nowhere and bounded up the staircase. He greeted Jed with a fist bump of sorts, then flashed a luminescent smile as he bypassed me. He reached up above and pulled the hatch door until it was firmly shut.

'Don't worry,' reassured Jed as he observed the look of fear that I must have unconsciously expressed.

No sooner had we reached the bottom that I realised the

height of Jed's popularity. People fawned over him as though he were some sort of celebrity figure. While I redundantly lingered behind him, it dawned on me that our hands remained interlinked, so I released my grip.

A man with purple hair caught me off guard as he pulled me into a tight embrace. As he squeezed me, a pungent odour eluded from the rolled-up cigarette that he held between his fingers.

'Lio's really friendly,' laughed Jed as the man excitedly strutted towards another acquaintance. 'You alright?'

So much was happening at such a speed that I had no idea if I was alright or not. I wasn't sure how to answer, so I didn't.

'Come.'

He led me through the archway to another open plan area. Though it was far from being overcrowded, the number of people was sufficient to create a stimulating atmosphere. There was a low hum of chatter beneath the sound of the music from the adjoining room. There were several sofas, a couple of armchairs, an oversized Mongolian rug and a beautifully designed ethnic fabric draped across the walls. While there was no mistaking the dank setting, a great deal of effort had been expended in creating a humble retreat.

Several crates of beer were stacked on cheap plastic tables and a selection of bottles positioned nearby. Ordinarily, the appearance of alcohol would fail to stir any interest in me, but I felt an overwhelming craving for something to take the edge off. As if he'd read my mind, and not for the first time, Jed produced two beers and handed one to me. I eagerly accepted and took an unusually large swig.

My eyes scanned the posters that donned the walls. Words and phrases such as "Protect Your Own!", "Who's Next?", and "Freedom!" stood out in bold, bright print.

Freedom. The word had been utilised abundantly.

It was fair to assume that I was in an underworld of sorts. Presumably, the individuals present formed a subculture and used this space as their secret hideaway. I chose not to prematurely judge, which was a value that Mum had instilled in me. Whatever their reasons, they were surely justified. I was yet to establish how credible they were, however.

We had all experienced a groundbreaking phase in life when we'd grasped at something that we believed in and developed a passion for all that it stood for. We'd seized the opportunity to have an opinion, to take a side and to be taken seriously. It was all part of our eternal quest to find an identity. Everyone had a story, and our experience was integral in shaping our opinions. I suspected these changes occurred more frequently than I realised, as the ages of the gatherers varied greatly. Some looked to be in their early twenties, while others appeared to be in their fifties or sixties. Perhaps we were never too old to fight for our beliefs.

In spite of the differences in age, they shared an apparent commonality. Amongst the group was a contemporary coolness that screamed of edginess and urban living. I could see a multitude of varying hair styles and colours, understated garments that implied an effortlessness while boasting a humble expertise in modern fashion. Tattoos, grungy vests, loose, ripped jeans and oversized boots seemed to monopolise the choice of attire. I glanced down at my clothing and felt hideously out of place. My long, rain-tousled hair and unmade up face did little to eclipse my plain white t-shirt and mud sodden jeans.

With my unease in overload, I took another swig of beer and emptied the bottle. A man directly opposite caught my eye. He was strikingly handsome; his hair was piled into a high ponytail, revealing a shaved lower half of his head. His short-sleeved t-shirt drew attention to the detailed tattoos that adorned his arms. I watched as he leaned into an attractive blonde female who lapped up his attention. Her perfectly formed slim figure modelled a cropped t-shirt, mini-shorts and biker boots, all worn as fantastically as any model. Her hair was long, blonde and fashionably messy, while her bold tattoos suggested an assured, no-nonsense attitude. Self-consciously, I twisted my hair. I wasn't used to being in the company of cool people.

The handsome guy spotted Jed and immediately headed in our direction. When he reached us, he and Jed embraced like long-lost friends.

Jed turned to face me. 'Raff, I'd like you to meet a very good friend. This is Zee.'

Zee had breathtaking green eyes and light brown skin. He beamed a huge white-toothed smile and kissed me on my cheek. Had I been less petrified, I would have blushed.

'Raff's good,' affirmed Jed as he held firm eye contact with Zee. There was a subtext to his words, of which I wasn't privy.

'I wouldn't think anything less,' replied Zee. There was a definitive gentleness about him. Or was I being naïve?

A man wandered by and caught my attention. Though I could only register his side profile, he looked familiar. When he turned his face towards me, my jaw fell open.

I tugged at Jed's arm like an excitable teenager. 'Is that…?'

A broad smile crept across the faces of both Jed and Zee.

'You recognise him? Good taste, girl!' grinned Zee as he raised his hand to give me a high five.

'You are kidding me!' I gasped as Jed waved at the vocalist of a very well-established English band. He waved back as though they were well acquainted.

The pretty, tattooed blonde had made her way over to us. She draped herself over Zee in an underhanded bid to enforce her ownership of her man. She pouted at Jed before she threw her arms around him and hugged him for a moment too long. I noticed Jed looked uncomfortable as he attempted to withdraw slightly. She was brutally aware of her sexual prowess and had no issue in expressing it. I smiled as she turned to look at me, expectant of the warm greeting that I'd received up to that point. Instead, she donned a sour expression as her eyes wandered up and down my body, consuming every last inch of my dishevelled appearance.

'Well then, who's this?' she sneered in a broad northern accent.

I felt my face flush with embarrassment. The prospect of an altercation in an unfamiliar setting was nothing short of fatalistic.

Jed sighed. 'Raff's fine.'

Whatever the subtext translated to, I had a feeling that it wasn't going down as well as it did with Zee.

'Raff, this is Myka.' I could see from Jed's pained expression that she knew how to ruffle feathers.

'You can't just bring anyone here,' she snapped. 'You know

this better than anyone.'

Zee tenderly touched her arm in a bid to calm her.

'Last time someone brought a random in here, there were dire consequences,' she snorted.

I'd always considered the northern lilt to have a certain warmth to it. That sentiment was about to change.

'That was different and you know it,' replied Zee in a softly spoken manner.

'She could be anyone!'

'She isn't anyone! She's a friend of Jed's. You need to respect that.'

In spite of the circumstances, I let out a nervous giggle. My timing was anything but ideal.

'Oh! You think it's funny?' she sneered as she pulled from Zee's grip and squared up to me.

I stepped back. My face projected anything but humour. I was terrified. In fact, I had no idea where I was, or who this temperamental woman was. I most certainly didn't want to establish what she was capable of.

Zee used his body as an obstacle while Jed pulled me towards him. They'd got their moves down perfectly. When Myka's nostrils flared with rage, I was happy to have protection.

'Leave it,' said a voice from behind.

Unanimously, we turned to examine the distraction, or the saviour in my case. Stan, the very person who had led me to safety just a few days ago, stood a few feet in front of us. Despite the unfolding surrealness, I was grateful for his intervention as it had sufficiently diffused Myka. She appeared to be slightly less animalistic than moments earlier.

'She's welcome here,' said Stan. His expression was stern and authoritative.

Myka nodded in agreement, though the gesture was veiled. Her reluctance was apparent as she rolled her eyes and defiantly folded her arms like a reprimanded school bully.

Stan stared at her. 'Okay?'

'Okay!' she mimicked. Her congruousness was as transparent as her vest.

Zee looked embarrassed as she interlinked her arm in his and led him away. She was suitably piqued by Stan's curtness.

Stan drew closer. 'Sorry about Myka. She takes some getting used to. She's alright. She just needs putting in her place now and again.'

Jed laughed. 'And then some.'

'Saving me once again,' I said. 'You're making quite a habit of this.'

He gave a warm, reassuring smile. 'It's good to see you, Raff.'

'Let's hope we don't have a repeat of last time,' I laughed.

'Here's hoping. I'm glad you agreed to come.'

'I wouldn't say that I agreed,' I insisted as I glared at Jed. 'More like forced. And I still don't have a clue!'

Stan eyed Jed with severity. 'You didn't tell her?'

Jed wriggled uncomfortably. 'Well, not exactly, but she wouldn't have come if I had.'

'Bad move, mate. It's not fair to throw her to the wolves.'

Wolves. Plural. Great!

'I know. I just figured that she wouldn't believe me. I thought she'd be better off seeing it for herself.'

'I am still here, you know,' I interrupted. 'See what for

myself?'

A man passed by and caught Stan's attention. I did a double take, certain that his cherub-like face and shock of red hair looked familiar.

'Excuse me, I need to disappear for a minute,' he said. 'Make sure you look after her,' he stressed, as he directed his gaze at Jed.

I glanced at Stan, who had quickly become engrossed in conversation. It looked important, judging by their serious facial expressions. He was a good man; of that I was certain, and I felt an unashamed fondness towards him. He'd looked out for me, and trust was a rare emotion in such times.

'You recognise him?' asked Jed as he followed my eyeline.

I nodded.

'Niall Richards. Chief advisor to Noah Payne. He was on the telly a lot during Payne's term.'

I nodded as I recalled his poor reputation at the peak of his career. Payne had proven to be a useless leader, and the mess we had found ourselves in was testament to that. Many blamed him for the downfall of the United Kingdom, the dissolution of the monarchy. It was his poor governing that had led us into a civil war. He had openly blamed "poor guidance" for the collapse, with Richards taking the brunt.

'Where exactly am I, Jed?' I asked.

Enough was enough.

It was time for answers.

*

Another archway led to an even larger section of the basement, where an enormous haze of cigarette smoke loomed in the air like a ghostly spirit. The walls were adorned with more logos than the previous; brightly emblazoned graffiti virtually covered the brickwork. In the brightest shade of pink and enormous font, the word Freedom took centre stage. Had I not have noticed it previously, I most certainly couldn't have ignored it here. A brick staircase led down, deeper into the earth. I shuddered at the prospect.

The setting resembled a scene from a cool music video. At worst, a deliciously modern, urban hangout.

Jed, having swiped another two bottles of beer, removed his backpack and sat himself down at one of two odd armchairs. I was far from pretentious, but it looked as though they'd been donated. They had shabby edges and worn seats.

His expression was serious. 'Sorry. You shouldn't have had to endure that from Myka.'

'No. I shouldn't,' I retorted as I cautiously sat myself down on the rickety chair.

He glanced around at the walls; his eyes lingered on the large Freedom logo. I followed his eyeline as I took another large swig of beer.

'Liberation for all!' I joked as I punched my hand in the air. The beer had begun to mildly take effect.

He smiled. 'You could say that.'

'I've never been in an underworld before,' I said. 'What are you fighting for? Human rights? Gender equality? What's Myka fighting for? I very much doubt it's…'

'This is the base of Freedom,' he stated, pragmatically.

'…freedom of speech. She definitely has enough of that.

Quite loud, at that…'

'Raff, did you hear what I said?' he interrupted.

'Yes, something about Freedom. I was just saying that…'

'Raff! This is the base of Freedom!' He looked sterner than I'd ever seen him. He took a large swig of beer and started to tap his fingers on the table.

'Can you stop with the tapping? It's so annoying.'

He stopped at once.

'So, Freedom. What about it? It explains why the word Freedom is all over the walls,' I waffled as I glanced around the room.

He leaned further in towards me and stared deeply into my eyes. I moved back an inch, unsettled by the close proximity. 'I don't think you heard me. This place, here, is the base of Freedom.'

I raised my eyes to the ceiling. 'Am I missing something because…?'

'Have you heard of the resistance movement?'

'Er… that would be yes,' I mocked. Of course, I'd heard of the resistance. Did he think I'd fallen off the planet?

'Freedom?'

His eyes remained fixed. He didn't even blink.

Unable to grasp the sentiment, and uncertain that I'd heard him correctly, I glanced back at the logo. There was no mistaking its bold message. I turned to look at the rest of the wall, at the murals that flaunted messages of peace, equality, hope, and liberty. I stared at a group of people that sat on the staircase and reconsidered their bohemian, punkish apparel, the cool and collected attitudes, the secret underground setting. I thought back to the gargantuan build up from Jed, the awkwardness and reticence in divulging, the secretive behaviour.

Everything started to fall into place.

Temporarily blinded by the realisation and void of articulation, my emotions responded as though I'd received an electric shock.

I felt instant fear. Pure, unadulterated fear. Freedom, sought after by every government and law enforcement agency in the country; my mere presence was an act of treason. My demise was imminent. I'd be flogged. Locked away. The key would be destroyed.

I felt anger. Immense anger at Jed for putting me in this position, for placing me in such grave danger.

Sadness. I'd left my dad alone for this. I'd let him down. My sweet, sweet Dad. He didn't deserve this.

Baring my teeth, I glared at him. 'How dare you!'

'I know you're angry, but please just hear me out,' he pleaded.

Not this time. He'd gone too far. Way too far.

'You ask me for my trust, then do something like this? You honestly thought I'd be okay with it?' I growled.

He slid his chair closer to mine. 'Listen to me. Just let me explain, please!'

'Listen to what? I think this speaks for itself!'

The sound of his pleas faded into the background like white noise. My single objective was to get out of there. I'd find a way to get home. I couldn't think beyond the present. For each moment I lingered, I ran the risk of being spotted or subjected to a raid.

I thrust my empty bottle at him and turned to leave. My

brain felt muddled and confused as I walked past groups of people. How were they so relaxed and comfortable?

The number of people present had increased at least threefold, which simply accelerated my anxiety and frustration. I reached the archway and roughly pushed passed an intertwined couple without consideration. One of them muttered something, but I didn't care enough to apologise. I had to get out of there.

I reached the staircase and attempted to navigate through the bodies that sat and slumped across them without a care in the world. Halfway up, I was forced to a standstill by a group of individuals that had claimed an entire step.

'Can you let me pass?' I asked. My voice trembled as I spoke.

No one so much as looked at me, much less move.

'Can you move, please!' I demanded. My sharp tone effectively yielded their attention.

The group had begun to disperse when I felt a strong hand on my shoulder. With my emotions on high alert, I spun around rapidly. Stan's face greeted me.

'I'm not interested!' I gasped. 'I don't care.'

'Raff, please…'

I turned my back on him and took a step. He gently pulled at my arm from behind.

'Stan! I need to go!' I protested. Hot tears stung my eyes.

He took a step towards me and turned me to face him. Placing a hand on each side of my face, he gazed into my eyes.

'I know that you're scared, but I need to explain why you're here. If you're still unhappy with my explanation, then you have my word that I'll take you home myself, no questions asked.'

My breathing was erratic. I needed air before I passed out.

He lowered his hands. 'I won't force you. You're not a prisoner. I'd like to explain.'

I glanced up at the hatch. My escape was just a few feet away from me.

'I don't know,' I muttered.

He spoke gently. 'No one is forcing you. Jed was wrong for not telling you, but I understand his reasons. I ask for half an hour of your time. That's all.'

I wanted to leave, that much was apparent. Equally, I trusted Stan, despite his affiliation with a criminal underworld.

What was I thinking?

I nodded. Glutton for punishment.

'Thank you.'

Gently and with no coercion, he placed his arm around my shoulders and led me down the stairs. My inner voice urged me to leave, but my legs willingly followed.

'Don't let me regret it.'

*

We were seated in the same place that Jed and I had been just a few moments earlier. He was nowhere to be seen. Coward.

Stan handed me a drink, which I didn't hesitate in consuming. The bitter taste made me grimace, though its calming effect was almost instant.

'I understand that this is overwhelming,' he said. 'Take a few deep breaths and allow yourself to step back into the moment.'

I couldn't help but laugh. 'And here we are again.'

He waved his hand at a passing woman and pointed to my

drink.

'You have waitresses?'

'Not really. We take it in turns.'

I shook my head in disbelief. An underground hideout with waiting staff, how things had progressed.

'Believe it or not, a few of this lot went through the same thing,' he professed as he glanced around the busy room. 'They were scared, too. Understandably, of course.'

He cast his eyes on me. 'I wholly appreciate that this isn't to be taken lightly and you must believe that you're not under house arrest. You can leave any time you want to. It's a hell of a lot to take in.'

'You think?' I mocked, pleased to have resumed a semi-normal breathing pattern. 'You and Jed had no right to drag me into this. I didn't ask for any of it.'

'I know. Let me explain and this will all make sense…'

'I'm sick of hearing that this will all make sense! You seem to think that you have the right to coerce people into your sordid little underworld. It's just… wrong!'

'You won't get into any trouble, if that's what you're worried about,' said Stan. 'If I thought that, then you wouldn't be here at all.'

'Really?' I asked, with a petulant tone. 'You have control of the military, do you? You can stop them from arresting me?' I shook my head. 'Don't answer that! I really don't want to know.'

'Couldn't be farther from the truth. But let me help you make sense of it.'

'Gee, thanks!' I mocked. I turned my face away, unable to look at him for a second longer. My affection for him was rapidly waning. 'You'll help me make sense of it after you've conned me into coming in the first place? Well, what about if I don't want it to make sense? How about if I choose not to know about any of this? Oh, hold on, it's too late for that, isn't it? Because you've made that decision for me.'

He dropped his head apologetically. 'I deserved that.'

When the waitress appeared, I stole my drink from her grip before it had a chance to reach the table. She turned away immediately, obviously used to making herself scarce.

'It'll only make sense when you make it make sense,' I continued before devouring the contents of my glass. 'If that makes sense.' I put my head in my hands. 'My God! You people are just abhorrent! I can't even think straight.'

'Jed wouldn't have brought you here if he didn't think you should know,' he said.

'You don't know Jed like I do,' I sneered.

'I know that he's trustworthy, and he's proven his worth on more than one occasion. He's been a very good friend to me. I think you'd be surprised at who Jed is nowadays.'

I glared at him, surprised to hear him vouch for an individual that had caused me so much frustration and aggravation. My life had taken a definitive downturn since Jed had reappeared.

'We had a discussion about you and your dad,' he said coyly.

'What's Dad got to do with any of this?' It was one thing to cajole me, but I didn't want my dad anywhere near it.

'To put it bluntly, that's why you're here,' he replied. 'Your Dad is unwell, and it puts you both in a very dangerous position. We want to open up to you. Believe it or not, Jed brought you here to help!'

'I'll choose not to believe it at this stage.'

'That's fair enough.'

'God, why are you so agreeable?' I asked angrily. 'Could you please just explain to me exactly what is going on?'

I was exhausted by the cyclic conversations that failed to answer a single question. Why was everyone so damn cryptic?

'Listen, when I saw you that day at the square, I was really saddened by what you told me about your Dad. Phil meant a lot to me and still does, as do you. It was my suggestion that he bring you here, to help you understand. Though I did assume that he'd have told you beforehand.'

The waitress passed by, so I raised my glass in a bid for her to fill it. 'You assumed wrong,' I protested. Under the circumstances, alcohol was the only thing that I could trust. At least I knew that it might get me drunk and rescind my newfound enlightenment. 'Maybe you don't know Jed as well as you think.'

The waitress poured the dark liquid into my glass and left.

Stan leaned back in his seat and looked at me. Begrudgingly, I turned away. I would no longer beg or plead with him. I'd have a few more free drinks and then depart.

'Did you tell your dad that you saw me?' he asked.

I continued to look elsewhere as I responded. 'No, I didn't. I forgot.'

'That's good. It's better that you don't.'

I looked at him. 'Feeling decent all of a sudden?'

'Ah, it's awkward. Long story.'

I narrowed my eyes. 'Is nothing straightforward with you, Stan?'

'It's complicated.'

'Did you know Mum died?' I asked as I surrendered to the failure of the previous conversation.

'Yes, I did.' His voice was barely a whisper. 'It saddened me greatly.' For the first time, he didn't look at me as he spoke. 'You remind me of her a lot.'

I'd have bet money that his eyes filled with tears. I was no psychologist, but his obvious discomfort at the mention of Mum roused something in him. Though strangely curious, I wasn't going down that road. Not yet. It'd be another "long story."

'Raff, I'll tell you straight. Not everyone can deal with stuff like this,' he said, as he conveniently changed the subject. 'In fact, few can. You're made of the right stuff and I think you could be an asset. You could really help us make a difference.'

I noticed Jed approaching in a stealth-like manner behind Stan.

'There are things going on that you need to be aware of. No conspiracy theory, all factual and evidence-based information. Not everyone will be affected, but I'm afraid that you're unlikely to be one of the lucky ones.'

'Affected? What do you mean affected?' I gabbled. 'Are we talking about a virus?'

'That's in-fected, not aff-ected,' offered Jed, who had safely tucked himself away behind Stan.

I scowled at him.

Stan continued. 'First off, you need to put your trust in Jed.'

'Good luck with that!' I snorted.

He glanced at his watch. 'Look, there's something going on downstairs and I need to prepare. I can assure you that by the end of it, you'll have a clear understanding of what we're all doing here. If, after listening, you want to leave, I'll keep my promise and make sure that you get home safely. You never need to look back again. No harm done. How does that sound?'

'It sounds like you're trying to sell me a timeshare,' I muttered.

They both laughed. At least someone was entertained.

'Just like your mum,' he acknowledged. 'Okay then, how about this? I saved you in the park and you're doing this for me, to say thanks? What do you think?'

I sighed. 'I think it's a crap proposition. But if you swear to me that you'll take me home afterwards, then okay. I guess.'

He placed his hand on my shoulder. 'Thank you. And yes, I promise.'

'Just don't expect me to buy anything.'

He smiled. 'I'll see you down there.'

Jed, no longer protected by Stan, lurked awkwardly. He reached out and handed me a bottle of beer. 'Peace offering.'

I snatched the bottle from him. 'It'll take more than a poxy bottle of beer.'

'I know you don't like me very much, but I swear that I'm doing this for you.'

'Time will tell,' I said as I stood and walked towards the staircase. 'But quit the pleading. It's embarrassing.'

*

There was not a single part of me that could have anticipated the next phase of the evening. Having been advised that something was taking place downstairs, I subconsciously visualised a bunch of seats, a lectern at the front of the room, and a rich profusion of yawning mouths. What I didn't expect was for the door to open to a colossal sensory overload.

The room was large and dark. A throng of individuals occupied the space in front of me as they danced to loud and energetic music. A female DJ was positioned on a raised platform with waist length hair that engulfed her tiny frame. Engrossed in her artistry, she sensually moved her body to her own beat. Behind her, an illuminated backdrop of brightly coloured lights danced across a projected screen that reached from wall to wall, while strobe lights and a smoke machine created an authentic club atmosphere. The loud, powerful beat poured out of the huge speakers and reverberated through my chest and feet. The damp smell of the basement was masked by the sweet, burnt odour of tobacco.

I gazed ahead as the scene unfolded before me; people danced, entwined; chemistry was conceived and inhibitions were lost. I should have been overwhelmed; I should probably have had a panic attack. Instead, I felt a rush of adrenalin as the energy of the room's atmosphere pulled me towards it. For a moment I was lost, hypnotised almost. No longer was I breaking the law, hidden in a secret dungeon and surrounded by members of a dangerous movement. I was seduced by music, captivated by an alluring atmosphere.

Many of us hadn't been to a nightclub in several years; the very epitome of youth culture had been denied due to the restrictions that had been bestowed upon us. The enthralling atmosphere enormously differentiated from the tension, urgency, and sorrow that had become so normative. Martial law had enforced so many constraints upon our lives that escapism and excitement had as good as been erased from our memories.

Jed moved with purpose as he guided me across the dance floor. We weaved around warm, moist bodies, each one consumed by its environment. Couples moved erotically, as though they were unobserved. Others held hands, embraced and kissed. Freedom, in its basic context, took on a literal meaning in the space that I found myself. It was so much more than a name; it was a true and valid description. Everyone looked free. Free from restraints and social order, free from misery and unhappiness.

We stopped in a small alcove that was positioned alongside the stage. The large screen behind the DJ booth flashed images of army trucks, riots, and violence. Much of it looked identical to those that I'd seen on the news when things were at their worst. I gazed in awe of the fantastical cinematography. The bright lights cascaded down and highlighted the DJ's silhouette like a perfect cover shot on a glossy magazine. The music vibrated through my feet, body and all the way up to my ears. It had awakened something in me that had been feared lost.

I felt more alive than I had since I was a child.

I glanced at Jed and caught him looking at me. Perhaps I misread his expression, but he seemed happy that I was there and that he could share the moment with me.

Abruptly, the music stopped, and the room went dark. My hearing was muffled by the unfamiliar explosion of loud music, but the sounds of voices could be heard from the crowd. A stark white light from the screen forced me to squint. The chatter gradually decreased until the room fell silent. In that moment, a pin dropping to the floor could be heard. Jed placed a reassuring hand on the small of my back. I didn't flinch.

The number ten appeared on the screen in bold, black print and began to count down towards one.

Zero. The screen faded to black. More silence. More blackness. In those few seconds, there was nothing.

A video played of a man and woman as they played with a small child in a park. They looked like a normal, modern couple; they looked happy. Despite their contemporary attire, the stilted motion of the picture had a faint nostalgic quality which gave the illusion of an old-fashioned movie.

The picture changed and showed moving images of idealistic nuclear families. A soundtrack played in the background; an upbeat instrumental that was slightly twee and annoying. The images continued; more people smiled; more people embraced. The words "Happy State" flashed onto the screen in bright neon shades. The music slowed and distorted, like the eerie sound of a child's wind-up toy as it loses power.

The serenity was replaced with army trucks. An unwelcome reminder of the times that we lived in. A truck drove down a suburban-looking street and a middle-aged man was violently pulled from his home. A woman screamed as she was thrown over the shoulder of a soldier, her arms fervently fought to break away.

It was apparent that the footage had been captured using a handheld camera due to the inconsistent angles and jerkiness. In the background, the faint sound of the camera operator's rapid breathing could be heard.

I turned to look at the crowd, at their fixated expressions and their unblinking eyes. A man next to me shuffled from one foot to the next as though he had boundless energy, yet his eyes remained transfixed by the images before him.

There were more similar scenes, many of a highly disturbing nature. Under normal circumstances, I'd have turned away, but for some reason I couldn't. While I was uncertain as to my purpose with Freedom, I felt compelled to witness the brutal scenes that played out.

A message flashed onto the screen. It read "Real Footage."

I glanced at Jed. I don't know why. Perhaps I yearned for reassurance that it was anything but real; that the bubble would burst, and things would become apparent at any moment. His expression gave me cause to doubt. As the light from the screen highlighted his side profile, I noticed his eyes were wet with emotion and his lower lip tremored. Whether he was deeply sentimental or delusional, I was yet to establish.

The shrill, horrifying sound of a woman's scream forced me to turn my attention back to the screen. It prompted a sharp intake of breath from both myself and several crowd members. We watched in unison as she was brutally dragged down a long driveway that looked stately in appearance. She fought and screamed as two soldiers vigorously pulled at her arms. I willed her to surrender to the force, for fear of her shoulders dislocating from their sockets.

As the camera zoomed out, an eminent and beautiful seventeenth-century house came into view. The vision in its entirety demonstrated tremendous ambiguity when beauty and cruelty intersected.

As the image faded, a vast expanse of grass came into view. A closer angle revealed a large mound with a stick in its centre.

The camera hovered for a moment. A burial spot, certainly.

A message replaced the haunting image.

'The Fallen.'

A shiver ran up my spine and gave me cause to shudder.

The Freedom logo exploded onto the screen with technical wizardry, simple but effective enough to be discernible; a circle with the letter F sprawled through the centre. As small boxes emerged, each one stated a location within The Happy State that had the logo emblazoned in its city streets. Prior to that moment, I did not know the magnitude of the group. According to the information provided in the film, they were firmly established in over twenty large cities and continued to grow.

The next film showed a selection of wanted posters in various buildings, outlets, and streets. A man in a black hooded top and a black face covering pulled down one of the posters and rolled it into a ball. His action was more than symbolic of Freedom's sentiment towards the posters. It mirrored my own feelings and actions to perfection.

That I shared a perspective with the country's most wanted resistance group did little to console me.

The eerie music continued until it soon became unbearable. A deluge of faces monopolised the screen, each with the word "missing" beside them. I thought of Layla, the young girl whose face I saw every day as she stared back at me from the walls of the café. Each day, I wondered if she was at peace, or urged me to find her.

As the picture faded to black, I closed my eyes. I wasn't sure how much more I could take. Stan was wrong. I wasn't built for pain and destruction. Even if I was, I didn't want to be.

When the black screen distorted with flashing white pixels, I refrained from asking Jed if there was a technical glitch. No doubt it was all part of the show. I was right, and within seconds, an oversized head and shoulders seemed to loom over us like a God of sorts. A faint piece of music started to play; it was haunting but strangely edgy. The crowd cheered enthusiastically at the new vision; the show wasn't over.

The presumed-male figure wore a sinister looking white mask that fit snugly to his face. His glare gave the illusion that he could penetrate the soul, so much so that I took a step backwards, intimidated by the enormity of him. The mouth was severely downturned, a feature that only served to magnify the element of macabre.

The room fell silent as he spoke. His voice was distorted, as though manipulated by a modulating device.

'Our government makes promises of a happy state to fill the void of an adrift nation. A nation that has been tortured by technology, drowned with celebrity culture and devastated by broken promises from previous governments. Thus far, they have denied us of our rightful agency, rid us of our resources. They have stolen our freedom.

How do they propose to utilise such vast promises?

The Happy State Government does not advocate mental illness. Commander in Chief, Nathaniel Frost, believes that mental illness is the catalyst for societal unhappiness, with its elimination the only resolution. The naysayers should be confined and manipulated into a self-enforced martyrdom.

Our film demonstrates the reality behind the sweepers.

Freedom's projected estimate is that fifteen thousand people will have been taken by the end of the year, with more Zones appearing by the day.

Nathaniel Frost seeks an idealistic race, a race that comprises serene, stoic, unburdened individuals, free of depression, anxiety and all other mental illnesses. For him, there is no place for mental illness. Depression and anxiety, aggression and dementia do not serve a thriving country. Mental illness neither contributes to, nor compliments their vision of a sublime, indefectible state.

What are human beings if not their emotions? Should we be deprived of all sentiment, of feeling? The greatest of beauty has been created with compromised minds in the darkest of times. It is struggle that creates. Nothing has been gained from bare and empty souls.

At this moment in time, the confidential medical records of the population lie in government offices, privy to lengthy sifting processes.

How long will it be before someone we care about is taken? How long before we, ourselves are taken? How long before we become walking automatons, free of conscious thought?

Freedom is now the most sought-after radical group in this country. We are viewed as terrorists by a corrupt and amoral government. The faces of many of our freedom fighters are now widespread on posters and leaflets, with generous bounties on our heads. It is a dangerous time for us, so we must move forward with great vigilance, allowing no thing nor person to create obstacles in pursuit of our goal.

Know this. We will not forgive. We will not forget. But we will fight for justice.

We are not terrorists. We will continue to refrain from

violence in our bid to absolve Frost of his position. Those that proclaim such injustices need to be ousted.

Freedom will not be prevented from exploiting the reality behind the Happy State Government.

Freedom will not be prevented from fighting to save its people.

Freedom will not be prevented from having a voice, however, that must be enforced.

Together, we are Freedom.'

An explosion of applause and cheer erupted from the crowd. From the back of the room, the rumbling of a chant echoed like a low hum;

'Freedom! Freedom! Freedom!'

They roared the word with pride and conviction. It was more than a word to them. It was a sentiment, a weapon. It had become their war cry.

The collective action rendered it impossible to remain unaffected. It had been a while since I'd experienced unity. Whilst a distinct greyness clouded my judgement regarding the validity of Freedom, the temperament behind it had heightened my sensibility. I felt a part of something powerful, even if it was to be short-lived.

As I turned to glance at Jed, I was aware that I was smiling. It was as though I had a painted smile that I couldn't remove, natural and unforced. When I failed to see him, I felt disappointed. Perhaps I wanted to share the moment with him, maybe I hoped he'd be watching me. Either way, I wasn't surprised when I spotted him chatting to an attractive female nearby.

'One minute,' he mouthed as he spotted me lingering like a lone wanderer.

In truth, I graciously welcomed the hindrance. It offered me a minute or two to collaborate with the startling images and rhetoric that had been hurled at me. I moved myself away from the crowd and leant my back against a cold brick wall. The cool sensation against my spine was a refreshing interlude from the humidity of the room.

I wasn't naïve. I'd never believed that we lived in a true and authentic democracy. The agenda had always been in favour of self-serving politicians and journalists. It was whether I could swallow the concept that mentally ill individuals were being captured and killed, cast aside in a random plot of land. It struck me as a winning cinematic plot, but certainly not a part of my life.

There was one aspect of the speech that had firmly embedded itself in my mind. The masked stranger had talked of dementia as a burden to society. For myself and my dad, the sentiment was salient. Should there be truth in Freedom's words, then I had good reason to be alarmed.

There had also been mention of a sifting process with regard to our medical records. I thought back to my recent experience in the doctor's surgery, the upheaval, the removal vans, Min's declaration. Yet, I believed in coincidence. Min's idle gossiping could have inadvertently fed an already established conspiracy through the medium of her son. It was easily explained.

Jed approached me. 'Hey, are you okay?'

Before I could respond, a young girl of no more than

seventeen appeared before us. With a radiant smile, she effortlessly balanced a tray of shot glasses that contained a blue, syrup-like liquid in her hand. If nothing else, happy faces were abundant. Were they all as upbeat as their expressions would have me believe? Who was I to judge?

I picked a shot glass and devoured the contents in the traditional manner. I tilted my head back to allow the magical liquid to take effect as quickly as possible. The pungent flavour stung my lips, and the warmth embraced my throat.

On cue, the lights dimmed, and the music once again spilled from the speakers. The crowd reacted with urgent vigour as they moved wildly and utilised the space. Jed handed me another shot and clinked his glass against mine before devouring its contents.

'We need to talk,' he shouted over the deafening music.

'We will,' I replied. 'But not now.'

There was plenty of time for talking. In the meantime, I had an overwhelming urge to live for the moment and forget about tomorrow. I moved towards a small, clear space and began to move with the music. In spite of everything, a powerful and visceral reaction forced me to surrender to the moment, to allow the music to possess me. I'd earned my slice of freedom, even if it was just for a short time. It had been a long time coming.

Tomorrow, I would return to being Rafella Crowe; café owner, daughter of an ailing father.

Until then, I would be someone else.

*

After exorcising a few demons on the dancefloor, Jed and I took leave of the sweat ridden room. Jed had declined the dancefloor which had come as little surprise. He was way too cool for that. Instead, he'd remained on the sidelines and eyed me like a hawk. I can't say it bothered me, even if I had demonstrated unscrupulous abandon. I felt more energised than I had in months, if not years.

He guided me upstairs, where we took our rest upon an enormous Mongolian rug. Pleasantly drowsy with a thin layer of perspiration across my brow, I lay back for a few moments as I allowed my body to drown in the soft texture. Jed followed suit and lay next to me. I stared at the ceiling, temporarily mesmerised by the flickering of the candles as they cast mysterious shadows against the walls. Their flames were hypnotic and their scent seductive.

'I like this room,' I whispered as I stretched my arms above my head.

'Me too.'

We stared overhead like stargazing teenagers, both lost in our own secret worlds. I was tired of thinking and feeling. I liked the numb feeling that the alcohol and adrenalin afforded. My eyes closed, and naturally, I felt the corners of my mouth turn upward. I allowed my mind and body to descend into a relaxed stillness as I became aware of only my breathing.

'Raff…?'

I wanted to kick him for disturbing me.

'Raff?'

'Yes?' I sighed.

Before he could answer, a loud and familiar voice dissipated the moment in its entirety.

'Hey, lovers!'

I opened my eyes to see Myka and Zee as they loomed overhead. Myka seemed to effortlessly epitomise self-righteousness as she posed with one hand on her hip and a perfectly bombastic jutted chin. I failed to see how someone as seemingly placid as Zee could abide being in her company.

'Looking cosy there,' she teased as she proceeded to ingratiate herself by dropping to the floor beside us. 'Not disturbing you, are we?'

I wanted to say yes. 'Not at all.'

I bit my tongue as I remembered a verse that Mum used to quote, something about empty vessels making the loudest noise. It seemed fitting under the circumstances.

Myka relentlessly tugged at Zee's arm until he was forced to the ground beside her. I didn't miss the apologetic frown that he threw my way.

We made small talk for a while, but it didn't take long for the conversation to take on a political stance. With my mood still suitably sedated and my subject knowledge sparse, I leant back on my elbows and granted them the latitude that they desired.

As several more individuals trickled into the conversation, I gazed at the camaraderie amongst the group. It reminded me of the warmth that emanated between myself, Jo, and Dahlia. I could often be mid-conversation with a customer when one of them would affectionally drape their arms around my neck. Watching from afar as an outsider, the undeniable sense of togetherness within Freedom simply highlighted the extent to which social disconnection had come to exist. Outside the walls in which I was hidden, human emotions were barricaded behind a metaphorical barbed wire. As a nation, we had experienced so much hurt, rage and frustration. We lacked trust and avoided associations on any level. We lived in anticipation, as though the worst was yet to come.

In time, I found myself involved in a conversation with a few random souls that had taken an apparent interest in me. They greeted me by name, like we were friends of old as we spoke of mindless and irrelevant matters. At some point, I found myself on the receiving end of dietary tips for dementia, courtesy of Lio with the purple spikey hair. His intentions were pure, so I chose not to ask how he'd come to learn of Dad's illness. News travelled quickly within resistance groups, it seemed.

As the alcohol flowed, conversations livened. At some point, Myka had taken to her feet and animatedly paced back and forth as she spouted diatribe towards our new government. Before long, she had commanded the attention of the room.

'It's time. I can feel that it's time,' she announced with abundant energy. 'I personally know over thirty people that have been captured. They seem to think that no one will notice in the city, but they're starting to. It's getting closer.'

'Yes, we know, Myka,' interrupted an exasperated Zee. He apologetically smiled at the rest of the group, which was something he seemed to do often. 'Come and sit down, will you?'

'So why aren't we stepping up, then?' she demanded, as she rejected his touch. 'Why the hell are we continuing to send them these futile threats? They aren't bothered! They don't care!'

At the mention of the word threat, she had my full attention. For the two hours prior, I'd dispelled the reality of my circumstances with surprising ease. I referred back to the harsh reality. I wasn't with friends at all. I was amongst a highly sought-after resistance group.

'We can talk about upping the stakes until we're blue in the face, but how many people have to die in the meantime?'

'In time,' said Stan coolly.

'People are dying, don't you see that?' urged Myka. 'We're like an army of ants that are trying to annihilate a city of giants. It's impossible.'

Jed moved to a cross-legged position as his interest heightened. 'And what exactly do you propose?'

Stan threw him a dissatisfied look. Opened the proverbial can of worms, perhaps?

As Myka spun to look at Jed, her wild eyes suggested that she was excited at the opportunity to speak freely. He'd offered her a loaded gun.

'You really want to know what I think? Okay, I say we bypass everything we've been doing and go straight to the endgame.'

Although I had no concept of the endgame or even the initial game for that matter, I detected that her announcement had sparked controversy amongst the group. Stan rose to his feet and walked away. A couple of others followed, less than impressed.

'Are you kidding?' balked Jed. 'We aren't terrorists. We can't go around…'

'Killing people? We can't kill the people that are killing our own people?'

Zee shook his head. 'Oh, come on. It's not as simple as that, Myka.'

'It's not as simple as that? Yes, Zee. It really is. Because let me tell you this. We'll try Plan A and C and F and G and, ultimately, come straight back to my plan because it's the only one that's effective.'

Jed frowned. 'But your plan is to resort to violence. How does that make us any better? You have to at least give people an opportunity to make changes, or you're nothing short of a terrorist.'

'Play fairly?' Myka snapped. 'Is mass genocide fair? Don't act as though these people are human, because they're not!'

'And we're trying to negotiate,' interrupted Zee.

Myka let out an oversized laugh. 'They're murdering people. This is a holocaust! You can't negotiate with people like that.'

To put it mildly, the atmosphere had become strained. Myka was quite skilled in that domain. The few that revered Myka and all that she stood for openly supported her comments. Others looked on with disdain. As for myself, all rhetoric spouted within the subterranean world that I found myself in had ceased to affect me on any emotional level. I could only assume that an unconscious defence mechanism had kicked in to protect me. Whether it would hit me in spades at a later date, I had no idea.

Jed leaned in to me. 'Hyperbole. Ignore her.'

'We're peaceful protestors,' stated Stan, who had returned to the conversation. 'A non-violent organisation. We negotiate until we can no longer negotiate. Then we look at other methods of interaction.'

'But it isn't working!' insisted Myka.

Stan took a deep breath. I sensed that Myka had pushed his buttons.

'When Johnny started this group, he was a staunch advocate for non-violence. He always said that the day may come when our tactics must change. But, for now, we remain a peaceful group, and not you or anyone else is going to change that.'

Myka laughed. I was certain that she could antagonise the most placid of individuals. 'What's the point? We might as well give up now.'

'As long as I'm around, that's the way it is.'

'And if you're not around?'

My eyes widened at her audacity, and a few audible gasps informed me that I wasn't alone in my thinking. Stan's ability to remain calm was commendable. He eyed her intensely. His voice remained cool.

'I am around. So, I'm afraid you'll have to keep your amateur tactics under wraps. Otherwise, you know where the exit is.'

He turned his back on her, which only served to aggravate her further.

'Frost will be eliminated,' she stated. 'Maybe not now, but I'll make damn sure of it.'

Zee rose to his feet and firmly wrapped his arms around her from behind, a desperate bid to ease the tension.

'Okay, Myka, we've heard enough of your voice for a while.'

He manoeuvred her away from the group and disappeared through the archway. Stan rolled his eyes at the remaining group members. There were a few shaking heads and choice gestures in response to her incendiary rhetoric.

'The gift that keeps on giving,' remarked Jed as Stan took a seat alongside us.

'I respect the man who gave us the opportunity to be a part

of this movement,' he responded in a low voice. 'We aren't about to become terrorists because she happens to think our strategy isn't working. She's been here five minutes. I've been here three years.'

'Ignore her,' said Jed, an attempt to appease him. 'She knows how to make waves, that's all.'

Stan turned to face me. 'And how are you?'

'Great!' I balked. The adrenalin and alcohol had begun to wear off, which had made way for an overwhelming tiredness.

'Allow yourself some time to consolidate everything. It's too much to think about straight away.'

I attempted to conceal an enormous yawn.

'I think you need to get this one home,' urged Stan as he rose to his feet.

I summoned the energy to lift myself to my feet and desperately tried to eliminate the fleeting thoughts of the marathon walk that lay ahead.

A shrill voice called out from behind. 'So great to meet you, Raff.'

I didn't need to look to recognise the dulcet tone.

'Do you have to be such a bitch?' snapped Jed.

'What? I was being nice!'

'Keep your thoughts to yourself, yeah?'

I tugged on Jed's arm, urged him to walk away. I refused to acknowledge such insipid behaviour.

'For the record, your girlfriend shouldn't be here. She's not one of us.'

'Is that right?' asked Jed.

'Look at her. She's privileged and wouldn't have the first clue about struggle.'

'Jed, please…' I begged.

'Well, considering she's about to be an orphan, I'd say that's a pretty rich projection!'

I glared at Jed. How dare he use my personal life as a cheap jibe to win points in an argument. And how dare he announce my circumstances to a room full of strangers. Frozen to the spot, I could feel the intense glares from the room. I wanted to curl up, to disappear. I hated him for making me look so vulnerable and weak.

'Doesn't change the facts,' stated Myka, unphased by Jed's admission. 'She still doesn't belong here.'

Jed lunged towards her. Zee and Stan intercepted at once.

'You need help,' he shouted as Stan pulled him away. 'There's something seriously wrong with you!'

She stood her ground with confidence, unaffected by the retaliation.

I immediately marched in the opposite direction and towards the staircase. With Jed beside me, I could almost smell the fresh air that awaited me. I'd never longed for the open air as much as that precise moment.

'Raff! I'm sorry.'

I turned to see Stan, just a few steps beneath me. 'I don't know what you want me to say.'

'Tensions are high right now. Myka isn't usually like this. She's just passionate.'

I wasn't sure if he believed his own words, but I nodded. Had I attempted a polite smile; it would have been a grimace.

'Your Mum would be proud, Raff. She'd support you being

here.'

The anger surged, so I took my cue to leave. He was undeserved of a response. He'd already used Dad to manipulate me, then had the nerve to try with Mum. I wasn't about to be radicalised, not as long as I had my sanity.

I followed Jed through the hatch and out into the open air.

*

We walked the entire journey home in silence. I wanted to let rip at him, but I had a mild headache and felt exhausted. As we walked side by side, I sensed his unchained fury, which made him walk at an impossible speed. Too stubborn to ask for a breather, I breathlessly continued.

We followed the same route as the inward journey. Jed governed the imperative timings to avoid any unwanted interaction with a sweeper. Other than the faint spotlight from the torch that highlighted the area in front of us, we were surrounded by blackness. The only sound was our heavy breathing as we powered towards our destination.

We froze as two sweepers crossed our path in the near distance. They were several hundred metres away, but nothing justified even the smallest of risks. I should have been terrified, but my tiredness had somewhat diluted any imminent fear.

We crossed the field and spotted two dark figures as they leapt behind a large oak tree. I panicked and froze to the spot. Jed shone the torch on his hand as he raised a fist; his thumb stuck out to the side, like a signal of sorts. When one of them returned the gesture, we continued. I suspected they were teenagers, sneaking out for an adventure. I couldn't judge them. Their objective seemed far more cogent than mine.

Midway, I began to dither with cold; the cool spring chill compounded by the late hour had started to penetrate my bones. I must have made a sound, as Jed stopped briefly to remove his coat. No words were exchanged as he handed it to me, and I denied him any gratitude. It was the very least he owed me.

It was gone three in the morning when I arrived home. I unlocked the front door with the stealth of an insubordinate teenager as Jed lingered outside. As soon as the door closed behind me, I crept upstairs and checked in on Dad. He slept peacefully, wholly innocent to my audacious behaviour.

A tear fell down my cheek as I watched him sleep.

The man that lay before me was my prime focus. I didn't need anybody else.

*

Chapter 19

The next morning, I was woken by the warm sun as it burst through the fine drapes in my bedroom. Groggy and overly warm, I climbed out of bed and opened the windows as I allowed the gentle breeze to cool my flushed face. Each time my mind wandered to the events of the previous night; I blocked the thoughts as quickly as they entered. Jed had occupied too much of my headspace of late, and it was an unnecessary distraction.

It was only after showering and dressing that I noticed the time on the kitchen clock. Five minutes past six, and I was unmistakably charged with a superhuman energy. Had I have overlooked the insufferable treatment that I received at the hands of Myka, my taste of freedom seemed to have served me well.

By the time Dad rose at seven, I'd blitzed the kitchen from top to bottom and prepared his scrambled eggs. The patio doors were opened to full capacity to enable the glorious sun to enter our home. The smell of freshly brewed coffee lingered in the air. As soon as I saw him in the doorway, I wrapped him in a tight embrace.

'What a perfectly lovely way to wake up!' he said as he kissed the crown of my head. 'Something smells good.'

'I'm making you breakfast, and we're going to spend the morning together. Maybe we could take a walk? It's a gorgeous day outside.'

Dad frowned. Not quite the reaction I was hoping for.

'Min's taking me to an art exhibition in the village,' he sighed. 'Oh, sweetheart, I'm so sorry.'

I tried my hardest to conceal my disappointment. 'It's okay. Well, at least you'll eat breakfast with me?'

He smiled, and ruffled my hair like he used to. 'You bet I will.'

The events of the previous night had triggered something in my subconscious. My desire to have him close by was heightened. I felt like an injured child that pined for the attention of a parent.

'Why are you staring at me?' he asked as he lowered his glasses. He peered up at me with large blue eyes.

I shrugged. 'I love you, that's all.'

My Dad. My world. I'd go to any lengths to protect him.

We ate a breakfast of scrambled eggs and toasted brown bread. A couple of years ago we'd have added fresh avocado, but the country's newfound independence had put paid to that. There would never be a day that we would eat this meal and fail to mention the loss. We drank coffee and chatted about his latest painting. He didn't like it very much, but he always said that. So did Michelangelo, apparently.

Min arrived as I cleared the plates, all hustle and bustle, overly mollycoddling Dad which, I too, was guilty of.

'Jed insisted on delivering me, but don't get excited,' she declared. 'We're walking into the village and soaking up this sunshine. You need the Vitamin C!'

The mention of his name prompted a visceral reaction, a metaphorical knife had been plunged into my innards. When he sheepishly appeared in the doorway, the knife turned. I made a conscious effort to avoid eye contact.

Their exit was as chaotic as usual, which simply magnified the silence that we were left in. Eventually, I muttered an awkward greeting, poured two mugs of freshly brewed coffee, and beckoned him into the garden with me.

I pulled out one of Mum's white antique garden chairs from under the table and took a seat. It was the first time I'd sat in the garden after a long and laborious winter and the emotional jolt wasn't lost on me. Many memories had been made at Mum's prize table; card games, board games, rich and philosophical conversations.

Jed took a seat opposite; his movements were slow and precise. 'How are you this morning?'

'Really well,' I replied as I pushed his coffee towards him. 'All things considered.'

He looked hyper-stressed as he wiped a bead of sweat from his brow. He fidgeted for a moment or two, then removed his jacket to reveal a thin cotton t-shirt.

He didn't take a beat. 'I'm sorry. Really sorry. I've been awake all night thinking what an absolute idiot I am. I honestly do not know what I was thinking of taking you there. If I had a brain, I'd be dangerous.'

I said nothing as I watched him squirm. Let him suffer.

He rolled up the sleeves on his t-shirt so they sat high on his shoulders; his slim, tanned arms were fully on show. I shifted my gaze to the garden.

'I thought I was doing the right thing. Stan thought the same. I realise now that I was wrong. We were wrong.'

I silently commended his mindful use of "we". I was almost

certain that he felt that the inclusion of Stan would lessen the blow.

'And then, you're insulted by Myka who accuses you of having nothing to fight for,' he continued. He enunciated the last few words with a whining, effeminate lilt. 'You, more than anyone I know, have everything to fight for. That's why I took you there. That's the only reason. So, you could see it all unfolding, so you could see…'

'Jed…' I interrupted.

'…how you and your dad could be in danger and we, or you, or we, together maybe, could make sure that…'

'Jed?'

'…there's no way they could get to your dad.'

'Jed!' I barked.

He stopped; his eyes were fixed on his coffee cup as they refused to acknowledge me. 'And now I'm doing your head in again…'

'Will you just be quiet?' I begged. 'Dude, you need to breathe!'

That I was the person offering advice on breathing techniques was nothing short of ironic. It was pleasantly apparent that he was devastated by his actions and burdened with remorse. It wasn't painful to watch. Not even slightly.

'I understand.'

His head remained bowed, but his eyes met mine.

'Why are you being so alright about this?'

'I don't know. But I understand why you wanted me to go.'

Curiously, he tilted his head. 'Really?'

'Really. If all that stuff is true, I'm glad I know. I wish I didn't have to know, but I'm glad I do.'

He leaned back in his chair and roughly rubbed his hands over his face. 'I am so relieved. I expected you to throw me out.'

'I thought about it.' I'd more than thought about it.

'You're strangely quiet,' he said, narrowing his eyes. 'Am I missing something?'

I shook my head. 'Nope!'

He leaned forward and gazed at me. 'Look, I wish I could tell you that we're a bunch of bored, frustrated juveniles who've had tough lives and just need a sense of purpose, but I can't. Everything that you heard last night is true.'

I turned my body and glanced up at the garden. A stunning pink lily had begun to sprout from the flower bed.

'Doesn't it scare you? Being a part of it?'

He took a deep breath as he considered his answer. 'Not as much as it should.'

'You realise you're highly sought after? I even have a poster on my wall at work.'

'Yeah. I noticed.'

'You're actually one of the most wanted groups in the UK.'

'Happy State?' he corrected. There was more than a touch or irony in his tone.

I couldn't get used to thinking of my country in those terms, let alone saying it.

'Whatever.'

'It's too easy to sit back and complain. I want to make a difference. That's what drives me.'

'I guess.'

I wondered if I'd ever wanted something badly enough to compromise my existence. My heart skipped a beat as I realised that I'd do anything to protect my dad. Anything.

'Do you have any questions?'

It dawned on me that I should probably have a long list of them.

'There's only one thing that I don't understand,' I said.

'Anything.'

'Why involve me? What on earth can I do?'

'It affects your dad. It won't be long before…'

'So, you keep telling me,' I interrupted. 'I have a question. What's with the creepy mask?' A desperate bid to divert the conversation from my dad.

He smiled. 'Traditions. Weird. Alpha's thing, not mine.'

'Alpha?'

'Forget it, too complicated.'

'That's one thing we agree on.'

'I'm sorry about Myka. She's had a bad ride, that's all. She's angry.'

I lowered my chin as I glared at him. 'You reckon?'

'It comes from a passion for change. No one can blame her.'

I paused for a moment as I tried to understand Myka and her vulgar demeanour. Perhaps a better person might give her the benefit of the doubt. Would I treat a polite stranger with disdain if I felt threatened?

Absolutely not.

'Any more questions?' he asked. 'You must have loads.'

'I do have another one. How do you all communicate?'

He laughed. 'Of all the questions…'

'Comms Wall?'

He shook his head. 'Word gets around. We know how to

reach each other when we need to.'

'I just wondered if those weird squiggles might be some sort of code. I've always been curious.'

He refused to answer and turned his attention to a floating leaf. I suspected it was an affirmative response to my question.

'I was expecting you to say you use a mobile.'

'Haven't used one of those for two years. They're illegal,' he winked.

I half-smiled. 'Oh, the irony!'

'The world was at war long before mobile phones came into use, and they managed alright,' he said. He drained the remnants of his coffee, glanced at his watch. 'I really have to go.'

I welcomed the respite. It was time for me to consolidate some of my newfound information.

As we entered the house, I stopped in my tracks. 'Why did you tell me all of this, Jed? You didn't need to. You could have carried on doing your thing, with me not knowing any of it.'

'Because I like you,' he replied. 'I always have. Maybe someday you'll see that.'

An awkward moment, felt by both.

'What would happen to you? You know, if you got caught?'

'We don't talk about things like that. That's why getting caught isn't an option.'

I walked him to the front door, and after he'd gone, I retreated back into the quiet house. With Dad and Min absent, it took on an eerie silence. I glanced at Dad's empty chair, and for a split second I imagined that he was gone forever.

Yielding to the extreme possibilities, I cried for my vulnerable and ailing dad.

Chapter 20

Having waited in a small reception area for over an hour, Aron was led into a large conference room. He was clean shaven and dressed impeccably; a simple black suit and a granite-coloured tie. He looked nervous as the polite woman led him to a seat.

'They'll be here in a moment. Make yourself comfortable,' she said.

He thanked her and waited for her to leave before exhaling. He'd unknowingly held his breath for the last fifteen minutes, anxious about his meeting with Edwin Oakes. He glanced at the images on the wall, which showed a series of portraits of previous prime ministers and leaders.

He braced himself as the door rattled and immediately stood tall and poised.

'Aron, a pleasure to meet you,' said Oakes as he reached out to shake Aron's hand.

Aron was visibly nervous as he reciprocated the gesture. 'The pleasure is mine, Sir. Thank you for inviting me.'

'Please, sit,' urged Oakes as he gestured towards a chair.

'Thank you, Sir.'

Oakes took a seat and spent several moments sifting through a folder that had been handed to him before entering. Aron wrung his hands in anticipation.

'Apologies,' said Oakes as he eventually replaced the papers and closed the folder. 'Work never seems to stop round here. I hear that you're a member of the police force, Aron. How's that going for you?'

Aron shifted in his seat and cleared his throat. 'Very well, thank you, Sir. I've been with the force for just under three years.'

Oakes smiled. 'You've been quite up against it with the transition. Can't be easy?'

'Not always, Sir. But we do what we can to keep the peace. Obviously, the military take on most of the work at the moment.'

'Yes, indeed they do.'

Before he could respond, the door opened, and Frost entered. Without forethought, Aron rose to his feet and saluted with the vigour of a rookie recruit.

'Commander.'

Oakes looked suitably taken aback at the gesture, while Frost looked him up and down. 'Quite the greeting. And you are…?'

'Aron. Aron Roux, Commander.'

'Yes, of course. The police officer from Thendra?'

'That's correct, Commander.'

Frost walked over to Oakes and whispered something in his ear. A second later, Oakes excused himself. With just the two of them remaining, Frost took a seat and urged Aron to do the same.

'I believe you have some information for us, Aron.'

Desperately in awe of Frost, he fidgeted in his seat.

'Relax, you're not on trial,' suggested Frost. 'On the contrary, I believe you're here to assist.'

'Yes, absolutely. I mean… sorry, I'm a bit taken aback. I think you're a fantastic leader and it's such an honour to meet you,'

Aron garbled.

'Not the leader,' he corrected. 'That's Edwin's role. But I appreciate the sentiment.' Frost leant forward in his seat. 'Let's get to business. How can you help us, Aron?'

'Yes, of course. My girl… ex-girlfriend works at a popular coffee shop in Thendra. She used to tell me that the owner was determined to be awkward in terms of assisting with the resistance. A government official has since visited her, I believe.'

Frost frowned. 'And you think this is relevant because…?'

'I don't understand why she won't comply. There are rules, and she isn't abiding by them.'

'You're a stickler for the rules, I see,' smirked Frost.

'With all due respect, I'm a police officer, Commander.'

'You'd be surprised. What are your feelings towards the resistance, Aron?' he asked.

Aron didn't take a beat. 'Pointless anarchists, commander. They're fighting a battle that doesn't exist. Anyone can see the good work you're doing. What's to resist?'

Frost beamed. 'I like your perspective. And this coffee shop owner, do you have reason to believe that she's involved with the resistance?'

Aron hesitated. 'Nothing specific. There are rumours that her boyfriend is a friend of Stanley Wallace, but I don't know if they're true. Stanley used to be good friends with…'

'Johnny McLaydon, founder of Freedom. Yes, I'm aware of him.' Frost looked up at him with wide eyes. 'Have you had a sighting of Stanley?'

'No, commander.'

'Right. And what's her boyfriend's name, this café owner?'

'Jed. I don't know his last name. He has a real ego. Anyway, my ex-girlfriend, Jo, tried to talk her into abiding, but she talks of freedom of speech and all that rubbish. She even puts missing posters up. Jo doesn't like her at all, thinks she's a right pain…' He stopped himself abruptly. 'Apologies, Commander. I spoke too openly.'

'Freedom of speech,' mocked Frost, as he scribbled something in a notepad. 'What a thing that has become in recent decades.'

'I agree. The rest of us are doing all that we can to clean up the mess left by the last government, to move forward to The Happy State. I have no doubt that our country will become great once again, but people like her feel she can make it up as she goes along.'

Frost leaned his hands on the table in front of him. 'Your attitude is refreshing, young man. Especially for someone so young. Have you ever thought about joining the military?'

'I'd like nothing more,' replied Aron eagerly. 'It would be an honour to serve The Happy State.'

Frost nodded. 'Leave your details and we'll be in touch. For now, work is pressing, so I must cut our meeting short. Thank you for taking the time to inform us. I'd appreciate it if you could also leave the details of the café with Edwin's secretary before you leave?'

'Of course. Anything.'

Frost stood, and Aron followed. 'It's been a pleasure, Aron,' he said.

'It has been a pleasure to meet you, Commander.'

As Aron left the building, he felt satisfied that he'd made a good first impression. He'd had to elaborate slightly, stretch the truth here and there. The outcome would be worth it.

*

Following the meeting, Frost stopped by Oakes' office. He was visibly stressed, deeply engrossed in a telephone conversation. When he'd finished the call, Frost closed the door behind him.

'I have eight meetings scheduled. What's the problem?' asked Oakes bluntly.

'I thought you'd want to hear the outcome of my meeting with Aron Roux.'

Oakes was distracted as he spoke. 'What did he have to say?'

'Not a lot. His intelligence was benign, to say the least. But he has a good attitude. I'd like to consider recruiting him. We need more like him.'

Oakes nodded. 'Yes, whatever you think.'

Frost smiled. 'Good. I'll leave you to it.'

He left the office and collected the information that Aron had left with Anneka.

Rafella Crowe, owner of The Café. Thendra.

He'd enrol Aron in the fast-tracked recruitment process to the military on the grounds that he rekindled his relationship with his ex-girlfriend.

With Thendra homing their largest Zone, he couldn't put a price on reliable informants.

Chapter 21

'You have mail,' announced Dahlia. She pointed to the work counter as I walked Winnie to the front door.

Winnie had been particularly fussy all morning, and I'd lost my temper with her. I'd felt terrible almost immediately and apologised, but her constant complaining was starting to wear very thin.

I turned my attention to Dahlia. 'What is it?' I hoped it wasn't important enough to have to look at it.

'That'd ruin the surprise,' she said, a huge grin on her face.

Instinctively, I reached for the mail. 'These are application forms?'

'Surprise!'

I rolled my eyes. Dahlia knew how I fervently disliked the interview process.

As I casually sifted through, I counted fourteen applications from my recent advertisement for staff. Instinctively, I pushed them aside to deal with later, but Dahlia shunted them back towards me.

'Don't put off until tomorrow what you can do today!' she barked. 'We need staff!'

She was right. I was a terrible procrastinator; always putting things off until the last minute. I poured myself another strong black coffee and sat myself down at one of the free tables.

I was bored before I even started.

*

Jed had proven to be quite the stranger.

After our previous conversation, he'd put some distance between us and though I was grateful for it, I was solitary in my resolve. Despite Freedom's passion in all that they stood for; I was unable to embrace the intrigue as they did.

I'd spent night after night sifting through the surplus information that occupied my brain. Sleepless hours had passed as I'd blindly navigated my way through the process of reason. One minute, I'd believe that Freedom were nothing short of a terrorist group, the next, I found myself empathising with their plight.

I thought back to when it all started, to the birth of The Happy State. While I was less than a novice with my understanding of politics, the conception had failed to cohere with archetypal political policies. Why had our government taken such extreme measures for the sake of societal happiness? It had never been an agenda before and we, as a nation, had become somewhat accustomed to political pantomime and the inevitable fallout that came with it. We had low expectations, and would survive whatever they threw at us. We always did.

Still, it didn't justify the maniacal theories of Freedom. Could they be yet another group of fervent conspiracy theorists that were brainwashed by their fanatical cult leader? Should I be trying to help Jed, rather than the other way around?

In spite of the fleeting enjoyment I'd experienced, I'd gained nothing but an increase in anxiety ever since. Each time I left Dad, I feared it might be the last time I'd see him. On one occasion, I'd even convinced myself that I was being followed by an innocent bystander.

Unable to discuss the matter with an unbiased source, I'd been forced to consider simple logic for the sake of my personal sanity. Powerless, I had no choice but to deem their information as nothing more than propaganda, borne from the mind of a sad, bitter or lonely group of individuals.

I wondered if avoiding Jed might be the best solution of all. I could bury my head in the sand and pretend that it hadn't happened. If what he said was true, then I'd soon find out. We'd all find out, and there was absolutely nothing we could do about it. But to merely be associated with him in these disturbing times, much less having visited the home of the resistance, I firmly placed myself and my dad in grave danger. One outcome was a certainty, the other was dubious at best.

And it was then, armed with this realisation, that I knew what I had to do.

My dalliance with danger had made me realise that nothing was more important than Dad and I. Nothing or no one was going to get in the way of our safety. It wasn't going to be easy, and Dad was going to take some convincing, but I had to eliminate Jed and Min from our lives. Poor Min. If she had any knowledge of her son's predicament, she'd be devastated.

A storm was coming, and I had to find the strength to ride it out.

*

'So, when can you start?' I asked, elated that I hadn't wasted yet another forty minutes of my life.

I'd interviewed nine potential staff members over the last three days, and my brain was close to imploding. One of the interviewees had disliked coffee and claimed to have an allergy to it. Another spoke in monosyllables, which made conversation virtually impossible. The rest had been acceptable, but no one stood out as both friendly and efficient.

That was until Edie had walked in with her application form.

I was all but ready to throw the towel in when she appeared at the counter, glowing with confidence and smiling from ear to ear. I'd decided to interview her there and then, and beamed with delight when she ticked every single box I required.

'As soon as you want me,' Edie replied as her eyes lit up.

I arranged for her to start the following day. Ideally, I'd have liked a few more staff, but her ability to work full-time hours, flexible shifts and overtime in addition to her vast experience of public service was a positive start. Dahlia tried to convince me that I was kidding myself with just one new employee, all because I hated the interview process. I told her she was wrong.

She wasn't.

*

The subsequent days offered me solace from the stress of running the café. Not only did Edie prove to be a hard worker, she'd also been forthcoming with her ideas to smarten up the interior and give the place a minor overhaul.

The other girls hadn't taken to her quite as well as I'd hoped. Jo had described her as being overconfident, Dahlia labelled her as insincere. I sensed a bit of damaged ego. I understood that it was a transition for the girls, but I needed the help and Edie seemed to effortlessly fulfil the role.

By week three of Edie's trial, things ran more seamlessly than they had in a while. By no means was this a poor reflection on Jo and Dahlia, but Edie brought a fresh perspective that the café had lacked. Midweek, I'd even been able to pop to the local salon and cash in the facial that Rex had gifted to me on my birthday.

I remained aware that my head was deeply rooted in the sand as far as Jed and Min were concerned. I knew I needed to address the issue, but had yet to summon the courage to have the conversation with Dad. I'd tried to subtly introduce the idea of "just the two of us," but he'd disregarded it as a silly idea. 'You need to focus on your work,' he'd said.

I knew it was his way of saying that he didn't want to hold me back, but if I could maybe convince him that I wanted to look after him, then maybe we'd have a chance. I was yet to establish how I'd overcome the difficulties associated with losing Min. That was at the end of a long line of things to deal with.

Towards the end of the week, I attended an appointment at the hairdressing salon just a few doors down from the café. In a bid to lift my spirits, I'd let one of the salon girls talk me into a haircut while she'd been on the daily coffee run. Despite my reticence, it was an injection of energy; to kick back and relax whilst being cosseted by the staff, not to mention my numerous split ends. The conversation was inconsequential and light as one of the girls combed my knotted hair, while another pushed back my overgrown cuticles.

I'd been there for approximately an hour when the receptionist drew my attention to the window; a military truck had pulled into the pedestrian area outside the small row of shops. Suitably relaxed in my stress-free bubble, I remained in place as they delivered a running commentary on the action.

'They don't ever do things like this,' the girl said. 'It must be something really serious to park here.'

There were several gasps, a sharp intake of breath.

'Raff, they're going into the café!' the receptionist blurted. 'You need to come and look!'

My bubble had burst.

The first thing that crossed my mind was that I'd been caught. The lid had been blown on Freedom's big secret and I'd been roped in. My heart raced uncontrollably as I made my way to the window. A soldier was stood by the truck with an oversized gun; tall and brawny with a mean expression that worked to repel. Another soldier headed in the direction of the cafe.

I opened the salon door and sprinted towards the café. The gown, attached only by a necktie, wavered behind me like the cape of a low-end superhero. For a split second, I wondered if I should be hiding, running in the opposite direction.

A loud voice bellowed from a megaphone. 'Do not enter the building. Step back from the building!'

I was going to prison for the rest of my life. This was it. Any moment, I'd be forced to my knees and handcuffed, right in front of the gathering of nosey shop owners and snooping customers.

Instinctively, and somewhat defiantly, I reached for the door handle to continue forward. Despite the imminent situation, there was a natural inclination to protect what was mine. The soldier repeated his order as I took a step inside. The mental picture of prison life played out so powerfully in my mind that my reality had become skewed, and when I walked into the café, I was unsure if the scene I faced was legitimate, or my mind playing tricks on me.

Jo and Dahlia, suitably distressed, stood back as a soldier pinned a girl to the floor. Her face was awkwardly squashed to the side as she lay flat on her stomach. At a glance, she looked to be no more than twelve or thirteen years of age. The door flew open as a further two soldiers stampeded into the café. They moved as though a violent criminal was on the loose. I held my breath as they approached the area where I stood. My last moments of freedom. I did all but raise my hands to surrender.

They bypassed me without so much as a glance and headed straight for the action. The stockiest of the threesome assisted in holding the girl down while the other demanded that everyone stand back. The girl cried out in discomfort; her arm was tightly pinned behind her back.

I waited. No one looked at me, much less approached me or, worse still, handcuffed me. I looked at Jo and Dahlia questioningly. Their expressions displayed no hint of hostility, more, a mirroring of exhaustive confusion. Perhaps it wasn't my time, after all.

The young girl screamed out, louder this time.

'Is that really necessary?' I asked. I was conscious that the girl made no attempt to resist and required minimal force, if any at all.

Embarrassed at my outburst, Jo hushed me. I was ignored

by the soldiers.

I slowly edged my way towards her as she tentatively moved behind the counter.

'What the hell is going on?' I probed.

As I spoke, I became acutely aware of the cold, damp gown that remained tied around my neck. I attempted to loosen the tie but my hands shook with such ferocity that I was unable to get to grips with the small knot. Conscious of my growing frustration, Jo intervened. Her voice was low as she spoke.

'The girl came in and ordered a drink. Next thing, Edie said she was calling the emergency services. I asked why and she said the girl was part of the resistance. Before I knew it, it had all kicked off.'

'What? That's insane!' I protested.

'Keep your voice down,' whispered Jo whilst maintaining a perfectly neutral expression. 'Edie just mumbled something about a backpack and then she made the call.'

Irritated, I brushed Jo's hands away from me. Her well-intentioned interference made me feel claustrophobic amidst the chaos.

For the first time since I'd entered, I glanced around the café. Full to half capacity, the customers conveyed panic-stricken expressions as the scene unfolded. I spotted Edie perched on the edge of a table. She had an almost smug look about her. I felt anger rise from the pit of my stomach.

'Can the customers please leave?' I protested. A hint of confidence had returned, and I felt angry at the liberties being taken on my property. My tone was sharp. I wanted to be heard.

'No one is entering or leaving,' replied the youngest of the soldiers. His eyes were fixed on the young girl.

A few inaudible comments went back and forth between the soldiers before the stockiest of the three forcefully yanked the girl to her feet by the fixed handcuffs. Several people winced at the force in which she was hauled to a standing position. Her arms twisted awkwardly, while her legs fought to ground her.

I looked at her small and fragile face. She was so pale and thin. She wore dark, skin tight jeans that clung to her pitifully thin frame and a black oversized hoody that seemed to drown her. Her expression remained blank and emotionless, and at no point did she attempt to struggle. It was as though she had willingly accepted her fate.

The young soldier moved to the door and boldly stood in the entrance; a gesture of authority, to block the only available exit. It served to unsettle a few of the customers. One lady begun to cry and Dahlia stealthily made her way towards her.

The remaining soldier lifted the girl's backpack and pulled the zip with more vigour than necessary, then shook the bag until its contents had fallen to the floor. He knelt down and roughly skimmed the items. The girl remained in place; her eyes focused on the area ahead. Unflinching.

A bottle of water, a plastic pot of food, a packet of biscuits, several bars of chocolate, and a torch lay scattered in front of him. He peered into the bag, seemingly unsatisfied with his findings. His audience surveyed the action with trepidation, curious as to what it was that he so desperately sought. Once again, the bag was tipped, and an opened box of sanitary items fell to the floor, one by one. I cringed for the poor girl. Despairingly, he opened a side pocket, smiling as he removed a small, swiss army knife.

Quite justifiably, I assumed the knife to be the source of his frantic search. A young girl carrying a dangerous weapon evoked numerous potential outcomes, none of which offered a lawful explanation. Yet, this discovery, while sufficiently incriminating for the girl, was of little consequence to the soldier. He cast the knife aside and, once again, manically foraged through each pocket of her bag. The girl remained statuesque, with her frail arms tightly pinned behind her. Perhaps she practiced meditation, as it appeared as though she'd transcended into another plane as she vacantly stared at the wall in front of her.

At last, the soldier's self-congratulatory expression informed us that he had found what he was looking for. In his hand was her identification, immediately discernible by the familiar red plastic cover.

We all carried them. As part of the transition to The Happy State, it had become mandatory for every civilian to bear their I.D consistently.

'Fake I.D. Yep! She's our girl.'

He kicked the items beneath him to clear his passage, marched to the girl, and thrust her identification in her face.

'Nice try. You've had it.'

He roughly took her arms and pulled her towards the door. She winced in pain as she was pushed and pulled, back and forth. As she passed me by with a blank expression, I was certain that I noticed a single tear fall down her cheek.

The door slammed shut, and the café lay in still silence, interrupted only by the intrusive sound of the truck's roaring engine as it escorted the prisoner to an unknown location. A customer started to cry.

'Please get her some water,' I said as I sprung to action. 'Let's get this place cleared up.'

The chatter began. It was inevitable, of course. I just hadn't been sure how long it would take. Though impossible to decipher entire conversations, the topic of choice was obvious as customers pointed to the door, glanced at the floor, and waved their arms melodramatically. It was more drama than the village folk were used to and would provide them with superfluous material over the coming months. Thendra was like that, a mere sniff of action was substantial to distract the occupants, and myself and the staff would hear each individual's perspective at least once. Even the invasion of martial law had become yesterday's news, with people seeking more recent scandalous topics to dissect.

The not-so-good aspect of the job.

Having mentally determined to close for the remainder of the day, I cleared the tables in a bid to silence the humdrum of gossip. It wouldn't serve me well to the hear the incident recapitulated for hours on end. Quite unaware of my intentions, Jo briskly ushered the customers to the door and changed the sign to closed. I clearly wasn't the only one who longed for some semblance of normality. When we'd cleared the tables and emptied the café of scandalmongers, we made ourselves a pot of tea and caught our breath. Edie was nowhere to be seen.

'Did that really just happen?' I asked. 'I'm not sure if I'm dreaming.'

Jo shrugged. 'I literally have no idea. It all happened so fast.'

Dahlia pointed to the ceiling. I frowned, confused at what she was referring to. That happened a lot with Dahlia and her mystical messages. She leaned forward in her seat as she prepared to indulge me when Edie appeared from the back of the café.

'I suppose I can go now?' she asked briskly. 'We're not opening for the rest of the day, I assume?'

She was all but ready to leave with her coat buttoned up and her bag over her shoulder.

'Edie, what happened?' I asked, perturbed at her lack of empathy.

'I did what needed to be done,' she replied nonchalantly.

I looked at her quizzically. 'And what was that?' I shifted my position to face her. Her arrogant demeanour aggravated me.

'She was only having a drink,' protested Jo. 'She didn't do anything!'

'She was quite blatantly with the resistance!'

Jo and I exchanged a glance. Dahlia let out a disapproving grunt.

'How on earth did you come to that conclusion?' I asked. 'She was a kid.'

Edie rolled her eyes at me. 'You are so naïve! She was acting really suspiciously. She wouldn't take her hood down and her eyes were all over the place. She wouldn't have paid for that drink; she was ready to do a runner.'

'That doesn't make her a member of the resistance!' I argued.

'The backpack was the real give away,' she added.

I took a breath. The girl was a real piece of work.

'Are you joking?' I spat. 'A backpack? That's your theory?'

'They all carry a backpack.'

I paused. She had my attention. Is that why Jed carried a backpack? Before I allowed my thoughts to spiral out of control,

I stopped myself. I was stupid to even entertain such a ridiculous concept. Why on earth would resistance members need to carry a backpack? It was sheer coincidence, nothing more.

'Why would resistance members carry a backpack?' asked Dahlia. I was glad that she'd asked the question.

Wide-eyed, Edie glared at us. She turned to Jo, apparently seeking some sort of recognition.

'Oh God, you're serious, aren't you?' A patronising grin unfolded on her face. I disliked her more and more by the minute.

She dumped her bag on the floor, sat herself on the table, and rested her feet on the chair. I would have lambasted her had I not been so dumbfounded by her boldness. She leaned forward and rested her elbows on her knees, addressing us as though we were a classroom of preschool infants.

'Do you guys know anything about the resistance?'

'Funnily enough, no!' sneered Dahlia.

'I figured. They're all on the military watch list, so they need to be ready to run. It's fairly common knowledge that they carry backpacks around with them.'

Jo glared at her. 'I have a backpack. Does that make me a part of the resistance?'

'No, dummy. But when you put it all together, the dark clothes, the hood, the suspicious behaviour, it's obvious. Well, it is to me anyway.'

Jo looked furious. 'Did you really just call me a dummy?'

'According to a friend of mine, who knows everything about them, they carry things like food, weapons, torches, burner phones, and money. I think she had a fake I.D which gave her away. They knew who she was. That was a big mistake.'

'I can't believe you just said that…' fumed Jo.

'Well, you're acting like a dummy,' she laughed. 'Everyone knows this stuff. I don't see how you can work in the busiest café in town and not know this?'

I've worked with the public for a long time and hear about anything commonplace. I'm often the first to hear of local tittle-tattle. Beside the odd rambling, largely prompted by the posters on the wall, the resistance wasn't a subject that tended to circulate. I certainly didn't know about the stuff that she referred to, and I'd been pretty up close and personal with the resistance. How I'd love to have declared that, just to see the expression on her smug face.

'You're so rude, you know that?' argued Jo. She'd never been Edie's greatest fan. Perhaps I'd overlooked her reasoning.

Edie raised her arms in fake retreat. 'Hey, don't shoot the messenger. I don't make the rules.'

'You made the accusation, though!' said Jo, intent on demonstrating her wrath.

'What will happen to the girl?' I interrupted.

Edie shrugged. 'Dunno. She'll be arrested and placed in a detention centre or something, I suppose.'

'But she's so young. Doesn't that bother you?'

Regardless of her crime, if, in fact, there was a crime, I couldn't condone such a harsh punishment for someone of her age.

Edie jumped off the table and collected her bag. 'Look, it is what it is. I'd be more worried about not reporting her. Have you even read those posters that you put up?'

Of course, I had. They said something or other about aiding and abetting, serious repercussions in the event of non-transparency with regard to… okay, I'd half read them.

Edie tossed her bag over her shoulder. 'It's her own stupid fault, if you ask me. Anyway, I might get a reward.'

Dahlia sighed. 'You really are something else, Edie.'

Even at her angriest, Dahlia had a God-given ability to remain calm and collected.

'So, can I get off?'

I nodded. As she reached for the door handle, I called after her. 'And I think it's better if you don't come back, Edie.' My heart raced at the mere prospect of confrontation.

'Suits me,' she shrugged. 'I don't think much of it here, anyway.'

As Edie marched out of the café, I let out an exhaustive sigh.

'I knew she had a bad aura from the beginning,' muttered Dahlia as she gathered the teapot and cups.

Jo approached me and smothered me in an enormous hug. 'You did the right thing, Raff. She was bad news.'

I felt like I needed to take a twelve month sabbatical.

'And there is some comedy to all of this,' Jo continued.

'What's that then?' I enquired.

She placed her hands on my shoulders and walked me towards the large mirror at the back of the café. I glanced at my reflection. My hair was frizzy and unkempt, mascara was smudged underneath my eyes. The hairdressing gown remained in place over my shoulders and flared out into a cape. A large pink hair clip was attached to my shoulder.

'Oh, God,' I muttered.

Even in the darkest hour, Jo had the ability to find light.

'Let's go to the pub,' I said. 'I need a drink.'

*

Min remained deathly quiet as she carefully sliced three generous pieces of cake. It was a rare moment when Min fell silent, and only tended to occur when food was being prepared, eaten, or discussed. The daughter of a lady she'd once nursed had hand delivered a home-made chocolate cake to her, eternally grateful for Min's care when her mother was ailing.

Min handed me a plate. 'Poor thing lost her mother last month. Lovely lady she was.'

'Shame. Kind of her daughter, though,' said Dad as he shovelled an oversized piece of cake into his mouth.

She looked at the buttercream that was smudged all over his chin. 'You look mortified.'

It was mid-afternoon, and I'd returned home after a brief visit to the pub with Jo and Dahlia. The girls had tried to convince me to make an afternoon of it, to knock back a few cocktails and dissect the surreal events of the morning. I'd declined and stopped at two small glasses of wine. I was suitably repelled from excessive drinking.

'Where's this young girl now then?' asked Min, desperate to know how the story unfolded.

'Who knows?'

She lapped up the cream from her fingertips. 'There's no accounting for brutality in my book, regardless of the crime.'

I nodded. 'Agreed.'

'Hang on, don't let her age fool you,' protested Dad. 'Some of these young kids are lawless. In my day, you were admonished for leaving the dinner table without permission.'

Min rolled her eyes. 'Oh, stop being so stereotypical, will you? Not all kids are like that. Look at our Raff.'

'I think I've outgrown kid status, Min.'

'Well, my Jed was never like that. I made damn sure he knew the difference between right and wrong. He turned out alright.'

I took an obscenely large bite of my cake to prevent myself from saying something that I'd regret.

Min smacked Dad's hand away as he licked his finger and picked the crumbs off her plate. 'I wonder what she did to warrant a scene like that.'

Dad pulled a face. 'Well, I doubt she nicked a bag of crisps from the supermarket.'

'I don't think anything justifies the way they treated her,' I said. 'It was awful.'

Dad picked up his plate and walked past me. 'Your problem is that you care too much. Think about yourself a bit more,' he soothed as he planted a kiss on the top of my head.

Min nodded. 'He's right. Not very often, but of that, he is.'

'It happened right in front of me,' I said defensively. 'I wasn't given a choice!'

'Well, whatever she did obviously warranted the response.'

I spun my head to look at him.

'Dad, I can't believe you just said that. They had her pinned to the floor. She could barely breathe!'

'Just let it go,' he urged. 'It isn't your problem to solve.'

I shook my head in disbelief as Min reached out and touched

my hand. 'I agree, love. I don't trust any of that military lot. More brawn than brains.'

I stared at Min, conscious of the fact that I'd been hearing the word "trust" a lot lately. Aware of my gaze, she instinctively licked the areas around her mouth; her finger moved to her lips to remove any suspected remnants of cake.

'Who do you mean?' I asked.

'Well, government, military. I think they're all up to a lot more than they let on.'

I slid my plate to the side and leaned my elbows on the table. 'Do you? Really?'

'I've never pretended to believe anything less. Corrupt, the lot of them.'

I was keen to have a conversation with someone that I knew and trusted. Someone who I believed to be grounded. Ordinarily, I'd have discarded her comments as throwaway; her opinion was not uncommon when it came to the government. But the inner battle that I faced had given me cause to question everything.

'Do you think we're in danger, Min?'

She pondered for a moment. 'I think we're in danger of another poor government. But I don't think we're likely to have a repeat of the riots again. Martial law has seen to that.'

'But... do you think we are in danger?' I asked.

She picked at a broken piece of cake. 'Why would we be in danger, love?'

I spotted Dad out of the corner of my eye. He'd stopped what he was doing and was leaning against the kitchen unit. He gazed at me with great concern in his eyes. I needed to be cautious. It wouldn't serve me well to say too much.

'I don't know, just thinking out loud,' I said dismissively.

'The only thing I'm in danger of is getting fat if I keep eating this cake,' she mocked. 'Then again, I'm already fat, so who gives a stuff.'

I attempted a smile.

'What do you think about The Happy State?' I asked. 'Do you think it could really work?'

Min let out an enormous laugh.

'Over my dead body,' said Dad as he resumed his task. 'Doubt there'll be much that's bleeding happy about it. You can hardly breathe for all the tension out there.'

'Do you think it's all the usual governmental rubbish?'

Shut up, Raff!

'Yes!' said Dad and Min, collectively.

Was I looking for a reason, any reason, to believe Jed?

I stood and tucked my chair neatly under the table. As I brushed past Dad, his hand reached for mine.

'Be careful, love,' he whispered as he gazed at me.

The sentiment was loud and clear.

I squeezed his hand. 'Always.'

I'd said too much.

I needed to speak to Jed.

Chapter 22

Jed paced back and forth across Min's kitchen floor.

'I can't believe that… despicable man. I can't believe he got hold of her. Anyone but him. Stupid girl!'

'It's hardly her fault,' I reasoned. I tried to keep my voice as low as possible. If I was calm, maybe he'd be calm. 'I very much doubt she intended to get caught.'

'What? Are you mad? We told her to stay hidden. We told her so many times. I can't believe it.'

Nothing was going to placate him. I'd been there for precisely twenty minutes and he had incessantly paced, stomped and shouted from the moment I'd arrived.

I lowered my voice to almost a whisper. 'Who is she, anyway?'

He took an over exerted deep breath. 'Do you have any cigarettes?'

'I don't smoke. Neither do you.'

Clearly out of sorts, he paced a little more before hurling himself into an armchair. His twitching leg and rapid eye movements informed me that his brain was in overdrive. I chose not to fill the silence, but patiently waited as he unconsciously tugged at a stubborn thread on the arm of the chair. Eventually, he gave up.

'Freedom was formed by a guy called Johnny McLaydon. He and Stan served with Frost. They hated him, a real dictator sort. An avid supporter of Mussolini and Hitler, apparently. Stan said he was always reading books about The Third Reich. Johnny could see what was happening a long time ago and wanted to do something about it. The group sort of organically evolved. He didn't go out looking for it. Frost worked his way up the chain and Johnny knew what that meant.'

I listened intently, grateful that he'd stopped to take a breath.

'Frost got light of what Johnny was doing and had him earmarked. Johnny managed to get out before they caught up with him. No one knows where he is.'

I slowly lowered myself onto the chair opposite him. 'How do you know they didn't arrest him?'

'We don't, but it's unlikely. He was too smart. Johnny had… has a daughter. She was a young kid at the time. Luka. Cool kid. Her and Johnny were cut from the same cloth. Both opinionated, sarcastic and wild, really wild. Luka was devastated when her dad left. Me and a few of the others helped out as much as we could, but it isn't easy, you know? You have to be careful doing what we do. Any one of us could have been arrested or interrogated. I was only a kid myself. We needed to stay away from her, but… well, that wasn't an option.'

'Where was her mum in all of this?'

'Physically, she was there all the way through. She was a decent mum, I think. But she couldn't replace Johnny, and that's all that Luka wanted. She knew Luka blamed her.'

I nodded. I was all too aware of the emotional impact of losing a parent.

'Luka went a bit… crazy, off the rails. Got involved in all the wrong stuff. Bad friends, bad decisions. Like any messed-up kid does, I guess. In the end, Zee took her in, so she wasn't sleeping rough.'

'Wasn't that her mum's job?'

Jed shrugged. 'Probably. Luka didn't make it easy, though. If your kid won't even look at you, what can you do? Anyway, Zee took her in, him and his girlfriend.'

My eyes widened. 'Myka?'

He nodded.

The thought of Myka going near a vulnerable child made me feel nauseous.

'She's alright,' he laughed. 'She's actually great with kids.'

'I'll bear that in mind.'

'Anyway, Luka begged Zee to teach her about the resistance. She's a smart kid. She knew what her dad was into. Seems her mum used to talk about his involvement to turn Luka against him. How he was endangering them and stuff like that.'

I shook my head in disbelief. 'Of all the things to share with a kid.'

'It backfired. It just made her more eager to learn about it. When Zee refused, she ran away, and eventually, we felt like we had no choice. Leave her on the streets or take her in. She never threatened us, but she did make us nervous.'

'Nervous how?'

'Like her dad, she'd perfected the art of manipulation. She knew how to pull the right strings.'

He walked to the fridge and removed two bottles of water. He handed one to me as he took his seat.

'She had us over a barrel. A young kid, holding us ransom. Mad, eh? She knew enough to implicate us, but I don't think she'd have acted on it. You can't take that risk, though. It made

Zee really vulnerable. We had no choice but to include her, regardless of her age.'

'Did she know... everything?' I asked.

'No. She thought she did, but she didn't. Way too dangerous.'

'So how did it get to this?'

He took a long swig of water and leant back in his seat. 'She was under strict instructions to stay inside Zee's house until we'd worked out a plan. Except she didn't. You know the rest.'

'Where do you think she was going?'

He shrugged his shoulders. 'Wouldn't have the first clue, but she's in serious trouble. And so are the rest of us.'

'Do you think she'll talk?'

He shook his head. 'No. I don't. She's young, but she's got her dad's spirit. She learnt a lot at a young age and coped alright. Not all kids could do that, but...'

He stopped abruptly and stared at the floor beneath him.

'But what?'

'She's still a kid. Once they start with the interrogation techniques, they could make her say anything. There's nothing we can do either.'

'How do you mean?'

'I mean, there's literally nothing we can do to help her.'

'You can't just leave her, surely?'

'We can, and we are.'

I was taken aback by his harsh resolve. 'Seriously? I thought you were all about saving people and changing the world. And now you're going to just abandon her?'

I knew I'd said the wrong thing. In order to placate someone, you certainly didn't oppose them. He sprung to his feet as his calmness rapidly mutated into anger. If nothing else, I'd learnt that Jed's temper rose from nought to sixty in a matter of nanoseconds.

'I'll just swing on in through the windows and save her then, shall I? What do you expect me to do? This isn't the movies, Raff! She's only got herself to blame. If we get involved, the whole outfit goes nuclear!'

I rose to my feet. 'Jed, it's okay. I'm sorry…'

'Frost will tear her apart, Raff. He's been after us for years and he'll make an example of her. He'll manipulate her, get her to talk and then destroy her. Then he'll come for the rest of us.'

I walked towards him in a bid to soothe him. As I placed my arm on his, he looked up at me. His eyes brimmed with tears; his lips trembled. For that moment, I felt an overwhelming desire to protect him, to make him feel safe. I placed my arms around him and he fell into my hold. His head rested against my shoulder.

'This is all my fault.'

And then, like a vulnerable child, he sobbed in my arms.

Chapter 23

Oakes slammed the office door, walked over to his secret drawer and poured himself a glass of whiskey. The entire situation was impossible. How could he ever condone the interrogation of a fourteen-year-old girl?

Frost had been elated when the call came through. It was from a waitress at a café in Thendra. With Thendra already on his radar, courtesy of Aron, his new golden boy, Frost must have felt a tremendous sense of self-satisfaction.

The girl's father had been number one on their hit list for over eighteen months. He'd created and founded the resistance group, Freedom, which continued to grow in both size and notoriety by the day. The father, it seemed, had somehow evaded capture and skipped the country, despite the apparently impenetrable security measures in place.

That the daughter was a curved ball, an unexpected surprise, was of grave concern for Oakes. The annihilation of Freedom had become something of a personal mission to Frost, and it was likely that he'd unveil his wrath on the young girl. Oakes hoped that the kid was nothing more than a teenage fantasy seeker, that she'd spill her guts straight away and be dismissed. She could hardly be considered a threat at such a tender age.

Oakes reflected upon the time that Frost had insisted he was present at a military meeting where several interrogation techniques were discussed. He had vowed never to return to another after intricate details of highly successful techniques had been shared. He was not accustomed to such a world, nor did he intend to be. He feared that the time to utilise such methods was upon them. And she was a mere child.

Frost had advised him that the prisoner was in transit. She was on her way to the city and would arrive within the hour. He would call when they drew closer. A car would be dispatched to take Oakes to the scene.

He reached into his drawer for an indigestion tablet, dropped it in his glass of whiskey and watched as it bubbled to the surface. He loosened his belt as his stomach gurgled and churned with stress. One day, when he had the time and the inclination, he'd see a doctor about his constant gut problems.

Once satisfied that the tablet had melted, he consumed the drink in one; the bitterness made him wince. He poured another and consumed it without taking a beat, visibly relaxing as the whiskey mildly stung the back of his throat.

Whatever course of action Frost suggested for the girl, he knew he had little option but to endorse it. Despite his position as leader of The Happy State, the military presence condemned his policing powers null and void. Frost would be the leading man in this one, and he'd milk it for all it was worth.

Shamelessly, he let out a loud belch and felt immediate relief in his chest and stomach.

He jumped at the sound of a ringing phone. It was time.

'I'll be there in five,' he muttered as he replaced the receiver.

Frost and his team were waiting for him.

*

Thirty miles south of the government headquarters sat an old, barren warehouse. Once used for stockpiling consumer goods, the building had ceased to prosper with the termination of online consumption. Frost had temporarily earmarked the warehouse as an ideal space for interrogations; suitably distanced from civilisation but close enough to the Zones for immediate transportation.

The warehouse was sparse and cold. Water dripped through holes in the ceiling and a faint stench of damp and urine lingered. The conditions were ideal to implement the extra pressure required for prisoners.

In the centre sat a white plastic table with three matching chairs. Luka sat on her own. Her body was hunched forward, her frail arms tightly folded to protect herself from the cold. Opposite her sat Frost and his second in command, Crawford Nielson.

Frost had served with Crawford during two tours of Afghanistan and he hadn't hesitated to recruit him when he gained his position as head of military. He made a loyal soldier, with a relatable ideology of how a country should look. Crawford had been branded the "battalion bully" during his time served. He'd belittled soldiers that had witnessed atrocities and fallen prey to mental illness. In Frost, he identified an ally and, in time, they forged a solid friendship, destined to continue long after they had served overseas.

Frost was almost unrecognisable as he spoke to Luka in soft tones; a cruel necessity in offering her false hope. There was no benefit to harsh pressure at this stage of the game. She was tired and hungry, premature harassment would merely cause her to collapse with exhaustion. Once she ate, she'd regain some energy. Then they'd give her a hot drink. Much like ambush predators, they would attract and entice their prey before the final capture.

Frost rose from his chair and rifled through the carrier bag that he held. 'Are you hungry?'

She didn't respond.

'Crisps, chocolate, sandwiches?'

Her teeth chattered as she stared at the floor.

He placed the bag on the table and rested his hand on her shoulder with the concern of a caregiver. 'You're freezing.' He turned to the soldier that guarded the door and spoke in an urgent tone. 'Can we get a damn blanket round here, please?'

When the blanket arrived, he tenderly placed it round her shoulders. 'There you go, kid. You'll feel better soon. Then you can get some food down you.'

*

She'd been held for so long. Days, maybe. She didn't know anymore. She was sleep and food deprived; cold and exhausted.

The first few hours were in a different place. It was informal, more like an office. Then she'd been blindfolded and taken on a long car journey to the second location. She felt the bumps as she lay in the back of the car, so it could have been off-road. She couldn't tell. It was much colder at the new location and the damp made her limbs ache. Thank God they'd given her a blanket. She hoped it might stop her teeth from chattering.

They were being more affable than previously; they used her name a lot or called her "kid." She knew it was an interrogation technique. They'd acted like vultures when she'd arrived and couldn't harangue her enough. They'd thrown endless amounts of questions at her, one after the other, some of which she genuinely couldn't answer.

She'd recognised Frost immediately. The military leader with the dangerous objective for The Happy State; the one that Freedom always talked about. She didn't know the other one. He just sat in silence and glared at her with his black, soulless eyes.

The sharp pains and rumbling in her stomach reminded her that she hadn't eaten for hours. Thus far, she'd survived on adrenalin, but she was ravenous and weakening rapidly. Why were they just watching her? Why couldn't they ask her what they wanted to ask her and let her go home? She'd told them she didn't know anything, that Freedom wouldn't indulge her due to her age. It wasn't strictly true, but they weren't to know that, and it sounded perfectly feasible. She'd tried to convince them that Freedom merely humoured her, that they only allowed her to do petty and inconsequential duties for them.

She couldn't stop thinking about Zee. By now, he'd be desperately worried and oblivious to her whereabouts. She felt a tremendous sense of guilt for storming out on him. Leaving the house hadn't been on her agenda; it was nothing but a childish and unprovoked act of rebellion, all because he wouldn't disclose sensitive information. He'd tried to protect her, he only ever tried to protect her. The situation in which she found herself was no one's fault but her own.

She glanced at the bag of food that lay in front of her. Her friends at Freedom had warned her about the acts of kindness.

It was nothing short of psychological trickery. She'd attended a Freedom meeting with Zee once, and Alpha had talked about arrests and interrogation. 'It's going to happen to some of you,' he'd said. 'And you need to be prepared. It'll be the biggest challenge you'll ever face.'

At the time, she was the last person that he was referring to.

Having served in the military, Alpha had explained the different techniques that they were likely to experience. 'They'll change their tone, flit from hot to cold. You'll be freezing, tired and hungry. Confused. You won't know what you're thinking. That's when they'll attack. They'll do whatever they can to make you talk. You either tell them what they want to know, or risk the consequences of not telling them. That's the price you pay for being a part of Freedom.'

Luka knew what Frost was doing. His cunning was painfully transparent. He thought she was a stupid kid, but she'd seen and heard more than most people of her age. Her Dad founded Freedom, and she held him in the highest regard for doing so. While most people spent their lives complaining about the state of things, her dad had gone out and tried to do something; tried to make the country a better place. She was so proud of him and all the wisdom he'd imparted on her. He'd taught her to remain independent, to trust few people, but to hold on to those that you learn to trust, as they would be invaluable. And he'd taught her to be tough, to never divulge her weaknesses.

Don't let them see I'm weak, she told herself. Stay. Strong.

It was only going to get harder, but there was no way that she'd threaten the safety of her family at Freedom. That was all that she could focus on, not her ineffectual Mother who'd failed to see the enormity of her dad's sacrifice.

The pains in her stomach were getting worse.

*

Frost walked round the table and sat down next to Luka. As a tall, well-built man, he barely flinched as he lifted her chair from the ground and turned it to face him.

He casually leaned in towards her and spoke in a calm tone. 'I know you're cold, and I know you're hungry. If you expect to get through this, you need to eat something. Otherwise, it's going to be a very long and painful process for all of us.'

As he forced her chair towards the table, it made an unpleasant, high-pitched screeching noise as it scraped against the hard floor. He lifted the bag of food and emptied the contents onto the table.

'Now, eat!' he demanded.

He took a seat, and they watched as she eyed the food. It would be seconds, like clockwork.

It took less than six seconds. As expected, she reached for the drink bottle, unscrewed the lid and poured it down her throat in one go. She discarded the bottle and reached for the crisps, pulled the packet open and forced them into her mouth like a scavenger. With her mouth brimming, she ripped open the sandwich and took a large bite.

For several minutes, they watched as she gorged on junk food. Frost's eyes met with Crawford's as they exchanged a knowing glance. She'd throw up next. They usually did. Following a period of starvation, the stomach was unable to bear such copious amounts of food, and would usually reject it.

Crawford reached behind his chair and picked up the bucket in preparation. Luka paid no attention as she continued to feed her empty stomach.

They sat. They waited.

With the food devoured, she stopped and leant back against her chair. Her breathing was laboured from the frenzied binge. A moment later, her hand shot to her mouth. Crawford placed the bucket next to her. Patiently, they waited as she threw up the remnants of two sandwiches, three bags of crisps, and two chocolate bars.

Frost glanced at his watch. There was still no sign of Oakes. Having spoken more than fifty minutes ago, they'd dragged things out with the girl as much as they could. Enough was enough. They were going to have to proceed without him, regardless of his rules and regulations.

He didn't wait for anyone.

*

She felt better after she'd been sick. Perhaps it was the energy provided by the food. Maybe it was a surge of adrenalin at the prospect of another round of interrogation.

Frost wasted no time in getting to the point. 'Do you know where your dad is?'

He'd already asked her this, and she really didn't know. Not that she hadn't tried. She'd asked Zee and Jed numerous times, but they'd said they didn't know either. It was better that way. She couldn't be tortured for information she didn't have. At least that's what she believed to be true.

Frost repeated the question. 'Luka, do you know where your dad is?'

She ignored him, aware that she couldn't maintain silence indefinitely. Before long, she'd have to speak up, even if it was a lie.

'I'll ask a final time. Do you know where your dad is?'

She shook her head.

'Tell us about your friends at Freedom, Luka.'

Alpha's words resonated in her mind. 'Play it carefully. Think before you speak. Buy yourself time. Do what you have to do.'

'Which friends?' she asked, unimpressed at her own meek attempt at coyness.

Frost and Crawford laughed.

'Oh, I'm pretty sure you know who I'm talking about.'

'What do you want to know?' she asked.

Crawford rose to his feet and headed to the water cooler to fill his cup. She eyed him suspiciously.

Frost clicked his fingers to redirect her attention. 'Hey! Come on, what can you tell us?'

She shrugged. 'I don't know.'

'This is getting boring, Luka. Surely you don't want us to treat you like a kid. Your Dad was, well… a legend I suppose. I'd be proud of a dad like yours.' He turned to Crawford. 'Wouldn't you be proud of a dad like that?'

Crawford nodded. 'I sure would.'

'There you go. You're a lucky girl. So, how about we just cut the crap and get to the point? You help us, we'll help you.'

She nodded. It was time. She couldn't hold back any longer.

Give them something. Anything.

Frost stared at her with piercing, unblinking eyes.

'They've been good to me. Really kind. Zee is the best.' Use your strengths. You're a kid, act like a kid.

'Zee?'

'Yes.'

'What's his full name?'

'I don't know. That's all I know him as.'

'How about Alpha? Do you know Alpha?'

'Yes.'

'He's the leader, right?'

'Kind of. There isn't a leader, not really.'

'What other names do you have?'

She purposely selected the least prominent members in the hope that they'd be of little benefit to her interrogators. 'Oz, Bee, Ali, Lio… I don't know everyone.' She knew at least another fifty names.

Crawford scribbled something in a pad, and Frost raised his hand to stop him. 'Don't bother. They won't be real names.'

The thought had never crossed her mind; that the people who had, in part, raised her, may well have lived under an alias since she'd known them. It made her feel uncomfortable that they couldn't be truthful with her. But that was all part of joining the resistance.

You made sacrifices. You compromised your soul. You never really knew anyone.

'Where do they meet?'

'Erm… different places.'

'No regular place? Someone's house, maybe?'

'No,' she lied. It was partly true, though the old communications building had become more commonplace in recent months. The group had grown in size and required somewhere more sizable. She had no intention of disclosing such information, however.

'You've been staying with Zee. What's his address, kid?'

There was no way she would part with this information, despite the fact that his address was permanently etched in her brain.

It was time to accept her fate, whatever that may be.

*

Frost was beyond agitated. The kid was tougher than he'd imagined. He hadn't anticipated that she'd crack easily, but he'd vastly underestimated her tolerance. They'd had her in custody for twenty hours and she'd given them nothing. She hadn't even been close to disclosure. Tiring of her resilience, he realised that it was time to raise the stakes.

Over time, he'd developed something of an intuition for those that had the greatest resilience. It was usually a look in the eye that told him how far he was likely to get, a blackness, a void. The durable types didn't come along very often, but this kid was one of them.

Defiantly, she sat in silence and, all the while, her confident glare remained fixed. That was a rarity in itself. Others would deny them eye contact or stare at the floor. Some would have caved in, their head too heavy to even hold upright. She was suitably primed for a moment like this.

Frost rose to his feet. 'Let's go.'

Ready for action, Crawford lifted the bucket in which she'd expelled her waste, walked to the water cooler, removed it from its station and emptied the contents into the bucket.

'I'm going to ask you one more time,' said Frost. 'What is Zee's address?'

He waited. Nothing. He glanced at Crawford and nodded.

She cried out before they made their move. Anticipation was often the cruellest aspect of torture.

In the briefest amount of time, they moved to either side of her. Frost forced her arms above her head as Crawford forcibly removed her outer clothing. She wriggled and fought, but remained an inferior opponent to a man twice her size. Crawford unzipped and removed her jeans to expose her underwear, then forced her arms behind her back and tightly bound her wrists with duct tape. Frost bound her midriff to the chair before tightly securing her ankles. The speed at which they worked was seamless.

Denied of all movement and no longer able to writhe, the fear in her eyes became alarmingly apparent. For the first time that day, she took on the appearance of a frightened little girl.

Frost stepped aside as Crawford tipped the cocktail of cold water and vomit over her head. The shock forced her to scream. She dithered profusely, so much so that her limbs jerked as though an electrical current charged through her body. Soon, she'd beg them to stop.

Frost took a seat. 'Give her a minute. Let her smell the stench of her own vomit dripping from her hair.'

He watched as she trembled with cold. Once in a while,

she would raise her head and attempt to look at him. He couldn't help but smile. He liked a challenge, and he admired her tenacity. He'd interrogated ruthless prisoners that were one hundred and eighty pounds of muscle. They'd never beaten him. But this kid was something else. He half wished she was playing for the other side; in a few years' time, she'd have been an asset to his team.

He waited long enough for her to calm a little, all part of the plan. As her breathing regained a semi-normal pattern, Crawford filled another bucket of water. Whether they would use it or not was of little consequence. It served to enhance the prisoners' anticipation; the fear of what was to come. Every move had purpose; nothing was based on chance.

'You need to start talking, kid,' he demanded. 'I'm afraid you're not leaving until you do.'

She remained silent. Every once in a while, her body would jolt as the cold penetrated her bones. As her breathing slowed and she calmed, Crawford tipped another bucket of ice-cold water over her head.

She didn't utter a word.

It was time for the next stage.

*

Every inch of her body ached. She had never experienced pain of this magnitude. Her neck was so weak it felt as though it might break, and her head throbbed with excruciating pain. She was so, so cold. She was scared. How long would she be able to endure this?

They continued to push for Zee's address. She suspected Zee would be in hiding. Maybe he'd be at the safe house. Perhaps she could get away with sending them off track, buying herself some more time. But what if he wasn't? What if he was still at home? She couldn't risk it, and what good did buying herself extra time do? No one was going to rescue her. It would take a miracle to get her out of there.

She'd always embraced Freedom and all that they stood for. What she hadn't prepared herself for was martyrdom. A part of her blamed them for not preparing her, for not taking her seriously enough. Had they have listened; she might have found peace with her inevitable fate.

The man with the dark eyes kept throwing water over her. Each new drop felt like it might kill her. The repugnant scent of her vomit was highly deplorable, yet it was of little concern under the circumstances. It was the bitter cold that throbbed through her veins. That would be her downfall.

She recoiled as Frost approached her. He placed a set of headphones over her head and left the room. Instinctively, she wriggled her body to free herself from her constraints, but relented almost immediately. Her attempt was futile. Were they leaving her there to die?

Then, blackness. Somehow it seemed colder in the dark. She couldn't stop her body from shaking. Her head spun from left to right as she attempted to catch sight of something.

And then it started. A loud, piercing tone screeched through her ears.

She was going to die.

Alone.

*

They left her for ninety minutes.

Despite his rich experience of interrogation, he never knew what to expect when he turned the lights back on. Sound torture was always effective, but some were more resilient than others. Some became disorientated and even hallucinated, others lost their sense of hearing. But they would all scream and writhe as if they'd been physically tortured.

Luka's head was heavily slumped on her chest. Fresh vomit lay on her chest and lap, and trickled down her thighs. He checked her pulse; her heart rate was slow but strong. She was unconscious. They usually were. When he slapped her round the face, she didn't respond. He hit her again and again.

Her head moved and her eyes half-opened as she regained consciousness. She moaned as her head rolled from side to side. Crawford took hold of her shoulders and shook her vigorously.

'Come on, kid. Get it off your chest. You'll feel so much better when you do.'

He smacked her face again, harder this time. Her cheek flushed a bright shade of red almost immediately.

'Come on, Luka. Surely you want to save your friends, don't you?'

Her moaning grew louder.

He was satisfied. She was close to breaking.

*

She couldn't take any more.

Each time they shook her, her brain seemed to drift in and out of consciousness. She didn't know where she was. At one point, she was convinced that she was in the back of a moving car. In another fleeting moment, she was certain that she was back at the café where they'd found her.

It was time. She couldn't take another second of agony.

'Okay,' she mumbled.

Her voice sounded distant as she spoke, as though it came from someone else's mouth. All she could hear was the high-pitched sound in her ears. Was it still playing? Maybe she hadn't spoken.

'Okay,' she repeated, uncertain that her mouth had even moved.

Frost pulled up a chair next to her. He delicately moved her wet hair out of her face and placed it behind her ear. 'That's a good girl. You can talk to us. Where does Zee live, kiddo?'

'Okay,' she repeated. 'Okay.'

'Come on, girl. You can do it.'

She wracked her brain for Zee's address, concerned that she was unable to access any information from memory. The sound was too deafening to think straight. She had to be close to death.

Frost rose to his feet. 'You want some more, do you kid?'

She forced her head upright. Though she could barely focus, she could vaguely distinguish a blurred figure in front of her.

'Wait…' she slurred. 'Astor Passage.'

'Number?'

'I don't know. It's the second house.'

As the words involuntarily tumbled out of her mouth, she couldn't even be sure that she'd given the correct information.

A loud bang at the door made her jump. She looked round to investigate the imminent threat. The scary one had left the room; she was safe for now.

'Good girl, there we go,' whispered Frost. 'Your Dad, where is he, Luka?'

'I don't know.'

He laughed. 'Good effort, but I doubt that very much.'

'He's… dead,' she groaned. The announcement alarmed her as much as anymore. Was he dead? Had she made it up? She'd lost touch with all reality.

'How do you know he's dead?'

With that, she loudly sobbed.

Chapter 24

Some days, I had no time for other people's problems. I'd frequently listen to customers complaining about such trivial matters that I wanted to shake them and say, 'you have your loved ones, it's all fine!' But life doesn't work like that. However small or mundane our problems, they have a way of suffocating us in their midst. But as Jo blew her nose and wiped her tears after ending her brief encounter with her boyfriend, it was a welcome distraction from my own thoughts.

'I'll be fine,' she spluttered as she wiped the mascara from around her eyes. 'I'm just being a girl.'

The café was quiet. There was a slow trickle of customers, but a farmer's market in the village had temporarily stolen our custom. It happened once a quarter, so it had little impact on trade. On this day, I was grateful for it, and used the time to move some of the furniture that Edie had rearranged; a chore that I'd continuously avoided. I needed no reminder of her time with us.

'Doesn't stop it hurting though,' I said as I adjusted a picture frame that hung eternally to the left.

'He was controlling, Raff. And literally obsessed with Nathaniel Frost!'

My ears pricked up. For one reason or another, it was a name that I couldn't seem to escape in recent times.

After my recent conversation with Jed, rightly or wrongly,

I'd come to believe that Freedom were fighting a genuine battle. During the initial few days, I'd almost drowned in doubt as I suffered with the heavy burden that I carried. Yet when I'd watched him grieve the young girl that had been arrested, I had no doubt that his emotions were anything less than authentic.

I'd been there when Luka was brutally wrenched from the café. I'd listened to Freedom expound the disappearances of numerous individuals; whose only sin was their compromised mental states. I'd sympathised as Jed cried on my shoulder; tortured by his guilt, of the belief that Luka was somehow his responsibility.

Jo's mention of Frost had gained my interest, but I ensured that I remained blasé. The last thing I needed was a potential future discussion between her and Aron that centred around my suspicious interest in Frost.

'What do you mean?' I asked as I relentlessly shifted the doomed picture frame.

'It's all he ever talked about. Frost this, Frost that...'

I attempted to sound far less enthused than I actually was. 'Really?'

'Can I tell you something?'

Frustrated at my futile attempts with the picture, I turned to face her. 'Of course.'

'You know that day, the one when I hung that resistance poster up? The day that you...'

'...shouted at you?' I interrupted.

She scrunched up her nose. 'Yeah. That day.'

I nodded apologetically.

'He made me do it. He said that you were breaking the law.

He even asked me if I thought you were pro-resistance! Have you ever heard anything so ridiculous in your life?'

My body shivered at the mere mention of the resistance, much less for my apparent involvement with them. Whilst my entanglement with them was by no stretch bona fide, it was more than enough to land me in considerable trouble.

I laughed awkwardly. A body language expert would have had me banged to rights with my meek attempt at covering a lie. But Jo, in the throes of grief, overlooked the strange shriek-like noise that emerged from my mouth and equated it to my growing list of quirks.

'I know. You're like the least likely person to do something crazy like that.'

I glanced at her curiously. 'Am I?'

For the first time during the conversation, she smiled. 'Hell, yes! It's too hilarious.'

I took a seat opposite her, satisfied that my cover-up was working sufficiently, but equally disappointed that I was deemed to be so boringly predictable.

'Why on earth would he think that?'

'Oh, who knows? He thought it was strange that you wouldn't put them up. I told him it was your café, your choice, but he thought it was really weird. We even had a row about it, would you believe?'

I widened my eyes in fake shock. I couldn't have her know I was pinned to the wall a mere four feet away from the said row.

'He couldn't understand why you didn't want to be part of making our country... The Happy State, a better place. He wouldn't let it go. Honestly, he hounded me about it. "Make her put them up," he'd say. I told him it wasn't my place to do that.'

'How very strange,' I mused.

'Yeah. Very. He was just infatuated with Frost.'

'I'm sure.'

I sensed that Jo needed to let off steam, so I allowed her to do the talking. Had I chosen to engage in discussion, I risked implicating myself. I'd never been particularly good at keeping things to myself.

'He had it in his head that you were seeing Jed, too. He thought you were a couple. I told him you weren't, but he didn't seem to believe me.'

'Me and Jed?' I laughed. 'God, no!' My reaction was entirely authentic.

'That's what I said. He didn't believe me. He could see how much Jed was into you, so just assumed that you were together.'

'Jed is so not into me,' I choked. 'We barely even like each other! It's just… his mum, my dad. It means that we can't really avoid each other.'

Jo raised an eyebrow. 'Are you kidding me?'

I remained deadpan. 'Not even slightly.'

'Raff. That guy is absolutely nuts about you. Don't tell me you can't see that.'

I wondered how the conversation had turned to me and Jed. The concept that he had any feeling other than loyalty, perhaps an obligation to look out for a friend of his mum's, was irrational to say the least.

'Oh. My. God! You have no idea, do you?'

I shrugged. I didn't want to talk about such futile nonsense. I wanted to get back to Frost, and Aron's fascination with him.

'Anyway...'

'Seriously. You are delusional if you can't see it. He's crazy about you. He stares at you with those huge puppy eyes.'

I hated the way she emphasised "huge puppy eyes" even more than her use of the term.

'Okay. Whatever,' I replied bluntly. I was over the conversation. 'But what's that got to do with your boyfriend?'

'Ex-boyfriend. Who knows! He had some real thing about Jed. He didn't like him, but wouldn't tell me why.'

The alarm bells almost deafened me. I was no detective, but my brain involuntarily spun into overdrive as it pieced together an intelligence network. A policeman who hero worshipped a corrupt military leader. A policeman that disliked someone who happened to be a member of the largest resistance group in the country. Could Aron have suspected Jed's involvement with Freedom?

There had been too many coincidences of late, so much so that I was no longer prepared to take any risks.

I casually picked at the leaves from the artificial flower decoration that sat between us. 'What did he say then?'

'That was just it. He didn't say anything. He just made it clear that he didn't like him. Kept telling me he had it coming, whatever that means.'

My heart started to pace. If Jed was at risk, Dad and I were at risk.

'I wonder what he meant by that?'

'No idea, Raff. But he's got big issues with that boy, that's for sure.'

As the frantically picked flower came loose in my hand, I

spread my fingers and allowed the petals to fall between them. My brain worked quickly as Jo's voice faded into the distance.

I felt deeply concerned for Jed. I hadn't seen him in a few days, not since his meltdown over Luka. I felt the need to warn him, to advise him to lay low for a while. Perhaps it was selfish of me, but his safety ensured my safety.

The sound of the front door opening instantly jolted me back to reality. I looked up to see Min peering around the door. 'Can I have a quick word?'

Min never popped into the café.

'What is it?' I blurted, as I jumped to my feet.

'Don't get yourself worried, love.'

Too late!

'Your dad's perfectly okay. Please, don't worry yourself.'

'Min!' I shouted. 'Please, what is it?'

'Sorry, love. Well, he had a funny turn earlier.'

I leant back against the counter as my legs weakened. 'What do you mean, a funny turn?'

'We went to the park, had a lovely picnic in the sunshine. He had to nip to the loo, which was only a few feet from where we were sitting. Well, after twenty minutes he hadn't come back, so I started to get worried. You know, he might have wandered off...'

'Go on,' I urged. Min had a habit of taking the scenic route with her storytelling.

'Well, I waited and waited. No sign of him. So, I packed up the tubs and flask...'

'Min!'

'Sorry. I went looking for him and found him sat by the

pond. He was in his own world, bless him. Away with the fairies, he was. He had no idea where he'd been, accused me of leaving him on his own.'

My legs started to buckle as Min's story unfolded. I clung to the counter tightly. 'Where is he?'

'He's in the car, love.'

As I darted to the front door, I felt like I was running through treacle. My legs had weakened so sufficiently that each step required great effort.

Min's car was illegally parked outside the café in a non-traffic zone, but I couldn't have cared less. I dashed around to the passenger side and spotted Dad gazing out of the window. He saw me immediately.

I pulled the door open. 'Hi, Dad,' I said breathlessly.

He looked tired and pale, and I was sure he looked thin. 'Hi, love.'

I squatted on the pavement so that I was level with him. 'Are you okay?'

'Yes, we've had a lovely afternoon. Min ate all the cake, as usual.' He smiled. That beautiful, cheeky smile.

'How are you feeling?' I asked as I reached out to touch his hand.

He cupped my hand in his. 'Me? Top of the World, love.'

I attempted a smile despite the desperate urge to sob. Whether he was unaware of what had happened or simply wanted to protect my feelings, I couldn't determine. Either way, it was cause for concern.

I stood and kissed him on the top of his head. 'Dad, wait here for me. I've just got to pop back inside for a minute.'

I pushed the door and returned to the café.

'I'm going home, Min. There's no way I'm leaving him.'

'I'll be with him. You don't need to worry, you stay here…'

'Not a chance.'

I turned to Jo with her red, puffy eyes and held her hands in mine. 'I'm so sorry that you're upset and I'm here for you anytime, but right now, my dad needs me. Could you cover for the rest of the day? Double time?'

Jo hugged me. 'No need for that. Go and be with your Dad.'

'Girls, you don't need to…'

'Min. It's decided,' I interrupted.

I gathered my things and headed to the car with Min trundling behind me.

As she reached for the door handle, she leaned into me. 'I'm getting him into the doctor's first thing,' she whispered.

I froze. 'Wait!'

Under the circumstances, there was no way that Dad could go within a mile of the doctor's surgery. If it was indeed true that medical records were being investigated, Dad's attendance would merely highlight his condition. I wasn't ready to consider the implications beyond that.

I tried to reduce the tension in my voice. 'Oh, I don't think we need to do that.'

As I said the words, I knew what Min's reaction would be. If Dad so much as breathed in the wrong direction, I panicked. It was usually Min that had to convince me to have faith, to relax a little. My behaviour was alarmingly out of character.

She raised her eyebrow cynically. 'That's precisely what we need to do.'

She urged me to move to the back of the car, where she lowered her voice so that Dad was out of earshot. 'If his health is in decline, we need to consider increasing his medication. It's not like you to take any risks.'

Min was absolutely right, of course, but it didn't help my predicament. I needed to think on my feet.

'I suppose I just don't want to hear the worst,' I sighed as I attempted to appease Min's concern.

She took my hand in hers. 'I understand that, love. But better to know and treat accordingly, eh?'

I nodded.

Think, Raff. Think!

'I've already planned to take a few days off and spend some time with him. How about you let me deal with it while you take some time for yourself?'

Stubbornly. she turned to walk away. 'No need for that, that's what I'm here for.'

Christ!

I gently tugged at her arm. 'But I want to. Please, Min, he's my Dad. I spend so much time at work that I want to do this.' My voice sounded desperate, but not for the reason that Min suspected.

Her face softened. 'I understand that this is difficult for you, but denial isn't a healthy thing. We'll get through this together. If you want me to step back for a couple of days, so you can spend some time with him, that's okay with me, love.'

I breathed a small sigh of relief. Imminent disaster averted.

In the meantime, I had to work out the logistics of spending a few days away from the café, the few days that I hadn't planned on taking off at all. I was back to square one with the same staffing issue as pre-Edie. But I'd committed, and I was prepared to do anything to keep Dad away from the surgery.

One problem down, another hundred to deal with.

Chapter 25

Oakes held two ties in front of him; one was red and the other blue. His eyes darted from one to the other.

In ten days, he was delivering a speech to over fifty thousand people at a large, open park in the city. It would be a groundbreaking moment; an opportunity to appeal to the public, to convince them that things were moving in the right direction. The announcement that the United Kingdom, now to be known as The Happy State, would mark the beginning of one of the greatest political overhauls in history, and it was his government that would make this possible. He could be the next Winston Churchill; leading his country from the brink of failure to victory. No more existential depression, and no more adversarial systems that had devastated their country.

Though he had been averse to the Zones in the initial stages, he had come to realise that, as an important figurehead, he would make history for enabling the birth of a new and unspoiled state.

Whilst his government had somewhat unorthodox methods of creating a state of such proportions, a state that would remain as untainted as it began, he was swimming against the tide. Few politicians had dealt with post-civil war leadership, so the precedent was up for grabs. In this, he saw an opportunity to utilise a pure foundation, a chance to design a state that encouraged political unity amongst its people. They would no longer require war provoking and divisive religious affiliations.

They would trust that their Happy State protected their needs and requirements.

His speech had to be pioneering. His diction, his mannerisms, and his clothing needed to be perfect.

He looked down at the ties.

It had to be red.

*

Frost fronted the security briefing. They'd gone over it countless times, but given the current climate and Freedom's determination to cause trouble, they needed to increase manpower tenfold. As much as Oakes incensed him, it was in his interest to keep him safe until his plans came to fruition. He'd wanted this for too long to be disabled by obstacles of any nature.

He wasn't naïve. He understood that a eugenics movement would take decades, centuries even. With vast generations of families that carried the gene for mental illness, it was unlikely that he'd even see his work come to full fruition during his lifetime. His main concern was to see the Zones up and running, with the body counts reducing.

'Let's go over it again,' he sighed.

It would be the seventh time that morning.

*

Oakes was chain smoking. He'd vowed to give up alcohol until he'd delivered his speech, but there was no way he could quit cigarettes. Besides, they gave his voice an attractive huskiness, or so he believed. He craved a shot of whiskey, even a cold beer, but he needed to keep a clear head. It's what all the great leaders had done.

He and Frost were discussing Luka, a subject that made Oakes particularly twitchy. He tried to brush around the edges, to avoid any in-depth, graphic details about the interrogation.

'She's steadfast, I'll give her that.'

Frost nodded. 'More than we could have anticipated. We've had her for three days and still nothing.'

'Do you think she's lying about her dad?'

'Definitely. There's no record of his death, though that doesn't categorically prove anything. I suspect that she joined Freedom to find him. There'd be no need if he was dead.'

'Unless she wanted to carry on his work?'

'Unlikely. Whichever way you cut it, she's still a kid. I doubt very much that her dad is dead. I think she fed us something in the hope of throwing us off scent.'

'Damn girl!' said Oakes as he vigorously pressed the button on his lighter, which had seemingly given up on him.

Frost walked over to him and took the lighter from his hand. With one gentle action, it lit with ease. As Oakes leaned in to light his cigarette, his hands visibly trembled.

Frost perched on the edge of Oakes' table. 'I'd like to propose that we take alternate action.'

'Such as?'

'If we consider the ways in which we can use her to our advantage, we're limited with our options. However, there is one way.'

'Go on?'

'She's valuable to Freedom, not to mention that she's a liability to them as long as we have her. We could suggest a trade. They give us Alpha; we give them the girl.'

'The leader? He's even less likely to give us anything. If anyone will die for the cause, surely it's him?'

'Undeniably, lesser members tend to be more valuable. They lack a certain tenacity. They're easier to persuade. Apart from the girl, of course, but she's the exception to the rule given who her father was. Even if we get anything from her, we have to question the validity of it. There's no doubt that they'd keep her away from certain aspects of their arrangements. Alpha is a bargaining chip; it compromises the rest of them by removing him.'

Oakes thought for a moment. He could see little logic in removing the most valuable member of Freedom. If they were battling with a young, vulnerable girl, they'd have a war with him.

'There are benefits in detaining the leading member,' said Frost.

'Then please elaborate. I fail to see them.'

'We give Freedom the chance to trade the girl and they'll take it. They're not going to let a kid take the fall. Guaranteed, the trade will be Alpha. We don't need to choose him, they will. No one else will do the exchange. The captain goes down with his ship, so to speak.' He offered a sarcastic smile. 'They are humanitarians, after all.'

Oakes frowned. 'This is entering territory that I'm not particularly comfortable with.'

'I see no other way, unfortunately. We can hold her, but she's useless to us. If we have Alpha, we have a chance of busting a hole in their plans. Take the one at the top and the rest fall like dominoes.'

'Won't someone else step up, take his place?'

'Eventually, yes. But it'll take time for the dust to settle. It's likely to create in-group conflict and weaken them. That's valuable time for us.'

'And what about repercussions? I very much doubt that Freedom will willingly accept that we have their leader. We might be opening ourselves up to all kinds of potential danger.'

'Like I said, our options are limited.'

Oakes paced back and forth. He wanted a drink to calm his nerves, to allow himself a moment to make a reasonable decision. Freedom were a curved ball. They'd caused him all kinds of stress and would likely continue to do so. The time had come for a decision to be made, a conclusion of sorts. He had a job to do. He needed to prove his worth, and they were vastly interfering with his plans.

He glanced at Frost. 'You can arrange this?'

'Yes. We have a contact that can carry the message to Freedom.'

Oakes raised an eyebrow. 'A contact? That knows where they are?'

'Not quite,' laughed Frost. 'A mutual contact that benefits from being a go-between, no questions asked.'

Oakes stubbed out his cigarette in the overflowing ashtray. He wouldn't pursue it; he was on a need-to-know basis.

'Get things moving,' he ordered before he allowed himself

time to ponder.

As soon as the door closed behind him, Oakes was overwhelmed with a burning rage. He was all too aware of the catalyst for his constant churning gut and pounding head. Despite his indignant feelings toward Frost, he remained quite unable to deny him. His own actions made him feel small and incapable; was he even capable of being a leader?

Deeply immersed in self-pity, he clenched his fist and struck his wooden desk with all of his strength. The pain seared through his hand; his knuckles turned purple immediately after impact. Profoundly frustrated, he removed his bottle of whiskey from the drawer and took a lengthy swig.

A swig didn't count.

Chapter 26

I'd spent three days with Dad, and I was already worried about the café. With Jo's mind fixated on her on-off relationship with Aron, and Dahlia in her dreamworld, it wasn't an ideal time to be absent from my own business.

Within a mere seventy-two hours, my stress levels had reached an all new high. I hadn't left Dad alone for even ten minutes in fear of another episode. That's what I'd convinced myself, anyway. In truth, it was more a fear of letting him out of my sight. I hadn't been able to ask Min to watch him while I popped to the café, just in case she decided to sneak him to the surgery. I had considered taking him with me, to give the place a quick once over, but I'd become so neurotic since learning of the Zones that I didn't want him to be seen in public. I felt safer behind closed doors. For now, anyway.

I received regular updates from the girls who assured me that things were fine, business as usual. They told me I was a control freak, insisted that I switch off and relax a little.

If only it was that simple.

I hadn't seen Min since the night after Dad's incident. It was then that I'd asked her to send Jed over to see me. He'd failed to appear and all sorts of scenarios had busied my mind.

Something else to add to the list.

*

As I hauled two heavy rubbish bags out to the bin, my neck severely strained from the sheer weight, I questioned how two people could produce so much waste in so little time. Dad ate fresh, home cooked meals, and I largely ate elsewhere due to my hours spent at work. It rendered me clueless as to what the bags actually contained.

When Jed appeared from behind my car, I nearly jumped out of my skin.

'Wow! Some warning might have been nice,' I gasped.

'Sorry. Mum said you wanted to see me.'

His eyes looked wild as they darted from side to side. He repeatedly glanced over his shoulder as though his emotions were on edge. I pulled the front door to, so that Dad wouldn't overhear. When I'd done so, I revealed my conversation with Jo, and Aron's apparent dislike for him.

'What's the problem with you two?' I asked.

'I don't know. I've never even spoken to him. Just seen him round and about.'

'He couldn't know about your involvement with Freedom, could he?'

'Of course he could. Nothing is impossible, and the military and police are pretty close knit. Why else would he have such an issue with me?'

'You don't seem very concerned.'

He glanced over his shoulder again. 'Least of my problems right now.'

'Maybe he just doesn't like your face,' I joked, in a meagre attempt to lighten the strained conversation.

There was no sign of a smile, or even a retort.

'I can only assume that he knows something. Maybe I am on their radar, after all.'

Suitably taken aback at his reticence, I raised my eyebrows. 'Doesn't that worry you?'

He shrugged. 'I guess. Can't be that much of a priority though, I'm here talking to you.' He paused for a moment, another glance over his shoulder. 'Was there anything else you wanted to tell me?'

I was astounded at his self-assurance and underwhelm. Unlike the compassionate person I'd come to know in recent weeks, there was a considerable change in his character. I wondered if it had all been an act. Perhaps this was the real Jed.

I breathed out heavily, 'Well, I thought that was significant enough.'

He looked at his watch. 'We have an emergency meeting. I really have to go.'

'Any news on Luka?' I asked hastily. It didn't take a genius to establish that I'd encroached on his valuable time.

He shook his head. 'She'll be in the Zones by now, I imagine.'

I closed my eyes; the concept was too great to consider.

There was a long, uncomfortable pause. Jed continued to survey the slightest movement while I watched on.

'I haven't left the house in days,' I declared. 'I'm scared your mum will turn up and insist on taking Dad to the doctors after his turn. Did she tell you?'

He nodded. 'You're doing the right thing. That would be a really bad move at the moment.'

I tilted my head. 'Would it?'

'What, you don't believe me now? Then go for it, take him

to the doctors!'

'Sorry. It's just… I'm worried about him. He might need meds and…'

'Yeah, I know. Like I said, up to you.'

'What the hell is wrong with you?' I blurted, no longer able to ignore the strained conversation. 'You're acting really strange.'

He shrugged his shoulders. 'I don't know what you want me to say, Raff. There's a lot going on. I have to go, but my advice is to filter what you say to Jo for a while. Break-ups have a way of becoming make ups, and people tend to talk when they're in the throes of it.'

'I wouldn't discuss any of this with Jo. Or anyone else, for that matter,' I snapped, startled at his sudden lack of trust in me.

'Good. Just keep it that way.'

'What's wrong, Jed?'

'You're really asking me that?'

He tugged at the straps on his backpack, as though the contents were weighing him down.

'Is it true about the backpack?' I asked.

He looked at me blankly.

'Emergency supplies, in case you get caught?' It sounded ludicrous when said aloud.

He frowned. 'How do you know that?'

'It's true then.'

'You seem to believe it, so who am I to argue?' He looked over his shoulder once more before offering me a quick glance. 'I really have to go. See you, Raff.'

As I watched him walk away, I had a really bad feeling.

*

Jed arrived at the prearranged location, a small house that Freedom rented for meetings and secrecy when the need arose. He walked past three times before finally slipping through the back entrance and into the back door. He couldn't afford to take chances at the moment, and if the police were on to him, he needed to be all the more scrupulous.

The bright and sunny morning abruptly diminished as soon as he entered; the low hanging blinds and drawn curtains cast dark shade throughout the downstairs area. There were clothes and empty food packages strewn across the floor.

Alpha and Zee were already present.

Locking the door behind him, Alpha marched through to the lounge area and peered through the blinds. 'You weren't followed?'

Jed shook his head as he took in Alpha's unusually dishevelled appearance; his chin was covered in heavy stubble and his hair looked wild. His clothes looked creased and dirty.

'What's the emergency?' he asked as he sat down on an old, ripped sofa.

Alpha strained his neck as he peered up and down the road. 'We've heard from our contact. Frost has sent a message.'

Jed shunted to the edge of his seat; his eyes were wide with anticipation.

'Luka?'

Neither of them responded.

'What's the message? Have they done something to her? I swear I'll kill…'

Alpha waved his hand dismissively; his eyes still firmly fixed on the outside of the house. 'She's alive. It's a bit more complicated than that.'

'Complicated, how?'

Alpha released the curtain and turned to face Jed. 'He's demanded that we trade. One of us for her.'

'That's ridiculous!'

'We don't have a choice.'

Jed turned to Zee, desperate for reinforcement. Zee lowered his gaze.

'Wait. You're not actually considering this?'

There was a delayed silence as Jed waited for someone to appease him.

'This is stupid! For five years we've evaded them and now, just like that, you're going to give someone up. Where's your backbone? We don't give in to people like Frost!'

Alpha's face hardened. 'You think I want to do this?'

'Well, it seems like you're rolling over pretty damn easily.'

'You're good with them punishing Luka then, are you? Because make no mistake, that's precisely what they'll do.'

Jed paused as he carefully considered his words. 'Has he threatened to hurt her?'

Alpha shook his head. 'Not yet, but he'll have already put her through hell. Some things don't need spelling out. The fact that she gave Zee's address shows how tough it's getting.'

Jed was startled. Having not seen them for several days, he had no idea how things had played out.

He looked at Zee. 'You okay, bro?'

Zee nodded. 'It's cool. I don't blame her for giving the

information. She knew I'd be lying low. I'm just concerned about her safety at this point.'

Alpha continued. 'It's only a matter of time before they do some real damage. He said there will be consequences if we don't do the exchange, but that seems pretty obvious to me.'

Jed considered the implications and racked his brain for an alternative. 'There has to be another way.'

Alpha shook his head. 'There is no other way. I'm going to hand myself over.'

Jed gasped. 'Oh, come on! You can't even consider it!'

'So, what do you suggest then, brainbox?'

'I suggest you think a bit harder. Where's your loyalty? Where's your dedication?'

Alpha darted towards him and stopped just short of Jed's face; their eyes were inches away from each other. 'You know exactly where my loyalty lies,' he snarled.

Zee placed his arms in the middle of them as he attempted to urge them apart. 'Guys, this won't solve anything.'

Jed pushed his weight against Zee in a bid to move closer to Alpha. 'It'll make me feel better though.'

'Give it a go, tough man.' Alpha's eyes were fixated and unyielding.

'Will both of you just quit!' bawled Zee. 'This is pathetic and doesn't help. As if we haven't got bigger problems than two bloody egos battling for first place. Go ahead, beat the crap out of each other, see if that makes you feel better. And then, when you're done licking your wounds, we'll come back to the very same conversation that we're having now.'

Taking heed of Zee's words, Alpha took a step back.

'We don't have time for this,' sighed Zee. 'We're on a crazy time constraint as it is.'

Jed turned to look at him. 'Why? When's the deadline?'

Zee's voice was faint and barely discernible. 'Tonight.'

Jed ran his hands through his hair. 'So, you're telling me that tonight we are handing ourselves over to Frost?'

Zee nodded.

Jed blinked frantically as hot tears welled up in his eyes. He roughly removed his jacket to reduce the overwhelming feeling of claustrophobia. Alpha slowly walked over to him and placed his hands on his shoulders.

'I don't want to fight with you, brother. You and Zee mean everything to me. I love you both. This is an impossible situation that none of us wants to be in. But we have to do this. It's not a decision that we've come to lightly.'

Jed tried to pull away from Alpha's grip, but he dug in deeper as he clutched his shoulders. 'Do not fight this. It only makes things harder. It's decided. I am going to the meet.'

Jed dropped his head to hide his tears. Alpha had said enough to convince him that the seeds were sown. He was respected for being a man of his word, and this situation would be no different to any other.

The room fell silent; each member was sombre, aware of the imminent inevitability. Alpha would be taken, undoubtedly tortured and possibly taken to a Zone; that was the best-case scenario. Each of them understood that it would be unlikely they'd ever see each other again, yet no one had the courage to say the words.

'You know what'll happen…' whispered Jed as the tears fell.

'It doesn't matter about me. You need to look after Luka. Teach her, nurture her. Don't let her mess up again,' he laughed. It was an awkward laugh that, by no means, hinted at joviality. Despite Alpha's size, authority and conviction, they both knew that deep down, he was terrified.

'Don't do this,' pleaded Jed. 'Please.'

Zee placed his arms around Alpha and Jed and pulled the three of them together. It would be the last time that they would all stand in the same room.

They embraced each other and silently allowed the tears to fall.

Chapter 27

The location was an hour's journey from the Thendra Zone. The area that was once the home of a busy cinema complex now stood as an isolated and derelict site; an eerie setting with a sprinkling of reminders of the thriving environment that once existed. Posters of fictional and cartoon characters adorned the brightly coloured walls; empty counters that previously housed popcorn and ice cream were redundant. As a standalone entertainment complex, there was little else in the area to attract civilians, so the chances of being disturbed were slim to none.

Frost wouldn't take any chances. People always had a way of appearing in random places at inopportune moments. To be certain, he had ensured that armed soldiers were stationed at every potential entry and exit point. It was too great a moment to sacrifice, and he wasn't going to risk failure due to some dim-witted individual. If anyone was stupid enough to turn up, then they'd face the consequences.

Frost's men were briefed, armed, and fully prepared for the exchange. He'd played it safe with ten men, as he couldn't take the chance of an ambush by Freedom.

Oakes had made it clear that he wasn't attending, which suited Frost perfectly. He didn't need a whiney so and so clinging onto his arm, overlooking his every move. The mission would be more efficient without him.

The joy he felt at the unfolding development was immense.

He couldn't have predicted a set of circumstances of such magnitude. The arrest of the youngest member of Freedom, exchanged for the leader of Freedom; the fortuity was too great. Had he been a religious man, he'd have believed that God was watching over him, supporting and encouraging his work. If he was spiritual, he'd put it down to fate. As it went, he was neither, but he believed wholeheartedly that this was meant to be. A greater force than he, mystically authenticating his plans.

Luka was being guarded by two armed men in a small room at the back of the cinema. When Alpha arrived at nine o'clock, the guards would assess the situation, ensure that he was alone, and only then would the exchange go through. The instructions were short and simple.

Crawford, Frost's closest ally, was positioned approximately one hundred feet from the entrance with his sniper in position.

He was ready to go.

*

Alpha sat in the parked car in silence. Jed was in the driver's seat, nervously tapping his finger on the steering wheel. Alpha glared at him, and Jed stopped immediately.

Alpha; the man he'd looked up to for so long; the father figure in his life.

He knew that this was the sacrifice. You didn't join a political group without accepting your fate should things go awry. He just hadn't had time to digest the information before delivering Alpha to the exchange point. He failed to comprehend how the group would exist without him.

Jed glanced at his watch. 'It's quarter to.'

Alpha nodded. He was calm. Too calm.

'We don't have to do this,' blurted Jed. 'I can turn the car around…'

'And what do you think they'll do to Luka if I don't show?'

A rhetorical question. They both knew exactly what would happen to Luka if they didn't go through with the exchange. Frost would be angered at the betrayal and take it out on her. She'd be made an example of.

None of them wanted that to happen.

'We should have kicked back,' said Jed. 'We've given in way too easily. What Frost wants; Frost gets. It isn't right.'

'He is head of the military,' mocked Alpha with a vague smile on his lips.

'Don't remind me.'

Alpha took a deep breath. 'It was always on the cards. You knew this.'

Jed stared out of the windscreen. It had turned to dusk outside, and the hazy sky looked a warm and beautiful shade of orange. Everything beneath it seemed to glisten like gold dust. It almost looked too picturesque, too perfect against the ugly backdrop of reality. How could nature's innocence and beauty shine down on such barbarism?

Alpha released his seatbelt. 'It's time.'

Hot tears pricked Jed's eyes like sharp needles. His chest felt tight and the lump in his throat was so great that he feared he might choke if he were to swallow.

Alpha pulled him towards him and forced him into an embrace. Jed kept his head low as he submitted and leaned into his chest. He couldn't let him see his grief. He needed to show warrior-like strength. He would lead Freedom. Alpha believed in him.

The passenger door opened and Alpha climbed out of the car. Jed didn't dare look up; he couldn't watch him walk away. That was a bridge too far.

It was time to wait. Luka would be there soon.

It was now his job to protect her and every other member of Freedom.

*

Crawford was the first to spot Alpha in his line of vision. He radioed down to Frost to alert him.

As instructed, Alpha stepped into the main entrance of the cinema foyer. He took his time; he was in no rush to be captured. After a few steps, he stopped and raised his arms above his head before he dropped to his knees.

Crawford, with his gun in position, continued to watch him from across the street, gratuitously enjoying the moment. Frost signalled for Luka to be brought out of the small room. Still blindfolded, she was guided down the corridor and placed several feet in front of Alpha. Frost removed her blindfold. Immediately, she began to cry, her relief at seeing Alpha so great.

'Should we move in, Commander?' asked one of the soldiers. He was ready to apprehend Alpha as planned, then await his next instruction.

Frost didn't respond.

'Commander?'

Frost lifted the radio to his mouth. 'Clear to engage.'

The soldier stepped back, blindsided by Frost's instruction that clearly wasn't meant for him. Despite the brief, Frost appeared to have a different agenda.

*

'Copy that.'

Crawford lowered his radio. He clutched the gun with both hands and peered through the eyehole.

He'd waited a long time for this moment.

*

There were no sudden, rapid movements. There was no action-packed drama. In fact, nothing happened for a few moments. The scene was eerily quiet and calm.

Alpha stared at Luka like a father to his daughter; his eyes warm and unwavering. She appeared to be safe and physically unhurt, which relieved him greatly. He didn't want her to cry. He didn't want Frost to see the slightest vulnerability. He wanted to use his final moments on earth to reassure her and make her feel safe. She'd had a tough ride, but she was destined for wonderful things.

He knew what had to happen. From the moment he'd been made aware of the exchange, he'd made peace with his fate. Luka would be safe. That's all that mattered.

When he heard the sound of a car backfiring, he instinctively turned his head towards the noise. Out of nowhere, a powerful force hit him in his spine; the power so immense that it pushed him forward and onto his side. He thought he heard a scream and tried to look at Luka. He couldn't see anything clearly, only bright lights, like perfect silver stars. As he lay on the cold floor, it crossed his mind that whoever had kicked him had superhuman strength. He could feel his back almost reverberating from the impact. That wasn't a fair fight. You don't kick a man from behind. As soon as he was able to lift himself to his feet, he'd give them everything he'd got.

He pushed down on his hands to lift his bodyweight, but he was too weak. His limbs felt peculiar; they failed to react to the messages from his brain. It was almost as though he'd been paralysed. Quite suddenly, he started to dither with cold. The temperature seemed to have dropped rapidly within a matter of seconds. He thought it strange for the time of year. A dampness dispersed across his back and around to his stomach, like someone had poured cold water over him. As soon as he had the strength…

And then it all went black.

*

After fifteen minutes, his anxiety had become unbearable.

He knew and trusted Alpha implicitly, but what if he'd overshot the mark on this one? What if he'd had a lapse in judgement and both he and Luka were now being held? Multiple scenes played out in his mind, and none of them offered a comforting conclusion. He decided to give it another ten minutes before he went to explore, despite the firm instruction to remain hidden. He couldn't just willingly accept it; he wouldn't be able to live with himself.

A movement in the near distance caught his attention. On closer inspection, he realised that it was Luka bounding towards him. He flung the car door open and ran towards her. As he drew near, he heard her cry for help; a disturbing guttural sound that seemed to come from deep within. When he reached her, her legs gave way beneath her and she fell to the ground. He attempted to support her, but her malnourished body was so limp that she slumped at his feet. As she sobbed, he lifted her head onto his lap and examined her body for signs of injury. Tears trickled down her ghost-like face. Her eyes were wide and haunted.

He lifted her tiny frame and placed her in the passenger seat of his car. Her bodyweight was so low that it required little to no effort.

Concerned that they were being watched or followed, he hastily headed to the driver's seat. They needed to evacuate as quickly as possible. As he turned the key in the engine, he noticed that his hand shook vigorously. He clenched his fist and tried again. The engine powered up.

The tyres made a loud screeching noise as they rapidly reversed several feet down the passageway. When he was able, he spun the car around and swiftly weaved through the winding roads. Until he reached a main road, he wouldn't feel safe.

Now and again, he glanced at Luka. Her sobbing had reduced to a faint snivelling, though her tightly coiled body continued to violently shake. He couldn't begin to imagine what she may have endured.

He racked his brain as he attempted to recall the instructions that Alpha had given him.

'When she's in the car, no physical contact. She may lash out and spin into a frenzy. She'll be out of touch with reality. Just speak to her softly, let her know she's safe. Drive straight to the safe house. He'll have someone there who can check her over, calm her down. Don't stop for anything or anyone. Just drive.'

'He's dead,' whispered Luka. 'Alpha's dead.'

*

Chapter 28

Min glanced at the clock as she waited in the surgery. They were running over forty minutes late. She was under tremendous pressure, particularly since Raff had firmly instructed her to remain at home with her dad while she popped to the café. Something about a leaking pipe.

Min had felt unsettled since Phillip's turn, so she'd seized the opportunity to have him looked over. Raff would understand. It was only fear that had prevented her from doing the same. Easing her burden was a kind gesture.

She glanced at the clock again; one minute later than the last time she'd looked. Five more minutes and she'd abort the operation. Phillip's patience had already worn thin, and he'd threatened to leave twice. Next time, he'd head for the door and make a scene, of that she had no doubt.

When the doctor called Phillips' name, she couldn't jump to her feet quickly enough. She followed behind as he trundled into the room like a bad-tempered child.

The doctor took a seat. 'Sincere apologies for your wait. We're running behind.'

'You're always bloody behind,' groaned Phillip as he hurled himself into a chair.

Min tapped him on the arm and cast a perplexed look in his direction.

The doctor looked suitably embarrassed at their

inconvenience. 'Perfectly understandable. How can I help?'

Min was well acquainted with the doctor that sat before her. She carried a reputation for being kind, patient and thorough; traits that kept her in high demand. Yet on this occasion, it struck her how agitated she appeared as she rigorously shunted several overfilled files to the back of the desk.

Min wasted no time in divulging the details of Phillip's recent episode. Though he continued to take his medication, she firmly advised the doctor that she wanted it noted on his records. Agreeably, the doctor undertook a few tests and asked him a few questions, all of which he answered with ease and a hint of sarcasm, and determined that she was content with his progress.

'I'm satisfied that you're doing well, Phillip,' she soothed. 'We're still in the early stages, so there's no great concern. Keep up with the healthy meals, they seem to be working for you.'

He nodded. 'Whatever you think, doc.'

'So, nothing I should be concerned about?' asked Min.

'Often, these lapses are stress related. Does that sound likely?'

Min glanced at him. 'He spends too much time in his studio. I'd like him to rest a little bit more.'

He rolled his eyes.

'And he's a cheeky whatsit,' she added. 'Got anything for that?'

Phillip leant forward in his seat. 'Right, happy now? Can we go?'

As he made his way to the door, Min laughed. Even in his grumpiest mood, he could make her smile.

Min lingered for a moment after he'd exited. 'How are things here?' she queried. 'Calmed down a bit?'

The doctor relaxed as she spoke. 'Oh, these people coming in and out, interfering with everything; now, they want certain ailments flagged, and it's giving us tons more paperwork. It's driving us all insane! Some get immediate prescriptions; others have to go through a long-winded system and wait days for them. And they've reduced our staff, as you know. I'm here for twelve hours a day at the moment.'

Min shook her head in disgust. 'You're overworked and I'm on fewer hours. I just don't understand what they're trying to achieve.'

'Making it a smoother system, apparently,' she mocked. 'Ensuring that certain patients get the extra attention they require, sending them to specialist facilities. Time wasting, if you ask me. And those patronising night staff are…'

The door opened, and Phillip's head appeared. 'Are we done gassing, ladies? Might I be able to go home at some point today?'

'Yes! Sorry, Phillip,' said the doctor. The corners of her mouth turned upward. 'Still got a sense of humour, I see.'

'Well, someone round here has to,' he muttered.

Min winked at the doctor. 'Miserable old goat, isn't he?' She patted her arm as she turned to leave. 'Get in touch if you need anything. You know where I am.'

As they made their way to the car, they were oblivious to the fact that they had rapidly accelerated his fate.

*

The GP surgery sat in stony silence apart from the two

individuals that were seated at the reception desk. It was eleven thirty at night, but they were both exempt from martial law constraints due to their high-level governmental positions.

As highly trained analysts, they had spent several months on the gruelling task of amalgamating patient records and dividing them into specific categories. Thus far, they had covered nine regions and their latest stop was Thendra.

Due to the small, close knit community, their presence had caused distress to the staff and patients at Thendra Medical Centre, but they remained unnerved by it. They were there on government business and weren't looking to make friends.

Having compiled their areas of interest database, they were able to begin sub-filtering patients. These areas consisted of patients that had been diagnosed with any form of mental illness from a list of one hundred. Then, there were those that had reported more common disorders, such as depression and anxiety. Finally, there was a further category for patients that had a diagnosis of dementia in any one of its numerous forms. When complete, the list would be electronically transferred to a governmental team that would discuss individual cases before deploying intervention strategies.

The list was compiled weekly in each surgery and on this day, the medical centre had just five cases. Four of the patients had presented on several occasions with anxiety-related symptoms. The fifth, a gentleman in his sixties, had been accompanied by his carer who was concerned about his ailing dementia.

The female official read through his patient notes. Mr Phillip Crowe. He had been diagnosed with a genetic form of dementia, definitely one to flag.

The initial phase of the operation involved highlighting those that visited their GP regularly or semi-regularly. Later, with Phase One complete, they would set to work on a full patient data analysis, where all patient records would be scrutinised, regardless of the number of visits. Frost and his advisors had called it the top-down system; they'd filter out the obvious, then dig deeper.

Unlike similar patients with dementia, Phillip Crowe rarely visited his GP, and it dawned on her that he could have quite easily slipped through the net. This happened occasionally and was unavoidable, but it was her job to ensure that it occurred as rarely as possible. She'd address this record with her superiors; ensure that they were made aware of her impeccable analytical ability.

The official was pleased with her work. She was being paid twice her usual salary to undertake this operation and, providing she continued to deliver, would be continuing in the role for the long term. She glanced at her long, glossy fingernails as they efficiently tapped the keypad, musing at how she'd developed a taste for expensive manicures in exclusive salons. She liked being able to buy more expensive clothes and visit the pricier shops. People were impressed by her, and women envied her. As long as she did a good job, she'd be pursuing this lifestyle for quite some time.

'Silly you, Mr Crowe,' she smiled as she moved her cursor to the tick box next to his name and opted for priority.

'You've just moved yourself right up the list.'

Chapter 29

Frost hovered beside the projector screen at the front of the classroom. A large, semi-circular table, of which seated thirty-five high-ranking members of governmental security detail, dominated much of the room.

Despite having little to contribute to the session, Oakes had insisted that he was present. Eager to ensure that he had a transparent understanding of his own security detail, he wanted a guarantee that he was to remain highly protected during his speech in three days' time.

As he glanced around the table, he noticed how many of his staff had been replaced by Frost's workforce in recent weeks. In contrast to the amiable faces that he was privy to, he laid his eyes upon an assemblage of oversized men. Few looked even vaguely familiar to him. Albin was present, but barely. Having been relentlessly disquieted by Frost, he was nigh on invisible.

The lights dimmed as a bird's-eye map appeared on the screen. It covered the vast vicinity in which he was to give his speech.

Frost pointed a pen at the screen. 'We have a total of two hundred military deployed within three miles of the location. At least one hundred more will be positioned both at, and within, five hundred feet…'

'Has everyone been vetted?' interrupted Oakes.

Frost looked suitably taken aback at the interference. 'Yes, all staff have been through detailed security vetting.'

Oakes was unperturbed at his requirement for information; it was a matter of life or death.

'We will employ two decoy vehicles...' continued Frost.

'And who will be driving?'

Frost narrowed his eyes. 'Isaac will be driving you.' He pointed to a member of the group, who raised his arm in acknowledgment. 'He's an experienced and highly skilled driver. We're not taking any chances.'

Oakes glanced over at the man in question.

Isaac. A thin and average looking man. Geeky, almost; the only man present that lacked muscle and brawn. He started to perspire at the gaunt appearance of his potential getaway driver.

'The carrier for Mr Oakes will be explosive and bullet proof,' continued Frost. 'Minimal chance of penetrating the vehicle.'

Certain that Frost was taunting him, he removed a handkerchief from his pocket and dabbed the sweat on the back of his neck.

Frost continued to wave his pen around and highlight areas of interest as he talked in detail about the operational logistics. It might as well have been Japanese for all the sense it made.

'We'll brief again in two days' time,' he concluded as he dismissed the group.

Oakes glanced at his watch; the briefing had failed to exceed sixteen minutes. Was sixteen minutes all that his life was worth?

'You have this under control, don't you?' he asked as the others left the room. 'Given recent events, I can imagine that certain people might have an axe to grind.' He hoped Frost picked up on the underhanded jibe.

'You'll be safe. That's all you need to concern yourself with.'

As the door closed behind him, a familiar fury blindsided him. He was still deeply resentful at Frost's secret operation with Alpha. Arguably, he'd dictated that he was on a "need to know" basis, but a mission of such extravagant proportions necessitated the approval of a leader. He was certain that the assassination would provoke Freedom into retaliation.

For the first time in his life, he felt vulnerable.

Vulnerable and terrified.

Chapter 30

Several miles from home in a seedy back street, Jed sat in the back of a car. His contact sat ahead of him in the driver's seat; a man of few words. It was gone three o'clock in the early hours and the roads were silent. He was cold and tired, desperately tired.

Since the incident with Alpha, he had remained haunted by Luka's expression. She had described the brutal murder of their leader with such alarming clarity that he had relived the incident as if he were present.

He had expected her to be traumatised for several days after collecting her from the exchange point. Exchange. That was a joke. A lie. Frost had no intention of exchanging Luka for Alpha; his objective had been to ensure that Luka witnessed a live assassination.

He'd never allow himself to be blindsided again.

Under the circumstances, Luka had been surprisingly coherent. After eating two large platefuls of warm food and sleeping for twelve hours, she'd been able to describe her interrogation with relative ease. The kid was tough, that much was apparent. But when Alpha had fallen to the ground and sounded a blood curling scream, that had destroyed her. It would stay with her for all eternity.

Jed rubbed his hands together to emanate some heat. It didn't seem appropriate to request a blast of warm air from the car heater. His recent lack of sleep and sustenance had taken its toll. In order for his next mission to be successful, he had to be in better shape.

The rear passenger door opened, and a man climbed in. A black scarf covered his nose and mouth and the protruding hood from his coat cast a dark shadow over his face. His presence alone emanated a brooding and dangerous air.

Jed knew nothing of these people. What he did know was that Alpha had outlined a plan of action and provided him with the necessary contact details should the moment arise. He would only come face-to-face with them in the worst-case scenario.

The worst-case scenario was upon them.

The driver lowered the rear-view mirror to ensure that he could see into the back of the car. Jed glanced up momentarily to see the man's dark, penetrating eyes staring back at him. 'These men are extremely dangerous,' Alpha had warned him. 'Get in, get out and say very little.'

He slowly pulled a thick envelope from his inner-coat pocket and handed it to the man next to him. With his eyes firmly fixed on Jed, the man forwarded the envelope to the driver, who proceeded to remove and count the thick wad of monetary notes. Jed shuffled in his seat, uncertain where to cast his gaze.

The still and empty street offered a sinister backdrop for the exchange. The faintest of sounds seemed to magnify to the power of ten. He could hear the man's breath next to him, the rapid rustling of bank notes from the front. It seemed like twenty minutes had passed when the driver finally spoke.

'All there,' he growled in a deep, gravelly voice.

Jed glanced out of the window and allowed his lungs to

slowly release.

Though he and Zee had checked, double checked and triple checked the contents of the envelope, it offered little solace during the tense exchange. Had there have been a complication, he would have been executed there and then.

The man reached into his pocket and produced a small, black box, then slowly and methodically lifted the lid. Embedded in the box's padding lay a small, clear vial that contained a liquid. It struck Jed how much it resembled an expensive perfume from one of the more upmarket stores. It couldn't have been further from the truth

The man lifted the vial for Jed to see. Though he was no expert in the field, he nodded.

He placed the vial in the box and handed the package to Jed before rapidly exiting the car. With the box held in front of him, Jed glanced into the driver's mirror. Dark, sinister eyes stared back at him.

'Get out!' demanded the driver.

With his eyes on the box, he nervously scrambled for the handle. His chest pounded as he fervently sought his way out of the sordid situation in which he found himself. When the door eventually opened, he climbed out and made his way to his car. Every second that he remained in the open, he half expected something to hit him from behind; a weapon, a fist, a bullet, even.

He hadn't expected it to come to this so soon.

Alpha's last resort had come to fruition.

*

Forlorn, tear-stained faces were abundant. In spite of their hazardous roles that came with dubious consequences, Alpha's execution had come as a tremendous shock.

The death of their impenetrable leader had incited a newfound fear amongst Freedom; if they could get to Alpha, they could get to any of them. Gathered at Freedom's base, the mood was sombre; the air was riddled with a collective tension.

Jed was consumed with anxiety as he considered his forthcoming dialogue. Never had he doubted or second-guessed Alpha's guidance, yet as he stood in his place, he felt like an imposter. He could never replace him; he wouldn't want to replace him, despite the unequivocal faith that Alpha had in him. A lump formed in his throat as he visualised Alpha taking to the stage, effortlessly guiding and nurturing individuals like himself. He roughly wiped a falling tear and took a long swig of beer. Dutch courage.

'In two nights from now, Edwin Oakes will be delivering a speech to thousands of people at a city stadium. Frost and his military will dominate the area, so security will be as efficient as we've ever seen. Freedom is going to be there, to complete the work of our leader.'

He was interrupted by the cheering of his comrades. They were with him every step of the way, but as they began to chant Alpha's name, he became inconsolable. Falling to his knees, he bowed his head and allowed himself to sob.

Alpha's voice in his mind spoke with clarity. 'It doesn't matter what you feel, it's what you show others that counts. No one needs to know what's really going on inside.'

He took a breath and rose to his feet. A sea of familiar faces stood in front of him.

'Alpha requested that in the event of his death, we are to remain strong. We are to move beyond our previous approach. Freedom aren't terrorists, but in order to maintain our position, we have to take more extreme measures if we truly seek justice.'

'In two days' time, we will not avenge the murder of our leader. That is neither our purpose nor our practice. Instead, we will destroy the heart of The Happy State. We will eliminate the individuals that are intent on torturing and murdering our people. A Neo-Nazi party with toxic visions of a Happy State; visions that are untenable, barbaric and evil.'

His voice cracked as a wave of emotion showered him. The pain was too immense to suppress.

'This… this is Alpha's last wish. Alpha's legacy. You will not be judged should you choose to recuse yourself from this mission. The stakes are high and the risk of capture is great.'

Several hands went up in the air while others chanted his name in support. Fearful of floundering, he quickly raised his hand to quieten them.

'This is not a decision you must make without forethought. Take some time and come to me throughout the evening. Tomorrow, you will learn of your positions should you choose to be involved. Please remember, for this is what Alpha desired. He would not want his death avenged. Revenge is an act of anger and weakness, and this is not the purpose of our mission. As we stand, we are weakened, but we will become strong again. We are doing this for our people and for our country. We are saving lives and saving futures.'

Jed raised his beer bottle above him. 'To Alpha!'

In unison, they echoed his motion.

'To Alpha!'

Chapter 31

Dad had been bad tempered for a few days. He'd woken each morning in a relatively jovial mood, eaten his breakfast and then, instantaneously, his mood had turned sour. I'd made a joke that it was something in his food, but even that had failed to raise a smile.

It hadn't helped when he'd told me about his doctor's visit. My reaction was of nuclear proportions, to say the least. My sole concern was for his safety, but I shouldn't have taken it out on him. I'd let rip, accused him of being a pushover for allowing Min to talk him into it, told him he was stupid and foolish. In truth, it was Min that I really wanted to admonish, but I couldn't, not without prompting her into suspicion. I'd apologised profusely, told him I was having a bad day, and didn't mean any of it. It hadn't eased my guilt.

Despite my overbearing regret, I realised that I had little option but to ride it out and accept that I was at fault. I was solely to blame for allowing Min to babysit while I dealt with a minor flood at work. As it turned out, Jo had already called in a plumber and my journey was futile.

I should have known that Min would take matters into her own hands. Perhaps, somewhere in the depths of my subconscious, I wanted her to. I couldn't think of another logical explanation for my foolishness. I couldn't blame her; she was only looking out for Dad. But with Dad's regular mood changes, my petulance had been forced to take a backseat.

'All part of the illness,' Min had advised me. 'It's nothing personal.'

What Min failed to realise was that I wanted it to be personal. I wanted Dad to be angry or snappy because of something I'd done. I'd have taken that gladly. What I didn't want was for it to be due to his illness because that meant that his health was in decline.

I wasn't ready for that.

*

It was early morning, and I decided to execute a cathartic house clean. I'd come to learn that scrubbing stubborn stains with aggression and vigour did wonders for the mind. As I tossed my second bulging bag into the waste bin, I heard my name being called. I glanced up to see Jed at the bottom of the driveway. Even from a distance, he looked gaunt in appearance; his eyes and cheeks were almost sunken into his face.

'We have to stop meeting like this,' I said as I closed the bin lid.

He attempted a faint smile as I drew closer.

'You look like something out of a vampire film. Have you seen daylight recently?'

He didn't take the bait.

'Do you want to come inside? No pun intended.'

He shook his head. 'I can't stay. I just wanted to say… er… you might not see me for a while.'

'Okay…'

'…and I want you to take care of yourself. Your Dad. And Mum. Please look after Mum.'

I laughed nervously. 'What are you on about?'

'Raff, will you just make me that promise?' His tone was firm and forceful.

I wasn't doing cryptic again. 'You can't turn up out of the blue and expect me to just accept that. What's going on, Jed?'

He gazed at me with bloodshot, red-rimmed eyes that hadn't seen sleep in a while; a watery glaze that suggested he might cry at any moment.

'Talk to me, Jed,' I urged, as I took a step closer. 'You're freaking me out.'

'Alpha's dead.'

I'd never met the man that they called Alpha, yet I knew how much he meant to Jed from the numerous times he'd brought him up in our conversations. I'd always sensed that he was something of a father figure to him.

'I'm sorry,' I whispered. 'Really sorry.'

He looked to the floor like a man defeated.

'I know he meant a lot to you. I didn't know him…'

'Yeah. You did.'

'Sorry?'

He paused for a moment. 'Stan. He was Alpha. Stan… is dead.'

Shocked to the core, I took a step back. Though I couldn't profess to have known Stan in recent years, he had meant a lot to me and my family when I was younger. He'd also shown me nothing but kindness during our last two encounters. I felt deeply saddened by the news.

'What happened?'

'Best you don't know,' he answered. 'I just wanted you to know.'

I nodded. 'Thanks. I guess.'

'I have to go.'

I took another step towards him as my concern heightened. 'Where to? Please, Jed. What's going on?'

'I'm sorry for bringing you into all of this, but I hope that with the knowledge you now have, you'll be extra vigilant with your Dad. That's all I ever wanted. That's all I ever... meant. Try and keep him with you whenever you can. I know that isn't easy. I promise, this wasn't supposed to be selfish in any way.'

'Jed...!' I interrupted.

'Let me finish. I honestly don't know if I'll see you again. But I need you to know...'

'Seriously, Jed!' I crowed. 'Talk about laying on the dramatics.' For some reason, I could feel my throat thickening with emotion.

'I... God, this is hard, but I really care about you. I always have.'

I froze. There were far too many unresolved issues hurling themselves at me in the shortest amount of time.

He took a step towards me and gazed into my eyes. There was a distinct vulnerability in his expression; his eyes had softened, the hard edge had all but diminished.

An excess of saliva in my mouth forced me to swallow. I hated spontaneity, I always had. With his face just inches from mine, I shifted from one foot to another.

'Where's this coming from?'

Before I could so much as anticipate his response, he placed both of his hands on my face and fell deeper into my eyes. It was much too awkward for my taste, but when he gently placed his lips on mine, I found myself surrendering to the moment. Every instinct I possessed wanted to fight against it, yet I remained glued to the spot.

Releasing his touch, he took a step back.

'I've wanted to do that for such a long time,' he whispered. A hint of a cheeky smile. There he was.

I was speechless, dubious at best. I feared my mistrustful emotions and their apparent inability to feel anger at his actions. Why didn't I want to punch him? It wouldn't be the first time I'd tried. Why didn't I push him away, berate him for beguiling me, for abusing my trust? I was shocked, but definitely not angry or appalled, as I'd have predicted under such circumstances. The only thing that was certain in my mind was that I didn't want to like the fact that he'd just kissed me. I didn't want to like the fact that I liked that he'd just kissed me.

I eliminated any further intrusive thoughts by focusing on my surroundings. Jed returned to sombre as he reached out and took my hand.

'Bye, Raff.'

Without any conscious reasoning, my eyes filled with tears. Perhaps it was the empath in me, my heightened sensitivity at the emotions of others. Given that I didn't particularly like Jed, I assured myself that I'd found the solution to my predicament. My emotions had simply mirrored his. Nothing more.

'Please be careful,' I croaked.

I watched him as he walked away, wondering if that fleeting moment had been a figment of my imagination. Reality had crossed too many lines of late, and nothing seemed impossible any more.

I resisted the urge to call after him, to stop him from going wherever he was going; to tell him he didn't have to do any of it. I simply hoped that he wasn't going to do anything stupid.

When he had disappeared from view, I went back inside with a heavy heart.

Chapter 32

The Day of the Event
9.00 am.

There was an air of excitement as Frost briefed his men at the governmental headquarters. He had undertaken more briefs in the last few days than he had over a twelve-year span in the military. Oakes had insisted that staff were regularly updated on both significant and inconsequential changes, so Frost was depleted before he'd even started.

For the occasion, all borders, main roads and motorways had been opened to enable access from across the United Kingdom. It came with tremendous risk, but it was necessary in appeasing the public and building admiration for Oakes and The Happy State.

The location had been manned by the military for forty-eight hours prior to the event. An event of such proportions would be a likely target for anti-governmental associations who would revel in the downfall of Oakes. He wasn't taking any chances.

He gathered his belongings and locked the door to the office. It was going to be a long day.

*

They travelled in two separate cars. Jed, Zee and Myka were in the first, and three other members of Freedom followed closely behind. They had faced numerous roadblocks on the way to the city. Each time, military had checked their I.D and demanded a justifiable purpose for travel.

They were confident that their faces had yet to reach the wanted radar, but in light of their rapid rise in notoriety, they couldn't take anything for granted. Discretion was key.

Their initial concerns were greatly reduced thanks to Myka and her exceptional performance skills; her sickly sweet charm had the soldiers eating out of her hands.

'We're just so excited to be given an opportunity to meet Edwin Oakes,' she cooed in a sweet, feminine tone that lay in stark contrast to her usual abruptness. 'I've dragged all of my friends here too.'

One of the soldiers was a jobsworth. She sensed that immediately; the sort that followed the rules to the letter and proudly protruded his chest as he did so. He'd be difficult to penetrate and wasn't worth the effort. It didn't take her long to identify the weak spot. According to Myka, every situation, regardless of the manpower, had a weak spot. She swore by it. Unfortunately, for the opposite sex, it was usually in the form of a weak male that couldn't resist an attractive and mildly flirtatious female.

As she untied her fair hair and allowed it to cascade past her shoulders, she registered Jobsworth's partner as he less than subtly stole a glance.

They sailed through the checkpoint. She hated it when people were so predictable.

After a four hour journey, they arrived at the location; a tailback of traffic determined that they would gradually creep towards the metal arch that marked the entrance to the park. Between the entrance and the car park, an additional three checkpoints slowed things further. It would take at least thirty minutes to reach their destination.

In the back of the car, Zee slid his body down the seat and made himself comfortable.

'Time to get your heads straight, kids.'

*

Oakes glared at himself in the full-length mirror and recoiled at his unsightly appearance. He'd barely slept the previous night due to a sub-standard hotel bed; the pillow was too flat and the feather quilt had triggered an allergy that gave his nose and eyes a definitive ruddiness. As if that hadn't been sufficient to keep him awake, his speech had looped in his mind from the moment his head hit the pillow.

'In what has been a period of uncertainty…' he uttered as he stared at his reflection.

He stopped.

'To the people of The Happy State. In what has been…'

Exasperated, he stopped. The butterflies in his stomach appeared to be auto-charged. If he wasn't careful, he'd have indigestion to add to his list of concerns.

He thrust his shoulders back and elevated his chin. 'People of The Happy State,' he gushed. An awkward smile distorted his expression. 'In what has been a daunting period of… great…

absolute… bloody rubbish. Crap!'

He slammed his cue card down in temper. His memory seemed to have evaded him, and if he couldn't get past the first sentence, he didn't hold out much hope. He reached into his pocket for a cigarette and fished around for his misplaced lighter.

'God, give me strength!' he shouted, as he spotted it directly in his eyeline.

With fumbling fingers, he lit his cigarette. He closed his eyes as he inhaled the nicotine that he'd come to rely on so greatly.

It was an important day. It was the day that he'd face the people, his people, and attempt to convince them that the disarray both behind and ahead of them was necessary for the long-term goal. 'Play down martial law,' Frost had told him. 'Let them see that it's just a short-term necessity for the greater good.'

He tried to tell himself that they were just a bunch of nouns and adjectives, but they were so much more than that. It was he who needed to do the convincing. It was his job to bring them to life. It was on him to reassure the people, to be transparent, honest, and trustworthy. It was him that would advise them that The Happy State was to be a historical breakthrough, remembered for centuries to come. We are making history; he would tell them. For our children, our grandchildren, our great-great-great grandchildren.

He grunted at his own thought process, perturbed at his newfound lack of belief in the overall vision. It would be so much simpler if he didn't have to consciously eliminate euthanasia from his brain for the duration of the speech; if he could erase the image of Tegan in her pitiful state. Frost had ushered him into this lucrative position. He could hardly turn against him and refuse to deliver.

He stubbed out his cigarette and glanced at his watch. His car would be downstairs within ten minutes.

Once again, he looked in the mirror.

'People of The Happy State…'

*

12.00 pm.

'Affirmative. Everyone is in position.'

Frost disconnected the call. It was the first time he'd spoken to any of his unit in over an hour due to Oakes and his incessant whining. He had insisted on a brief telephone discussion with him, just to go over a few things. Another call for a quick check, a question, a query, a question. When he'd attempted to have a face-to-face chat, Frost had lied and said he wasn't dressed. He was military, of course he was dressed, and had been since five that morning. Oakes had believed him, nonetheless.

His preparation for the day had been as thorough as any mission he had undertaken. He had organised and overlooked all security detail, which he could have quite easily delegated to an experienced and lower-ranking officer. Naturally, Oakes had wanted him to personally take charge. He didn't trust anyone else. Reluctantly, Frost had agreed, if not solely to give himself a break from Oakes' relentless moaning. It hadn't worked out that way. Every single day, he'd insisted on an update. Paranoia was prevalent in positions of such distinction, but Oakes had set a new precedent. With minimal self-belief and a reluctance to embrace change, it made Frost wonder how he'd ever accumulated such a following.

And his chain-smoking was likely to give him lung cancer, much less Oakes.

'We'll escort you to the stage in forty-five minutes,' Frost had gabbled, eager to abort the conversation.

'You'll be escorting me?' Oakes had asked.

It was a rhetorical question. Naturally.

He bit his tongue. 'Of course.'

With silence as his only companion, Frost took a moment to disburden himself from the stress inflicted by external sources. Unlike most, he didn't rely on alcohol or cigarettes for clarity. A couple of minutes of solitude and he was as good as new.

'Think of the prize,' he told himself. 'Think of the prize.'

*

A private golfing range on the outskirts of the city marked the location for Edwin Oakes affluent after-party. No cost had been spared by the lavish golf club; it would be a celebration to honour the success of the new government. It was far more likely that they were being paid hundreds of thousands of pounds to hold a high-profile and prestigious event, which meant that they could double their membership fees for the next season.

The catering was well underway and perfectly on schedule for the three o'clock arrival of Oakes and his entourage. There would be a five course meal with full table service and a large selection of expensive wines and spirits to choose from. The staff had been hand selected for the event to ensure an impeccable, high-quality service. A small security team was present, predominantly to monitor over-enthusiastic drinkers.

As the staff busily prepared tables, a smartly uniformed waitress sat outside on a bench as she smoked a roll up cigarette. She had a look of contentedness about her as she gazed at the clear sky.

It was the first time she'd felt tranquil in a long time; she felt blessed to be where she was at that precise moment in time. It struck her as fate-like, despite having gone to the ends of the earth to make damn sure that she was there. To her credit, she had an abundance of waitressing experience from her teenage years, so a few nudges here and there had ensured that she was present at one of the biggest events of her career.

She smiled to herself. She had spent so much time following their careers and, at last, she would come to face to face with Edwin Oakes and Nathaniel Frost.

She stubbed her cigarette out on the grass, popped some chewing gum into her mouth and headed back inside.

'You've got this, Myka,' she whispered to herself.

*

Having practiced his speech fifty times over, consumed an early but healthy lunch, shaved and showered, Oakes felt suitably improved from the earlier part of the morning. Aside from the unflinching fear of stumbling over his lines, his nerves had settled somewhat.

Undoubtedly, there would be hostiles present. It was an activist's prerogative to follow all that they despised. He had faith in Frost and his security protocols, particularly as he'd relentlessly hounded him to the point of annoyance. It was Frost's recklessness with Alpha that had turned him into the nervous wreck that he'd become; some reassurance of his safety was the least he expected in return.

He looked forward to three o'clock when he could finally break his sobriety of sixteen days. He felt tremendous pride for abstaining, even if he had smoked his bodyweight in cigarettes. He'd think about that tomorrow. First, he had to make history.

And drink copious amounts of whiskey.

*

1.55 pm.

Frost casually sauntered around the backstage area. There was nothing accidental about his slow pace. He wanted to take it all in, to embrace the manner in which people responded to his presence. Oakes carried the title, but he didn't command attention and respect. Power had to be earned.

He watched Oakes as he lingered in the wings, silently mouthing his speech to himself. As he glanced outward, a glimpse of the endless crowd offered him pure and indulgent fulfilment. He stared ahead and pondered at his imposition, how his reductionist state would be celebrated in years to come. Oakes could never have achieved it on his own, but he was a necessary pawn. A pawn that the people seemed to like.

Oakes had earned his fifteen minutes of fame. The people would cheer his name, even if prompted by the stooges that they'd placed throughout the crowd. His speech would be a pinnacle moment. The people would embrace him and place their trust in the man that would salvage their country.

Frost smiled, a rarity in itself. Soon, he could return to his work; the work that was necessary to make his country thrive once again.

On this very day, The Happy State would be born.

*

Jed was positioned halfway back from the stage area. The area was full to brimming with families and individuals that had flocked to see their leader. The atmosphere was upbeat as they awaited the arrival of Oakes. He couldn't help but smile to himself. There was a certain irony in seeing so many happy faces. The banners that surrounded him were largely of a positive nature as they warmly welcomed their new government. He'd spotted a handful of less than flattering messages. It was always inevitable.

He watched as parents occupied their excited offspring with endless tubs of ice cream and bars of chocolate. They were too young to understand, but someday they would talk of this day for a number of reasons. A young boy of no more than four years of age excitedly waved at him from his father's shoulders. Jed offered a half-smile as he considered the young boy's future.

'Good luck, kid,' he mouthed as he enthusiastically waved back.

He thought of Zee and the others. They were somewhere in the crowd; suitably embedded amongst the masses as they mimicked the enthusiasm of those around them. His mind wandered to Myka, and he silently prayed for her safety and success.

Amidst the drone of chatter, he took a deep breath and looked at the vast blue sky.

'We can do this,' he whispered.

Real change only came when people opposed.

*

Oakes took his place at the lectern and was overcome with stage fright. The endless positive affirmations and empowering mantras had all but drowned in an ocean of nerves.

He glanced down at the cue cards; a unified swirl of blurred, black writing. He placed a hand on either side of the lectern to balance himself and slowly glanced up at the crowd. His largest crowd to date; the image that lay before him resembled a giant patchwork quilt, scattered with a multitude of bright colours.

'You'll walk on stage and feel paralysed,' his assistant had advised. 'Your mouth will become dry; your hands will shake. You may feel an urge to go to the bathroom. Focus! Find a point ahead of you and use it as your object of attention throughout. Smile. Wave. Take a deep breath. Then begin.'

'People of The Happy State,' he began. 'Let me thank you, and welcome you to the city. I am overwhelmed at the masses that have travelled to be here today. Your support means everything.'

His voice trembled as he spoke. He licked his moistureless lips and took another deep breath.

'The United Kingdom. Strong, powerful, united, and stable. The last two decades have not exemplified this. Four-yearly elections have offered a plethora of leaders the opportunity to build, maintain and nurture a nation that is synonymous with a good quality of life for all. They have failed.'

'As a highly developed and forward-thinking country, that should do nothing less than thrive, we have merely survived, and accepted the scraps that have been thrown to us.'

'Those with low incomes have suffered brutally with substandard living; over twenty five per cent of our population continue to live in poverty. What has been done to correct this? More importantly, what has been done to address this? These immense inequalities have promoted crime; the less fortunate were no longer willing to accept a divide of such proportions. Do we blame these individuals? While we, as a country, will not endorse crime of any nature, we must attempt to understand and rationalise the mentality of those that dwell under such circumstances.'

'Past governments made promises to the people that changes would be made; that new laws would be implemented to protect them. We have lost an immeasurable number of people to violent acts of terrorism. Where are the laws that will lessen the chance of such acts occurring?'

'The United Kingdom, as an independent country, is a sobering and somewhat isolating prospect. At the time of its execution, the concept was ill-advised and poorly researched. As a result, we fell. We witnessed civil war. To each and every one of us, it appeared as though our country was broken and unfixable. Money could not save us. It was our self-belief and faith that saved us. We helped and supported one another until slowly, we were once again able to stand. The people showed tremendous resilience and kindness, a debt that no monetary figure could ever repay.'

'When martial law became the only means necessary, it was received with understandable reticence. We feared notions, such as domination and control. I am here to advise you that such notions would be detrimental to our cause. Our soldiers work to protect you, to restore peace, and to keep you safe. We do not live under a dictatorship and we are all entitled to our freedom. The military presence, though daunting for all, is necessary to clear the debris left by failed governments. It is them that failed you. They watched you suffer and did nothing to intervene. As a country united, we were tragically overlooked.'

'In time, we began to build a government and, in doing so, remained conscious that no government could ever replicate what had once been. It could no longer be the enemy or the dictator, but, in fact, a true reflection of what was best for our country. We could no longer speak of policies and manifestos, taxes and GDP. These factors would not rebuild the foundations of a fallen country. False promises, ignorance and self-serving policies were the very things that destroyed us.'

'We have chosen to listen to the people. We have chosen to hear the muted voices. We have chosen to focus on the most important aspect of this phenomenon that we call life. That thing is happiness, for without that, we have nothing.'

'And now, we strive towards a future where the people of The Happy State are asked a simple question. What is it that you want? You have spoken, and we have listened.'

'No longer will we be dictated to. No longer will we merely accept what we are offered. No longer will we accept the leftovers.'

'We ask for change. We ask for hope. As your new leader, I understand that this does not come without fear for our futures, and for those of our children.'

'As we move towards The Happy State, I ask for your patience. I ask that you search deeply for any faith that you still possess. Let us move forward together and support those that guide us in bringing a future of hope and happiness.'

'We are The Happy State, and we value the wellbeing of our people over and above all else.'

'I would like to conclude by thanking you. Thank you for your understanding at a time that has brought about many changes. Thank you for being strong and kind to your fellow citizens. Thank you for your support.'

'The United Kingdom, as we once knew it, has been laid to rest and, on this very day, The Happy State has been born.'

'I would like to finish with a passage from the Bible. You do not need to be of any religious affiliation to understand its message. It speaks to each and every one of us.'

'I can do all things through Christ who gives me strength. I will not let fear stop me, but I will boldly step out and do everything God puts in my heart to do. Philippians, 4:13; Deuteronomy, 30:11.'

'Thank you.'

The rapture was electric, the applause from the amassed crowd was nothing short of hypnotic. Oakes stood back and watched the people, his people cheering for him.

He'd done it.

2.45 pm.

There was a buzz of excitement at the golf club as news spread that Oakes had arrived. Waitresses fought for mirrors as they straightened their uniforms and neatened their hair. At any moment, they would welcome their new government.

Myka, both nervous and excited, felt a rush of adrenalin.

On this very day, she too would be a part of history in the making.

*

As his driver pulled into the golf club, Oakes allowed his body to slump against the seat. He cracked his neck to release the pent-up tension that had accumulated in his back and shoulders.

Having being consumed with an overbearing and visceral fear for several weeks prior, he had failed to consider the prospect of gratification. He hadn't anticipated the cheers or the warmth that had projected from the crowd. He had felt supported and respected.

The car came to a halt outside the back entrance of the club and Oakes stepped out. He'd insisted on having a cigarette to calm his nerves; a brief moment of isolation to consolidate his success.

And then he planned to really celebrate.

*

As food was served and drink flowed, moods and emotions ran high. Frost was relieved that Oakes had performed well, largely due to the fact that it was one less thing to worry about. He watched as Oakes sipped on expensive whiskey and relished in the attention. He was already on his third glass, so he'd have to keep him in check.

Oakes' excessive drinking had become something of a concern. Alcohol loosened tongues, and he often feared that Oakes might overshare. Somewhat reluctantly, he'd ensured that he was positioned right next to him, so that he was within earshot of all conversations that took place. He would possibly allow himself one alcoholic drink, but after that, he'd stick to water.

Oakes was mid conversation with Albin as they gratuitously dissected his speech.

Let him gloat, he thought.

The real work starts now.

*

Myka watched as Oakes crowed to all and sundry. She observed the way people clung to his side and hung on to his every word, like he was some sort of celebrity. The table of eight reacted to his comedic attempts with overblown and affected laughter. It left her wondering how many of them knew about the Zones. How private was his work?

She noticed that Frost said very little. He merely threw an occasional half smile across the table from time to time. With a simple glance, she could see the vitriol in Frost's expression as he glared at Oakes; the others were too sycophantic to notice. How she despised him. Every inch of her soul wanted to march over to the table and tell him exactly what she thought of him, just as she would in any normal situation. But this wasn't a usual situation and it wouldn't serve her well.

Oakes waved his empty glass in the air in a pompous bid to draw attention to the waiting staff.

She raised the perfect smile and dutifully walked over to his table.

*

With great triumph, Oakes had been able to devour a meal without it causing too much abdominal discomfort. He leaned back and drained the remnants of his whiskey glass.

A waitress arrived at his table and removed their main courses in preparation for dessert. He did a double take as he watched her work. It had been a while since he'd paid attention to a member of the opposite sex, especially one as attractive as her. Young and blonde, he was able to clearly ascertain her slender figure beneath her well-fitted uniform.

He reached over and touched her arm. 'Did you enjoy my speech?'

She smiled politely, though her eyes remained on her work.

'I didn't hear it, I'm afraid.'

He released her arm in disgust. 'How on earth could you miss something as important as that? Don't you have a television in here?'

'Afraid not,' she muttered. She lifted his plate and added it to the perfectly balanced pile between her hand and forearm. As she attempted to move away, he tugged at her apron, which forced her backwards. She steadied her arm to ensure that the plates remained intact.

'You know who I am, don't you, sweetie?' he drooled.

She spun around. 'How could I not? You're the most famous man in The Happy State. Can I get you another drink?' she asked sweetly.

He smiled.

The most famous man in The Happy State.

He liked that a lot.

*

Myka virtually threw the plates into the kitchen before stepping outside into the cool air. Her eyes welled with tears as she inhaled the cool, fresh air.

She hadn't anticipated how difficult it would be, being up, close and personal with the people that murdered her mentor. She'd managed to remain civil and polite when all she really wanted to do was to tell them who she was and that she knew of their merciless plight.

She missed Alpha more than she could bear. He'd been a father figure to her when her mother had kicked her out at sixteen. She had been too caught up with a string of boyfriends to watch over a child. After meeting Zee through mutual friends, she'd soon become a member of the movement and they'd been the best days of her life. Alpha had nurtured her, encouraged her to redirect the misguided anger and resentment that had manifested throughout her childhood. He'd taught her how to invest her emotions into something meaningful.

She allowed herself to silently cry. It wouldn't be favourable to let anyone see her upset and could draw unwanted attention. She thought of Alpha and his determination, his strength in bringing people together, in fighting for justice and what was right.

She would do right by him.

*

9.00 pm.

Frost was bored. He'd had enough of listening to Oakes and his minions rattle on about his wonderful leadership skills. He was surrounded by a bunch of dull creeps who wouldn't understand real power if it hit them in the face.

Oakes staggered towards him, his face aglow from an obvious rise in blood pressure. His eyes wandered in different directions as he attempted to manoeuvre his way to his seat.

'I think I did us proud, Nathaniel,' he mumbled as he slumped to his chair like a dead weight. He leaned in towards him. 'What do you say, old boy?'

Frost shifted his body a few inches in the opposite direction.

'I particularly liked the religious quote,' he offered, entirely uninspired.

Oakes grinned. 'I thought you might. They love that crap… so I added it especially.'

Frost forced a smile, despite the pungent alcoholic fumes that were enough to knock him sideways. He was ready to leave. He'd drunk more water than he could handle and it didn't look like Oakes was leaving anytime soon. Summoning the waitress, he decided to opt for something stronger.

Sometimes, even he needed a crutch to get through.

*

Myka had subtly stalked the table all evening, so when Frost raised his hand for service, she was the first one there.

'Scotch,' he demanded, devoid of any pleasantries.

She smiled and graciously accepted the empty glass that he thrust in her face.

It was time.

She had to work quickly.

Quickening her pace, she headed out of the restaurant doors, down the corridor, and into the bathroom. She glanced under each cubicle. There was no one else present.

Without hesitation, she entered a cubicle and locked the door. Removing her apron, she unzipped the small pocket at the front of her skirt and pulled out the fine latex gloves. She slid them onto her hands, stopping only for a moment to control the overbearing shakes that she'd suddenly acquired; a small tear in her glove bore catastrophic consequences. She paused, took a deep breath, and unzipped the bag that lay on a belt around her waist. With tremendous caution, she extracted the copious amounts of tissue that served to protect the hidden content. She stared at the box for a moment before she carefully lifted it.

Every background sound seemed to penetrate her soul and increase her heart rate. A closing door, a distant car alarm, a glass as it hit the floor and smashed into a hundred pieces; her hearing had become supersonic.

'Take your time,' she whispered to herself. One bad move and it was game over.

She opened the box and removed the vial. Steadily, she lifted the lid and poured a few drops into the centre of the glass, careful to avoid any overspill. She pulled a tissue from the dispenser and thoroughly wiped the sides and edges of the glass, laying it down on the toilet lid before she removed her gloves. Her movements were slow and deliberate. They had to be.

'Hello?' she called. 'Anyone there?'

She'd devised a suitable retort should anyone respond. She'd say she had women's problems and ask if they had anything. As it happened, there was no response. She was safe to exit.

She lifted the glass, balanced it on the palm of her hand, and opened the cubicle door. Slowly, she moved to the sink, lay the glass down and washed her hands. Her breathing was shallow. A moment of panic could be fatal. She took another deep breath as she allowed the excess water from her hands to drip into the sink. It took three lengthy hand washes before she felt satisfied that all traces were gone. Only then did she carefully replace the vial inside the box and into her waist bag.

With the glass in her hand, she stood before the bathroom

door to compose herself. She willed the muscles around her mouth to morph into the obligatory fake smile, then opened the door and exited the bathroom.

Amidst the chaos in the bar area, she squeezed herself behind the counter and reached for a bottle of whiskey. She clutched the glass tightly, but not too tightly. The rapid pace at which the staff worked made it virtually impossible for anyone to register her presence, so she patiently poured the measure into the glass.

A hand on her shoulder made her heart beat out of her chest; too many disturbing thoughts hurtled through her mind for her to make sense of them. Several beads of perspiration formed at the back of her neck; her palms were dangerously clammy. She stared at the glass in her hand.

It took one droplet.

'Crazy, isn't it? I still can't believe I'm here!' said the excitable waitress as she elbowed her way in beside her.

Myka attempted a smile, but it felt forced and unnatural. Her palms became wetter by the minute. Dangerous.

She added two large ice cubes to the glass. 'Yeah… yeah, it's nuts,' she stammered.

'We so need to meet up sometime. I think we'd get on really well. I like your vibe,' the waitress continued.

Myka smiled. 'Yeah, sounds great.' She hadn't heard the word vibe since she was thirteen.

She made her way from the bar and breathed a sigh of relief as she reached Frost's table. To her fortune, he hadn't grown impatient and summoned another passing waiter. She approached him; the sound of chinking glasses and cutlery deafening in her heightened state of anxiety.

She repeated Alpha's name over and over in her head like a mantra.

'Your drink, Commander,' she offered.

'About time,' he snapped.

She made a gesture to place the glass on the table as he simultaneously reached out to accept it. For a brief second, their hands intercepted, and the glass tipped to the side. Myka withdrew it immediately.

Sensing her discomfort, Frost eyed her. 'It's only whiskey,' he sneered.

It was an excruciating moment as she stared at the glass. Every second counted, what she did next could make or break the mission.

'Always better to drink it than wear it,' she giggled.

She continued to hold the glass until Frost reached out and stole it from her tight grip. Had she done enough?

Aware of his gaze, she offered her warmest smile.

'Is there something else?' he sighed.

'Nothing. Sorry. Anything else, Sir?'

'No.'

'No problem. Enjoy.'

It was time to leave.

Her work was done.

*

Jed pulled into the layby that was situated a few metres from the entrance to the golf club. His leg twitched incessantly; his hands drummed at the steering wheel.

'Where are you, Myka?' he whispered.

Zee shifted his position in the back of the car. 'She'll be here.'

The waiting was torturous. With no means of communication, he had no knowledge of whether or not she'd been caught, if they were being hunted. He'd become somewhat acquainted with the notion that a military team could surround them at any given moment, blinding them with flashlights while forcing them to surrender. It didn't make it any easier, though. There was little option but to sit and wait; hope for the best and face the consequences if necessary.

The meeting had been arranged for ten o'clock. It was ten minutes to. In just a few minutes, he would be forced to fire up the engine and drive.

If Myka was with them, they'd return home; continue life as though nothing had happened. If she wasn't, they'd drive to the safe house and remain there for as long as necessary.

'Look… there!' blurted Zee as he pointed towards the front of the car.

Jed lurched forward and squinted his eyes, unable to see clearly in the dark of night. As the figure drew near, he recognised it as Myka.

He turned the key in the engine and fastened his seatbelt. 'That's her!'

Myka opened the door and climbed in.

'It's done.'

Jed started the car, eager to put some distance between themselves and Edwin Oakes.

Fearful to speak or move, the trio remained mute until they reached the main road. When they were out of the highly secured danger zone, Zee broke the silence.

'You think it went alright?'

'Yeah. Fine.' She wound down her window to allow some fresh air into the vehicle. 'God, it's boiling in here.'

Jed tensed his shoulders as a sharp gust of wind caught the back of his neck. The temperature in the car was anything but warm.

'No suspicion?' he added.

'No, we're good.'

He placed his foot on the accelerator and headed towards Thendra.

The war had begun.

*

The young waiter watched on as the pompous politicians drunk themselves half to death. He was only eighteen and had no interest in politics. All he wanted to do was earn his money and go home. He hadn't wanted to be there, but the catering agency he occasionally worked for had suggested him as a waiter, and he'd been successful. He could hardly say no with all the big gigs they were getting for him.

He didn't like working around rich celebrity types. They were all the same; desperate to attach themselves to some nondescript, inferior prey that they could drown with stories of success and riches. He'd had it happen to him on more than one occasion and he couldn't have cared less. What he did like was people watching. He loved being the insignificant fly on the wall; the person that was so irrelevant that they could openly discuss their big plans without fear of repercussions.

He'd been privy to all kinds of conversations over the last few years; a famous actress having an affair with a cameraman, a well-known author who'd miscarried three times, a doctor that was under investigation with the General Medical Council for sexual harassment. He'd heard it all.

As a waiter, he'd come to realise that his status was on par with slavery.

This lot were no better than the rest. They ordered drinks by the dozen and left them untouched on the table. The entitlement made him feel sick. He hadn't been born into a wealthy family and the recent changes had left his dad out of work. He didn't like to see waste, so he'd taken to cheekily knocking back the odd abandoned drink to soften the blow. After downing two glasses of wine and a vodka mix, his edges were suitably softened, and he'd stopped caring when he was spoken down to.

He watched the politician, Oakes, or whatever his name was; he was completely inebriated and had made himself look like a royal idiot. In time, he was going to have a tumble. It's the way these events always went. Oakes was engrossed in conversation, his fake raucous laughter rumbled like an earthquake. He was leant against the table to steady himself, but he didn't look stable. It wouldn't take much for him to fall over a table, leaving a gargantuan mess for the menial staff to clean up.

The waiter had cleared several full glasses from the table to avoid an accident. It always came back on the staff if the guests were injured in any way, even if it was down to their own stupidity. On numerous occasions, he'd seen famous people fall over, which usually resulted in some form of injury. A couple of times he'd even had his pay docked to cover costs, and he wasn't risking that again, not with a university course to save up for. That was his ticket out of there when the restrictions were lifted.

As if on cue, Oakes staggered backwards. The waiter darted towards the table.

'Alright if I move these?' he asked as he pointed to the three glasses that lay in the line of fire.

Frost rolled his eyes. 'Take them, he's had enough for one night.'

The waiter lifted the glasses from the table and grinned to himself as he walked into the kitchen. Two full glasses of whiskey. That should see him through to the end of his shift just nicely. He glanced around to check that no one was watching and knocked back the two drinks. The potency of the whiskey nearly triggered his gag reflex.

'Gross!' he muttered to himself as he shook his head in disgust.

And then he heard the crash from the dining area.

It was inevitable.

*

They had driven for forty minutes in silence. Zee had dozed off in the back of the car and let out the occasional grunt. Myka and Jed had simply stared at the road ahead, the road that led them out of the city.

Myka felt agitated as she played the scenario over and over in her mind's eye. It had all gone swimmingly until that final moment when Frost struck the glass. The consequences could have been catastrophic. He'd commented on her exaggerated response and she'd attempted to play it down, to embody the starry-eyed slave that she was supposed to be. It perturbed her that he might have seen through her act.

Occasionally, she glanced in the rear-view mirror, just to be certain that they weren't being followed.

'You doing okay?' asked Jed. 'Myka…?'

She turned to face him. 'Sorry?'

'I asked if you were okay.'

'Oh. Yeah. Tired.'

She slid down the chair to deter him from further conversation. Her mind was far too active to sleep, but it was crucial that she consolidated the events of the day; play them over until she was resolute that her fears were impotent. Her mind wandered back and forth as she mulled over potential outcomes. Should Frost survive, her thoughtless reaction was significant enough to lead to a more thorough investigation. It was inevitable that the staff would be questioned, and she was prepared to withstand it along with the others. Zee would want her to go into hiding, disappear off the radar, but that would draw attention to Freedom and destroy their efforts.

She decided there and then that she wouldn't mention her minor indiscretion. She'd suffer the consequences of her actions. She'd do what was needed to ensure that Freedom were unharmed.

She just hoped that Frost wouldn't live to tell the tale.

Chapter 33

Four Days Later.

The members of Freedom had seen the news. It would have been impossible not to. It had been on three times a day as opposed to the usual ten-minute, pre-curfew snippet that they had become accustomed to.

Commander-in-Chief of The Happy State, Nathaniel Frost, was in a critical condition after falling ill three days prior. For the first two days, he had been in intensive care, but early that morning, they had announced that he was stable and would likely survive. Any long-term damage was yet to be discovered. The news anchor stated that he was believed to have ingested a toxic substance. The amount was small enough to do no more damage than cause internal burns.

An eighteen-year-old male had also been admitted to hospital. Toxicology specialists had confirmed that he had imbibed the same substance as Frost but the volume was far greater. He was unlikely to survive. It was believed that he had worked at the private party that Frost had attended.

Myka felt instantly sickened when she saw the news. She recognised his face as soon as it appeared on screen. The young waiter was the only person who she'd conversed with that night. He'd made an underhanded comment about inflated egos, and she'd laughed.

'Look at them, don't they make you want to vomit? They have more money in their wallets than I have in my bank account.'

She'd laughed. 'Probably.'

'I wish someone would knock them off their pedestals. Egomaniacs.'

He'd mentioned that he had plans to go to university and was only doing these jobs to save some money. She felt guilty and confused. How had he been poisoned? She'd seen Frost take a sip as soon as the drink was in his hands. It didn't make sense.

A young, innocent man would lose his life because of her, and Frost would live to tell the tale.

He would continue to secrete his deadly rhetoric throughout the streets of The Happy State.

*

Oakes had been an emotional cripple since the event, jumping at every sound, unable to sleep, terrified to go anywhere unaided.

Under no circumstance could it have been mere coincidence that an eighteen-year-old waiter had been poisoned at a political event; it was clearly intended for him. As unethical as it may have been, he'd hoped that the drink was meant for Frost and not himself. His advisors had convinced him that this was the case, but that he should remain vigilant.

Whatever that meant.

Frost had been quarantined while further tests were carried out and was unable to receive visitors. It was likely that he would survive, they'd said. But he would probably endure long-term tissue damage to his throat.

Frost had been vigilant with security for the event; extra military and security staff, numerous stop-checks for drivers and pedestrians, all staff fully vetted, yet it hadn't been sufficient. Somehow, there had been a glitch; an overlooked loophole that an accomplished infiltrator had recognised and embraced.

He took a seat at his desk and pulled out his notepad. He turned to the page that listed a selection of names; all possible contenders in his attempted assassination. Most were individuals that he'd come to blows with over the years and posed as unlikely candidates. Others were anti-establishment groups that would likely slaughter their own mothers to gain recognition. Undoubtedly, there were members of the public that deemed him amoral, and while a lone actor couldn't be discarded, the methodology indicated unparalleled sophistication. This was not the work of an opportunist. It had professional written all over it.

He thought back to the staff at the party, or at least those that he was capable of recalling. He had been served by numerous waiters and bar staff, to identify a single one would be impossible. In truth, his consumption of alcohol had put paid to any recollection.

His first job before he proceeded with government business was to identify, arrest, and prosecute the perpetrators responsible. He would make a public example of them; demonstrate that no one would elude punishment. It was time to raise the bar and execute his authority; to substantiate his power and illustrate the consequences of treason, even if it did contradict the sentiment of their objective. There was no pathway to The Happy State without the elimination of unruly dissidents.

Having stared at the list of names for over ten minutes, he picked up the phone and dialled his new secretary.

'I'd like an itinerary list of all staff present at the party,' he demanded. With Anneka gone, he owed no pleasantries to her replacement. 'Get them to me as soon as possible.'

As soon as the list arrived, he would arrange a rigorous interview process.

As he stared at the series of names in front of him, one name in particular persistently nagged at him. He drew a bold, black circle around it and leant back in his seat.

It was not the work of a lone agent. Nor was it the work of an irked civilian.

It was the work of Freedom.

Chapter 34

I felt my eyes become heavy as I watched an old and unfunny romantic comedy. I didn't mind. It was pleasant to have something uplifting in the background.

Over the course of the previous days, we'd watched the news break along with every other citizen of The Happy State. Frost was hospitalised after being poisoned at an event. A young waiter was critically ill. It had affected Dad on a much greater scale than I could have anticipated. He'd spouted a few things about freedom fighters and their futile efforts; it always did more harm than good, or words to that effect. He'd talked of Mum and her silly ideas, rolled his eyes a lot.

On this night, he'd been particularly irritable. Freedom had been mentioned numerous times and his mood had gone from bad to worse. Eventually, he'd taken himself to bed earlier than usual. I hadn't argued. His constant ranting had started to unsettle me.

With my composure suitably agitated, I made several attempts to escape into the world of unrequited love and heartbreak, but failed miserably. As much as I attempted to remain in denial, my mind was fixated on one thing only.

Jed. His parting words.

I was resolute that Freedom had been involved in the Frost incident, and I feared for Jed's safety. Their plight had reached such an alarming scale that he would never escape.

I yawned for the third consecutive time and decided that I was ready for bed. I'd had a particularly mind-numbing day at work after listening to numerous hypotheses with regard to Frost's potential assassin.

I stretched my tired arms in front of me to ease the tension in my shoulders. I glanced at my hands. They were dry and cracked from the obsessive cleaning that I'd recently undertaken. It was at that moment that I noticed my wrist was devoid of Mum's bracelet.

The panic set in at once. I frantically searched the sofa, reaching between the cushions before I tossed them aside for a more thorough inspection. I studied the ground beneath me, emptied the contents of my bag onto the table, then retraced my steps from the moment I'd arrived home. My brain raced as I attempted to relive my daily movements. Earlier that day, I'd rigorously tidied the area behind the counter at work, my hands had been immersed in various pots while I cleaned them.

I glanced at the clock. It was ten past nine. I knew I should wait until morning. I also knew that I wouldn't get a minute's sleep with worry. Before I could reason, my coat was half on and I was in my car.

To my immense frustration, the monsoon-like rain denied me the opportunity to slam my foot on the accelerator and drive at fifty miles an hour. Instead, I ambled along the empty roads while my windscreen wipers worked ten to the dozen.

Eventually, I pulled up outside work and let myself in. I searched in obvious and less obvious places; empty coffee mugs, the dishwasher, beneath the tables and chairs. The more I searched, the more my panic intensified. The prospect of losing something so valuable was too much to process. My bracelet was my only link to Mum and without it, we'd be disconnected. I wasn't ready for that.

I searched for twenty minutes before I noticed the clock. Twenty minutes to curfew. Frighteningly aware that I needed to terminate my search and head home, I fell against the counter and burst into tears. Had the circumstances allowed, I'd have stayed all night, roamed the streets and undertaken whatever was necessary to find it. The curfew dictated that I was unable to, and for that alone, I felt a momentary and visceral hatred for Edwin Oakes and Nathaniel Frost.

I composed myself and solemnly clambered into my car. Quite half-heartedly, I turned on the overhead light to inspect the seats. As I scanned the area around me, I spotted the bracelet innocently perched between my foot and the brake pad. I awkwardly contorted my body to reach for it, then kissed it several times before I held it close to my chest.

'Thank you! Thank you!' I gleefully declared to the deathly silence that surrounded me.

As I slid it onto my wrist, I made a mental note to have it tightened at the first available opportunity.

When I arrived home, it came as little shock that the front door was ajar. My exit had been in such haste that I'd half expected to find it wide open, swinging in the wind. I walked past the coats that hung neatly on hooks, the shoes that sat in neat rows. I lifted and repositioned a pair of my trainers that were randomly scattered at the bottom of the staircase; no doubt I'd kicked them mid-panic.

It was then that I spotted the wet, muddy footprints on the

hall floor. I took a sudden, sharp intake of breath as my body became consumed by sheer, unadulterated panic.

I slowly followed the direction of the footprints, through the kitchen, then into the lounge; stopping just a couple of feet in, as though the recipient had changed their mind.

It made me wonder what they were looking for.

I shivered and called Dad's name a few times. He didn't answer.

He'd had a turn and disappeared into the night, the only logical explanation. I wasn't stressed so much as angry. He couldn't have done it during the ninety per cent of the time that I was with him. He had to wait for the one occasion that I popped out.

It was then that I caught sight of a second set of footprints, and for a moment I was bewildered. I lifted my foot to check the treads of my boots. They were several sizes smaller than those that lay in perfect walking symmetry ahead of me. Whilst I was no expert in the imprints of footwear, it was apparent that two distinctly different sets of shoes had left their muddy impressions on the tiled floor.

I'd heard of home invasions and the spine-chilling tales that people had been subjected to, but that was long before martial law had taken effect. Petrified, I called Dad's name as I darted up the stairs, two steps at a time. As I ran towards his bedroom, I braced myself for the vision that might greet me. I steadily opened the door; his bed sheets were pulled back as though he'd risen from his slumber. But Dad was nowhere to be seen.

Whatever my previous heart rate had amounted to, it had since doubled. I charged back downstairs in fewer steps and checked each room, including the small downstairs toilet. I tugged at the back door, satisfied that it was locked before opening it and calling his name. Nothing. I pulled it to, and ran to the front door; the lock was intact.

My panicked breathing was loud as I double checked each and every room. I continued to call out, yet all the while I knew that only silence would respond to my cries.

'Don't do this to me, Dad,' I pleaded. 'Where are you?'

I opened the front door and ran down the drive; the rain soaked me in an instant. I looked up and down the road, ran several feet each way until I realised that my search was futile. As I sobbed, warm tears fell down my cheeks until I eventually fell to my knees.

I wasn't worried that Dad had lost his mind. I wasn't concerned that he'd wandered into the road and taken a wrong turn.

Somehow, and I don't know how, I just knew.

They'd taken him.

They had taken my dad.

Chapter 35

I don't know how long I stayed on the ground for. Neither do I know how I summoned the inclination to lift myself to my feet. All I knew was that I was running down the street towards the unknown, and at any moment I might fall and never get back up again. As long as I was moving, my mind was unable to think, to process any semblance of logic, practicality, or emotion.

I urged myself to run faster, to enforce an uncomfortable breathlessness, to counter my dark and disabling thoughts with a physical discomfort. At least that way I was protected from my own mind, from doing something stupid. Every time an inkling of a thought entered my brain, an image of Dad or of the unfolding situation, I ran faster to depress it into the depths of my soul. I didn't care about the sweepers; they could take me and do whatever they wanted with me. My life served no purpose without Dad in it and, to my misfortune or fortune, of which I couldn't decipher at that moment, I almost willed one to drive past me.

I'd somehow managed to run as far as Liaison, which I knew from my regular runs, was approximately a mile, and it was only then that my laboured breathing forced me to stop. The rain, which I'd remained oblivious to, bounced off the top of my head with force, and the cold from my sodden clothes began to take hold. I leaned forward and placed my hands on my knees as I attempted to control my breathing.

The moment that I stopped; I opened the door to my brutal reality. Engulfed in a paroxysm of grief, I stood still and allowed the rain to drench me. I was lost and alone. I couldn't see a way out of the abyss.

A random thought crossed my mind that at some point in the future, if I were to survive this, it would be the rain that I remembered when I thought back to this moment. The ice-cold droplets trickling down my face and into my mouth, the rumbling of thunder, the distant sparks of electricity that seemed to threaten me with their ferocity.

I allowed myself those few seconds of desperation before I summoned the strength to compose myself. It wasn't the time for ego-driven emotion. I needed to formulate a plan of sorts.

A bright headlight in the distance caught my attention. The light was blurred and fuzzy in the heavy rain, but of what it was, I had no doubt. A sweeper was headed in my direction and I needed to act. Despite the instinct to throw myself in front of it and wave my arms around, to beg them to take me wherever that might be, I instinctively glanced around for a place to hide; a humanistic desire to survive despite having nothing to live for.

With Liaison situated alongside me, I ran towards the outside area and hid myself awkwardly under an outdoor table in the decking area. I didn't dare move an inch, and the stillness caused me to dither uncontrollably. Though unable to see the sweeper pass, there was no mistaking the large, heavy tyres as they splashed through puddles, the brightness of the lights as they highlighted the area around me. I reached my arms around my folded legs and clung tightly, desperate to rouse some bodily heat. I could no longer feel my fingers or toes, and with no drive or willpower present, part of me wondered if I should stay in place, to live out my final moments in that very spot.

My options were limited. I probably couldn't walk the streets all night, and in light of the circumstances, there was only one logical thing to do.

With a vague plan and a dubious geographical direction as my guide, I took to the street. As I ran, I became aware of the unequivocal euphoria that fuelled my plight. My body and soul were inadvertently protecting me from endangerment, guiding me towards the only person that I could trust.

I turned onto Willows, past the school, and kept on until I reached the end of Jed's road. He'd be long gone, no doubt; hidden away securely, but Min would be there, and she was my best option.

At some point, the rain had lightened, yet the ice-cold sensation against my back, legs and backside had become more apparent. It was only as I reached his front door that my legs seemed to buckle and I knew at that moment that I couldn't run another step. I mustered the last of my energy as I hammered at the front door, seemingly unconcerned about alerting any neighbours to my presence at such an hour. Harder and harder I pounded, so much so that I feared I might penetrate wood.

The door opened, and with Jed standing in front of me, I crumpled to the floor in a heap.

I remember he reached down for me. There was a sensation of weightlessness as I was lifted into the air. I could hear two voices, one male and the other female, though I couldn't decipher what they said. Gradually, they faded into the distance until the only sound present was that of a continuous high-pitched tone.

And then it all went black.

*

It was Min's voice that I heard first.

For a couple of seconds on waking, I was unable to make sense of my surroundings, but the gentle tone of her familiar voice offered immediate comfort and assured me that I was safe.

'She'll be alright in a minute or two, the poor love.'

The first thing I spotted were my feet, perched on several cushions and elevated just a few inches above the rest of me. Min was knelt on the floor beside me as she gently rubbed my hand.

'Oh, here she is! Jed! The kettle is boiled. Go and pour the tea,' she ordered.

Instinctively, I attempted to lift myself from a lying position, but Min raised her hand to stop me. 'Gently does it,' she urged as she placed a cushion beneath my head. 'No sudden movements.'

I could see that my physical body was present, but my mind appeared to be elsewhere. I felt safe, that much I knew. I tried to understand how I'd come to lie on Min's sofa, but my brain prevented me from free-flowing thought. The more I tried, the more impossible it became. There was nothing but an infinite black hole where my memory had once been.

In retrospect, it was my body preparing me for what was to come.

Out of nowhere, a multitude of images flashed through my mind's eye. They came at me with such force that I felt temporarily harangued by them. The lost bracelet, the empty house, the footprints, my cold body as it dithered in the rain.

It was just a little chattering of my teeth at first. I didn't feel cold, quite to the contrary. Within a matter of seconds, my body followed suit until I relentlessly shook from head to toe.

'She's in shock. Hurry up, Jed! Loads of sugar!' Min shouted as she quickly wrapped a blanket around my unruly body.

That was the first time I saw Jed, as he sped-walked through the doorway with a cup in his hand. His other hand was placed over the top in an attempt to secure the contents. He handed the cup to Min, and I noticed that he looked more terrified than I did. Min held the cup to my mouth and encouraged me to take small sips. It took several attempts, as my body seemed to virtually spasm each time she tried. Eventually, I managed a small mouthful. Sweet tea. Too sweet. So much so that I recoiled and pulled a face.

She held the cup about an inch from my face. 'You must sip this, love,' she prompted.

I glanced at Jed's pale expression, his rigid posture and star-struck eyes. Even in my vulnerable and compromised state, I somehow knew that he knew. Sometimes words weren't necessary.

It took an entire cup of tea, much of which had dribbled down my chin and clothing, and numerous soothing words from Min for the shaking to subside. Whilst my strength had diminished, my condition had improved sufficiently to vocalise my position.

'They've taken him,' I blurted. 'Dad... he's gone. He wasn't there when I got home. I just saw... I don't know...'

I swung my legs off the sofa and tried to stand, but I was too weak. Jed caught me as I floundered and carefully guided me back to a seated position.

'Jed, what are we going to do?' I pleaded.

The numbness had dissipated, replaced with raw emotion. Like a tsunami of water, the words poured out of me.

'He was in bed… I just went to get my bracelet… I was gone… footprints… he's gone… Dad… they've taken him…'

I clung tightly to Jed's arm as I cried. I wasn't sure that he understood. My ability to articulate so seriously compromised. Why wasn't he jumping to action? Why wasn't he pacing, or doing whatever it was that he did when he was stressed and angry?

'Say something!' I begged, as I squeezed his arm a little tighter.

'Calm down,' he soothed. 'It's okay.'

That was far from the desired response. Everyone knew that you didn't tell a panic-stricken person to calm down. Jed clearly didn't get the memo on that one. I felt anger surge through my stomach, an overwhelming and desperate urge to lash out at him.

'Are you kidding me?' I snapped. 'Did you hear what I just said? Don't you dare do this to me now! Don't you dare! What are we going to do? What's your plan, Jed?'

He pulled his arm away. 'I don't know! I really don't know!'

I was as weak as a baby bird, but my rage provided me with enough adrenalin to withstand the torture.

'I ran all this way to hear you say, you don't know?'

Min let out an audible gasp. 'You ran here? Oh, good grief! No wonder you were soaked through. Why on earth would you do that?'

I stared at Jed. 'Is he even alive? Come on, you're the expert in all of this. You should know where he is. Tell me and I'll go, right now!'

The pacing started. As frustrated as it made me, it was a reaction. That was something.

'Jed! Will you speak to me, for God's sake?'

I jolted to my feet and knocked a glass of water. The contents spilled onto the carpet. Under usual circumstances, I'd have been mortified, and apologised at least six times. On this occasion, I didn't give it a second thought.

Min stepped in front of me. 'Raff, will you please sit down? You're getting yourself all worked up again.'

Instinctively, I shunted her to the side of me, all the while my gaze remaining on Jed. 'Are you going to speak? Are you going to give me some answers? Or shall I just run back home and get my car and hope for the best?'

His lack of response enraged me further, and no longer able to practise patience, I ran at him. My hands repeatedly pounded at his chest in a fit of fury. He did nothing but remain glued to the spot as he simply pacified my anger and frustration. It wasn't enough. I needed him to feel my pain.

'I hate you!' I sobbed. 'This is all your fault. This is you and your stupid people; do you even know what you've done?'

As my weak arms tired of hitting him, he pulled me into an embrace and held me tightly. I made a few futile attempts to resist, but eventually submitted to his tight grip. With my head against his chest, my arms dropped to my sides like lead weights as I sobbed profusely.

I was defeated.

It took several minutes for the crying to subside. When he was satisfied that I'd calmed, he released his arms and placed his hands on my shoulders.

'I am going to do everything in my power to find him. I promise, Raff. I am going to find your dad and bring him home to you.'

'How?' I asked, my voice a whisper. 'How, Jed?'

He took a deep breath. 'We'll find him. I need you to believe me when I say that I am going to fix this.'

With my head hung low, I noticed that I wasn't in the clothes that I arrived in. I glanced down at my body and saw a pair of grey, oversized jogging bottoms, a white t-shirt on my upper half.

Jed's, presumably.

He spotted my confusion. 'Don't worry, Mum changed you. You were soaked through.'

I looked at Min and noticed her grave expression, the sadness in her eyes as she stared at the floor beneath her. I felt terrible for misdirecting my anger.

'Sorry, Min,' I whispered. 'You don't deserve any of this.'

She looked up at me and attempted a smile. 'Has he really… gone?' she asked.

I turned away. I couldn't allow myself to break down again.

'I just didn't think it would really happen,' she said in a barely audible tone. 'Honestly, I didn't.'

I spun on my heel to face her. What on earth was she talking about? Min couldn't possibly know. But given that my life had taken such a surreal turn in recent weeks, I couldn't negate anything. I looked at Jed. His equally puzzled expression alerted me to the fact that he was as confused as I was.

'What do you mean, Mum?' he questioned. 'You didn't think what would happen?'

Min wiped a tear from her eye. 'They'd talked about it. You know, the assisted living homes? But I didn't think it was official. He hasn't even announced it yet so…'

As her sentence trailed off, Jed looked bewildered. His confusion acted to further compound mine. Nothing seemed impossible anymore.

He moved closer and knelt on the floor in front of her.

'Start at the beginning, Mum. I don't know what you mean. Just tell us what you know,' he urged in a soft voice.

She reached for my hand. 'I'm so sorry, Raff. I'm so sorry. Maybe I should have told you, but I didn't want to scare anyone unnecessarily.'

I took her hand, and she pulled me towards her, positioning me next to her on the sofa. Her hand clung so tightly to mine that my fingers uncomfortably pressed against each other.

'They said he wasn't introducing it until next year. Oakes, that is. Well, it's probably nothing, but apparently it's going to be mandatory for the elderly or terminally ill to live in these assisted living homes. Something to do with removing the pressures on the family. It's a big strain, makes them depressed or something. All part of this Happy State stuff.'

Jed and I glanced at each other. She had our attention. 'Go on,' he urged.

'Well, they're amazing, these homes. Apparently. A wonderful way of living, with care around the clock. They said there might be jobs for us nurse folk, but there was some silly vetting process you had to go through. Nothing like the other jobs we do. None of the girls at work were interested in all the fuss and bluster, to be honest…'

'What else do you know… about these places?' Jed interrupted.

'Besides them looking like five-star hotels? Nothing. They showed us some pictures, like something from The Great Gatsby.'

'Do you know where they are?' I cut in. 'These assisted living homes?' I said it with the vitriol that it deserved.

Min shook her head. 'We weren't allowed to know for some reason, just that there were going to be a lot of them. Might not even be built yet. I don't know, they sounded pretty fancy, all walking and talking, you know? Didn't like the idea myself.' She paused as she stroked Jed's hair, clutched my hand even more tightly. 'Family should always be together.'

'Do you have these pictures?' asked Jed cautiously.

'No, someone showed them to us just the other day. It was all supposed to be very hush-hush until Oakes announced it. As I said, we signed forms. That's why I didn't…'

'Who told you this, Mum?'

Her brow wrinkled as she thought for a moment. 'Some woman came into the surgery. Stuck up, to be honest with you. We didn't take to her at all. She was all made up and…'

'Mum!'

'Sorry. She was from the government, I think.' She stopped and looked at me, her eyes widened. 'But it makes sense as to why they were looking at all the medical records. It was bedlam in there, remember, Raff?'

Slowly, I nodded.

She was right. It did make sense. But not for the reasons that Min had been led to believe.

'If I'd told you sooner, maybe we could have done something. Stopped this from happening?' Her eyes welled up again.

Jed rose to his feet. 'Jesus, Mum!'

'I'm so, so sorry, love. I thought I was protecting Raff by not saying anything. She was stressed enough.'

'It's alright, Min,' I soothed.

Min couldn't have done anything differently. She knew a fraction of the truth if, in fact, anything was to be believed.

She gazed at me. Her eyes were wide and innocent. 'Raff... what do you mean they've taken him?' A mere glance at her saddened expression told me that she was clueless.

'What else haven't you told me?' snapped Jed. 'Anything else you know about these care homes?'

Min shook her head as she visibly forced back tears. 'I'm so sorry. And I'm so worried.'

'Bit late for that,' he sneered.

'Alright, leave it alone, Jed,' I urged, conscious of Min's sensitivity.

I didn't agree with Jed's harsh tone. Min had been fed a half-truth as justification for the Zones, but she certainly couldn't be held accountable for any wrongdoing. There was no way that she was privy to knowledge about the darker side of the truth; the zones, the abductions, the euthanasia.

I shivered at the prospect of my dad being locked up in a care home, much less a Zone.

'I'm just eager to know if she knows the real truth. Maybe she knows precisely what's going on, but it slipped her mind to mention it.'

'Enough!' I snapped.

'It's okay, love,' soothed Min. 'He's right to be angry.'

'You're damn right I am!' he shouted. 'Maybe, if she'd decided to impart this information sooner, we might have been able to protect him!'

'Don't you dare!' I interrupted. My voice was hoarse, but there was no denying the rage that it contained.

Min rose to her feet; her eyes were wet with tears. 'Do excuse me for a minute.'

I waited until she was out of earshot. 'How dare you treat her like that,' I snapped. I attempted to keep my voice at a low level whilst projecting the necessary amount of vitriol. 'She's done nothing wrong and you know it!'

Jed opened his mouth to speak, but he instantly stopped himself.

I took a step closer to him. 'Do you realise how upset she is? You're despicable, you really are!'

'Look, I'm sorry, okay? I'm just... just angry. That's all.'

I turned my back on him and marched to the other side of the room. 'This isn't about you,' I said as I fought the tears. 'For once, this isn't about your anger or your battle. It's about my dad, and right now that's all I give a damn about!'

'Sorry,' he whispered.

I turned to face him. 'You know what, Jed? It's not me you should be apologising to.'

I stomped past him and out into the hallway. I spotted my

trainers, neatly positioned on the radiator, in a bid to dry them out. Jed followed behind, so I defiantly shook the cold water from them and slumped on the bottom step of the staircase. One by one, I forced my feet into the tightened leather, determined not to let him see the discomfort I was in as my feet squelched inside. As I tied my rain-soaked laces, I spotted a large travel bag next to the front door.

'Going somewhere?' I asked.

'I was. I decided it wasn't safe to leave Mum.' He looked to his feet and shuffled them nervously. 'She's worth it. I'll take the hit.'

For a split second, I considered consoling him, offering a few words of comfort, but quickly recognised my naivety. He wasn't prepared to help me; I certainly shouldn't waste another second on him. I was angry at myself for asking.

'I don't need to know,' I snapped.

I'd had enough drama for one evening. No longer was I even curious about the Frost debacle and Freedom's likely involvement. Experience had taught me that I was better off not knowing. I had one objective, and Jed wasn't going to call the shots this time.

I rose to my already frozen feet, courtesy of my sodden trainers.

'Where are you going?' he enquired.

'Home. I need to do something. I can't sit around wasting time.'

'It's torrential out there.'

I shrugged my shoulders. I needed him to see that I was prepared to do it alone.

'And it's curfew.'

I snorted with laughter despite myself. 'Since when did that bother you? Tell your Mum I said thanks,' I muttered as I tiptoed towards the front door. The fact that I could barely walk in my trainers gave me little hope.

As I pulled the door open, the wind blew the rain at my face with the force of a sharp and painful slap. Instinctively, I pushed it to. I braced myself and tried again. This time, Jed stepped in front of me and forced it shut.

'I'm not letting you do this,' he said. His arm blocked the door. 'You need my help.'

I attempted to reach past him and pull the door handle. 'I don't, actually. I'm more than prepared to do this alone.'

He shifted his entire bodyweight in front of the door. 'Just think, we could use this to our advantage.'

When Jed had a plan, it usually spelt danger.

'Can you please move?'

He leant back against the door. 'Didn't Mum say they were offering jobs at the care homes?'

I pulled a face. 'Are you serious?'

'Very. Think about it. She gets in and the rest is just logistics.'

I raised my hand to silence him. I couldn't listen to anymore of his blunder. It was insulting to both myself and Min.

'Just hear me out,' he pleaded.

I stopped in my tracks. I knew him well enough to know that he wouldn't quit until I heard what he had to say.

'You have literally two minutes before I leave,' I spat as I glanced at the watch that I wasn't wearing.

He clasped his hands in front of him. I could almost hear

his brain ticking as he unveiled his plan. 'Right. Mum finds out about the vacancies and applies for a job. I can pull a few strings, don't worry about that. Once she's in, well, she's in.'

'What if the jobs have all gone?' I asked. The notion was simply ludicrous.

'They won't have. They'll need tons of people at the Zones.'

'What if she doesn't get the job?'

He smiled. 'Of course she will. Have you met my mum? Everyone loves her; she's got a great reputation.'

I wracked my brain for further obstacles. The quicker the torture was over, the sooner I could formulate a plan of sorts. 'She mentioned vetting. That takes weeks. Months! We don't have, sorry, I don't have the luxury of waiting that long.'

He rolled his eyes. 'Look, it's at least worth considering, isn't it?'

'No, Jed! It isn't worth considering at all. You're actually prepared to send your mum into a place like that? You're worse than I thought.'

I pushed past him, but he stepped in my path.

'Listen…'

'No!' I shouted. My patience had long dissipated, replaced with outright fury. 'I won't listen to another word that comes out of your mouth. Just when I think I know you; I realise how wrong I am. I want my dad back, Jed! That's all I care about, and if that's the best you've got, then it looks like I'm doing it alone.'

He glanced up the stairs before he lowered his voice. 'But she doesn't know the truth, Raff. This is just Frost's way of making his plan more seamless. It's a cover up. She doesn't need to know.'

My hands cupped my face in sheer horror. 'You really are as monstrous as them. How long before she realises what's really going on? Do you think she'll thank you for allowing her to do something like that?'

'No! I don't know. It just seems like a way in. What else have we got?'

I could sense his frustration. His desperation was so great that he was prepared to compromise a person he held dear to him. Perhaps his recent shock had compromised his cognitive functioning, and he wasn't thinking clearly. It was the kindest explanation for his hyperbole. Either way, I'd never consider such a foolish notion.

'I need to leave, Jed,' I demanded. 'And quite honestly, I don't know if I believe anything you say anymore. How do I know that you haven't made it all up?'

He raised his eyebrow. 'Fine. Knock yourself out,' he said as he stepped aside. 'But if you really don't believe me, speak to Luka. Maybe see what she has to say first.'

'Luka?'

'Yeah, Luka. She's currently in our care, and I'm sure she'd be more than happy to share her experience with you?'

'She's been released?' I asked, shocked that he hadn't thought to mention such a relevant piece of information. Before he responded, I reconsidered my question. I was on a need-to-know basis. I raised my hand in front of his face. 'On second thought, don't tell me. I don't want to know.'

I took a step towards the door. Jed didn't block me, but a sharp intake of breath suggested that he was about to speak.

'Before you go, just remember that the only thing we have

going for us is Mum. She could help. It's the only viable option you have.'

'I'll do it,' said a voice from behind.

Min was halfway down the stairs. Her hand rested on the bannister. With her face red and blotchy from crying, I hoped Jed felt guilty. She slowly descended the staircase towards us. 'I want him back, Raff. I love him too, you know.'

'I know you do,' I sighed. 'But this isn't the way.'

'I'll do whatever it takes to find him. Maybe we could appeal? Tell them we want him at home with us?'

My heart sank at her lack of comprehension for the matter. She didn't know that Dad had been torn from his bed, and I wasn't about to correct her. In Min's innocent mind, she no doubt assumed that it had been a clean undertaking.

'We'll think of something,' I assured her. A bid to convince myself as much as I did her.

'Now you listen to me,' she croaked as she cupped my hands in her own. 'You're not going anywhere at this time of night. You'll have a good night's sleep, a decent breakfast and if you want to go home by then, that's fine.'

She glared at me until I conceded. She was right. It made no sense to wander the rainy streets during curfew.

'And if it means going in there and dragging him out myself, then so be it. I'm an old-fashioned nurse, we're tougher than we look.'

She turned to Jed and reached out for his hand. He embraced it and offered a rueful smile.

Grouped together in a close-knit circle, we held hands. All but me and Jed, that was. That was until his fingers crept across my palm and clutched my hand tightly. Out of pure exhaustion, I succumbed.

At least that's what I told myself.

Min smiled. 'There we go, the power of three. As long as we have each other, nothing can get in our way. Now, I won't take no for an answer. I'll go to work in the morning and start the ball rolling. We will find him.'

Tears rolled down my face. Though deeply touched by Min's offer, the implications of such an act were not without consequence. Min was the closest thing I had to a mother figure, and I loved her dearly. I wanted to deny her, to tell her to stop being so irrational, yet I simply nodded. Perhaps it really was the only feasible proposition.

'It's been a long night. How about we have some hot chocolate and get our heads down. We can look at this in the morning,' she said as she gently patted my cheek.

As she walked towards the kitchen, I heard her mutter under her breath. 'Who could come up with such a barbaric idea? Forcing people into care homes to take the burden from the family? Rotten, it is. Blinkin' rotten.'

Jed and I glanced at each other.

If only she knew.

'Looks like we might have a plan,' he whispered.

A plan.

I never wanted a plan. I never thought I'd need a plan. I wanted Jed and Freedom to be nothing more than a group of fantasists that thrived on conspiracies and corruption. That's how the story should have unfolded. It's certainly how I expected it to unfold.

At heart, I'm not sure that I ever fully believed him, but his perpetual conjecture had allowed me a sort of escapism from reality. It would have been easy to hate him for lying, yet I hated him more for speaking the truth.

Perhaps I'd see sense tomorrow. Perhaps I'd tell Min everything and disable her plan. Maybe I wouldn't.

I hoped that sleep would give me the strength to make the right decision.

Sleep.

I feared sleep as I may not wake.

I feared sleep in case I did wake.

I had lost my Mother. I had lost the freedom that I once knew. I was slowly losing my dad to a cruel and incurable illness.

No more surprises. I knew the way things would play out now.

I had an overwhelming feeling that things were only going to get worse.

*

The End.

Reviews are the most powerful tools for a publisher and an author. They help to gain attention for the books you enjoy reading. Honest reviews of our books helps to bring them to the attention of other readers.

If you have enjoyed this book, or any of our other books, we would be very grateful if you could spend just five minutes leaving a review. These reviews can be as short or as long as you like.

Music is a journey, and they're lost in the lyrics.

When musicians Matty and Sandy crack open a dusty old book of folk songs, they hope to escape into the whimsical stylings of the past. They don't expect to actually be taken there.

Yet just a few notes sung from its cursed pages whisks them away to the world of Old England and all its hey-nonny-nonnies, myths and magic. In a dire twist of fate, Sandy is taken prisoner by the heartbroken Lord Donald who seeks to sacrifice her in the hope of resurrecting his lost love.

Knowing he must find Sandy and stop the murderous Lord before May Day, Matty needs allies now more than ever. Can a lustful witch and a plucky swordswoman guide him through the musically-induced mayhem of this strange - yet oddly familiar - world? Or is Sandy well and truly folked?

Drake Banks is a 12-year-old boy who is used to moving from one army camp to another. After the death of his father, Drake and his mother have to get used to living a normal life in the town where she grew up. This proves challenging for Drake as he misses the army life. Drake finds an old arcade in his new town. He loves video games! One day, after arriving at the arcade, Drake discovers a new game called Death Trap. He did not know how his life was about to drastically change. After pressing Start, Drake is sucked into the video game.

Upon entering this new world, Drake has to face a series of dangerous challenges and survive if he wants to get back home. But he soon realises that he is not alone. There are two other competitors, Scott Vent and Crystal Moon, who are computer programmes. The race is on! However, it isn't long before they realise that they cannot face these challenges alone. Can they put their differences aside and work together?